250

V. J Baker
Greenville, Ill.

The Beachcomber

A NOVEL

WILLIAM McFEE

The Beachcomber

A NOVEL

DOUBLEDAY, DORAN & COMPANY, INC.

Garden City, New York

MCMXXXV

PRINTED AT THE *Country Life Press*, GARDEN CITY, N. Y., U. S. A.

TO RICHARD

CONTENTS

BOOK ONE

IT WAS A SHOCKING NIGHT, down where the Hamilton Avenue car used to reach the end of its journey in Erie Basin. The rain came down with an unremitting vindictiveness that was, Mr. Spenlove reflected under his streaming umbrella, almost theatrical. He remembered such a scene many years before, in a theater. His first ship had been in the Surrey Commercial Dock, and he had gone to see an old-style melodrama of the 'nineties. The rain had poured down realistically at the end of the third act, when the heroine had been driven out. Stage thunder and lightning had entranced Mr. Spenlove's youthful imagination as she stumbled away, the child in her arms, from the door she was never to darken again, until act five.

Mr. Spenlove smiled as he stumbled away himself, into the night of the Erie Basin, to find his ship. He recalled Oscar Wilde's remark that Whistler's nocturnes had been imitated by nature. It seemed to rain more furiously nowadays, he thought, since the movies had adopted a downpour as a symbol of tragedy.

In that pandemonium beyond the quiet of the gatehouse he paused and felt his wet cheeks and beard. The clang of metal, the whine of pulleys, the gasp of compressed air released, the stuttering of pneumatic riveters, the hiss and glare of oxyacetylene torches cutting through the plates of a steamer with high bows that leaned, as though rearing in agony—all these things were visible to Mr. Spenlove through the downpour of rain. So too were the drab buildings, the maze of tracks, the loom of lofty derricks, and the lighted windows of the offices. A sailing ship with her yards cock-billed, her bowsprit dismantled and her bows splotched with red paint, made Mr. Spenlove think for a moment of some shabby genteel spinster forced at last to a life of shame in mean streets.

But he saw all this only because he had seen it so often before and because he knew it was there. He was not thinking of it. He stood for a moment peering into the murk beyond the damaged steamer and made out the upper structure of his own ship in the drydock. There she was, the old Camotan, who had carried troops to Brest and whose quadruple-expansion twin-screw engines were supposed to be out of date. They ran like sewing machines, he thought fondly, all the eleven thousand horsepower of them. They had become to him what the memory of a classical education is to some men. Damn these newfangled turbines, he went on thinking, for he knew that it was only a matter of months now before he would be sent away to bring out a new ship, a ship so perfect in her mechanism that he might become no more than a glorified head chauffeur in her.

Perfect she would be, he reflected, whereas he himself could never reach perfection. That was reserved for the young. He had several juniors on the Camotan, who seemed to have achieved that stage of development. They were tempted neither by wine, women, nor song, it appeared. Mr. Spenlove thought with affection of riotous and dissipated companions of past days as he ascended the steep gangway. He received a correct salute from a hygienic quartermaster with Y.M.C.A. written legibly all over his features, which had the classical beauty of a collar advertisement. As he stepped into the working alleyway Mr. Spenlove thought some of the young men must use make-up and patronize fashionable hairdressers. He was starting downstairs to reach his own quarters when the young man said someone had called to see the chief engineer. An old friend, he described himself. He was down below now in the engineer's mess. He had a pass from the up-town office. "What's his name? I'm not buying any more insurance just now," said Mr. Spenlove patiently. He was slowly removing his dripping garment. The lower entrance hall of the Camotan was covered with brown paper on which he was leaving watery trails.

"Name he gave was Sidney, sir. He said he was an old friend."

"Oh! Thank you, thank you. I'll go down and see him."

There was a great deal of subdued activity on the Camotan. Presently Mr. Spenlove would begin to participate in that activity. He would be disguised in heavy overalls with a Puck-like hood attached, goggles, sea boots, and thick gloves, and he would be in obscure and almost inaccessible corners of his machinery. He would disappear into boilers and wedge himself into narrow tombs between combustion chambers to meditate for long periods, with a magnifying glass, upon signs of corrosion. He would climb a rickety ladder in the drydock and embrace his propellers while he examined, also with a magnifying glass, their respective shafts. This was his life, and he loved it. The longer he lived the more comfort he derived from his association with ships and their machinery, and the less he thought of the much vaunted society of men. It was borne in upon him that as society became more complex and interlocking, men became less interesting to the philosophical mind. Because they were so predictable, he supposed.

He went down. He passed through kitchens where workmen had made messes, and the usually spotless floors were covered with dirty canvas. He saw the second steward supervising the arrival of stores. Men like gnomes, in clothes of astounding filthiness, saluted Mr. Spenlove as one of themselves, and he returned the salute as though they were worthy of his regard. So he came into his own region and stood at last before his own door, at the forward end of a narrow passage, where he brought out his key and gained admittance. He stood staring into the cabin, aware of a quick step behind him, the step of a man he had known for twenty years.

"Yes?" he said, without turning. "What is it?"

"It's me, Fred. Sidney Nevile, Fred. How are you?" They shook hands.

"Come in," said Mr. Spenlove, without any expression at all in his voice. He closed the door and turned the switch of the ceiling light. "Sit down, Sidney."

The man addressed as Sidney stepped lightly across the cabin and sat down on the settee, laying his raincoat and dark green fedora beside him. Almost unconsciously he drew out an expensive cigarette case and opened it to take out a cheap cigarette. He had dark hair, delicately touched with gray by his ears, and his eyes were a gray-blue that was repeated in his necktie. And he had good but slightly ravaged features. Mr. Spenlove sat down in his chair by his desk and looked at his visitor.

"What brings you down here, Sidney? You know they'll never give you a ship again. That was definite. They admitted you had bad luck, but they refused to try it again."

"I know. But I'm in luck now. I've got a job. I'm going down with you as a passenger."

"Some woman get you the job?"

"No sir! There's no strings to it at all. I'm starting a new life down there, Fred, and the past is all behind me. I've always wanted to make a clean break. I never wanted to live ashore in the States. You know that."

He sat looking at Mr. Spenlove, who had switched off the strong ceiling light. Now the soft green-shaded bulb on the desk threw strange romantic shadows across the room, and Sidney Nevile's face became young and lyrical. Mr. Spenlove had a vivid memory of him twenty years before, in the Mediterranean, acting third mate of a tramp steamer, sinewy, slender, and with the handsome candor of unawakened youth.

Now he was thirty-eight, and he still had that strange gift of seeming to be without experience or cunning in the ways of men. There was a frank sincerity in his voice as well as in his face when he spoke, so that one believed him.

"I dare say, Sidney, you think you didn't want to live ashore, but you made out pretty well. You've done pretty well, so far as that goes. Why do you come down here? Just to see me?"

"Don't you think I would?" He was hurt. "I've no friends I care about in New York. You've been my best friend."

"I've been your frankest, I admit that," said Mr. Spenlove. "I haven't been a very good one lately. I have to draw the line somewhere, you know."

"I suppose you mean Mrs. Olivierra. That's not what you think, Fred. Tell you the truth, it helped me a lot in the office, the contacts I made through going to her apartment. When she was in the hospital her husband called me up and asked me to go and see her. It was her husband's brother who told me about this billet I've got in the West Indies, as a matter of fact."

"So it *was* a woman put you into it, after all! And what's this billet, as you call it?"

"It's a club for rich johnnies who want to go fishing," said the other man. "It's a manager's job. I have to make all arrangements."

His eyes were shining now, and in the half light Mr. Spenlove saw again the youth for whom he had conceived so great an affection in those days before either of them had known the strain of American life. Mr. Spenlove had never told anyone about those days, or the exact spiritual relation between himself and the young fellow. Sidney Nevile had been so exactly the youth he had imagined as his son that he had been frightened. He had been forced to mount a stern guard over himself. Two voyages they had been together in the old Manola, and Mr. Spenlove, leaning over the rail while the ship was in dock in Glasgow, had seen young Nevile in his natty uniform and with his neat luggage wave his hand as he got into a cab to drive away to sit for his first mate's ticket in London.

And now, looking at Sidney Nevile twenty years later, he was dismayed again as he thought of how he would be in desolation if this were indeed his son. He was desolate anyway. So few of those he had loved were left in the world. They were bones in the sea, or part of the soil under French crops, or illegible names in distant graveyards. Only Sidney Nevile had been spared, as if in irony, and sat across the cabin describing with shining eyes the new billet he had secured.

"It's just what I've always wanted," he said. "A job working for men. No women. It's what the Yanks call a stag affair."

There had never been, Mr. Spenlove reflected, anything quite so noble as young Nevile in those days. He remembered his coming out of the transparent glass-green water in a cove of white sand enclosed by black marble cliffs in the old island of Ipsilon where they had been swimming. His profile had been like the intaglio of a Greek god. The sunlight reflected from the water upon the dark stone had made his features seem smilingly transparent. It had been the nobility of that young man's face which had stirred Mr. Spenlove to a sort of ferocity of protectiveness, as though he had discovered a miraculous specimen of a new and more glorious humanity. Or perhaps a miraculous survival of a golden age whose existence he was privileged to cherish and preserve.

It was a noble-looking face at this very moment, Mr. Spenlove thought, pushing up his graying short beard with the back of his hand. But where had the soul inside hidden itself? he wanted to know. Had all the women of those twenty years nibbled it away, as dogfish nibble away the body of a wounded enemy in the sea? Young Nevile added, smiling:

"I really mean it, Fred. I'm absolutely sick of women."

He says that, and believes he believes it, thought Mr. Spenlove, and he will go on believing it when he is actually in bed with the next one. And it will be true, which makes it all the more damnable for me, because I have loved him, because for me he is still that young Nevile who came up from the glass-green caverns under the cliffs of Ipsilon and made me believe in a golden age.

But aloud he said, heartily:

"You came down here in this damned rain to see me? Couldn't you have waited until tomorrow? I'm busy tonight."

"I say, Fred, couldn't I stay here? I won't be any trouble, you know. It's just that I don't want any fond-farewell business when the ship sails. My things are expressed to the dock."

"Is that why you're sick of women?" Mr. Spenlove was leaning over a drawer in his desk, and he looked up over his shoulder.

"I'll explain all about that when we get to sea. It's absolutely the last favour I want to ask of you, Fred, but it would be a kindness to both of us. I'm serious about this. The new job is a godsend because I've lost my bearings rather, living ashore among all these people. If they'd leave me alone I'd leave them alone. I know that."

"Is that your excuse? It's a very old one, Sidney. It came glibly off the tongue in the Garden of Eden."

"Don't you believe me when I say I don't want to have anything to do with women?"

"I do, Sidney. I'm the only one who would believe it, too. And the funny thing is I wish you did want to have something to do with women. It's because you can say that, and mean it, that you never get anywhere."

"I'm going to get somewhere now. I'm leaving the company for good. Down there, with men, I'll find a career. I should never have taken a shore job, after what happened. I was finished then, with the company, if I'd only known it. Old Spottiswood had it in for me all right. You know what old Spottiswood is."

"I do. I had him here some time ago. He said Virginia is engaged to Trumbull, who's going to open the new office in Montreal, so the old man said."

"I know Trumbull. That's a good thing. Just the thing for Virginia. He's just the man for her. He used to be old Spottiswood's personal secretary. Better than a prince!"

Mr. Spenlove sat up with a half-empty bottle of Jamaica rum in his hand. Nowadays he rarely drank anything else. It was, he maintained, unfashionable, and therefore unadulterated by blends or cuttings. He twisted the cork as he looked austerely at young Nevile, young Captain Nevile, who had been booted out of his command for affronting lady passengers through no fault of his own at all.

"You can talk like that about Virginia Spottiswood, the senior vice president's daughter!" he said. "Sometimes I don't know what you're made of."

"I'm what I always was, Fred," said young Nevile. He got up and took two glasses from a rack. "I play the game, and when they're tired and drop it, I'm glad enough to put on my coat and go home. They needn't play if they don't want to."

"She didn't drop it. She wanted to marry you, I'm certain."

"I was married—to Ada. I know Virginia wanted to get the old man to pay for a divorce, but that was a bit too thick. And I didn't want a divorce. I was satisfied with things as they were. It was Ada who wanted the divorce. Or said she did. Women never know what they do want, in my opinion."

"Well, you ought to be a good judge by now." Mr. Spenlove poured out the noggins of rum, and young Nevile went

over to the big thermos flask that hung by the bathroom
door. "Rum and water—a good drink for pirate or parson."

"Can I stay here, Fred?"

"I'll fix you up somehow. I want you to notice I don't
ask you who it is you are dodging now."

"You ought to give me credit for dodging, Fred. Ninety-
nine men out of a hundred wouldn't want to dodge—the
person I'm trying to avoid. It's because I know she'll be
glad, some day, that I welshed on her. And because her husband is one of the decentest chaps I've ever met in the States.
Fred, do you believe women have souls? I mean, do you believe they're ever anything more than animals? Of course I
know Ada is, and Virginia too. They are far too good for me,
really. But most of them don't have any scruples. Here's
luck."

"Plenty of them have, Sidney, but they don't run around
in your parish."

"I'm not dumb enough to believe you're absolutely right,
Fred. I've seen glances."

"I'll bet you have. You don't miss a trick, and I'll grant
you've had reason to think as you do. But you aren't fooling
me, not even when you act so nobly toward the decent husband."

"Damn her husband, if that's what's worrying you. I tell
you, I'm thinking of myself. I've got to. I'm afraid of losing
my self-respect. In this new job, I'll be safe. I'll never be in
love with a girl again, anyhow."

"Better for you if you were, and made it stick. I don't believe you'll ever amount to anything until you have a wife."

"What was Ada? Wasn't she a wife?"

"Yes, she was a wife in the legal sense, but the only person
of any importance in the world to Ada is Ada. And I give you
credit for being a gentleman in that matter too, my boy. I'd
never have stood it as long as you did. You weren't cut out
for a Greenwich Village husband. And she might have fooled
you all your life. It was a risk that worried me when I was at

sea, that you might be fooled all your life and never wake up to see her as she was."

"But we were happy for a while, anyway. I mean I was. I'd have let things go as they were. We didn't get in each other's way at all. She had her work. After all, I knew what I was doing."

"No, Ada simply wanted you. She was too absorbed in her own career to be a wife. She has a certain number of tricks that give her a sort of glamour. Like that habit of calling herself Aïda and saying her mother was an Egyptian princess. When your novelty wore off she turned back to herself. She'd been married before, and she is getting married again. Don't forget I saw more of Ada than you did several times. I mean while you were away and I was over here, looking after a ship."

"Yes, I remember. She tried later to make me believe she had made you fall in love with her. I'm never jealous."

"If you were you would never have got yourself into this state," said Mr. Spenlove.

"I haven't the faintest idea what you mean by that, Fred. What state?"

"Well, you are too young to remember, but in the old days religious people would have said you were unregenerate."

"What does it mean? Degenerate? I'm not that." He spoke with a certain flash of pride. "I've never even been able to understand degenerates, Fred. You remember that purser we had on the Aramaya?"

"Oh, I wasn't accusing you of anything like that. I was using a theological phrase to explain how you seem to have got into a way old-fashioned people didn't believe in. They'd make allusions to the flesh, and Apollyon the destroyer of souls. This is all very unfair to you, Sidney. I ought to have told you I agree about quitting that office job. It will make a clean break for you, and you can make a new life for yourself. Can you save any money out of your salary?"

"Of course, because it's all clear. I have quarters and all found, and entertainment allowance as well. And a month or so off in the summer, between the seasons. I'll arrange to come up with you, Fred, and go to the country."

"Oh yes! You have the luck of the devil, Sidney. There isn't a sailorman in ten thousand could be kicked out the way you were and come back as you are doing. And yet you have to hide down here because some idiotic creature has listened to your tripe and thinks she's the only woman you ever loved!"

"That's not so, Fred. I never gave this girl any encouragement whatever. It was one of the fellows in the office told her I was sailing on this ship. Fred, I give you my word this is the truth. I went there to tea once. She has one of those big imported cars, with a chauffeur, also imported. I never had any desire to run with those people."

"That all you did, went to tea?"

"She went with me to Sherry's. And then, I told you, her husband is a splendid man and trusts her absolutely. I had to pull out, on his account. That fool in the office blew the gaff. So I know she'll be down to see me."

Mr. Spenlove looked hard at young Nevile for a moment. "It's like that time we took the job in the yacht. You remember?"

"Yes, something. Only here I can get away from it, and I shan't lose my job. I've always had a dislike of private yacht work since."

"You never did come clean about what took place while you were on that island," said Mr. Spenlove.

"Well, it wasn't my secret entirely," said the young man. "Maeve was so dominating. I had nothing to gain by blabbing other people's affairs."

"You were indiscreet," said Mr. Spenlove. "That's the unforgivable sin on a private yacht. You are always letting women maneuver you into those situations."

"What else can I do?" Nevile demanded, and even his resentment against women was without any real fire. It was not, Mr. Spenlove thought irritably, genuine. He was too interested in them ever to hate them, and they had lost their power to hurt him. "What else can I do? You tell me. I might go into a monastery. I don't see why, though. I've as much right to live in peace as the rest of you. I haven't backed out, have I? Ada, I mean."

"Well, I have a rendezvous with the underwater connections," said Mr. Spenlove, getting up. He began to take off his shore clothes. "You can turn in on the settee, Sidney. Nobody will disturb you."

"You're always the same, Fred. You've been a father to me."

"Stepfather at times. You've needed coercion. I've had plans for you and you always did something to make them impossible. I'm getting old and cantankerous, Sidney. I think I hate women, sometimes, when I see what they've done to you."

"That's just where you get mixed up. They never do anything to me. I'm absolutely independent of them since that time in Malta. You remember that, Fred. I could never feel like that about a girl again. As I did about Elli."

"Like what?" Mr. Spenlove was standing in his underwear, his muscular hairy limbs bulging in vigorous curves as he held out his boiler suit in order to step into it.

"You know what I mean. Love. I was mad about that girl. I was absolutely ill with it. People joke about anybody suffering from love, but I did on that occasion, Fred. I remember it just as I do having brain fever when I was at school."

"I saved you from perdition that time, my boy."

"Yes, I suppose you did. It has never really left me, that experience. I mean it's always there, no matter what happens. I might have married Elli Phalère. By Jove! I get the wind up when I think what I escaped because you were there."

"You escaped perdition," repeated the figure in the heavy brown union suit. A pointed hood that hung behind him gave

Mr. Spenlove the appearance of a Carmelite monk with puckish, slanting eyebrows. Young Nevile nodded.

"Well, the reason I can never be in love with any of these girls is simply that I'm still a little in love with Elli. I never met any girl like her, somehow. . . ."

"You'd better snap out of it," Mr. Spenlove remarked, pulling on sea boots and tying the laces of his trouser ends close. Then he reached for a pair of formidable gauntlets and a large electric torch. "She must be fifty now." He smiled.

"Sure I won't be in the way?"

"No. I said Elli must be fifty now. You're in love with her as she was when we were in Valletta in 1911."

"I know it well enough. I have her picture here." Young Nevile showed a gold watch and snapped the back open. "As she was that day we went to Cività Vecchia."

"It's no use talking to you," said Mr. Spenlove testing the torch. "You are making the worst of both worlds. It's all topsy-turvy. Go to sleep." He pointed to a roll of blankets over the wardrobe. "I'll see you in the morning, my boy."

"Fred, you're the best man in the world. You'll never regret it either."

The door closed behind Mr. Spenlove, and Sidney Nevile, taking off his coat, smiled to himself. He knew no woman could ever care for him in the way Fred did. No woman could shut out the cruelty and treachery of the world and make him feel safe. In a way he had the same sensation that good people had when they spoke of "the everlasting arms." Fred had saved him from Elli, the only girl he had ever really loved! Modern people would say Fred had been jealous of Elli, which was a lie.

He lay down, after opening the scuttle and starting the fan to freshen the room, and pulled a blanket over him. He lay thinking and intending to get up and stop the fan in a few minutes.

He lay thinking of the new departure he was making. He was leaving all those people, the wives with good-natured husbands; the daughters whose parents liked him and invited him to their homes; the girls who were married but separated and who were so desperately lonely. And he reflected that he had not been entirely frank with old Spenlove. He was really too experienced and too well acquainted with himself to believe he was never going to have anything more to do with women. Of course, old Spenlove hadn't believed it either. What he himself did want was a complete clearance of old emotional baggage. He wanted to be alone, at sea, with old Spenlove, whose tart skepticism and rambling intelligence had made life amusing in the past. Then he could trust to his usual good fortune to throw an interesting woman, who would not make too imperative demands upon him, in his way. There was always one such, he knew by an experience which he had never sought but which had been forced upon him. The world seemed everlastingly full of women seeking a man. Not, he thought without cynicism, a particular man, but just a man—like himself—to work her wiles upon. Fred was disgusted because he had merely protected himself by playing their game and playing it better than they. There was the Wyatte family. What an escape that had been! Nobody could ever accuse him of self-interest or mercenary aims after that affair. Fred had been splendid with the Wyattes. Fred had nearly got involved himself!

Now all that was over and done with. The slate, once they got down the Bay, would be clean. Four or five days of pleasant indolence, interesting scenes and people, a new career and good prospects for the future. He would show Fred he was wrong. Of course, so long as they kept their friendship Fred was bound to be wrong. Fred was really romantic at heart about women. That was fatal in the long run.

Mr. Spenlove found him there, the light still on and the fan running, almost smiling in his sleep.

II

IT WAS A SOURCE of private amusement to Mr. Spenlove that he could never enjoy the spectacle of passengers on sailing day. They reminded him too painfully of children assembling for a Sunday-school treat such as he had endured in his Victorian childhood. The attitude of the stewards was, he told himself, exactly modeled on that of the servants of the local duke, in whose grounds the picnic was to take place. Everybody seemed to relish the temporary rôle of idle rich which was forced upon passengers nowadays. Mr. Spenlove's employers, who were no fools, had a slogan which appeared on every menu card, and all their other publicity. It even appeared in official correspondence addressed to Mr. Spenlove and his colleagues. The passenger was informed, gently but firmly, that "the Company is your host." Mr. Spenlove was directed to regard every purchaser of a cruise ticket as his personal guest. It was a pleasant device to distract attention from the rigid bureaucracy which is necessary in handling large bodies of people who have no knowledge of ships and who are practically helpless outside of their own social groups. It is to be feared Mr. Spenlove rarely bestowed the beaming glance of an old-time host upon the new arrivals who milled around in the alleyways and wandered unwittingly into perilous places and prohibited areas. It seemed at times to him that all these simple people had been the victims of illusion, that they had been swindled and fooled by the Company's dream pictures in magazines of impossibly lovely tropical places and unbelievably fascinating companions. He pictured them as believing that they really were going to experience something resembling the glamorous scenes drawn by unscrupulous artists and described by copywriters who, nine times out of ten, had never got beyond Asbury Park in their own travels. And he took a morbid pleasure in regarding them with asperity for being so fooled.

He thought of them, not as guests, but as simple savages lured on board by tinsel toys and bales of bright Manchester goods. What else was it? he asked himself as he threaded his way among the groups saying good-bye. What they wanted was not there. They expected to find the Spanish Main and they themselves were pirates, many of them, at home in Illinois, or perhaps Minnesota. For them to go to the Caribbean was like Sir Henry Morgan being driven from London to Bath in his private coach with postilions and outriders keeping him safe from harm. Mr. Spenlove had a weakness for believing these people never fooled him with their attitude of children at play. He was continually divining behind their ingenuous hilarity and alcoholic sailing parties a sinister blend of plutocracy and economic ruthlessness. As years passed he found it spiritually invigorating to despise the very people who paid him his salary and who were making him independent.

He was thinking something in this fashion—for he never fooled himself either, except during reveries of earlier days—when he saw a woman with a snub nose and the pale gray eyes of southwestern Ireland gazing at him in expectant good-humor, as though she were prepared to see him dance a jig. It was impossible not to smile into such a face, and Mr. Spenlove did smile.

"Are you the captain?" she said. It was a common error on the part of inexperienced travelers, and Mr. Spenlove was not offended.

"Nothing so contemptible as that," he said, smiling again, and enjoyed her sudden solemnity. "But I might find him if you want someone to run errands. He used to be a friend of mine."

"Ah, you're fooling!" said the lady with rich appreciation. "Come clean now! You're the captain after all."

"You ought to be more respectful," said Mr. Spenlove. "How can we keep discipline if you people talk like that?"

"It's me brother," she explained eagerly, for it was obviously on her mind, and she needed a friend. "He's not very well, and he's with a lot of the boys in some cabin."

"Then it's the doctor you want."

"No. It's just that he's had a few, you understand, and they're trying to see who drinks the most before they go back with the pilot."

"Newspaper men, I suppose."

"Sure. Me brother, he works in Washington for the *Globe*. And they're having a singsong down there. . . ."

"Ah! Well, what do you want me to do?"

"I thought the captain could get him out."

"I think there are other people on the ship who can handle that situation," said Mr. Spenlove. "Suppose you leave it to me. What name shall I say?"

"Oh, O'Relly. Me brother is Terence O'Relly of the *Globe*. I'm Mrs. Kavanagh. We're takin' a cruise to Jamaica, ye see. I'm so obliged to you, Captain. The cabin's number forty-seven. Terry's next to me with another man."

Mr. Spenlove, after he had been to the top deck to see what he had been going to see, went down the forward elevator to the dining-room level and slid inside the door of the chief steward's cabin. Mr. Romaine had come out from England with Mr. Spenlove. They had long ago hit upon an agreeable formula of friendship which irked neither of them and which left them free to serve their employers without friction.

When Mr. Spenlove explained what he wanted, Mr. Romaine made a notation on the dining-room plan on a table near him and opened a box of cigars. He was a large calm man with a passion for tropical fish, which he kept in a glass tank on a shelf over his bunk. He would switch on lights and lie watching the translucent glories of microscopic creatures through a large reading lens. Mr. Spenlove had twitted him sometimes with misanthropy. The contemplation of passengers for so many years, Mr. Spenlove said, had made old Romaine seek consolation in the abnormalities of the deep. Mr. Romaine did not deny this. He never denied anything.

He was a silent man. Even ashore, with a group of noisy ship-mates in the Canal Zone, or at some pub in Southampton, Mr. Romaine never said very much. He had a profound respect for Mr. Spenlove, founded on the latter's fortunate suggestion in 1929 that they both sell all their stock, which they had bought in fear and trembling in the early twenties. A most fortunate suggestion. Mr. Romaine had done very well. And the market had fallen like an avalanche since he had sold.

He pointed out to Mr. Spenlove that those two passengers were specially recommended by the office. He showed a letter. Mr. Spenlove nodded.

"I thought I'd seen the name," he said. "In a magazine it was. Yes—Norah Kavanagh; that's the name. I'll be glad to have them at my table. So she writes those murder things. I doubt if she ever killed a fly in her life. Now, Romaine, don't offer me a drink while we're in the Narrows. I'll be along later. Will you get that lady's brother out and put those newspaper lads over the side with the pilot? We have to be nice to them, with so much competition."

"There's another one specially recommended," said Mr. Romaine. "Do you want her at your table? There's Captain Nevile too. The skipper they fired that time. The old man said he wouldn't have her."

"Yes yes. I want him at my table," said Mr. Spenlove. "Who's the other?"

Mr. Romaine produced another letter, signed by the vice president in charge of operations. Mr. Spenlove read it. Miss Athalie Rhys. The writer of the letter directed that every courtesy be shown Miss Athalie Rhys, who would be met at Kingston by her father.

"No reason assigned," murmured Mr. Spenlove gnawing his beard. "Every courtesy, eh? She can sit in, Romaine. What? Wilmarth, you say? Ah well!" he added. "That makes my little circle complete. Two men, two women. You heard about Nevile? He has a good job, he says. He's given up trying to get back his command and has a good job."

Mr. Romaine heard this without comment. For him Captain Nevile had been "out" for a long time. It was all Mr. Romaine knew about young Nevile—that he had been put out for some row over the women passengers. He knew, of course, that old Spottiswood had his knife into Nevile. And a man might as well go and jump into the dock, in that case.

They sat there for a few moments, those two elderly, profoundly experienced men, far down in the cellular structure of the Camotan, ordering the lives of people they had not yet seen, like twin demiurgic beings. Over Mr. Romaine's bedplace gemlike creatures came to the side of the glass tank and peered with incredible glowing eyes at the two monstrous objects on chairs. Mr. Spenlove suppressed a smile as Pucklike thoughts passed through his mind. He rose and made some excuse about the engines.

Back in his own cabin he communicated with the engine room and sat listening to the news over the telephone. It afforded him a certain impish pleasure to reflect upon the way these young men were continually in a state of enchantment. What else could you call it when they were living completely happy lives and didn't know it? They would envy passengers and shore people generally, whereas it was a much better life at sea! They thought him cynical and malicious when he pointed this out to them, and they would even retort with allusions to his own lack of family ties. It was a poor argument, as he could demonstrate when some ship captain or officer got into a matrimonial morass. No, he would tell them, they were enchanted, and some day would wake up to discover they had been having the best time of their lives on the Camotan.

And he began to think again of young Nevile, who was now upstairs, a passenger. It was not possible to classify him in that way. He had come from so refined and genteel a home that the average seafaring man was uncouth in mind compared with him. He had never been a sissy, but on the other hand he had gone through life, up the ladder of his profession to a command, even through the war, in the Naval Reserve, without ever removing the mask of upper-class good breeding and showing what lay underneath. Perhaps, Mr. Spenlove thought, it wasn't a mask at all. Perhaps he had nothing to show. That was baffling. It made all these modern psychological dervishes go haywire if you were unable to postulate a dark crypt full of human bones. Young Nevile never drank or gambled. Professionally he had been one of those quietly efficient officers and unobtrusive commanders of whom nobody ever says a word. He never did anything spectacular and he never did anything foolish. He gave the lie to those effusive and romantic people who imagine the command of a ship to involve qualities heroic and romantic, as well as professional skill comparable with that of discoverers of new routes to the Indies. Young Nevile, of course, had had a good education, and he possessed the aforementioned upper-class good breeding. He had tact and had learned from one of his early skippers a lesson which many officers never learn until it is too late and they contemplate the harm they have done from the shades. He learned that the best way to govern men is to leave them alone.

He had, Mr. Spenlove reflected, every last qualification for success, and he had succeeded. He had been the youngest shipmaster in the service. And he had stepped out—by request—because of a woman's spiteful recrimination. He had lost his command, his career, and his position in his profession because women imagined they had a claim upon him. They assumed that they had a right to squabble over his favors, and that if he were ruined in the course of the row they had no responsibility.

Mr. Spenlove realized that even if one were able to sneer at that upper-class good breeding it was a useful substitute for Christian charity and stoical fortitude. When he was fired young Nevile had made no defense. He had expressed no views about the woman who had lodged a complaint against him and thereby created a situation which could only be solved by smashing him. Not a word. Mr. Spenlove wondered why that was, unless . . . hm! Mr. Spenlove remembered that episode as recounted in the many discussions he had heard among the Company's men in bars and cantinas. They varied in details, but Mr. Spenlove felt justified in believing that young Nevile had never foreseen the peculiar dual nature of a rich girl's mind. He might never have become aware of the inevitable feline savagery with which she would use the only weapon civilization had left her. The only weapon! Mr. Spenlove repeated to himself in a sort of ecstasy. She couldn't even ask some other man to horsewhip her ravisher. There were no horsewhips, and the other man in any case wouldn't want to get mixed up in a mess like that. The economic stiletto was all she had left. She had him fired. If she had been living in the sixteenth century she might have had him burnt. Manners changed, and the phrases lived on. What was that one about the torture of the boot? And the Iron Maiden who crushed the wretch in her sharp embrace? Yes, the economic poniard had done for young Nevile that time. Esther Davidge's father was a person of immense social and financial importance. The professional career of a foreign-born seaman was nothing to Davidge. Mr. Spenlove was often entranced by the rich men whom he carried in the Camotan. Their smugness and arrogance, the obvious pleasure they derived from the silent worship every man and woman tendered them, was colossal. What complicated that affair, Mr. Spenlove saw now, was that if young Captain Nevile had been despicable, Esther Davidge could have bought him. Davidge would have bought him for his daughter and given him a tinsel position in one of the Davidge companies. Mr. Spenlove had a suspicion that young Nevile had not thought of that and would not have done it if he had thought of it. Then why was he such a disappointment? Why, asked Mr. Spenlove of himself irritably, did it seem more honorable for him to have eased himself into such a marriage than to have been fired at the request of an irate parent? He hadn't even avoided a flare-up with the Spottiswood girl. He had incurred Esther Davidge's rage because he was being attentive to Virginia Spottiswood. It was an extraordinary jam to get into for a young shipmaster, and he had never said a word about either girl afterwards.

Mr. Spenlove had seen the other one too. While young Nevile had remained below, the chief engineer had taken a walk around on his way to Captain Wensley's cabin for a professional word. He had seen a girl hurrying up and down the promenade deck looking for someone. He had seen her again at the purser's office, pestering a harassed young man who could do no more than say he did not know who Mr. So-and-so was or where he was. She brushed past Mr. Spenlove, glancing sharply at him for a moment, as she went down the stairs to the next deck. A handsome dusky siren, with glasses that somehow made her more seductive, Mr. Spenlove thought. He was amazed, for he noted her vigor as she prowled along seeking. It was obvious that she was capable of bearing off the man she wanted almost in sheer physical energy. She was predatory. She was not above tearing him from another woman's arms. Mr. Spenlove smiled as his imagination rose to the possibilities of that baffled woman's powers. He saw her pause irresolute in the palm court; chin on gloved hand she stood imagining the scenes that would take place in that secluded romantic region, at night under a tropic moon, while she herself was far away and forgotten. She stamped an expensively shod foot and rushed out of sight. Mr. Spenlove did not try to follow her. The whistle was bellowing above them. Stewards were shepherding the visitors to the gangways. Good-bye, good-bye! Bon voyage —good-bye! When he got to his cabin, Mr. Spenlove saw young Nevile watching the colored paper ribbons that streamed from the rail of the Camotan to the dock.

"Good-bye, good-bye!" Mr. Spenlove chanted in a falsetto voice. People on the dock were behaving dramatically with handkerchiefs. They were flinging up arms and blowing kisses with faces contorted into masks of conventional emotion. Each member of that polite mob was oblivious of the rest. The Camotan's whistle trumpeted in deep vibrating bass notes, with hysterical treble overtones like a maniacal war whoop. In between, as the echoes fled like stampeding armies, the clash and squeal of the ship's orchestra, the tup-tup of the drum, were dwarfed by that immense clamor. Good-bye! Good-bye! The ship began to move astern with a faint tremor of her hull.

"I must go down," said Mr. Spenlove, taking a cigar from a box on his desk. "You escaped from the siren by remaining in the hull of the sharp-prowed ship as she left the shores of the fatal island," he remarked.

"You always try to make me out a rotter about women," said young Nevile, turning. "Sirens lured men to destruction. Mrs. Rossiter knows all about how I came to be in that up-town office and she got her husband interested too. She didn't destroy me. She's given me a new career. Mr. Rossiter is financially interested in this new club. He's a keen sportsman and a thorough gentleman."

"Then why do you have to dodge Mrs. Rossiter? Or rather, why does this lady bountiful have to come down and see you off?"

"You needn't be so sarcastic, Fred. She'll be all right in a few days—forget all about me. She's a bit upset . . ."

"Oh, good-bye, good-bye!" said Mr. Spenlove. He went out and put the door on the short hook, his deeply set dark gray eyes, almost black at times, gleamed through the narrow opening, and his black oblique brows made him look more like a Puck in uniform than ever.

The whistle began again. Vast slabs of sound seemed to float away down the river and collide with other noises, from towboats and ferries. Mr. Spenlove, standing between his two quadruple expansion engines, told himself that he no longer understood the new generation. He wondered whether this was the key to young Nevile's uncomplaining attitude. Could it be that, when a desirable, finely bred woman like this Mrs. Rossiter could run after a lover and bulldoze her husband into befriending him, the lover naturally developed a new and peculiar discretion of his own? They were so uncertain in their reactions, these women, that they seemed like leopards and panthers. It was necessary, even in their moments of affection, to be extraordinarily careful to avoid being clawed.

The sudden peremptory jang-jang of the telegraphs signaled full ahead on both engines. They were out in the stream now, going down on the tide; down that mythical pathway that was a continuation, on the chart, of Broadway. The sound of the accelerated pulsations always thrilled Mr. Spenlove. His imagination had never become jaded, perhaps because these responsive and exquisite engines were the only things he lived with in close communion. So long, he would reflect, as you do not give your soul into the keeping of men and women, you were safe. Only young Nevile had somehow hung on, he thought, and saw at once that such a description could no wise fit young Nevile. He had been always the same. Gaps several years in length he had bridged with an occasional letter to his friend, resuming the friendship at once after the war and never trespassing on anyone's privacy. That was a curious feature of his adventures with women— he seemed to respect their private lives. At any rate, he never seemed to know anything about them save the essential facts that they gave to him. They never got hold of him so that he turned on them and told tales about them. Possibly because he was a gentleman, Mr. Spenlove thought. And he couldn't be really weak, either, if he kept them spiritually at a distance. His question last night, demanding if women had souls, had been inspired by his experience. Young Nevile was impervious to philosophical speculations. He kept his attention on the outside world. You could tell that by the extraordinary lack of interest he had in reading. He would promise to read anything anybody recommended, but he only glanced at a few pages. Outside of his school classics and one or two plays of Shakespeare, Mr. Spenlove could make no definite statement about Sidney Nevile's resources. He was like a great many young officers nowadays, he got it over the radio. Mr. Spenlove supposed that as a substitute for thought that was far better than reading.

With the final full away order Mr. Spenlove felt able to go upstairs and sit in his cabin. He never went far away from the telephone until the pilot was dropped and the gear snugged down for the run. The socialists, the communists, and the intelligentsia who visualized Mr. Spenlove as a slave to a machine and to capitalistic society, misapprehended his attitude. He enjoyed much more liberty of speech and security of tenure than the average trade union delegate, and he derived much more sensuous pleasure from his engines than the composers of advertising found in their fraudulent productions. The propulsion of fast vessels on a schedule, he had once told a perplexed executive, was the nearest thing to absolute truth and honesty in the world. Deviation from strict virtue on the part of anybody imperilled the enterprise. The executive, who had been unusually successful in selling stock at prices scarcely justified by the earnings of the companies, smiled. It was obvious to him that a man who had grown gray in the service of other men was an inferior. He gave Mr. Spenlove a box of perfectos and advised him to buy all the Continental Soothsayer common he could get at the market.

Mr. Spenlove had at that time given Mr. Romaine his advice about selling while the selling was good, and Continental Soothsayer was not bought by either of them. He smoked the perfectos and attended to his job, which was to keep the Camotan going exactly on her schedule on the least possible amount of fuel. He considered he was better employed in this way than in playing the market.

Now he sat in his room, listening to the familiar sounds from below and watching the steam gauge and voltmeter on the bulkhead near the desk. Presently the boy who waited on him entered and laid the table for lunch while Mr. Spenlove mentioned what he wanted.

This was the way he liked to live, he told himself. This was what he would miss when he retired, if he did retire, to the place he had bought in the country, instead of merely going there for a couple of weeks and half-a-dozen week-ends every year. He would miss the thrum of the propellers and the pleasure of adding, voyage by voyage, to his professional reputation. He would miss even more the sights and sounds upstairs, those manifestations of human pride and folly among people whose chief troubles were too much money and a complete lack of repose. It was impossible, Mr. Spenlove suspected, for them to keep still in one place. They had traveler's itch, if there were such a disease. Even an overnight stay in some lovely harbor made them restless. They got off the ship in Havana and took the airplane home, not because anything at home needed them, but simply because they could not rest. They were beset by devils from hell who drove them on. Mr. Spenlove watched them delightedly, noting their furtive fornications and unabashed alcoholism, not in any spirit of censorship, but because he was fascinated by their lack of imagination. They never invented anything new! He often thought they might be the same unrestful people, in different clothes, every voyage. There were nice people, of course, as well, but they appeared like pure, disembodied souls beside the bright spirits of carnality who strummed their idiotic baby banjos and tooted obscenely on silver saxophones in the midnight darkness on the upper deck. It was strange, he thought, how like to the hereafter a ship was, and how, possibly, we were as mistaken about the hereafter as about a ship. Heaven indeed might easily turn out to be a vast celestial fleet driving on forever through the void, entering archipelagoes of shining spheres where tarried the souls of beings from other universes. Each ship would have its hell on board. . . .

His lunch came; consommé, smoked salmon sandwiches, a slice of Gruyère, and black coffee. Now that he did no manual work he kept to a rigid diet, and never drank liquor until after dinner. Not always then, he reflected grimly. Upstairs those people were stuffed like Strasbourg geese from their morning tea or coffee with biscuits clear up to the last caviar sandwich with stuffed olives in the smoke room at eleven at night. They had meals and meals between meals. They bought candies and fruit and brought crates of things on board with them. They lay on deck chairs in attitudes of animal repletion. And they wondered why they had dyspepsia. They drank several cocktails before dinner, and filled themselves with red wine, and stared pop-eyed and miserable at the blue Caribbean! Somehow the trip did not do them the good they had expected. Mr. Spenlove, smoking a cigar, watched them calmly from his favorite place at the after end of the promenade deck. It was close to the stairway, it was quiet, and the engineer on watch could make a signal from below on the after well-deck that meant nothing to anybody but his chief, who could descend in a few seconds without alarming a single passenger. He would sit on a folding chair and enjoy the scene.

When his lunch had been cleared away he sat smoking and thinking of young Nevile in the light of what had happened. To do justice to those we love is very hard, he reflected. We have an ideal of them and they won't live up to it! It would have been consoling to Mr. Spenlove if young Nevile had turned out a complete failure and gone to the dogs, as they say. But instead of running true to romantic form, he had stuck to his guns and kept up his end after being practically wiped out by being fired from his command. Instead of rushing to an extreme and, after Ada had gone down to Cuernavaca and secured that preposterous divorce, marrying some girl in a reaction of spite, young Nevile had kept his head and, as he said himself, played their game as long as they wanted. It was even possible, since the Company were far from being a branch of Cheeryble Brothers, that young Nevile was a sort of success in the uptown office and the social life he had organized around the Plaza and Ritz was financially approved. Mr. Spenlove realized with some dismay that he himself retained a lot of the old-fashioned horror of a man who had lost his job on a ship. It was evidently ingrained, to regard such a man as an untouchable, no matter what grit he might show. Why, to make a theoretical case of it, wouldn't most young Englishmen, after taking such a beating, disappear from sight? Wouldn't they develop a severe case of homesickness and drift back to England in the second class and go to sea again as bosun or third mate of a tramp? Young Nevile not only had never complained or railed at the unfairness of sacking him on a woman's furious complaint, but had made it clear to the people ashore he was the victim of circumstances. That was what he had been— another way of saying he had been one of the black sheep sacrificed to the Eumenides of our day. Mr. Spenlove took a mild pleasure in discovering classical parallels to his own experience. And because young Nevile had refused to be sacrificed, had in fact become a sort of Perseus in black-sheep's clothing, as it were, there was no sound reason for regarding him as a failure.

And yet that conviction would not down. Mr. Spenlove, by reason of his long observance of the rich, was skeptical whether anyone serving them, as young Nevile was going to serve them, could retain any character worth a penny. And young Nevile, with his handsome, slightly ravaged features, which Mr. Spenlove compared in his mind with those of a god who had been away from Olympus much too long for his own good, might not be on his guard against moral ravages in this new life. That early experience they had shared, before the war, in a millionaire's yacht, might have left seeds of corruption that could grow vigorously in the new soil. There would be pickings in a rich man's club as in a rich man's yacht, Mr. Spenlove suspected. Why had young Nevile been so secretive about that time on the island? He could have blackmailed the family of the Honorable Maeve if he had been a cad. He had, on the other hand, resigned the moment they put in at Cowes and now called it "losing his job." Of course, the damned ship was to be laid up until next season. Curse all private yachts! Mr. Spenlove intoned in his mind, smiling. The most insane extravagance any fool ever indulged in.

Yes, he had resigned at Cowes and had gone home to Ipswich and lived quietly with his people for six months. Must have saved all his pay while on the yacht. . . . And his sister, the candid Ursula . . .

Mr. Spenlove heard the door open and looked in a small mirror he had fixed on his desk to reflect the face of anyone entering.

"Sidney," he said without turning his head, "when you left the Moira, the yacht, I mean, that time in Cowes, why did you go home and stick around instead of looking for another billet?"

Young Nevile came into the room and sat down on the settee.

"They wanted me to. You know perfectly well, Fred. They were trying to bring us together—Maeve, you know. I was a week-end at Boule House, that time. She wasn't in love with me, really. She was in love with that chap she married: the fellow who took lessons in navigation from me in the mornings."

"You backed out? You never told me that."

"I said it wasn't my secret, Fred. I had nothing to do with it. I didn't want to stay all night away from the ship. You know well enough I have always looked after my job."

"I admit that."

"Well, she was the owner's daughter and she took advantage of being the owner's daughter. I don't like being patronized. She'd had several experiences before that voyage. I was just another experience to Maeve. It was a novelty— a night on a Greek island in a ruined temple!"

"Well, it was a novelty and an experience for you too, I should think."

"I ought never to have left the ship. I was still in love with Elli."

"You won't make me believe you are now. I discount that."

"I didn't say I was, in the sense of wanting ever to see her again or to be with her. It's a memory. I think of all these others as just *tarts* compared with her!"

"That's very unfair, Sidney, when you remember what Elli was."

"I know it seems so to you, to anyone. These others are very fine eligible girls to their own people. But they are only tarts to me."

"Hm. Did you have lunch?"

"I was the only one at the table. The other people were being served in their rooms. I saw the skipper on deck. He's getting fat."

"Well, he never does a stroke of any sort. No exercise, and he has three squares a day. I'd be the same if I ate the way he does. He's a good skipper though, Wensley is. I'd hate to change him for some of the others."

"Will you come up to dinner tonight?"

"I may. But you'll have company. There's a little Irish lady at my table. She's making the cruise with her brother. And there's a girl going to visit her father in Jamaica. An agreeable foursome for you."

"A girl? I hope she's all right."

"Specially recommended to the captain by the vice president in charge of operations." Mr. Spenlove rolled out the sonorous title with sardonic enjoyment. "But you know Wensley has no love for petting passengers. He has them up to his cabin once for tea and cocktails during the voyage, and apart from that they must find their own amusement. He thinks they get a better deal from me."

"Well, you come up, Fred. It sounds funny, but having been on these ships, I feel stage fright coming on, sitting among passengers again as one of them."

"That will wear off very rapidly," said Mr. Spenlove. "I've had it. It wears off in a day or so."

"It makes me feel how I've come down in the world after all." Young Nevile went on in a quiet tone. "Sort of losing caste."

"Yes, that's true, and no fancy job you get in a gentleman's club will ever satisfy you in the same way as the command of a three-legged tramp with coal dust all over the bridge. But you've made your bed and you'll have to lie on it."

Mr. Spenlove saw the door opening again. A bell-hop with unbelievably slicked hair came in with a parcel.

"Lady in number forty-seven, Chief, sent this."

"For me? You're sure she's a real lady?"

"Guess so, Chief." The buttoned brat permitted a grin to form on his smooth face. "She said it was for the officer with a beard and four bars on his cuffs."

Mr. Spenlove nodded to indicate the parcel might be laid before him. The boy went out. The string of the parcel was clumsily tied, loose yet with a snarled unpickable knot. When it was cut open a book appeared with a note inside. Mr. Spenlove scowled at the garish paper jacket and then smiled. He held up the book for young Nevile to see.

"Here's one of your companions as far as Kingston," he said. "*The Gilded Skull*, by Norah Kavanagh, published by the Clever Crook Corporation. Want to read it, Sidney? She's a lively little person. Plenty of vitality. I suppose this is by way of introducing herself to my august notice."

On the cover of the book was a glossy picture of two men with flashlights and revolvers peering down into a coffin in which lay a glistening skull. In the background, on a bench lay an almost nude girl with hair the same color as the skull and an oriental krise in her heart. Young Nevile took the book and opened it with the same polite attention he would have bestowed upon Shakespeare or Dumas.

"I read a lot of these," he said. "I find it leaves my mind clear to think of business. It's a sort of occupation. And there's always a chance of finding something really thrilling."

"You're an optimist," said Mr. Spenlove, opening the note that was in the book. He looked up at young Nevile quickly. "She says," he went on, "Mrs. Kavanagh says she hopes I'll give her a chance to pick up some local color while on the cruise and introduce her to as many interesting people as possible."

"You can leave me out," said young Nevile gravely. "I know that line. I was completely fooled by a girl who came down once from a newspaper syndicate with the same excuse."

"You're a passenger now, and you don't suppose I was going to let her interview you. You've never done anything, Sidney, that would interest a writer of that sort of thing. They want bloody murder, strangled blondes and green-eyed Chinamen in chains, my boy. We'll think up something for her."

He took the book back and laid it in his desk.

"I'd better read it myself before I go up," he said. "I liked her. She thought I was the captain, and we had a few pleasant words. She's got a brother on board who's in the newspaper business. Represents the New York *Globe-Messenger* at Washington. They're generally pretty easy to get on with. Pontifical but polite, I would call them. That leaves us only one unknown quantity at the table."

"The girl going to Kingston."

"To be met by her fond parent. Having received every courtesy at our hands, she is met by her father."

"Do you know anything about her?"

"Only that the captain wouldn't have her at his table,"

said Mr. Spenlove. "Wensley takes violent dislikes to specially recommended passengers. And he dislikes Wilmarth, our legal director. That's where he differs from you. He has all his women ashore."

"Perhaps that's the reason he doesn't want this one at his table—he's met her ashore."

"Well, upon my soul, I never thought of that," said Mr. Spenlove, and he gave his beard a pull. "You can ask her."

"I shan't," said young Nevile, with a slight frown. "I don't want to get too friendly with any of these people. I'm making a new start."

III

THE WOMAN with the white hair, pale gray eyes, and the bright scarlet spot on each cheek bone sat in Mr. Spenlove's cabin and looked at the door which young Nevile had just closed behind him.

"Tell me about him!" she said, waving her cigarette in the air. "Tell me! You say he used to be a captain?"

"He is still that, but he hasn't a command," said Mr. Spenlove calmly. "He resembles a monarch without a throne, you may say. I suppose you know there are many points of resemblance between the captains and the kings? I've often wondered whether Kipling hadn't a malicious as well as a poetic reason for coupling them together in his 'Recessional.' The captains and the kings depart! Naturally! I would say. They are very much alike."

"Ah, but that's only fooling," she said, her thoughts on the man who had departed.

"No! They are very much alike. They rule, some as despots and others as constitutional monarchs. Some are, I suspect, usurpers and tyrants. Some lose their heads, and others, like your friend, have to abdicate."

"*My* friend!" said the lady. "He told me he'd known you since he first went to sea."

"Not quite. He was a senior cadet acting as third mate on my ship when I first knew him."

"Tell me!" said the lady again, with a peculiar urgency. Mr. Spenlove looked at her and smiled. The three of them had dined in the saloon. Mrs. Kavanagh's brother was still under the weather, and the other girl had been seen by no one save a stewardess.

"I'll tell you," he said. "You're like all the rest of the women."

"Is he married?" she demanded. "Of course he'd be married," she said, half to herself.

"Not at present," Mr. Spenlove informed her. "He is a deserter from the ranks. In fact, he is leaving the world of women for a happier state of existence in a gentleman's club on a small island off the coast of Jamaica. He's had enough of you!"

"I don't believe it," she said. "He's charming!"

"Yes, he has charm enough, I grant you. I suppose that's all you know or ever need to know about a man. You remember the old song:

"A roving eye, a soldier's mien,
A pennon of the blue,
A doublet of the Lincoln green—
No more of me you knew, dear lass,
No more of me you knew."

"What's that? Tell it to me again." She dug down into her purse and brought out notebook and pencil. She looked up at Mr. Spenlove, who was lighting a cigar and suppressing a smile. He was laughing at himself for being so susceptible to the flattery of her interest. He had had many listeners to his tales on ships, but he did not recall any of them trying to make copy out of him. He repeated the verse, partly because he enjoyed the sound of his own voice.

"You said 'roving eye,' the first time," she remarked,

studying what she had written. "Not 'lightsome eye.' Which is correct?"

"I've forgotten," he told her. "I only quoted it to show you how superficially you regard men, in spite of the daily spectacle of men doing the same thing to women. All we think of is a pretty face, you say! And all you want is a lightsome eye."

"I'd like to see him in uniform!"

"I'll show you a photograph of him when I get time to dig it out. You mustn't fall in love with him, Mrs. Kavanagh."

"Ah, but I must!" she said in high delight. "It's what I came away to do—have some new experiences. We authors get into a groove."

"Thanks for the book. I'm going to read it."

"You'll never get through it. I'm going to do another when I get back."

"About a murder mystery on a ship?"

"How did you guess?"

"You're not the first author to come here for local color, Mrs. Kavanagh. Local color, I have discovered, consists of putting the same improbable characters in a hotel in Barcelona instead of a hotel in the Adirondacks. The body is found in Suite F on the promenade deck instead of in a Park Avenue penthouse."

Mrs. Kavanagh eyed Mr. Spenlove critically as her pale gray eyes danced.

"I can see you're a cynic," she said. "It just never occurred to me in my life before, how sick you must get of us passengers, with our crazy ways, comin' and goin'. . . . Yes, I can understand it."

"You're the only woman in the world who does, barring a few Scotch stewardesses," said Mr. Spenlove, amused.

"But tell me," she laid a finger on his sleeve, "tell me about him. I believe he has some unhappy past. You say he was married. I suppose there was a divorce. I bet she wasn't good enough for him. Did you know her at all?"

"Oh yes. I knew Ada Nevile very well. I don't know about being 'not good enough.' What does a woman mean by a remark like that?"

"Well, I guess she really thinks it." She laughed at herself and tapped her pencil on the notebook. "It means she's thinking of an ideal," she enunciated slowly as if to test a new idea out in the open. All this time she was contemplating Mr. Spenlove with wide pale gray eyes, behind which a busy brain was working in darkness, formulating and assembling the strange patterns of her trade.

"I dare say. Well, Ada Nevile was not the girl you imagine. She was good enough for anybody, if he happened to be able to keep up with her. She is a very ambitious person. I don't mean in social position or even in money. I mean for herself. She had the loftiest ambition and the feeblest equipment for realizing it I have ever encountered."

"You say the most provoking things. Tell me about her. I mean about her with him. What sort of ambition?"

"You could never be sure. She was a passenger when he met her, you know. They always are. We never have a chance to meet women of any significance unless they are traveling in our ship. And that explains a lot. But it doesn't explain how he came to marry Ada. By the way, her real name was Aïda."

"From the opera? Was she beautiful? And what do you mean—you could never be sure what her ambition was? It sounds as if you didn't like her."

"You are on the right track there. Plenty of other men do like her, however. She's married to Number Four, I believe."

"Then she must have something."

"It is possible, but I have no clear notion what it is. Yes, she must have something. She never revealed it to me because, I suppose, she knew it would never work. It is a sort of grave mendacity about irrelevant facts."

"I don't understand you at all," said Mrs. Kavanagh.

"Well, a great many women indulge in it. She transcended most women because she worked it so successfully on men who ought to have known better. Why, the man who is married to her now, or who was married to her last time I heard of her, worships the ground under her feet."

"And you can't see anything in her? Any woman who can do that—nowadays—is above the average. Did he, your friend, worship the ground under her feet?"

Mr. Spenlove watched the little woman in front of him busily making notes in fine handwriting in her book. He watched the habitual flicking of ash from the glowing cigarette, the nervous fidgets and incessant dependence upon drugs that mark off the genuine modern woman from those others who are only serene relics of a former age. He wondered how deep her interest lay and whether he was justified in talking to her.

"Worship? I don't think he did. Does your husband do that, if I may be so bold?"

The shrewd weather-beaten Irish face dimpled, and the corners of the humorous mouth were drawn down to make Mr. Spenlove smile.

"Ah, go on with you, Mr. Spenlove! Why, we're married, we are. Married forever and ever. You'd never understand, I suppose. You Protestant Englishmen are so stupid! We're outside all this."

"I suppose you are. I ought to have remembered. You're just taking a voyage because the good father gave you advice, eh? And your brother, his wife is all the better for a vacation."

"I'll be very glad to get back to my family, if that's what you're hinting. We're very devoted in our family. My brother Terry's been badly treated by his wife."

"Well, I only inquired about worshiping the ground you tread on, remember. Why should anyone else do it? Why did you infer that a marriage is unhappy unless the man is a fool?"

"Tell me about him. I've an idea, and I want some clothes for it. Tell me about how you came to be so fond of him."

"I'd rather hear about your brother Terry and his wife. Is he away on this cruise to punish her?"

"Oh, she left him. Of course, she wasn't a Catholic and it wasn't a real marriage. It served her right at that. She could have wound Terry around her finger if she'd had any sense. My brother's awfully clever, and he should never have tied himself down to a mere schoolteacher. She wouldn't even give up her job to devote herself to him, let alone what she calls her religion."

"Well, I hope he forgets his griefs and enjoys the cruise. Plenty of diversion on a ship like this, you know. He may discover consolation and balm for his wounded heart."

"Ah, but I'd never let him!" she exclaimed, alarmed. "No, no! I'll take care of him!"

"You reserve the adventures for yourself, I can see that."

"You'd never understand the Irish," she beamed.

"I had an Irish grandmother," he reflected aloud, not proudly enough for his listener.

"Now, that'll *do*, Mr. Spenlove! I want to hear about that friend of yours. He has a most interesting face, and what you've told me makes me crazy to hear more."

"I'll send for a drink. I only have Jamaica rum here. You won't like it."

"Why, I'd love to have some. I've heard so much about Jamaica rum. Sixteen men on a dead man's chest; though how they could all sit on one man's chest is beyond me."

"Ah! Then I'll make you some punch." Mr. Spenlove pressed a button near his chair and drew out a bottle from his lower drawer. "Sure your brother won't be looking for you?"

"He won't be looking for anybody for a long time yet," she said, shaking her head. "I know those villains he was drinking with. They had flasks, and they're all very fond of Terry.

You know, Terry's really clever. He won't be a Washington correspondent all his life."

"I thought that was a pretty good assignment," said Mr. Spenlove, cutting up some limes.

"Not for Terry. He's refused several splendid positions that would take him away from Washington. He's writing a book showing up the Administration. Several publishers have told him they would like to see it when he's finished it. He's got it with him now, and I'm goin' to make him work at it the whole time. After he's through with his hangover, I mean. Oh, he's awfully clever."

"It runs in the family," murmured Mr. Spenlove.

"You can't make me forget what I want to hear by making ridiculous remarks," she assured him. He gave an order to the steward and answered the engine-room telephone.

"I haven't mentioned this to a soul," he remarked and he went on preparing the two tall glasses of punch. "Because the dénouement of the story, as I suppose you would call it, was a great disappointment to me. It was a sudden and astonishing end to a career in which I had taken an interest ever since it began on that old Mediterranean tramp long before the war. Long before the war you remember, I mean. There was another war on then, one that you have forgotten if you ever knew about it. I refer to the Turko-Italian War. We were in the thick of it at one time. We saw history in the process of manufacture. We saw imperialism, a sort of baby imperialism, taking its first walk, watched over by several grown-up empires who were watching each other as well."

"It must have been interesting," said Mrs. Kavanagh. "I've never seen any great events. I envy anyone who has been all over the world."

"No, there wasn't anything very interesting. Seamen seldom see what you call great events. We saw Italian cruisers trying to catch a Turkish cruiser. We were overhauled by Italian destroyers, but when we broke out the Red Ensign they went away. Sometimes we saw, far away on the horizon, one of our own cruisers, very white and efficient looking. It pleased us to compare the fussy blustering of the combatants with the calm aloofness of our own chaps. I remember it was on one of these occasions that young Nevile said to me:

"'By Jove, our fellows are on top, eh?'

"He was quite emotional about it. It made me wonder who he was. Of course I knew he was in the deck department, but he had come suddenly to us one day in Glasgow, very neat and good-looking in his cadet uniform and with one of the neatest-looking sets of luggage I had ever seen on a dock side. Snowy canvas dunnage bags and a new Gladstone bag as yellow as gold. It was an altogether marvelous sight for anyone on a tramp steamer. But I had had other marvelous sights down below in the engine room that voyage, and the young fellow had dropped out of my mind. At Gibraltar a naval cutter flew alongside and gave us the information that Italy and Turkey were at war but would not harm neutrals. The skipper was given a course to Malta. As nothing happened we forgot all about it. We were very superior, in those days, about other nations' squabbles. We kept the ring. We told those two irritable children, the Italian Kingdom and the Ottoman Empire, to confine their tantrums to Lybia and Cyrenaica. When Italy wanted to bombard the Straits and capture Constantinople we said: 'Naughty, naughty!' Dreadnaughts, hidden in the creeks of Valletta Harbor, got up steam.

"So, one day, as we plugged along eastward at ten knots toward Malta, I saw a white warship on the starboard bow. And then another, and another. And a young fresh voice said, close beside me, 'By Jove! our fellows are on top, eh?'

"He must have been in his eighteenth year then. Possibly a year older, but I forget. He was very good-looking. Yes, I know he's good-looking now; but the bloom was on then. Don't be offended if I say it was because he'd had nothing to do with women then. There is a bloom. I think it's even more beautiful than the virginal freshness of a young girl. And I am, or I used to be, more abashed in the presence of such a youth than I could ever be with young girls. They, the girls, seem always so full of their own bright thoughts which are concentrated dazzlingly upon the impression they are making upon men that they give me a feeling not at all proper."

"Not all young girls are like that," warned Mrs. Kavanagh. "I have three of my own."

"Ah, not yours, of course. The nuns keep them ever between the walls of impenetrable thorny thickets. They are behind the high walls of an invisible convent."

"They try to be," smiled the lady. "And they are good girls, I am told. Never mind, I forgive you."

"I am speaking of heretics," went on Mr. Spenlove quietly. The punch was ready, and he offered the potent brew to his companion. "We still speak of seduction as a base practice of men. But seduction nowadays is a prerogative of young girls in their new freedom of movement and promiscuous cohabitation with unmaidenly ideas. It is the youth, nowadays, who is bashful and reticent, and who withdraws hurriedly from the bold huntresses on the highways."

"Nonsense!" said the lady. "That's only a defense mechanism the girls have cultivated. The best defense is an attack."

"I think I'm a better judge of heretics than you are, especially the traveling kinds," said Mr. Spenlove, taking a small drink. "Do you call going into a man's cabin and demanding . . . eh? demanding . . .? Come, come! The sea does strange things to young women. And the point I was trying to make was only that the first assault, the battery of eyes and voice, the clutch of a vibrating personality, is all the girl's. You can't deny that this makes a difference in the course of a year or two. You'll have a chance to see for yourself on this voyage. We have a few of all kinds. Local color you want? Keep your eyes open, dear lady, as we sail towards the Blue Caribbean. . . .

"Yes, he was proud and happy because our fellows were

on top. It wasn't prigism at all, as you call it. It was a pure flame of disinterested patriotism. He came from a home, a town, a school, where all the traditions of law, order and good government were impregnated with the idea of heroic achievement against outer darkness and savagery. For a couple of generations the conception of the white man's burden had been leavening all the thoughts of the class to which he belonged, the upper middle, as we say. It was an integral part of his cultural background, to feel glad the navy was on the job, always ready, yet never taking the offensive. We believed, in those days, that we really did keep the peace of the seven seas. It's our national hypocrisy to assume that we had a large measure of success. We had the knack of being Johnny-on-the-spot without indulging in provocative belligerence, like the Prussians."

"Ah, that's the British complacency of you!" Mrs. Kavanagh broke out as she waved her hand in Mr. Spenlove's face. "You make yourselves out snow-white angels and all the other nations black devils from hell. What about the seven hundred years you've trodden Ireland under the iron heel? I'll bet you can't answer that one. Provocative belligerence!"

"Well, I had no hand in it, and neither had young Nevile. In fact, like me, he had Irish blood in his veins rather than on his hands. And what I am trying to convey is not an impression of angelic purity, but virginal innocence in his young heart. There was, as I told you, a bloom on everything connected with him. That was what attracted me to him. I had been passing through a personal experience in that part of the world. I had lost something—someone, in fact, who was very dear to me, and I felt at a loss. I was like those elderly childless persons who want to adopt someone to fill the cavity in their own lives."

"Tell me," said Mrs. Kavanagh. "Was it your wife died?"

"No, the loss was more poignant than a wife could ever be to a seafaring man. We had been to Salonika the previous voyage, and it was the daughter of a man I used to know in New Orleans. She was killed in some street fighting in Salonika, accidentally, you know, and I happened to value her friendship very highly. Call it friendship, because she had her own special tragedy."

"Tell me," said Mrs. Kavanagh. "Tell me all about her. Was she pretty?"

"It doesn't matter much any more. She was dead when young Nevile came down to our ship in Glasgow and began to give us a tone."

"What do you mean, doesn't matter any more? It's perfectly plain to me you were in love with the girl, whatever her story might be, and she was killed. And yet you say it doesn't matter any more!"

"Only a little. The memory of these experiences dies away. Do you know, Mrs. Kavanagh, I'm not at all sure, if I were to meet that girl in the street now, that I would recognize her."

"That's callous!"

"No, only human. I don't even want to talk about her any more."

"Because you still love her."

"That's very charming and feminine of you, but it begs the question. We weren't talking about my love affairs, I hope. I was only explaining how I came to be interested in the young man who interested you at our table."

"And you watched over his love affairs instead of having any more yourself. Is that it?"

Mr. Spenlove set down his glass and smiled.

"Ha!" he said. "I can see I am in the hands of an expert. You want me to admit that when the young fellow had a love affair I saw myself in reincarnation? You mean I became a victim of middle-aged sentiment? Come, come! I wasn't forty then."

"Something like that, I'm sure," said Mrs. Kavanagh. "Your own love was born again."

Mr. Spenlove, looking at the floor between his feet, shook his head slowly.

"I wouldn't take the trouble to mention such things," he said. "The love affair he became involved in was something I had no experience of at all. Possibly you, as a writer of fiction, may know all about it, but not me. I wasn't at all pleased, I can assure you."

"I can see you're dying to tell me everything," said Mrs. Kavanagh, and she drank with deep satisfaction. She was one of those women who can gratify several senses at once, while their minds move swiftly, like complex mechanisms lowered into the subconscious. Mrs. Kavanagh, now that she was really at sea, and her anxiety about her brother Terry temporarily assuaged, was enjoying herself. She lit another cigarette.

"Don't be too sure about that," warned Mr. Spenlove over his glass. "I draw the line—well, you shall have this straight. We went on that trip with a cargo of Welsh coal to Valletta, which is the great naval dockyard of Malta. You ought to have seen the young fellow with his classy binoculars gazing at the fleet. He had his name engraved on those glasses, with an inscription. He had been top of his school —head boy, and captain of the first cricket eleven when he left to go to a nautical training school, and they had presented him with that costly article to show their appreciation.

"That was what made me ask him why he hadn't gone into the navy instead of the merchant service. It seemed more in keeping with his social standing. He told me his father had a haberdasher's shop in Ipswich and he himself had won a scholarship at King Henry the Eighth's grammar school at Saxhambury, which is in the very heart of East Anglia."

"That's in England, isn't it?" said Mrs. Kavanagh.

"Very much so, just as New England is in the United States; almost the oldest part of all. Well, that was where the young fellow was raised. He grew up in a cranny of the ancient edifice of England, with all the old-fashioned notions of class privilege and social order that you Americans love to laugh at. But you have to understand them before you can enjoy their really humorous quality. It was because of them that he elected to go into merchant ships instead of the navy. He was a shopkeeper's son and it was not, in his family, fitting to try to be a naval officer. Moreover, it was much less expensive to pay a small premium for apprenticeship."

"I never heard of anything so ridiculous!" said Mrs. Kavanagh. "He'd make as good a naval officer as anybody, I'm sure."

"He did, in the war. Did very well in the war. That's not the point. He, and his family, haberdashing in Ipswich, had no desire to climb out of their well-guarded position in the social order and hang precariously on the outer fringes of a world alien to them. You forget these people are very proud. I went down there once. I saw the haberdasher's shop, over which the family had lived in a narrow street over which the carved oak beams projected to carry the upper floors. I even went down with young Nevile to the new house his father had built at a place called Ufford.

"It was very illuminating. That was where they had come from. Young Nevile's mother had been a Wishant, and one of her very distant ancestors had fought at Agincourt. What interested me was that when Mr. Nevile had the money to build a country place he built a new villa, an early nineteenth-century house of red brick, with a bathroom. He did, in fact, what his ancestors had done, unconsciously however. There was neither philistinism nor snobbery in him. He was a haberdasher, not an antiquarian. I doubt if he knew much more of King Uffa, who had his capital on Uffa's Ford, than I did. His brother, young Nevile's Uncle Alf, was in Australia and doing well. They never heard from him save by a card about a month after Christmas, but they knew he was doing well. I suppose King Uffa, when he took the daring decision to cross the stormy North Sea from Jutland, and settled

down at the ford where all the Saxon trackways met, thought
of himself as a pioneer into the western wilderness. Possibly
he sent messages home to say he was doing well.

"What I am getting at is that young Nevile came out of
an environment that was as wise and as wholesome as existed in the world at that time. What? Crazy? You had better
wait and hear what I have to tell. He wasn't a Brushwood
Boy, I may remind you. He had excellent ideas on the subject
of democracy, for instance. He told me straight that strikes
were a rotten trick, but he would never break one by taking
a job until it was settled. Where did he get that idea from?
I have a conviction he got it from some inherited conception
of solidarity with his own kind. His explanation was that 'it
isn't decent,' to do that sort of thing. He had a code, if you
like, calculated to infuriate those who live by discussion. He
would not discuss things. He merely expressed his own personal attitude in simple, brief phrases. I remember, when the
second engineer of the Manola, who picked up the most
alarming ideas at times, only to drop them with a crash, said
the House of Lords ought to be abolished and the estates
given to sailors to raise chickens, young Nevile remarked
that there were two things he never argued about, politics
and religion."

"The very things most people argue all night about," said
Mrs. Kavanagh.

"Yes; and I am not sure they are doing us any good
thereby. Young Nevile listened, enjoying the controversies,
but nobody lured him into any confession of faith. It wasn't
necessary because he expressed his faith and his ideals in his
behavior. I fancy Captain Evans liked him more than he
would admit to me. Captain Evans and I had been together
a long time and you couldn't conceive a more dramatic contrast in backgrounds than young Nevile's and his captain's.
He was what Captain Evans would have liked his own son to
be, if you can imagine a shipmaster who can face the prospect
of having a son at sea. Jack Evans came up through the

hawse hole and bore the marks of the forecastle yet upon his body and mind. But he was aware of the tone the acting third mate gave the Manola. Oh yes, he liked him very much. He knew in his heart young Nevile would go into new fine passenger ships in the future, 'and leave us old shell-backs on the beach,' as he put it.

"So we came into Valletta to discharge our cargo of best Welsh coal, which was navy fuel in those days. All the warships were bunkered and ready to go out at an hour's notice, so we were tied up at the head of French Creek in that huge harbor to await the turn of events. We were told we might even be sent somewhere else, under escort. It was exciting and interesting for the young fellow. He got permission to go ashore. The other mates were married men, new to the ship, and without much enterprise. They were content to stick on board and watch the movement of the ships in the harbor. So he went ashore, and that was what did for him. He fell in love."

"It sounds terribly old-fashioned to hear you say that," said Mrs. Kavanagh reflectively. "You can't talk about people falling in love—in fiction—any more. The public is too sophisticated. Characters begin by going to bed together now."

"In your novels?" Mr. Spenlove laid his hand impressively on *The Gilded Skull*.

"Indeed not! I stick to murder thrillers. They're the only moral literature left for us to write."

"Or to read," agreed Mr. Spenlove. "Well, I have suspected for some time now that I was old-fashioned, and that is my excuse for insisting that he fell in love when he went ashore. He met a girl in a café, just off the Strada Reale, which is the main street of Valletta."

"Did you see her? Was she, you know, not very respectable?"

"Why, there you have me. She thought she was very respectable, and you would have the opposite view, I suppose. You see, she was not one of the regular girls plying for hire like taxis in that part of town. The social gradations of courtesans in a place like Valletta are well marked and very strictly maintained. From the girls who waited for blue-jackets and firemen down below the town, to the ladies who kept house for officers over in Sliema, which is across a long arm of the harbor behind the town, there was no trespassing on one another's preserves. But the fact was that this girl—Elli Phalère she called herself—was not in their ranks at all."

"Was that her real name? It sounds awfully romantic." Mrs. Kavanagh looked up from her little notebook.

"It was where she came from. She had drifted into Malta from Tunis, but she had been born on the shores of Phaleron Bay, which is the port of Athens. Yes, she was a Greek, I suppose, though her name was never revealed to us. She was Elli Phalère. If young Nevile ever learned it, he kept it to himself. Elli Phalère was like Betty of the Bronx or Nellie from Nyack. Just a professional moniker, a stage name. Elli had been a dancer in Tunis, she told me. But when the young fellow met her in the café on the Piazza Tesoreria she had a friend who was supporting her."

"Oh, I'm so disappointed!"

"Yes, I knew you would be. But I am not gilding any gingerbread for you. He fell in love with her at first sight. Knowing her later, drinking with her in that same café, I can imagine how she would capture his inexperienced and romantic heart. She was so lovely I didn't blame him at all. She had exquisite taste in clothes. She wore large-brimmed hats that made her large dark eyes darker and larger, made her pallor luminous and her smile full of exotic mystery.

"She sat apart in there. The friend, as she called him, was a Maltese merchant, who was married and lived in Italy most of the time. He was very busy making money out of the trade stirred up by the war with Turkey. I believe he had married a Genoese. Elli sat apart, for everybody who frequented the place knew her circumstances. Young Nevile fell in love with her and when she rose, smiling, to go out, he plucked up his courage and followed her.

"She told me about it, long afterwards. She spoke many languages surprisingly well and she said she had fallen in love with him too, a little. I wasn't surprised at that either, because of that bloom I mentioned. Elli was about twenty-six or -seven at that time, with a figure like a goddess or perhaps a nymph of her native Mount Hymettus, which rises to the southward of Phaleron. I asked her how she came to walk like that, and she told me when she was a child and lived up in the hills she carried a water jar on her head every day from the cistern.

"They were a very handsome couple. Her friend, she let me know, in a roundabout way, was well on in years; but that was inevitable. Young fellows hadn't the means to disport themselves in the rôle of a keeper of concubines, if you'll excuse the definition. She knew exactly what she was in for when young Nevile followed her out of the Café Regina and along the Strada Reale. She was amused and she was happy, I think, for she revealed to me with a touch of pride that she had caught an English boy."

"What complacency!" muttered Mrs. Kavanagh. "What incredible complacency you English have! Why should a Greek girl feel any such pride?"

"You ask me questions I could never answer," said Mr. Spenlove. "I don't know. I merely observe and contemplate. Why don't you ask one of them yourself some day? All I know is, they always do feel that sort of pride. Elli Phalère was entirely without self-consciousness about it. I fancy the young man suddenly filled a gap in her life, which was somewhat solitary while her merchant was away in Naples and Milan. I fancy he had a wife and family in Milan. And with so much at stake she would be extremely careful to give the other girls no reason for tale-bearing. She was, moreover, a wanderer. She couldn't speak the peculiar lingo of that old island. As a rule, those who can speak it never learn any other language.

It is baffling as Basque or Irish to a foreigner, and about as much use to its possessors."

"Ah now!" said Mrs. Kavanagh, but without real force or fire.

"We have to face these cases of suicide among languages," said Mr. Spenlove calmly. "There is no bringing them back to life. Elli Phalère said Maltese was the tongue of savages, in which she agreed with St. Paul, who got marooned there. He called them barbarous people but kind to castaways. Very hospitable, as I found them, those old Phœnician folk, and I love their island, which seems carved out of honey and cream. It was an ideal setting for that girl, the hellenic odalisque who held our young man captive for the first time in his life."

"Like Calypso and Ulysses!"

"Well, it was the same island, I believe. I've heard some-where Ogygia was the Greek name for Malta; and here was a Greek girl, a nymph if you like, from the shape of her and the power of her in the arts of love."

"Was that all it was? Just a dallying around while the ship was in port?"

"No, it was a pretty serious affair. I became very much alarmed when I realized he was completely carried away by his experience. Captain Evans said to me, one day on deck as he stood watching the ships, 'What's the matter with that young feller? I've had to speak to him several times. He's away ashore before supper every night.' I said something soothing. Good old Jack Evans stood staring, red faced and tun bellied, as concerned as he could be about anybody out-side his own precious family circle of mother and child. He really liked young Nevile, and he said, 'Don't let him get into trouble with these tarts ashore, Fred.'

"I'd have taken care of anything like that. But how was I to know what he was up to when I never saw him? He skipped ashore and vanished. He'd come on board at some godforsaken time of the night, or morning, turn in for an hour, and be up to turn the men to at six as smart as you please. What concerned us was his dreamy inattention while we foregathered in the saloon for meals. He didn't write a single letter home. He drew on Saturday all the pay coming to him. I think Captain Evans was quietly scandalized at that. He made no audible comments except to me, for old Jack had learned wisdom in his years at sea. He knew how to hold his tongue in spite of his forthright character and hot bloodshot eyes. He only wished the young fellow to keep out of harm. He sat at the head of our cabin table like a stout red-faced idol, his black mustache sweeping out in grand curves as he preened it. His eyes would be cast down as he became aware of the young fellow's empty seat at supper.

"But when I suggested he come ashore with me and take a look around, he refused. 'You go, Fred,' he said. 'I don't fancy the beach any more. I'll go ashore when I can take a train to Cardiff. Wish I was there now.' So I went ashore alone. I wanted to give the natives a treat, of course, but I also wanted to see the attraction that was keeping young Nevile engaged so continuously."

"And you saw her? Was she what you expected?"

"I didn't know what to expect. Most young men when they go ashore from ships are too timid or too furtive to do anything unconventional. They sit around in parlors, drinking tepid beers and soft drinks and indulge in not very refined orgies of conversation. What they really want is not love or even sensuality, but to be able to say they have been around. Young Nevile wasn't that sort of lad at all. I don't believe he ever went near such places in his life." Mr. Spenlove gave a short laugh. "He never had any necessity. And it was only a fluke that he happened into that Café Regina and followed Elli Phalère out. It was a fluke that she should have reached a point when she felt she wanted some diversion. So when I drifted slowly up the Strada Reale one night heading for the Opera House, which was advertising *Faust*, and saw young

Nevile in a carriage with a girl, I raised my hat. I couldn't see who it was, for she lay far back under the hood while he was leaning forward to speak to the driver. He saw me and was suddenly and very charmingly embarrassed.

"Defiant, too. The driver, on seeing me, stopped his horse, and there we were, in the main street of the city, facing each other. I said, 'Well, well!' and he smiled as he turned a rather nice shade of pink. Then he found his companion shaking his arm, and he turned towards her to listen. What she wanted was an introduction."

"You'd made an impression!" said Mrs. Kavanagh, much amused.

"I might have thought so, but she had other schemes besides conquest. 'This is Elli, Chief,' said the young fellow. She leaned forward, and I saw how lovely she was. Her gloved hand came out to meet mine. He told her who I was, and she smiled. 'Come to my place,' she said. 'I have a nice house.' She had a low, sweet voice.

"I said I was going to the opera, so could I come later? She said, yes of course, very pleased, and wrote the address on an envelope I gave her. She was so obviously glad to see me that I divined she wanted others to see us in such intimate grouping. She suggested I drive up the street with them, and I consented. I think she was awfully pleased about that. Some girls going by saw me get into that small vehicle and sit down with my back to the driver and with Elli's small, perfectly shod feet close to mine.

"She was wearing an immense hat so that her face seemed small and superhuman. She had features fine and regular, with great dark eyes that she kept bent upon me with an intelligent curiosity. Nothing but that, I assure you. I had fugitive thoughts at one time that she was only prospecting for a new middle-aged friend, but I was wrong. She was seeking to protect herself from gossip by being seen with such a respectable person as myself. Yes, that was her idea! The young fellow had persuaded her to go out for a drive, unconsciously desirous that all men might see him with the wonderful girl he had captured. Which wasn't Elli's idea at all. She hadn't the slightest desire for some girl at the Regina to tell Signor Vilhena, when he returned, that his girl had been having a lover. She received me into that small carriage with grave delight. Yes, I must come to her house. It was in Floriana, which is to Valletta what Yonkers is to New York.

"I got out at the Opera House. Well, I was relieved from most of my fears. You may think I am a pernicious person of depraved morals, but when I realized what had happened I entered the grand foyer of the Valletta Opera House in a state of elation. He had got hold of a first-class woman at the very beginning!"

"Ah, you're disgusting," said Mrs. Kavanagh. "How can you justify such wicked ideas?"

"By their fruits, which are fairly well known by now. By logic, if you like. What would you have, leaving out those who cherish a vocation for the religious life? I knew that after such an experience he wouldn't want any truck with the usual Jack-ashore women; and you complain because I was elated! You haven't yet understood that what I was beholding was a romance. He was in love, and to a certain extent so was she. I could even see the flame of it burning between them as they sat under the leather hood of the carriage.

"I enjoyed the music. I still prefer *Faust*, in Italian, to modern music, which I don't understand. I can't remember it; nobody can. I told you I was old-fashioned. And even in the opera I am in touch with the greatest mind of the nineteenth century, who conceived the story, and the character of the tempter of mankind."

"You remind me of him." Mrs. Kavanagh sighed. "You shouldn't have let that nice boy waste his youth on such a creature!"

"That's just where you make a mistake. I didn't look at it that way at all. I was assisting at a romance. You have to remember that, in order to grow up, a man must have a

romance. Young Nevile came from a social order with very
clearly defined traditions. His own place in that order provided him with a certain sort of romantic attachments. He
might marry in his own class, or below it, in which case the
romance would wear thin and shabby in no time at all. He
might marry above his station, and what that does to a young
man has never been adequately described. I was once ship-
mates with a handsome devil of a second officer who was
literally swallowed alive by a county family. He was never
seen again after he married the eldest daughter. Never seen
or heard of by any of us. And young Nevile, when we were
together on a private yacht—— I will tell you about that
presently."

"Wasn't he swallowed alive?"

"No, he escaped. That was one of his lucky adventures.
Besides, he was no longer a boy in his first love affair as he
was with Elli. What I want you to understand is the enormous influence the environment of a place like Valletta has
upon an impressionable young fellow from the cultured section of the middle classes, with its background of Greco-
Roman culture, its Renaissance traditions from Elizabethan
times, its heritage of maritime adventurers going out to find
new lands and seas, standing before kings and getting on
intimate terms with kings' daughters. . . . Figure to yourself
how Elli Phalère would appear to that romantic youth ready
for his first passion. She was beautiful, just so much older
than he to make the glamour marvelous beyond words. Her
name sounded like the bells chiming across the harbor as we
lay at anchor in the still dawn. He would even discover a
romantic and heroic quality in finding favor in the eyes of
another man's mistress. Oh yes he would. Romance, dear
lady, takes on strange and wonderful disguises sometimes.
He was a sailor, and he was ashore with a lovely Greek girl
in a fabulous isle of the sea. He didn't know it until I told
him long afterwards, but he was a young Ulysses ashore with
Calypso on Ogygia. You don't suppose Ulysses was the first

man Calypso had kept house with. You can see her cavern
at the other end of the island. We drove out there from
Cività Vecchia one Sunday, through the Bingemma Hills.

"That was the sort of expedition Elli loved, for it took her
away from Valletta without depriving her of young Nevile's
society. She was very discreet. The way she eluded the facts
of life was superb. Or rather the way she took them, put
romantic garments and regalia on them and presented them
to young Nevile, was masterly.

"After the opera, and I was enjoying my usual thrill over
the scene where Mephistopheles vanishes with Faust in a
blaze of crimson flames, I took a cab out to the address in
Floriana. I told you it was like going to Yonkers from New
York. Valletta is a small-scale model of Manhattan, while
Sliema, where the naval and consular swells live, corresponds
to Brooklyn, and the dockyards are on the Jersey shore. All
on a small scale. Floriana is more level and open than
Valletta, which is no more than a series of steep staircases
running down each side from the Strada Reale. Floriana lies
beyond the great gate in the walls of the ancient city. After
following the wide central avenue a while the cab started
down a narrow street towards the Marsamuscetto Harbor.
The moon, which was nearly full, threw intense shadows.
When we turned into a still smaller street that had a view
over the water towards Sliema the cab stopped within the
shadow of a high wall, and the driver, bending down to look
'at me, pointed with his whip at the house across the street.
He buzzed the bell he had on his dashboard, to call attention.

"It was a small house, with a door of dark wood, and a
window with closed green jalousies about six feet above the
sidewalk. I got out and glanced down at the harbor. A ferry,
like a beetle, was crawling across a polished mirror towards
the Misida Creek. Up at the corner a wine shop shed a faint
glow upon the shadow in which I stood. I thought to myself
that no young man in the world could withstand the on-
slaught of so much romantic glamour. You see, he had been

on a ship before, but he had never been to such a place as this. He had been to ports like Bremen and Galveston, which have no more connection with what I call romance than a London suburb."

"Romance can be anywhere," snapped Mrs. Kavanagh. She was enjoying herself, and the planters' punch was a novel excitement.

"To you. Not to us. We need that touch of neo-classical loveliness that we inherit from our eighteenth-century ancestors who had their honeymoons amid the autumn fall of leaves in Vallombrosa, or to the sound of Adria's gondolier whose voice swept along the blue and moonlit waters of the Grand Canal. You may say what you like, but to an Englishman, Byron living with the Countess Guiccioli in a palazzo, with a gondola tied up at the front door, is romance. I confess I am thrilled even nowadays by such adventures! Most of us, after we have passed the days of our youth, are afraid of them. We pretend we are too respectable and too moral to have romantic love affairs, whereas really we don't know how.

"I stepped across the street. Suddenly the jalousy swung open and framed Elli Phalère's face in the opening. She smiled and, thrusting the shutter away, leaned out and gazed down upon me. Now, she was saying to herself, anybody can look. I'm having friends in to see me. Behold this respectable person from one of the ships! An Englishman too! Well, something like that. How do I know? By what she said later. She said, 'Mister Chief, if you come it's all right because plenty girls want to get my friend away from me. I have to be careful all the time.' Oh yes, we understood each other at once, Elli and I. She smiled down at me and created, I may tell you, a very favorable impression. She had black hair that she was wearing loose, and when she put her bare arms up behind her ears it became a sable cloud. Artifice if you like, because, like the big hat, it made her face seem smaller, but it is the artifice of the artist who uses perspective and foreshortening to carry conviction. She gave me another glance of welcome and went away to open the door.

"We came together on a balcony at the back, where there was a view of the harbor. It wasn't really a furnished house, but there seemed to be everything one really needed. Young Nevile was in a long chair out there and he was reading a magazine. They had been drinking lemonade, for neither he nor Elli touched alcohol at that time. He never did drink much. Elli knew too much about human nature to offer the stuff to me. It wasn't that she thought I was likely to be a drinker so much as that she wanted me to know she knew how to be a hostess in such circumstances. She moved a chair around, called to some invisible menial, and presently I was able to remark, 'Well, here we are! and here's luck, you two!'"

"Didn't you feel embarrassed, coming in like that?" asked Mrs. Kavanagh.

"Why should I? They weren't. They were in love. She was watchful and discreet because she knew love was a temporary thing. She knew that ships sail away and sailors rarely fail to rejoin. She had to take care of herself. But she was in love with him. I could see it when she looked at him. And he was in that golden fog which envelops us when we are young and enamored of a woman of experience who is also outside of our social order. We have a feeling of desperate urgency in a case like that, because we are sure there never was such a chance to achieve supreme ecstasies. We are so proud of ourselves we are ready for any folly. We believe in the loved one and wish to possess her forever.

"How did I know? He told me as we went back to the ship. I was frightened to death. He told me he could not live without Elli Phalère, that he wanted her to come to England so that he could marry her.

"I don't exaggerate when I say this threw me into a panic, although I remained outwardly calm and silent on the subject. I was like a man who, about to reach for an admired flower in a tropical hothouse, sees an absolutely deadly snake asleep among the foliage. I knew enough to be aware that if I set up a great cry and went into a fatherly rage with him, young Nevile would be more determined than ever to make a muck of his life. I had to keep still and think how to circumvent him without making both of them my enemies. It wasn't easy."

"What did you do?"

"I waited until next day. I assumed a faint lack of interest. I said nothing to anybody, not even to the old man, who would have exploded like a bombshell. I was very frightened when young Nevile came down to my cabin after lunch and after getting himself inside the door, closed it. I was lying on my settee, meditating. I didn't want to be asked for sympathy or advice. I was harassed by a feeling I'd do what he was doing in his place, but that I wouldn't want to marry her. It made me less noble than he. For it was nobility of soul that inspired in him the horrendous notion of taking a woman of easy virtue, a wanderer of many ports, seven or eight years older than himself, back to the serene middle-class home in East Anglia.

"You see, what made it so damnably complicated for a man in my position was the extreme attractiveness and suitability of Elli herself once you ignored the young fellow's background. She was, as I suspected then and found out when I got to know her, a first-rate article. I fancy Ulysses would never have stayed all those years on that island with Calypso if she hadn't been something unusual. Elli was, as we say, smart as a whip. She had an attractive personality and a persuasive intelligence. Thinking of these things, I saw no reason why I should get myself into difficulties by barging in on the boy's business. But I am, as you may have suspected, English as well as human. And I couldn't bear the thought of him running such a risk at the very beginning of his career. So when he came into my room and closed the door I was in a state of irritable uncertainty."

"But what did he want?"

"Only a loan. He wanted me to lend him five pounds. He had two pounds ten left of what he had drawn, and his idea was to give Elli seven pounds to pay her fare to England. This, mind you, after seeing her about three or four times. He'd pay me, he said quietly, as soon as he got back home. He'd be leaving then, he said, to get married.

"I didn't refuse. I said I'd have to see if the old man would let me have it. We avoided the reason why he couldn't go direct to the old man. No, I didn't refuse and I didn't promise. I played for time. And as luck would have it they were moving the ship that evening to some buoys in French Creek which made it necessary for young Nevile to stay on board several hours. I was going ashore anyway, and they were only using the winches. Young Nevile rushed down and gave me a note to take to Elli Phalère explaining why he was delayed. Would I go out and deliver it? Yes, I said, I'd do that. I didn't tell him I was going there anyhow, that I was inspired with an idea and a mission. He was very wretched and gave me the impression that for two pins he would dive over the side and swim over to the Valletta steps. He was so absorbed in the romantic passion that he thought we were all insensitive clodhoppers. He was out on the forecastle head helping the mate with the ropes, and as I went down the ladder to the boat I saw him bent over a halliard, hurling the falls of the hawser away from him with the energy of disgust and despair. What, he was saying to himself, was the use of trying to make such people understand the glory of a great love? We laugh at the phrase, a grand passion, and we like to think humanity is grown out of such tantrums. It hasn't. We English like to think only emotional Mediterranean races give way to it. But it may happen to anyone. It may be beginning here and there right over our heads in this ship. I have seen men whom you would have thought immune shaken by the hot breath of it. And when we say love is blind we mean, I think, that it is blind to the spectacle it is making of itself; blind to the prudence and intelligence we claim separates us from idiots."

"You?" said Mrs. Kavanagh derisively. "I can't see you
throwing your hat over the moon! You're too self-centered,
too fond of seeing just where you're going. You gave me a
look when I spoke to you on deck . . . ! And so you went up
to see his girl. What was your real reason for that?"

"You needn't suspect me of ulterior motives. I have many
ways of diverting myself ashore, and what might have happened if Elli had been in different circumstances, if I had
crossed her path in some less embarrassing moment, I leave
you to figure out. Ulterior motives I said! Plenty of men
would have taken a soundly materialistic view of the situation and would have decided that the best thing that could
happen to young Nevile was for some virile person to take
his girl away from him. I couldn't do that. I was entranced
by the possible success of passion over prudence. But I was
daunted by the economic and professional aspects of the
contest. All very well in olden times for a young seaman to
grab a lovely wench from a sea-girt isle—once aboard his
lugger and the girl was his. Not now. Not even then, in 1912,
when the shipping magnates were merging the lines into vast
interlocked fleets managed by a supreme council of millionaires. Our old Manola had a fight every time she got a
charter! And even in those days, if you lost a job you had a
devil of a time getting another. Young Nevile couldn't buy a
schooner and go trading among the Greek Islands, or up the
Euxine Sea to get a cargo of black amber from Erzeroum at
some forgotten port on the Pontic shore. He couldn't go off
with his girl on a pirate galley and join the Sallee Rovers.
Nothing of that. I think it was because he had it in him to
be an adventurer then that he was so disgusted with the
prosiness of our attitude. No, he had to go home and get a
second mate's certificate of competency, and that depended
largely on the sort of character the captain gave him. If he

ran off with a girl he would lose all his service time and have to start as ordinary seaman again. There wasn't any way out, no matter how he wriggled."

"I went into the Regina before starting for Floriana. And she was there, quietly sitting in a corner, a glass of beer in front of her, smoking a cigarette and smiling up at me. There was nobody else in there at the time save two Maltese girls who took no notice of us. I sat down at Elli's table and ordered a beer. She was glad to see me in her own pleasant way. She was very agreeable to be with, I may tell you. She presented a smooth, civilized exterior to the world. To look at us, we were a couple of well-behaved bourgeois taking a refresher in a public café and conversing amicably on the news of the day. Only when I told her about young Nevile being detained on board that evening did she give me a long contemplative glance. I said:

"'You like him, don't you? He's very much in love with you.'

"'Yes,' she said. 'I like him very much. I see nobody else.'

"That was quite a lot for her to say. It was, really, all she had to give any man. There was no irony in her statement. I saw that.

"'Yes,' I said, 'but listen, Elli. He wants you to go to England.'

"'I know,' she nodded, smiling. 'He tells me he give me seven, eight pound. I tell him not enough.'

"'He wants to marry you,' I said.

"She gazed quietly at me and shook her head.

"'How can I leave my friend here?' she inquired gently. 'He do not understand I have a friend. I tell him, yes I have a *friend*, who give me house, clo'es, food, everything. Soon he will come back from Genoa or Palermo and this—' she waved her fingers to mean young Nevile—'this will be finish. I tell him—he don't understand. He say, you come to England. Me, England!' She put a long slim forefinger on her bosom and then spread her hands like fans, raising her shoulders a little. She drank her beer, drew on her cigarette and gazed without interest at the two Maltese girls.

"I said, 'That's about the size of it. He's so much in love he's a little bit off his head about you.' She nodded gravely. 'I like him,' she said again. 'But—no money.' 'Yes,' I said, 'you must make him understand you have a friend. Why not tell him your friend is coming home, so it won't be safe any more?'

"She said, 'It isn't safe now. I only know he comes—when he comes. There is a boat from Palermo tonight or tomorrow early. Another in two days.

"'Well,' I said, 'you don't want to have any trouble. By and by the boy will forget.'

"'Yes,' she said, smiling, 'he will forget—marry English lady by and by. He is a nice boy.'

"I was very relieved to find her so reasonable. Oh, she knew the world, I tell you. She gauged all of us to a shade. She had never even dreamed for a moment of going to England. What would she do there, she inquired of me, adding 'Leicester Square? Piccadilly? A French girl in Tunis tell me about London.' She shrugged her shoulders again and turned her head to look through the glass partition at the people in the bar. 'No!' she said, just shaping the word.

"We sat there talking a long time, having drinks. She said would I like to have dinner at her place? I said I would. She asked me to buy a bottle of whisky, as she had none in the house. The waiter brought it and soon she went out, saying she would have her cab wait for me a short distance up the Strada Reale. With the bottle, wrapped in brown paper, under my arm, I set out a minute or two later. I thought to myself—she doesn't even let the idea of marriage rest on the surface of her mind, let alone sink in. It slips like ice from glass. He was safe enough from her, it was plain; but he was coming ashore soon and then we would see if her resolution was equal to the job.

"For a while, after the cab started out to Floriana, she said nothing, only gazing out upon the people sitting beside the wide boulevard on stone seats or walking in the pleasant air of evening. Something was stirring in her mind. She was wearing bronze shoes with high heels. Unlike most Greek girls she had very fine ankles. She contemplated them on the small front seat. She leaned forward and touched a place where the bronze glazing had been bruised. At last she said, with a low laugh:

"'Love is a lot of trouble, Mister Chief.'

"'It is worse for him than for you,' I told her. 'He's a young fool, but it is worse for him than for you. He hasn't ever been in love before.'

"'Ah!' she said, turning away. Suddenly she looked back at me, as if to make sure I wasn't laughing at her. I don't suppose she believed me, you know. She couldn't quite see how a youth of nearly twenty could be so innocent that she was his first love. I nodded in vigorous affirmation. 'Absolutely,' I said. She nodded slowly. 'I like him very much,' she repeated. I said I did too, and didn't want him to make too big a fool of himself. Lose his job, for instance. Our captain was hot tempered and didn't approve of young fellows having girls ashore.

"It wasn't quite dark when we got to her house and I was able to see that she had neighbors. The houses were connected, with tunneled passages between them diving down from the street to the rear. A handsome red-haired girl, leaning from the window of the adjoining house, began talking in Italian to Elli while I was paying off the cab. It struck me that probably other gentlemen like Elli's friend had establishments on that street. The sound of their voices was musical and friendly. I enjoyed hearing them, although I had no notion what they were saying. There was an atmosphere of camaraderie, as though all the things you and I would be so insistent about were understood between them. Do you know, I have always preferred such women to ladies. Or rather, to the women who marry shipmasters, for instance."

"To passengers?" mused Mrs. Kavanagh tapping her wrist with her pencil. "I know what you mean."

"Passengers are not so much a species as a class," said Mr. Spenlove, but he did not seem entirely satisfied with the definition. "They have certain characteristics, but they arise from the environment rather than from the organic structure of their minds. I don't have to cultivate passengers unless I find them worth the trouble. What I was trying to explain is the comfortable feeling I experience among the unclassed, the benign parasites of the sea and sea commerce. I fancy married women dislike them for that reason—because they are often better at their job than married women. Well, that is as near as I can get to what I mean.

"Elli gave me a good dinner, but we had it next door. The red-haired girl had told her Mr. Vilhena was supposed to be in on the Syracuse-Palermo packet. *Her* friend, chief officer of that boat, had seen Mr. Vilhena on the dock at Palermo. I was persona grata with the red-haired girl, who came from Venice as soon as she heard I was off one of the English ships. How easily they made their dispositions! Their houses had a common yard at the back. The veranda affair was continuous, so that they could sit looking down at the Marsamuscetto Harbor and across to the lights of highly respectable British Sliema, and converse, each in her own domain. Like most dwellers in the Mediterranean they had good hearing. They could identify the sounds of the street. They could glance through the louvers of their closed jalousies and see who was outside.

"The other woman was under the impression at first that I had supplanted young Nevile. Oh no, nothing so ambitious, I said. I invented a wife and children to account for my position as a man without a friend. I am no misogynist, but I owe much to that mythical domestic hearth at Golders Green, London, N.W. They were interested and tolerant. So she, the red-haired girl, who was evidently Austrian, returned to the subject of young Nevile. She rubbed her forefingers together while Elli was not looking, to indicate the situation between those two. When Elli went back into her house to get a siphon of charged water I was told she was very much in love. When I said he would probably come up later on she clucked her tongue and looked grave. She talked in Italian rapidly to Elli, who looked grave too. I said, 'Do you want me to head him off?' They said they would tell the servant not to let him in. This didn't strike me as adequate at all. In the state he was in he might easily brush past several servants. The situation was serious enough without any encounters between young Nevile and a man who, after all, wouldn't appreciate the plan to steal his girl, even though he could be convinced that young Nevile's object was matrimony and appallingly honorable. After dinner I began to wonder.

"It was Elli Phalère's attitude which I was unable to understand. She smiled to herself and sometimes she favored me with a glance that was agreeable but enigmatic. I mean more enigmatic than usual. There was a quality of mystery in her demeanor always. I think it was this which had caught young Nevile so completely. I would call it a poetical quality in her. She had a style. The poise of her dark head, the movement of her strong arms, the upward thrust of her breasts, were not merely just that, but they made one think of women long ago, women of whom poets sang songs and about whom great muscular men quarreled over wine cups which were filled from skins hanging by the shores of Ægean islands. I'm not sure we haven't forgotten just how men felt about such women."

"Objects of men's pleasure," said Mrs. Kavanagh. "Nothing else. You can't fool me."

"Well, it was a profession," Mr. Spenlove pointed out mildly. "Almost an art, I would suppose. But you see, she was enough in love with young Nevile to become abstracted and dreamy. I have a notion she was indulging in a temporary romantic passion on the side, as it were. She had no intention of running any real risks. But some elderly protectors of beautiful women are indulgent. I knew that, long ago! I had had an experience of such a case."

"You?" Mrs. Kavanagh was incredulous.

"I told you I had had an experience of my own only a short time before this affair in Valletta. That was in Salonika and at home in London. She was there, in a hotel, and I was asked to call. The elderly protector left us together. I suppose he thought I was safe enough to be trusted! I was, too. But it was I who held her in my arms when she died of a stray bullet in her heart. . . .

"But Elli wasn't anything to me. We would sail in about a week, or even next day if we got new orders to follow the fleet to a new base. I thought it sound sense to tell her this about our movements. We were strays in Valletta. Why, I doubt if I've been back there twice since that time. Alexandria and Smyrna were our ports in the Manola, with a voyage to Salonika when we got a charter.

"'I know,' she said. 'Soon finish.'

"I said, 'I wish your friend wasn't coming up tonight. You could make it easier for the boy, then.'

"She looked at me for a while and then nodded.

"'Well,' I said. 'Let me stop him. I'll walk back. I'll see him coming.'

"She still looked at me. I could see she wanted him to come to her, although she knew I was suggesting the wiser course.

"She was shrugging her shoulders to indicate I could do as I pleased when we were all put on the jump by the sound of wheels against the curb and the buzz of a carriage bell. The two women sprang up, looked at each other, and then the red-haired girl vanished to the front of her house to reconnoiter through the shutters.

"She came back, and while she was telling us it was young Nevile, we could hear Elli's door bell jingling in the kitchen. It was one of those old things on a coiled spring that was operated by pulling down a hook in a slide on the door jamb. It went on tinkling in a way that brought to me a vivid memory picture of my mother's kitchen down at Threxford in Hampshire. She had a row of them there—one for every room in the house. They went on and on if anybody pulled the earthenware knobs upstairs. It brought back the queer homeliness of England and the sort of home young Nevile had come out of. And then we heard him in the house. Elli gave me a highly intelligent glance. Running down into the yard, she ascended to her own veranda and disappeared into the house.

"I thought to myself, now what? I might as well have stayed on the ship for all the good I had done. I was alone with the red-haired girl. She came in and sat down beside me. We began to whisper to each other. The coils of her heavy, copper-colored hair were close to my face as she leaned over towards me. Her breath bore a load of garlic, and she used a heavy, musky perfume. Her eyes were dark green rather than blue, in the light from the incandescent oil lamp on the table. Her voice was a hoarse contralto. In every way she was different from Elli, coarser if you like. She was more the type of her social order than Elli. She would be a good companion, but men would never become mad under her spell.

"I said, 'Do you think she can send him away?'

"She shook her head and smiled. 'No. She bring him in here. It will be all right. She don't want him to go.'

"'No?' I said faintly. All my old alarms and fears came to life again. You see, I wanted to remain a deus ex machina, and it looked as if I would have to step down into the dust of the arena and run a chance of receiving some injury to my personal dignity. I was willing to risk even that, if it were necessary, to get young Nevile safely out of this affair. I said to the girl, 'I'll have to go in. I don't want him there if her friend comes. You understand,' I went on in a whisper, 'he is an officer, and if the captain hears about this . . .' I gave her one of her own gestures. 'He is so young.'

"'That's why she like him so much,' said the red-haired girl.

"I got up and walked through to the veranda at the back. I went down the steps into the yard and ascended to Elli's house. I intended to walk calmly in and take command of the situation. But I found the door locked.

"I couldn't see anyone through the glass, and nobody offered to open the door. I walked down into the yard again through the tunnel leading between the houses to the street and rang the bell. I heard it jangle in the kitchen while the servant, a solemn Maltee wench, looked out of the window. Seeing me, she just went on looking. I asked where Elli was. She made a wide expressive gesture toward the harbor. Gone in a cab? gone for a drive? She nodded and vanished, closing the jalousy.

"I went back to the other house and poured myself a stiff go of whisky. The red-haired girl heard the news without much excitement, I must say. It suddenly occurred to me that I was wasting my time so far as young Nevile was concerned. I said, suppose her friend Mr. Vilhena comes up now? The red-haired girl shrugged. She said, 'You stay here with me.' I got up, corked the bottle, and pushed it over to her. 'No,' I said, 'what about your friend?' I told her I wasn't in the habit of trespassing. I found my hat and stick. They had been moved from where I had laid them to a more intimate part of the house. At the door she said: 'You want Elli, then?'

"I didn't answer that beyond a wave of the hand. I was discouraged as I walked up that intensely quiet and discreet little street to the corner where I could make my way up towards the main boulevard that led to the city gate. I felt a letting down of my spirits. I suppose I had credited both of these women with emotions they did not possess. Elli especially. She had been entirely unaffected by my solicitude for young Nevile. She was going her own road, like an experienced driver on a perilous, precipitous highway, ignoring the remarks of a nervous passenger in the back seat. I had imagined myself expertly extricating the young fellow from a difficult entanglement, retrieving him for some nice English girl of his own class. And here I was, going home with my tail between my legs.

"But when I was back on the ship, after a drink at the Old Dun Cow, I was more resolute than ever about rescuing him."

Mrs. Kavanagh leaned forward.

"I don't understand you at all," she said. "Why didn't you leave them alone?"

"Possibly for something of the same impulse that makes you take care of your brother. Ah, you see! Or it might be paternal feeling, or something that makes us love the young of our own kind. You know, I told you, there was a bloom, a virginal quality, and it appealed to me. Our thoughts have hardened into certain rather Hebraic and medieval grooves. I couldn't explain how I felt to Mr. Pecksniff, or to Dickens either, I'm afraid. St. Paul would have burst out at me. And yet, I don't know. There is Steerforth and young Copperfield. There isn't much in common between Steerforth and the middle-aged chief engineer of a tramp steamer, but he had something of the feeling for Trotwood that I had for young Nevile. And I waited up, long after the ship lay quiet on the glassy waters of French Creek, in darkness save for the riding light and a hurricane lamp at the ladder. I walked up and down the after deck, waiting for him to come aboard.

"And he didn't come. I turned in about three and he hadn't come. I was having my morning tea at six-thirty and I sent the mess boy along to make a discreet examination. The third mate, young Nevile, had not been aboard all night; hadn't come aboard yet. No, the old man was asleep and knew nothing about it.

"I got up. I told the second I was off for a constitutional and would be back before noon. The ship chandler's motorboat, delivering fresh stuff at the ship, took me ashore. I was going to find that young man and bring him down with me, or he would think the watch was out. This was a serious matter."

"I've always heard that for sailors it wasn't," said Mrs. Kavanagh with a smile.

"You've always heard! You're thinking of the riffraff, the fools and drunkards who go to sea because they cannot hide their folly or their liquor while on shore! The whole point of young Nevile's story is that he wasn't one of them at all. He never had the slightest tendency towards having a wife in every port. He was more inclined to leave them alone. But he was in love with Elli Phalère. He didn't know what he was doing at all. I got a carriage and started for Floriana."

"And you found him, of course, in the hussy's arms," said Mrs. Kavanagh. Her hands were clasped around one knee and she moved her body gently to and fro, as though waiting to hear of fleshly delights which she herself could never experience because of her religion and the tribal taboos of her race. Mr. Spenlove gave his graying, pointed beard a tug and brought his black brows together.

"That's melodramatic," he warned her. "I found them at breakfast. The supposed arrival of the elderly protector had been a false alarm. Mr. Vilhena was still transacting business in Palermo. I never met that estimable person, but he must have been a good sort. Yes, I found them at breakfast; and the embarrassing cheerfulness of those two almost put out of my mind how Elli had eluded my well-meant ministrations the night before. For she did not gloat. She didn't look at me defiantly or triumphantly. She had reacted, as they say, from instinct. The service of the senses was her special function in our complex civilizations, and the fact that she was in love with young Nevile did not deprive her of her sagacity and resourcefulness. She had avoided me as an expert driver avoids an obstruction in the road. I didn't know as much about women as I thought I did. I idealized them."

"You what?"

"Imputed to them purely masculine conceptions of love and honor. But she didn't show any feeling of triumph. I sat in my cab outside the house and I saw their two heads, one dark and the other fair, close together over the breakfast table set by the jalousied window. And after a pause young Nevile leaned out.

"'I say,' he said, 'is the old man in a wax?'

"I told him, not yet. I said I wanted him to come aboard with me at once. I made it quiet but emphatic. He threw away his cigarette, looked at me for a second and said, 'Righto. I'll come in a jiff. You won't mind if I keep you waiting just a sec.'

"So I had to sit there and wait for him. The main thing was to get him on board. I was ready for any humiliation to achieve that. Only when we were in a rowboat going out to the Manola did I try to make him see he was acting like a fool. He gave me a burning glance from the strange regions of passion where he was a prisoner.

"'Oh, I know what I'm doing all right,' he said in a high defiant voice which had a faint tremolo in it. 'I know. I don't care either. I'm going to get her, you know. I say, will you do what I asked? Lend me that fiver, I mean?'

"The old man saw us come on board together. It was nearly eight o'clock, and the breakfast bell was jangling at the cabin stairway. He turned away and went across to the other side of the ship. Nor did he make any inquiries about our adventures. He was one of the best men ploughing the ocean, was Jack Evans.

"And there we were, no nearer a solution than ever, it seemed to me. Jack Evans, however, was moving along his own groove. He made no allusion whatever to the young fellow, who wasn't the only chap sleeping ashore by a long shot. He called me up to his cabin and over a drink he said

he had stopped all shore leave. He was cagey enough to say
he had orders. He had orders to be ready to sail for a place
called Paphos, at the western end of Cyprus. That was where
the priests of Aphrodite lived, you know; but old Jack was
not guilty of that kind of irony. He sat there like a comfortable rotund effigy, his thick red lips holding a cigar under
his black mustache. He asked me what there was funny
about it. Anyhow, he insisted, nobody was going ashore. I
asked him, what about the work? We had cylinder heads
hanging in the chain tackle as usual, doing our routine in-
spections. 'Oh, take your time, Fred,' he said, 'but leave
'em lyin' ready for closin' up every night. Tell the crowd
all leave's stopped.'

"And so it was for two or three nights. We were a dis-
contented ship, I can tell you. Young Nevile shut himself
up in his room. He had divined, somehow, that I did not
approve of his behavior. He had also had a hint of derision
from someone on board. Some of my engineers had uttered
disparaging remarks about his exploits. I daresay they had
seen him in that carriage with Elli, and Englishmen often
disguise envy by being ribald. He shut himself up.

"And then the third night, when old Jack's pretended
alarms about sailing at an hour's notice were wearing a bit
thin, we heard murmurs at the cabin entrance. A deputation
was waiting on the old man for permission to go ashore. I
heard his sharp, clipped Welsh speech talking back at them.
No, the orders were definite. He had them in his desk, on
Admiralty paper. They could save their breath. No leave
until further orders. He turned his back on them. My third
engineer told me they had been left standing there. No
leave? they said, looking at each other.

"My room was on the port side, well aft, just the opposite
to this, and I usually took a walk on the well deck. It was
dark after supper, and I was startled to see the young fellow
come down the ladder from the bridge deck and join me.
He looked pale, with dark rings under his eyes, but he smiled

at me. He had just a patrol jacket on over his singlet, a pair of gray trousers and tennis shoes. No collar, no hat. He leaned his arms on the bulwarks and said it was very slow. Didn't I think so? I said yes, but I could stand it. He smiled again and gazed across the water. I was saying to myself, 'He's resigned to the inevitable' and felt pleased, when our attention was drawn to a mysterious collection of shadows on the poop, leaning over the side. I think young Nevile and I discovered at the same moment that those chaps were in touch with another shadow on the water under the counter. (Nobody lived aft in the Manola. She had a high poop containing a carpenter's shop, the tiller gear and some large store rooms.) The men who had gathered together at the rail behaved with extreme circumspection. They wandered slowly about between the boats and the skylight as though admiring a vessel they had never seen before. But they seemed to grow fewer in number.

"Suddenly young Nevile darted away from my side, up the bridge-deck ladder. I was astonished at his sudden change of demeanor. I could feel it! And before I could come to any opinion he reappeared with a shore coat and hat and he had buttoned the coat, as though bound on a desperate adventure. He had a collar and tie dangling from his pocket and a pair of shoes under his arm. He gave me a peculiar bright glance as he passed and ran rapidly along to the poop.

"A minute later I saw the shadow on the water detach itself slowly from the ship's counter and move silently into the deeper darkness beyond the faint radiance of our stern lantern.

"So he'd gone. The conspirators who had determined to take a chance and visit the beach once more had been joined by young Nevile, and I was able to admire myself as a first-rate failure when it came to managing another person's life.

"I went into my cabin and sat down to read. I was going through the *Anatomy of Melancholy* in those days. I remember the young fellow glancing at those three heavy volumes and saying, 'I say, that seems a jolly gloomy sort of book, eh?' I told him to take a look at it some time, and after he had had one volume he brought it back and said, 'Awfully interesting. I must finish it some day.' Books never sank into his mind. He read with the surface of his brain. He told me once, 'Of course I prefer light reading. Nothing like a good light novel, what?'

"I was reading old Burton when the doorway was filled by the captain in a dark blue serge suit, just the thing for a cold day in England, and a gray derby. He had his cigar in a gold-mounted amber mouthpiece, his barrel-shaped waistcoat had a gold chain across it, and he was carrying a walking stick with a gold band on the crook. He had a heavy gold ring on his finger. He only needed gold earrings. He was a typical skipper of his day, one of the best. He would have been horribly uncomfortable on a ship like this one, Mrs. Kavanagh, with passengers.

"What he wanted was for me to go ashore with him. 'Fred,' he said, 'I didn't have no supper. Didn't feel peckish. Now I feel I could take a walk up the street. Comin'? We can have a chop at a place I know.'

"'Oh, what about no leave?' I inquired.

"'I'm goin' to call at the office for orders,' he said. 'Get your coat on and come along. Master's orders.'

"I was curious that he should know Malta as intimately as all that. Oh, yes, he said as we rowed ashore in a boat he had sent for. He knew Malta, donkeys years ago. When he was in a sailing ship. He sat in the stern, setting the boat well down too, and with his hands clasped over his stick told me he'd been here in sail. He added that he had been a distressed seaman. Consul sent them home in a Messageries Maritime steamer to Marseilles.

"And do you know how that fat, purple-faced Welshman had come into Valletta? He'd come in pulling at the oar of an open boat while the mate, who was in command, steered and handled the sheet of a sail. They had been stove in by

a steamer on a dark night off Cape Passero, with a cargo of
currants, and had taken to the boats. And they had been put
up at a hotel. He was going to take me there now, he said,
for a chop.

"I was curious to see what our captain had up his sleeve.
So curious, indeed, that I forgot the young fellow. What else
could I do? He had rushed off like a rabbit, got into that
boat with the rest of the truants, and was now in the hussy's
arms, as you remarked. I might as well enjoy myself with
the old man.

"We had a cab, and we were hauled up the circuitous incline to the Strada Reale. I knew better than to interfere.
Jack gave the jarvey some complicated instructions. All I
could distinguish was the word Stretta, which means narrow.
Jack said to me:

"'That's all I can remember of it. This hotel is down an
alley called Stretta Street.' It was sufficient to take us there.
We arrived in front of a huge portal with a lamp over the
arch. Jack nodded. 'This is the place. We were here a week,
Fred, waitin' for the consul to send us home. I had a bedroom as big as number two hold. It's one of these old palazzos
I suppose.'

"The dining room was enormous. It had a ceiling covered
with Renaissance frescos; one of them, I observed, of a decidedly erotic character. We had sat down in a far corner,
and the chamber was so large it took me a few moments to
get my bearings. It was medieval, that Hôtel d'Angleterre.
Mankind was diminished beneath that lofty ceiling swarming
with mythological adventures. My gaze descended from the
erotic picture to the people far below, and I received a
shock."

"They were there, dining! I knew it!" said Mrs. Kavanagh. She glanced at her wrist watch, which had stopped,
and then at Mr. Spenlove's electric clock.

"No," said Mr. Spenlove. "It was Elli all right, and she
was with an elderly person in a light gray suit. He had a

bald spot on his head, just too large to be mistaken for a tonsure. I didn't see him very clearly, but he looked decidedly ascetic. Anyhow, they were dining there. I saw champagne in a bucket beside them."

"Elli had seen me when I came in, I fancy. As I stared across at her, about four tables away, she allowed her eyes to glance for a moment at me while she went on attending closely to her companion's conversation. I heard my captain ordering dinner.

"We had fried trout, a salmi of quails, roast partridge, a bit of mutton, and jam tarts. We had a bottle of what they call wine in Malta. We had reached the coffee and liqueur when Elli and her escort rose to go out. I was suddenly impressed with the fact that she had no hat. Old Jack was cracking nuts and telling me how he had waded into the grub there when they arrived in that open boat. He glanced up and remarked that this was a fine-lookin' gel goin' out. She wasn't a Maltee, he'd lay a sovereign. He seemed to have a poor opinion of Maltese girls. I said, yes. I was watching Elli standing at the entrance while her companion spoke to the head waiter. She made a slight movement of her head indicating that she wanted to speak to me. I got up.

"I made an excuse to my captain and went out. There was a corridor, and a waiting room at the end—where the seventeenth-century apprentice Knights of Malta sat when the turcopolier sent for them, I should say. It had immensely thick walls with windows set far back in square stone funnels and a groined ceiling. Elli was in there. She came close to me, her eyes bright and hard. She was wearing a stunning dress, and she had a new gold bracelet on her arm, above the elbow. It was a coiled serpent with emerald eyes.

"'Where is he?' she asked me, meaning young Nevile. I said I didn't know. Gone ashore somewhere.

"'He has not been to see me?' she said. 'It is no good any more now. He,' she pointed in some general direction that meant her escort, 'he has come back.'

"'You here?' I said, knowing she was, of course.

"'Yes. He wants me to stay here. He lives here when he comes to Malta.'

"'H'm. Well, that's all, then. I told him. I told him, but he wouldn't pay any attention to me.'

"'Tell him,' she said, listening intently and moving away. 'Tell him, come back next time. Tell him, Elli love him. . . .'

"She gave me a brilliant glance over her shoulder as she hurried away. When I got into the corridor she was gone.

"I went back to my captain and finished my dinner. He was smoking a cigar, at peace with the world. I looked at him and wondered whether he had fallen in love with some girl in a pub over at Senglea, across the harbor, when he was a young shipwrecked sailor. He had probably forgotten it. In the minds of men like dear old Jack memories sink into oblivion as gravestones sink into the earth and can be no more deciphered. We see them there, but we no longer know what they commemorate. He was a successful and benevolent man. I know, for I was with him for years. But he would not have appreciated the news that the girl he had casually admired as she passed his table was trying to wreck the life of his young third officer.

"We went slowly back to the Strada Reale, and when I suggested a last one at the Regina old Jack said, 'Yes, but I guess I'll go aboard, Fred, pretty soon. I'm gettin' sleepy!'

"I said, 'Thought you were going to the office.' He said, looking at me for a moment, 'That's right. I'll look in on my way down. The transport officer has an office in the Custom House.'

"So he called a cab and trundled off, while I went back and wondered what the deuce I should do. I wanted to find young Nevile and take him back to the ship. If the old man happened to ask for him it would be awkward. I decided to go out to Floriana. I felt a bit of a fool about this, because the girl next door would probably misunderstand my motives. But I went, in spite of my qualms. I took a cab out to the Maglio, which is a sort of long park leading to the Argotti Gardens, and then I walked. I didn't want to miss him if he was on his way back.

"It wasn't necessary for me to visit that house again. I saw him sitting on a seat in the gardens. He was alone. His head was sunk on his breast, and his hands hung across his knees. He gave me the impression, in the vague light of a neighboring lamp, of a man who was slowly regaining consciousness after a knockout blow. I mean a physical attack. I went up and sat down beside him.

"When he looked at me he showed no surprise. He asked me in a level, toneless voice, what I was doing there. Eh, what? How did I know he was there? I hadn't been following him, had I? Because it was a funny thing, by jove, a fellow couldn't come ashore without being followed by everybody on the blasted ship! His voice rose a little, and I saw his lip quiver.

"I said, 'Nobody's following you. I was going along to Elli's place to find you. I've news for you.'

"'What news?' he said. 'It's all over,' I said. 'She can't see you any more. I met her in the city. She gave me that message. All over. You know why, too. Better come back with me, have a drink, and get on board!'

"While I was saying this he sat perfectly still. Something happened to him then. He was crying. The tears were running fast down his face, dropping on his hands. He sat perfectly still, as though, if he moved ever so little, he would lose his self-control and start a scene. I didn't dare touch him. I let him weep. The sooner it was over the sooner he would be cured. He began to sob in his chest and shake, but he kept his mouth shut tight. Presently it eased. I kept my face away and watched the fireflies while he grew calm.

"All the way back to the ship he kept silent, and I saw no good in breaking into his thoughts. Now and then he drew a deep breath and caught a hiccup or two, but the storm was over. He never saw her again."

"Never?" said Mrs. Kavanagh. "And you?"

"Nor I either. We sailed for Paphos and put our coal on board a cruiser. And we didn't go to Malta again while he was in the Manola. He went up for his second mate's examination soon after that—about two voyages later. The old man gave him a very good reference. Said he was an extremely sober, competent, and trustworthy young officer, and expressed regret that he was leaving.

"'Of course,' our captain said to me after he was gone, 'he isn't a sailor, but he'll make a good officer for one o' these two-wheeled excursion steamers.' Which was old Jack's way of alluding to passenger vessels with twin screws. He always called the propeller 'the wheel.' It placed him perfectly in the maritime hierarchy, that phrase. Old Jack is dead now, buried up at Penarth, where he was born, and where he lived when he retired from the sea. And the young fellow became what Jack prophesied, if not worse. I mean he got a job on a yacht."

Mrs. Kavanagh rose and extinguished her cigarette in the ash tray.

"I must go and see after Terry. He may be wanting some supper, poor lamb. It's much later than I expected. Was it the yacht business which made you so disappointed in him?" she inquired.

"Oh no. The disappointment came much later. I'll tell you about it tomorrow."

"I won't know the way up to my cabin," said Mrs. Kavanagh, taking thought. "I didn't notice . . . I've never been on a boat except to Cherbourg." She stood up close to the desk to look at a photograph.

Mr. Spenlove made a gesture calming her fears. "Number forty-seven, which is on the port side of the next deck to this. You see, it's like New York. You always know that odd numbers are on the north side."

"It's not like New York to me," said Mrs. Kavanagh. "I wish Terry was here."

"We'll go and find him," said Mr. Spenlove. "I'll take you a short way. There's a locked door on this alleyway. We use it to take members of the crew to the doctor's surgery."

"You'll tell me about the yacht tomorrow?"

"I will. So you take an interest in yachts?"

"For my new book I need a scene on a yacht. My agent says the public want yachts."

"Murder on a yacht, eh? Well, there wasn't any murder on our yacht. More's the pity. I felt like committing one myself at one time."

"Were you on it too?"

"I was. A very remarkable experience, I may tell you, being chief engineer of a millionaire's yacht."

"Was he a millionaire? Oh, you're going to be terribly useful to me, Mr. Spenlove, with your yachts and millionaires and beautiful Greek hussies!"

He took her along to the locked door by the bar steward's storerooms, and she found herself suddenly ascending a familiar stairway. As Mr. Spenlove, following her, reached the top of the stairs he saw her run forward towards a characteristic scene. A gentleman in modernistic pajamas was being urged by two stewards to enter his cabin. A cigarette hung from his lips, and he rolled a severe eye upon Mr. Spenlove.

"Terry!" screamed his sister. "Go in now!" She took him briskly by the ear and led him into his cabin. The stewards looked relieved. "Thank you, thank you," said Mrs. Kavanagh, and darted into her own cabin. As she closed the door, Mr. Spenlove saw her bright, defiant gray eyes regarding him, as though flinging a challenge to his inevitable irony.

IV

MR. SPENLOVE found Mrs. Kavanagh next forenoon in a sheltered nook of the glass-enclosed promenade. She was sitting up in a deck chair and offering a cup of bouillon to a convalescent but still lethargic Terry, who lay beside her. He was securely wrapped up in one of the Company's rugs, and he had not yet shaved. The bristles showed in dark bluish patches on his sardonic Irish jaw. Mr. Spenlove was amused, but not startled, to note that the shoes protruding from the lower end of the rug needed soling. The Washington correspondent of the New York *Globe* looked remarkably like a corpse. The green beret on his rebellious head which had slewed to one side made Mr. Spenlove think of a patriotic corpse. There was something bohemian about Mr. O'Relly's appearance, something that recalled the figures of old-time foreign correspondents in Mediterranean ports. They wore old Norfolk jackets and always carried fat long notebooks with elastic bands on them in their patch pockets. Only those fellows, Mr. Spenlove reflected, never had sisters taking care of them on ocean voyages.

In reply to his inquiry Mrs. Kavanagh said she was very well so far, but Terry wasn't so good. He hadn't settled down to the voyage yet.

"Terry darlin'," she said. "This is Mr. Spenlove, the chief engineer. We're at his table in the dining room."

Mr. O'Relly gave Mr. Spenlove a vacant stare and shook hands. He said, "Pleased to meet you, Mr. Spenlove," thus proving that he was in possession of his faculties. Indeed, Terry O'Relly was always in possession of his faculties. He had a curious capacity for retaining his intelligence under adverse circumstances. He was aware, far more than his sister, of the life of the ship. He had a flair for news and scandal. Whispers in Washington invariably reached Terry's curiously convoluted and projecting ears. There were lewd stories down there, obscene exaggerations, of his uncanny knack of knowing the inmost thoughts and secret sins of statesmen, hostesses, and civil servants who were in society.

There was nothing happening at that moment on the Camotan to engage his attention, so he lay back, gently drinking the hot bouillon and refusing the crackers his sister offered him, and staring at the four bands of gold lace on Mr. Spenlove's sleeve. Mrs. Kavanagh withdrew her gaze from her brother's face, and her own was at once restored to vitality. It was as though the light of intelligence had been suddenly switched on inside of her. At that moment Mr. Spenlove perceived clearly what he had suspected—that her solicitude for her brother was of no significance to anyone in the world save herself. Terry O'Relly was quite capable of going his own road at any time.

"And now about the yacht," she said, smiling broadly. Her brother gave her a solemn stare and turned it on Mr. Spenlove. "He used to be on a yacht," she said, "and he was telling me all about it." Mr. O'Relly maintained his attitude of uncertainty and interest. Mr. Spenlove heard him say, under his breath, "How big a yacht?"

"How should I know?" said his sister. "He hasn't told me that yet."

"Whose yacht?" said Mr. O'Relly. "Anybody we know? In the news, I mean?"

"Not now," said Mr. Spenlove. "He's one of those Americans who abandon America and become British. Did you ever hear of Bunthorne's Chest Tonic? No, I didn't suppose you would. Bunthorne's Chest Tonic is an English superstition, though old Starnburg, father of Lord Sternborough, was a German-American and made his money out of American patent medicines which were disguised alcoholic beverages. They sold out their interests long ago, for millions. They are—or were—really very wealthy. It was old Starnburg, when someone asked him how much a yacht cost to run, who made the classical and perfect answer. His friend, another rich man, said he wasn't sure he could afford one. 'You can't, if you have to figure out what it costs. You can't afford one,' said the old chap, and began to laugh.

"That described the Moira perfectly. She was the most fabulously silly ship ever launched. Old Starnburg was

dead long before this. His son had spent nearly a quarter
of a million in charities and political support. He had raised
a cavalry regiment of country gentlemen during the Boer
War, paid for all the equipment and horses, and chartered a
ship to take them to Cape Town. He had built a hospital in
his grounds at Boule House in Suffolk for wounded officers.
So he became a baronet and then a baron. Baron Sternborough of Boule. And as one of the richest men in the world
at that time he had a yacht. He built a new one, a new
Moira, a larger, faster, more luxurious affair than his old
German-American Jew father had ever imagined.

"I was home at the time because I had to leave the
Manola to do my time at maneuvers in the Naval Reserve.
I had urged young Nevile, as a good move for his future
advancement, to join up too. We were rather poor relations
in those days. The regular naval people tried to discourage
us. They regarded us as something the cat had dragged in
if we managed to beat all their hurdles and were officially
accepted. I was told frankly, at my first attempt, that they
didn't want me. In those golden days of the upper classes,
if a first-class marine engineer had a bad tooth or flat feet,
he couldn't get into the Naval Reserve! I used to laugh during the war when they were short of men. Our King and
Country had precious small need of us in 1910 or 1911.
Happy days! We went on maneuvers and got all the dirty
jobs, the hard steaming ships, the breakdowns and the
mavericks.

"Never mind. I mention my patriotic efforts and my rank
as engineer-lieutenant of those days to explain that it got
me a job on the Moira then building. Lord Sternborough
pensioned off the old gray Scotchman who had served him so
long in the old Moira. I knew turbines, and the firm building
the yacht's engines recommended me. Young Nevile had
been away on another cruiser, and when he wrote me I
suggested him as a good fourth officer.

"He was twenty at the time, or twenty-one possibly, I

forget. But he was the type they wanted. The captain took him at once. That was how we came to be on a yacht. In 1911 or 1912. The Golden Age!"

"You say it was a golden age?" said Mr. Terry O'Relly sarcastically. "I was alive then, and it wasn't much of a golden age for me!"

"You wouldn't be of an age to appreciate it," said Mr. Spenlove, smiling. "We were. That's one advantage we Victorians had over you. I don't say we all understood our advantages. There was no boom, you know. But we had grown up in a pretty tough school in England, and we didn't grumble."

"Well, go on," said Mrs. Kavanagh.

"Ah, the yacht. Yes, we were a month or so in the Clyde, fitting out. We had everything in the way of luxuries the world had ever heard of. I can't give you some of the technical details. But I can mention that all our engine oil was specially treated so there would be no odor drifting aft to the passengers who reclined on the scarlet leather cushions abaft the dining room on the upper deck. In the engine room there was a small balcony leading out of the accommodation, a balcony of Florentine ironwork, where passengers could stand and look down at us and see the turbines revolving. I've seen them there in evening dress, chatting.

"The gadgets that ship had! She had a dome of colored glass over the dining-room table with little secret lights illuminating it from below at night, and the tablecloth was wired so that if you set the electric candlesticks on it, they had prongs that pierced the heavy silk and reached the wires and were lit. Lady Sternborough took a dislike to her suite, which was paneled in walnut, so it was all painted pearl gray for her. There was an illuminated globe in the smoking room, and the position of the yacht was marked on it by some intricate machinery from the bridge. The cabins were all suites, and the bathroom fixtures were gold plate. It was rather awe-inspiring if you allowed your mind to dwell on material things. I remember young Nevile came down after having a look, and remarking to me, 'I say . . . !' and stopping short. He hadn't anything to say. What *was* there to say? The captain, who had been in yachts so long he had forgotten what other ships were like, used to say, 'It's good for trade. Keeps the money circulating'—which was a common enough notion in those days.

"Then we took her down to Cowes to pick up our party. I soon became aware of a peculiar atmosphere in our part of the ship, an atmosphere very different from other ships. We all cultivate discretion, you know. If you tried to pump one of us about this ship we would be tactful and evasive. We wouldn't give away any confidential information. We say 'I'm not allowed to discuss that.' Or some such phrase.

"But on the Moira the discretion resembled the discretion of a seraglio, where eunuchs without tongues stand with drawn scimitars outside the great bronze doors. Everything was geared to run in a sort of blind silence. What went on upstairs was nobody's business. The owner brought his own servants, valets, maids, waitresses, and a butler who told the chief steward how the guests wanted their meals and so forth. Lord Sternborough was considerate enough to give even the captain and officers a separate life of their own. So when we started off from Cowes to join several other yachts at Monte Carlo, we had no more to do with our passengers than the driver of an express train with his. I didn't see them. I had a new crowd of engineers from the yard, all picked reserve men, and a new engine room. Turbines were rather a novelty in those days. Like wireless, they were just coming in for merchant vessels. The Moira had all the latest improvements and late improvements sometimes require attention. But I had twenty-five pounds a month and luxurious quarters. We had things like quails and partridges to eat in our mess room, amazing desserts, and a wine list. I was not complaining because of the atmosphere of the ship. I liked it. I thought it worked both ways.

If it had only been maintained we would never have had any trouble when we got to the Ægean. But there we were in Monte Carlo, unaware of what was coming."

Mr. Spenlove excused himself to go up and see his commander. He left Mrs. Kavanagh watching solicitously over her brother, who had fallen into a light sleep. Or rather he dozed. So he did not see young Nevile, in a smart suit of flannels, walk briskly along the promenade deck. Mrs. Kavanagh did, however. She returned his salute and watched him, entranced. She thought he was "terribly good-looking," as she put it to herself, and waited for him to reappear around the after end of the deck.

The sun shone on a sea of gray-blue wrinkled silk. There was no motion of any significance, and Terry was evidently recovering his usual spirits. If he still looked like a corpse, he was a very peaceful one, she reflected, with a humor she would have resented fiercely in any other human being. She liked Mr. Spenlove because he accepted her without commenting with his eyes upon her preoccupation with her brother. Everybody Mrs. Kavanagh knew had to accept her like that if they were to be tolerated. Nobody could possibly be good enough for Terry.

She sat with her gray eyes fixed on the far end of the deck where young Mr. Nevile would appear again. But he did not appear, and she fell to thinking of him as he was in that far-away place, Malta he called it, with the Greek girl, Elli Phalère. She was not sure anything so far away as that could be worked into the book she was planning. There had to be a mystery and a murder. The yacht seemed more promising, of course.

At the far end of the deck she saw a girl in a blue traveling cloak leaning over the after rail. She had suddenly appeared and then turned to the rail. She could not be identified. There were so many people appearing now whom nobody had seen before. The wings of the girl's blue cloak flew out in the breeze. She had a scarlet beret. But she was too far away to make out. Mrs. Kavanagh saw her swing around to face an invisible companion, and then young Nevile's head came into view. He was talking to the girl. He was, Mrs. Kavanagh noted with displeasure, making her laugh and turn away as though charmed beyond her will. And then they moved out of sight again, after the fashion of passengers not yet at ease on the ship, enraptured with the strangeness of leaning over the whispering mystery of great waters. Who was she? Mrs. Kavanagh asked herself, and wanted for a moment to go and see. She glanced at her brother. He was asleep, his mouth slightly open, and she resumed her search for a convenient motive for her new book. It was, she knew, a question of devising a puzzle, a jig-saw design which had to be carefully drawn and then as carefully scattered along the trail of a pair of lovers. Her public wanted a pair of lovers. Like many happily married women with a family of daughters, Mrs. Kavanagh regarded romantic love without enthusiasm. There was no room in her own imagination for any such emotion. She had sometimes thought it would be exciting to have a short love affair with some stranger, who would disappear forever when the affair was concluded, but many things had combined to prevent this adventure. She liked to think she could do it if she gave her mind to it. Men were easily fooled, of course. . . .

She rose on an impulse, and divesting herself of the rug walked slowly down the long deck to the after rail. There was no one visible. Even by crossing to the starboard side she failed to locate young Nevile or his companion. Mrs. Kavanagh began to retrace her steps slowly. After all, she told herself, he was probably only amusing himself for a moment. Yes, the romantic boy who fell for that Greek creature would grow into a man who could be attractive in a polite way to a passenger. He would be thinking of his conquests in the past and that would make him interesting. Then he would meet a woman who would want to kill him!

She sat down in her chair and drew the rug over her with

a sigh. Now she would have to figure out how the murder would take place.

It was shortly after this that the ship's bugler, sounding the first call for lunch, woke Terry O'Relly from his doze, and he began to make unmistakable preparations for visiting the bar. He thrust the rug onto the deck and scrambled hastily out of his chair. Before his sister could offer any remark he was off, unerringly winging in the direction of the smoke room. It was characteristic of him to leave her without a word, as an animal might leave his mate in the jungle. Between them passed unspoken signals, the tribal communications of a family united in racial and religious solidarity.

She watched him go, and sat contemplating the cover of the book her publishers had sent her with the suggestion that she would find it instructive in her own work. It was, of course, a book very much like her own, yet she was reading it with as much zest as if she had never written a thriller in her life. She was like that. She could never feel sophisticated for more than a minute or two. It was only when she sank herself in her husband, her children, and especially in her brother Terry, that she became hard and practical and a shrewd, unscrupulous personality.

She went downstairs and got ready for lunch. When she heard Terry making a noise in the next cabin she called out to him. Passing the door she saw a steward serving drinks to a group of men. She saw young Captain Nevile accepting a cocktail.

"We'll be right down," said her brother. She craned her neck to make sure there were no women in the room and went on to the main stairway. "I'll wait here for him anyway," she said to herself and took a seat where she would be sure of catching him.

She watched the women going down in twos and threes, mostly with new hats on. She had noticed that when she went to Paris. Her father had given her a trip to Paris for a graduation present. Why did they wear hats at lunch on a ship? But not at dinner! She smiled. She knew the answer, of course, but even to herself, being a woman, she refused to put it into words. She did not do these things herself. She would wear anything anywhere, and like many women who write, she always seemed to be wearing some other woman's hat. She was wearing no hat at all at this moment. She sat on a divan in a corner of the hall, her light gray eyes and white hair contrasting with the bright red spot on her cheeks. Her glance flitted from group to group as her mind worked ceaselessly with the problem of her story. Then she saw Terry and young Nevile, followed by Terry's room mate, coming along the passage. They were very cheerful.

Downstairs at the table she heard the two men talking of publicity. There was an odd sensation in hearing young Nevile, who scarcely glanced at her, remark that in his opinion publicity was all the better if it was indirect. It was, he said, like flattery: if you laid it on with a trowel it was resented. It had to be done with finesse and diplomacy. Even tact.

Terry O'Relly sat through this without flinching. He had the newspaperman's suspicion of press agents. He also had the newspaperman's lively awareness of the chances of landing a public relations billet for himself. He had been approached by several senators and at least one vice presidential nominee to accept such a position. That was politics, and Terry was a cynic about politics. He was, in the famous phrase, incapable of loyalty to the things he did not believe in. Captain Nevile, however, was talking about a business project.

Mrs. Kavanagh heard their voices without taking in the sense of the words. "Fishing!" she heard Terry say. She knew he was one of those romantic creatures who could go away to some unpronounceable place in French Canada and spend a solid week with other men, fishing. She had never understood that side of his character. If he had been a good

Catholic, or had gone off with other Catholic men, she could have understood that. But it was more pagan than Christian, the light in his eye when he gathered his fishing gear and made for Grand Central Station!

She wished Mr. Spenlove had not gone away. But of course he had things to do in his work. She wondered whether he would ask her to his cabin again. She wanted to hear what happened on the yacht. Lord Sternborough's yacht. She felt a peculiar thrill at being ushered, as it were, into that shadowy world of luxury and plutocratic privacy. It would be sure fire, she thought, if she could reproduce the atmosphere realistically.

Her glance went across to the empty chair on the other side of Mr. Spenlove's. That girl must be a bad sailor. Nobody seemed to have seen her yet. She watched young Captain Nevile. Why did one always think of some men as young? He had gray hair over his ears, very interesting, of course. She found she was thinking of him as Mr. Spenlove described him with that creature Elli Phalère, who would be no chicken now. Older than me! Mrs. Kavanagh calculated, and her smile was the least bit wintry. She was intelligent, and she saw without illusions the shockingly unfair advantage men had over women as the years passed.

She heard young Captain Nevile say, as he leaned towards her with a smile of apology:

"We're talking about my new job. I want Mr. O'Relly to come down and try the fishing. The tuna and tarpon are running very large now at the cays. I'm managing a fishing camp down on the coast of Jamaica. He says he goes in for fishing when he's on vacation."

"Sometimes," she admitted, thinking of Terry's professional standing. He had to be back in Washington in three weeks. "He hasn't the time now."

"Oh, quite. I think we can get him to make up a party. I have plenty of elbow room when it comes to publicity. I am going to submit a scheme for next winter."

"I'll bring the boys," said Mr. O'Relly simply, taking plenty of butter and pressing it hard upon the bread. Mrs. Kavanagh saw no reason to distrust Captain Nevile. He was entirely on the level. His follies and romantic adventures were behind him. He was now a business man. He might be useful to Terry. Her fears for her brother, who was the youngest of the family and whose little steps she had guided when he began to walk, died away. Very little harm could come to Terry on this ship, she thought, looking around at the women. He had no sense about women at all. The proof of that was visible in the wife he had married, a Protestant, a Greenwich Village creature who had offered him a companionate arrangement. Well, it served her right for him to leave her.

She left the table before the men were finished and went to her cabin. She was obsessed with the idea of using a yacht for her new murder novel. It was obvious the chance to talk to Mr. Spenlove was a slice of luck for her. She must find him at once. She left her cabin on a sudden impulse and started along towards the after end of the passage, which terminated, beyond the gymnasium and the barber shop, in a palm court and café. She could see a stewardess sitting in a wicker chair doing some sewing and talking to an invisible companion. She was about to turn back when she saw Mr. Spenlove's head appear. He was smoking a pipe and making the stewardess smile at what he was saying. Mrs. Kavanagh went forward into the palm court. Mr. Spenlove, sitting sideways on a tile-top table, rose to greet her, a Puckish look on his face.

"Meet Mrs. Cairnes," he said, offering a chair. "We were talking about the reasons passengers have for travel, and whether they ought not to be licensed after examination by a psychiatrist. Mrs. Cairnes tells me there's a woman on board who has requested the chief steward to let her open a shop of antique jewelry in the music room, as she wants to clear her expenses while she's making the cruise."

Mrs. Kavanagh looked from one to the other. She saw Mr. Spenlove beaming down upon her.

"I don't believe you like passengers," she said, meeting his mood. "You've been spoiled, being on that yacht."

"No," he said, but laughing at the idea she had picked up. "Oh no! I can assure you our passengers are far more intelligent than those I've met on yachts. It's only the peculiar ethic of some of them that staggers Mrs. Cairnes and myself."

"You remember that doctor, our last Mediterranean cruise?" said Mrs. Cairnes in a soft Lowland voice.

"I think so," said Mr. Spenlove, his eyes screwed up and showing a hard glint. "He sent his cards around to all the cabins and told the other passengers he could be seen in his own cabin from two to four in the afternoon."

"With a ship's doctor on board?" said Mrs. Kavanagh, slightly confused.

"Of course. Two, as a matter of fact. Both licentiates of the Royal College of Physicians. Both jolly hard up too, having lost their practises during the war. Our medical passenger believed in a little healthy competition among the sick."

"I suppose the captain would hear of it," Mrs. Kavanagh said.

"He did. Captain Wensley was just the man to hear of it. Nothing happens on the Camotan that our captain doesn't hear of. He took it in the day's work. The ship's printer ran off an emergency billhead, and the purser made it out to the passenger. A bill for rent of cabin as surgery. I forget how many hundred dollars he was to pay. About what he paid for his cruise ticket. Now, would you say such people should be allowed to travel without legal guardians?"

"Did he pay it?" Mrs. Kavanagh wanted to know. Mrs. Cairnes laughed and glanced at the lady.

"No," said Mr. Spenlove in a disappointed tone. "Nothing so poetically just. Instead he came down in the Riviera with

an interesting case of hives, due to too much wine and grapes.
Our doctors gave him the best of care."

Mrs. Cairnes rolled up her sewing and rose to go about her
duties.

"It was the chief who persuaded him fruit and wine were
good in large quantities," she said, smiling to herself.

"Mr. Spenlove, I want to know about that yacht," said
Mrs. Kavanagh earnestly. He held his elbow in his hand and
smoked gravely. He rose from the tiled table.

"I know you do," he said. "I was telling you about it
when duty called. Duty calls at times, you know. There are
things to do. But come upstairs to the solarium. Nobody
getting a tan yet."

Abaft the wireless quarters, on the high boat deck of the
Camotan, was a house with a glass roof, with divans and
low tables, where the sun worshipers would congregate in
a day or two to acquire their peculiar virtue. Mr. Spenlove
found the place empty, as he had foretold, and he drew
attention to the change of atmosphere.

"Here," he said, "you don't see quite so much of the
others. The sea becomes more benign, and you can think.
You'll find you can't think among a lot of people on a ship.
They are all so busy maintaining a social position just a little
above what they are at home. They don't want really to
live the way they do here, but they're afraid the world would
think them of no account if they didn't pretend to be used
to all this. You, for instance, have no solarium at home."

Mrs. Kavanagh sniggered. She thought of the ramshackle,
untidy house behind the big trees, far up a narrow road beyond Harrison, with the rope swing under the apple tree
that never bore any apples. She thought of her three rowdy
girls lying on the grass, or climbing the tree, or piling into
the old car to be taken to school. No, there was no solarium.
Only a great many beer and milk bottles by the screen door
and several cats sunning themselves on a dusty porch.

"So," went on Mr. Spenlove, "we needn't keep up the

pretense. They are all trying to find a cheap substitute for a yacht, you see. That is what lies at the back of the luxury advertising of our ships. The ship is yours. Every soul on board is your host. You lie in your superb bed, like an Eastern potentate or a sultan's odalisque, as the sex may be, and a host of willing minions serve you on bended knee—for a month in the cerulean tropics!"

"Snob appeal," said Mrs. Kavanagh.

"Partly," assented Mr. Spenlove, "but I don't use the word snob myself. I would prefer to call it idealism. These people all around you in America, Mrs. Kavanagh—I refer of course to the Protestants—are idealists. They are like the buccaneers who went in search of the City of the Golden Man. They toil in muck and sweat to reach a higher station in life. They will pay anybody who will tell them how to reach Eldorado, how to behave, and what to wear when they reach it. I suppose a yacht symbolizes the topmost lift of their dream world, because it gratifies at once their desire for show and the universal craving to have others as guests to share and envy their magnificence. The thing to remember is that there's nothing immoral in such a dream world. The majority could carry it off just as well as the people who happen to have yachts and several millions. That's where we come in. We are able to treat them as if they were Monte Cristos for a month. All our gadgets, swimming pools, solariums, orchestras behind exotic palms at dinner, our Tudor paneled smoke room, and our bar made to resemble a great sea shell, and so on, are merely to lull the average American family into a soft plutocratic trance and make them forget the humdrum and tragic fact that they haven't got a million dollars. We can give them everything they want, nowadays."

"Except the culture that goes with all that," said Mrs. Kavanagh. "Culture and breeding."

"Culture! Don't make me laugh myself to death. They have that; they have it. You forget that the aristocracy are all broke now. *They* can't afford yachts. They can be found in the student third class at times, but as a rule they don't travel at all. We could tolerate vast wealth in the hands of those who could make an original use of it. We could even excuse clever people having it. But the richer they are the duller they turn out to be. It was one of the things I discovered on the Moira when we joined the squadron at Monte Carlo.

"We lay off Cap Martin and one of the two large launches was always in the water running in and out and to the other yachts. I admit it was a fine sight. I can remember the Khedive's yacht close by, the Marroussia she was called. There was the Duke of Orleans' and the Duke of Savoy's and the Prince of Monaco's. There was a yacht belonging to some Maharajah from India and another owned by a Brazilian coffee millionaire.

"You should have seen the young fellow's eyes when he saw all those yachts. He had to keep his astonishment to himself on the bridge, for the other mates and the captain were all old hands at the yacht game, and his uniform impressed him too. When he came down to my cabin he was able to be as boyish as he liked."

"I like him," said Mrs. Kavanagh.

"I don't doubt it. Women always do," agreed Mr. Spenlove. "Without intending any sly innuendo, the fact that women like him has spoiled his life. They have bedeviled him all his life, so far. And it was on the Moira, I think, that he became aware for the first time that a woman will go after a man she wants, without scruple and without shame. Before that he thought only the hussies in Water Street went after men. He had preserved the illusion that girls had to be won by waiting and were timid tender creatures who knew only what Lord Tennyson had chosen to tell them. The Honorable Maeve showed him what a girl could do when she meant business.

"Maeve was Lord Sternborough's daughter. She came on board at Monte Carlo, where she had been staying at a villa at La Turbie. I mean, she had been sleeping at the villa, lying on the beach in the sun all afternoon and sitting in the Salle Privée of the Casino in the evening.

"She must have been twenty-one, because she had her own money, I heard later. There were two Starnburgs at first. One of them died in America, and his widow left Maeve a fortune in her own right. It hadn't made her any easier to live with, either. She was good-looking. I saw her coming alongside in the mahogany and teak launch with the brass funnel and the silver handrails. She lay back on the red-leather cushions in the stern looking up at us as I was looking out of my porthole. She couldn't see me. She swept past in a surge of blue-and-white water, and I noticed her arms were sunburned and covered with bracelets halfway to the elbows. The contrast was novel then, for she was an extremely modern girl. On the other hand, she never allowed her face to be tanned."

"Was she prettier than that Greek girl, Elli?"

"You couldn't tell for certain. It was impossible to say where nature left off and art began. Maeve had a different kind of beauty. She didn't appeal to me at all. What? No, I haven't made it clear. When I say she didn't appeal to me I wasn't casting any aspersions on her sex appeal, as you call it. She had that, I suppose; but remember, I was rarely in a position to speak to her as a companion. I kept down on my deck. No, I meant she was not the sort of girl I imagined ought to be the daughter of a millionaire lord. She was much more like the girls you see now around smart bars at cocktail time, sopping up hard liquor and showing off among the men, who in their hearts despise them and who like to see them getting inebriated."

"But what was she *like?*" said Mrs. Kavanagh. "I've a perfectly clear idea in my mind of that Greek hussy. I keep thinking of her because she was so successful. But what was this Maeve—a blonde?"

"Sort of sandy, with pale brown eyes, the color of amber

almost. She was thin, and very modern in her clothes. Why, her skirts, and this was in 1912 mind you, nearly twenty years ago, my God!—her skirts were more than two thirds of the way to her knees. Shorter than they are now. But if you want to know the impression she made upon me, I would say she had a damaged look. She looked as if she had been around much more than was good for her. A girl as rich as she was, of course, was damaged in the ordinary sense. She had her own maid, and she was enough to take one's breath away in her dinner gown under the silk-lined awnings of the after deck when they had a party. Often they took dinner out there.

"I mean damaged in her spiritual texture, frayed with sated desires. The way she glanced at the man who came on board with her showed she was spoiled. He was a nice boy too, in yachting togs and a monocle. He was the man she married. She had luck, that girl. She suddenly married him, a younger son without a cent. And look what happened. His father died, his brothers were killed in the first six months of the war, and he succeeded to the title. She's a countess, with more money than ever. I wonder if she remembers the Moira and the young fourth officer who took her fancy, and the island of Eupopyle. I wonder!

"We were going there because, although our owner and most of his friends were people of no importance in the world, one of the guests was a famous archæologist. He was going up country from Nauplia to show the party where he was un-earthing the house of Agamemnon at Mycenæ. He had been the guest of the Prince of Monaco. I remember him because of his beard, which was long and venerable, and because his name was so strangely suitable to his vocation. He was Sir Hector Digges, with most of the alphabet like a kite tail following his name. I saw it in the local paper as a news item from Paris.

"You understand, these people were playing. They went through all these motions of owning a yacht and going to Monte Carlo and then cruising in the Ægean, merely to pass the time in an agreeable way. They were entirely functionless organisms. They hadn't even the excuse of a vacation, for none of them had ever done a day's work or a day's house-work. They had not read Sir Hector's thirty-seven published works on Peloponnesian architecture and art. They would never have dreamed of attending the lectures he delivered regularly every year in London. But being rich they enjoyed the distinction of having this man of immense erudition and world-wide celebrity performing for them in private like a clever trained animal. He was a sort of archæological Jumbo, who could pick up queer facts with his trunk and balance himself on his front feet. He could toss theories of Attic origins in the air and keep them revolving.

"But the Honorable Maeve wasn't interested in men with venerable beards and a detailed knowledge of the family life of Agamemnon and Clytemnestra. She was so entirely preoccupied with the immediate present that a heap of cable-grams and thick letters from the man she had been in love with before joining the Moira lay unopened in her cabin after the cruise, when she went ashore in Marseilles and took the train to Paris. I'll tell you how I heard about that. That's the sort of girl she was. Without ever formulating in speech a cruel or callous impulse, she could drop those she had no further use for without a moment's regret. I found that out later also. I am summing her up. She had just completed a tremendous love affair in London, where she had been staying with a girl friend who had a studio in Chelsea. She was en-gaged in a vague way to the young chap who came on board with her, young Copelin. And she had an enormous number of social engagements with men on the other yachts. That was the situation when she had a quarrel of some sort with her fiancé.

"Was it important, all that?" said Mrs. Kavanagh. "Are such people important at all? I'm sort of disappointed in your yacht folks. They seem just common to me."

"They were. Even the peerage made no difference. I was

astonished at the narrow limits of their social activities. I
was puzzled at first. The secret was, the Sternboroughs were
climbing. They were too new. If they had had their home in
England for a couple of generations, it wouldn't have been
so obvious. But there was no way, apart from the arboreal,
of explaining why they had come to England at all! There
was even a touch of the gate-crasher about some of their exploits, as when they received advance news of the arrival of
a celebrated American prima donna in the Salle Privée and
were introduced by a celebrated Spanish novelist who
thought all English lords were alike. I am able to tell you this
because of a scrap of conversation young Nevile heard while
he was talking to the Honorable Maeve. Some people from
another yacht were talking about the supper at the diva's
villa afterwards and they said to Lady Sternborough, 'Were
you there? We weren't invited.' She said, 'Neither were we!'
There was loud laughter at this, and it turned out none of
them had been asked to go on. Young Nevile couldn't understand anybody doing a thing like that. I told him it was one
of the privileges of the upper classes, to be unconventional.
It was their prerogative to do things we of the middle classes
couldn't possibly get away with.

"Yes, they were common, if you like, but I think a better
word is dull. That was the reason behind their daughter's in-
difference to their ambitions and ideals. Even if they achieved
both, it was merely that they would be accepted by other dull
people who happened to have a great deal of money and no
responsibility. You might think that when they took up a
venerable savant like Sir Hector Digges they had ambitions
to be patrons of the arts and sciences. But their interest in
him lay in his fame. They contented themselves with knowing
him personally, ordering his latest book from London and
forgetting to read it, and talking about him. There was a pile
of books on Lady Sternborough's table where she sat under
the awning aft, but she never read them. She never had time.
There was always a new scheme to devise for the killing of

time. While we were lying off Monte Carlo, they had a treasure hunt in launches, a ping-pong tournament, a water-polo
match and a race between two Frenchmen on tricycles with
large pneumatic tires so that they could float, and paddles
turned by their feet. What they did on shore I never discovered save once when I went to the Casino, to see what it was
like. The captain gave me a pass. He said it was worth going
to see—once.

"I saw the Honorable Maeve at the table in the Salle
Privée, putting counters on the various numbers. She had
two important-looking personages, one of them with a dark
green ribbon across his shirt front, standing behind her and
bending down to make remarks. Her arms were sunburned,
and her diamonds contrasted strangely with the reddish skin.
So did her shoulders with the unscorched neck and face with
a thin band of gold set with emeralds on her hair. She had
won a lot of money. Her bag was stuffed with five-hundred-
franc notes. Outside on the terrace I saw the nice boy she
was engaged to walking up and down by himself smoking a
cigarette very fast. He took no notice of me. He didn't know
who I was. Thought I was some Frenchman with a beard, or
possibly a naval officer on leave. He looked at me as I passed
him and throwing his cigarette into the shrubs below the
balustrade he said distinctly, Damn, damn, damn! Then he
laughed and spun his monocle on its cord. 'I'm talking to
myself,' he said. 'That's a sign of weakness in the upper story,
isn't it?' 'It needn't be,' I said. 'Those who say so forget the
importance of the soliloquy!' 'Oh!' he said, 'who the devil
are you with your soliloquies?' 'I'm the chief engineer of the
yacht Moira,' I said. 'At your service, sir.' 'Well, I'm
damned!' he said and took a look at me through his Piccadilly window.

"I didn't go there again. The expression on the faces of the
habitués was not my idea of human nature at its best. I preferred walking about the upper town or looking at the marine
monsters in the aquarium. They were strange indeed, but

not so repulsive as the skinny crones in evening gowns with their dry claws trembling over the numbered squares.

"And was she after Captain Nevile even then?" asked Mrs. Kavanagh.

"No, she hadn't even seen him, I fancy, at that time. She may have, but she hadn't thought of him save as a possible diversion later on. He used to come ashore with me, and he was still in love with Elli Phalère. One day as we passed a lovely little villa that was to let, the terrace above the gate concealed with hibiscus and bougainvillea, he said, 'I wish I was rich, Chief! I'd fetch Elli here and live in that house, and I'd marry her too.'

"'Now, now,' I said, 'you couldn't do that. It would never work with her. Aren't you ever going to learn elementary sense?'

"'Oh, of course it's only a dream,' he said. 'I meant it that way. Sort of fairy story—because I'll never be rich!'

"Just for a joke I said, 'You can marry a rich man's daughter, can't you?'

"He gave me a quick, shy look. 'I don't know,' he said. 'I keep thinking of Elli, so I couldn't marry anybody's daughter. I don't think I'll ever marry, as a matter of fact.'

"'You mustn't keep thinking of her,' I said. 'You know what she is. She goes with whoever can keep her. You were in another man's house, you know, out there in Floriana. It seemed so romantic, but was it?'

"'Don't!' he said quietly. 'I know it's all despicable but I'm in love with Elli.'

"'Then I give you up for a silly young ass,' I said.

"He knew I didn't mean anything except that I was fond of him. When I told him I wanted him to marry an English girl later on, one of his own class, he didn't make any comment except that the girls of what I called his class didn't marry sailors. 'You won't be a sailor; you'll be an officer,' I said. 'Nor officers either,' he said, swinging his cane and looking out across to Cap Martin.

"You see, we were approaching a social cleavage at that time. I have always had a geological view of society."

"You mean British society," said Mrs. Kavanagh with a note of antagonism in her voice. "Snobs!"

Mr. Spenlove laughed as he pressed a finger upon the loose ash at the top of his pipe bowl.

"That's not a geological term," he pointed out. "I was alluding to the various strata into which all society in our two countries is forced by the economic changes. There are upheavals caused by industrialism in England or the Civil War in America.

"I saw a cleavage like that in formation in England at that time. We, who in the days of Elizabeth had been the backbone of the navy, were now reduced to the ranks of the lower middle classes. I mean socially. Our employers, who never went to sea, who hardly ever saw their ships at all save as items in statistical tables, went to court and became knights, baronets, and barons after they had accumulated a million or so and contributed to party funds or royal charities. We ourselves had no more chance in that lottery than the mill hands in the factories whose employers were also in the House of Lords, and the navy had gone up in the social scale as we went down. We almost disappeared from the articulate life of England altogether. We had no representatives anywhere. We hadn't a professional organization like lawyers or doctors, and we hadn't a trade union like a bricklayer or coal miner. We lived in segregated areas near the ships. We were supposed to be a pretty tough lot, like Captain Kettle, a fictional character of those days who was very popular with magazine readers. Legally we hadn't much of a position in the world either, because the captain had no right to his title. He was told, on the slightest provocation, that he was the master of the ship and his officers were only mates. The four great pillars of English social life had no intention of admitting any other vocations to their own stature. The Army, the Navy, the Church and the Bar didn't look down on us. They

were blissfully unaware of our existence. At that time, I recall, for I looked it up in an almanac I had with me, we had
ten thousand ships sailing all over the Seven Seas. Socially
they didn't amount to as much as one light cruiser.

"Young Nevile knew that as I knew it, but he recognized
it with the honesty of youth, whereas I was resentful and bad
tempered when I saw that holier-than-thou attitude dis-
played toward me. I still am. It reconciles me to living in
America. It certainly made it easier for both of us when we
came over.

"No, it wasn't snobbery in the sense you seem to understand it. We didn't criticize the social order. We only felt
that we had a right to more consideration in it. Our error lay
in imagining we were underlings in an aristocratic system.
The presence of our employer on the Moira, Lord Sternborough, born Starnburg, makers of patent medicines, should
have made it clear we were wrong. It was a plutocracy we
were confronting, and it is sitting comfortably on our backs
today, all over the world. So it wasn't snobbery. It was stupidity on our part. We had to get money to become Sternboroughs. And we never even thought of that.

"After a couple of weeks the fleet of yachts began to diminish. We were given orders to be ready for sailing at an
hour's notice. Plutocrats like to change their habitat on the
spur of the moment's whim. One of the curses of the new rich
is an incapacity to remain anywhere very long. Well, we were
ready. I had no more to do on that yacht than I would have
in winding a watch. There were times when I would have
welcomed some real problem of my profession. And young
Nevile chafed under the extreme futility of his professional
life on the upper deck. They had been doing a lot of gilding
in his department. The Moira had a figurehead, an allegorical
female, one of the Fates, I suppose. The figurehead, the line
along the deck strake, the name and scroll at the stern, were
all gilded with gold leaf under the supervision of the officers.
An expert French gilder was employed. I don't know how

many books of gold leaf it took. There was a lot of gilding in Lady Sternborough's suite to relieve the pearl-gray enamel she had made them put on over the walnut paneling. And young Nevile, what with special silk awnings to put up, and having the sailors work quietly at all times so as not to disturb the guests, was not so much in love with the job as he was at first. He knew he was lucky to get such a position without a master's certificate, but he was not happy. The time didn't count, he remarked to me gravely, for his next certificate. What he meant was he didn't like being a flunkey. Neither did I. I wrote some letters while we were in Monte Carlo, to that effect, to some superintendents I knew at home.

"There was another thing too. He mentioned it to me the last time we were ashore and sitting in the Casino Gardens. He asked me if I had heard what the second officer was saying about Lord Sternborough's secretary and the Honorable Maeve's French maid. No, I hadn't heard a word. The second officer was a rather jaunty young chap with a knack of worming his way into the affairs of the people in the cabin. Perhaps he used his imagination. He was about the only one of us who actually came in contact with Lord Sternborough. He was the ambassador, you may say. And he had not made up his mind that I was an admirer of his. I preserved a more or less diplomatic reserve when he came down to me with a message or an order. So I'd missed the scandal about the owner's secretary going over to Mentone with the French maid.

"'I don't like the way this job is panning out,' young Nevile said. 'There's a lot of gossip among the sailors. They're ashore with the men off the duke's yacht, and they say we're going to Yalta later on and lie there a long time. It isn't going to be much fun for us.'

"I agreed with him, though the secretary's behavior didn't strike me as worth throwing up a good job for. The French maid was very attractive and probably knew her own affairs better than we did. Of course we weren't supposed to see, hear, or know anything, and we were under agreement that our own behavior should be entirely above suspicion on pain of instant dismissal with a month's wages and second-class fare home. Note the second-class fare. We were like maids and valets to the owners. The captain gave us a memorandum before leaving Cowes.

"We were in the position of eunuchs, you see, in a sultan's seraglio. And it confirmed my doubts as to whether I was cut out for the yacht business as a permanency. So we started for the Ægean Sea.

"We were standing by to sail one evening at dinner time, and we stood by all night because the girl Maeve was ashore with her friends. She had had another row with her fiancé, who was coming with us, and she remained over at La Turbie all night. Launches were coming and going continually. There was a family council of war, I heard. Sitting in my costly wicker long chair on our own private after deck I heard voices raised in agitated debate upstairs. Lady Sternborough said, 'You must be patient!' I heard the words 'high strung, settle down, too much excitement, tables, money,' but all disjointed and merely tantalizing me with a desire to see those smug plutocrats as they paced to and fro upstairs. I wanted to hear more. I had a really genuine curiosity to learn how they regarded that girl. She was a portent of changes to come. She had that value in the world, whereas her parents were merely imitations of an aristocracy passing away.

"We stood by all night. Then, about ten, as the family and the other guests were at breakfast, a large launch came to the gangway with the Honorable Maeve in a stunning costume that was very characteristic of her. It was cream colored and deceptively simple in its design to conceal its extreme costliness. On her head was a cream-colored turban with a sort of plastron encrusted with emeralds. With her figure, her magnificent hair, and her amber eyes, she made me think of a disreputable empress. I was in the entrance hall as she came in through the ship's side from the gangway. My first good look at her.

"She was extremely pleased when she heard she had kept the yacht waiting. She had to the full what I can only call a passion for disorder. Each moment, each movement, each experience for her was isolated from all others. She would, I happened to learn later, kick off each of her shoes into different corners of her cabin and throw her corsets and under-clothing wherever they might fall, and in the morning she would put on some other garments without even glancing at the disorder. Because such people are in essence infan-tile in their mental processes. They have the small child's limited outlook. They live quite simply in the present mo-ment.

"At that moment she enjoyed making an impression on me. She walked upstairs, and at the top of that exquisitely curved and carved gold hand rail young Nevile suddenly ap-peared, on his way down to speak to me. She saw him there, and for a moment, close to me, she paused. I heard her say, 'Oh!' He came down towards us and saluted her with a charming smile. She looked at him, as she walked up past him, as if she had never seen him before. And I dare say she hadn't, in that sense.

"That was where it began. I know now she never left him alone until we reached Eupopyle.

"You don't know the Ægean, of course. It is a peculiar region, and its peculiarities, I always maintain, shaped the mythology of the ancient Greek world. You look at it on the map and it seems small, insignificant compared with other seas. But it is a stormy sea. Sometimes it has fogs and cold winds. Sometimes a squall will come whirling across like an enormous spinning wheel of wind and vapor, blotting out the sky and horizon. I have been days just trying to get around Cape Malea. There are islands by the score, specks of gold on the blue floor in summer, death traps when the weather is bad. They are the tops of tall pinnacles just showing above the sea. They will rip your plates off and sink you in a hundred fathom.

"Oh no, the Greeks weren't exaggerating at all when they talked of Æolus and his mountain full of terrible winds. With a boat such as Ulysses had a man might be all of twenty years reaching Ithaca. And it was still winter time when we left the Riviera for the Gulf of Nauplia. On the way Sir Hector Digges asked Lord Sternborough to put in at an island where he wanted to inspect the supposed ruins of a temple dedicated to the worship of Venus. An island called Eupopyle, a lofty hummock which is an outlying peak of the mountains of Argos. It lies within the arms of a craggy indentation of the coast, and the shores are steep cliffs except in one place, where there is a deep cleft leading down to a narrow white beach. At the head of the valley is a village of white hovels. Beyond them again, in a grove of ilex and almond trees, was a small temple, roofless and broken.

"I fancy the worship of Venus was fairly prevalent about those shores. It was certainly going on aboard the Moira while I was her chief engineer. As we sailed down past Corsica and the Lipari Islands we carried a number of love affairs. I suppose Lord and Lady Sternborough accepted these liaisons as part of the price they had to pay for being in smart society. The Honorable Maeve, however, became girlish and artless. She avoided the amorous guests and haunted the navigating bridge after dinner. We were off Stromboli, and I was showing the skipper through the telescope the red glow of the lava trickling down the precipitous sides of the volcano and bubbling in steam in the sea, when I caught sight of young Nevile showing Maeve how to take a position by shooting a star. She had his sextant, and he was holding her arms in the correct position. The old man saw them too and immediately applied his eye to the telescope again. When we reached his room he closed the door and slid the shutter over his ventilator.

"'What do you know about that?' he said, getting out a

bottle. 'She's after him all the time. We'll have trouble. You see, Mr. Copelin, that lad she's engaged to, is going to learn navigation from young Nevile, and she's going to learn navigation too. Only she takes her lessons at night.'

"I asked how young Nevile looked at it, and the captain said he seemed to be absolutely the soul of tact.

"'If she was to chuck herself at me the way she does at him I know what I'd do,' the old man said, and he was ferociously grim and realistic when I rose to his bait and asked him what he would do. I said I wondered young Mr. Copelin didn't object. The captain made a very peculiar face.

"'I'll tell you, Spenlove,' he said. 'He's acting under advice of counsel, as they say. He's very gone on her, and her parents have made him believe that if he lets her have her head a bit, she'll be all the easier to handle. If I was him I'd give her a thrashing within an inch of her life! I'd thrash any daughter of mine—and I've got four—who played the game she plays with him.'

"'But what about young Nevile?' I said. 'I don't want him to get into any mess. I am very fond of him. I was with him on his last ship. He's a good boy!'

"'Oh, you needn't worry about him!' the captain said. 'If he plays his cards right he can do very well for himself.'

"'He may lose his billet,' I said.

"'For a better one,' laughed the captain and gave me a drink.

"'No,' I said. 'No!'

"I didn't think so because I had found that our employers were not at all what I had imagined they might be. If the Honorable Maeve wasn't my idea of a lady of high degree, what about her parents? Instead of being aristocrats, a law to themselves and models for us, they were almost as preoccupied with wealth and position as if they had been middle-class suburbanites. Mr. Copelin was one of those distinguished young men who have not a penny of their own but whose families are wealthy and of ancient lineage. He is now

the fourteenth earl of his line. And Lord and Lady Sternborough, who were about as remarkable to young Copelin
as rich pawnbrokers, simply fawned on him. They fawned
because he was what they wanted to be, because they were
afraid the spell of love Maeve had cast over him would break
and he would escape. They fawned because he gave them that
faint but coveted seal of acceptance by the real upper ten.
They were Whigs who aspired to be Tories."

"It's revolting, that sort of thing," said Mrs. Kavanagh.
"We don't have that in America."

"Don't you?" said Mr. Spenlove. "I'll take the matter up
some time. We had it in England, anyhow, and the rich
Americans like the Sternboroughs were extremely sensitive
to it. So I disagreed with my captain about young Nevile. I
said about all he would get was the sack. I said people of our
class were fools to leave our class. It was particularly dangerous for us because we get thrown among passengers, and when
we are young we have dreams of marrying some rich girl and
getting a fine position ashore. We hear stories of men who
have done these things, who sit in offices and receive large
incomes because they have had that kind of luck. It's a sort
of fragrance in the air, and breathing it we all dream of such
fortune when we are young. Romance! Handsome young
sailor marries a peer's daughter! 'No!' I said to our captain;
'don't you believe it!' But he kept screwing up one eye and
nodding at me over his drink.

"'You'll see I'm right,' he said.

"Well, I had to leave it at that. I discovered, moreover,
that I could bear it if young Nevile had the luck his captain
foretold. I discovered in myself some of that complacent
British snobbery you say you don't have in America. It's a
very subtle pleasure, to contemplate being even distantly
connected with an aristocratic alliance. Most of us have
enough sense never to put the reason for our complacency in
plain words, but we experience the thrill, a sort of physical
titillation at the top of one's spine, just the same. I believe it

has something to do with our glands, so probably you in America are born without them. You're lucky. It's irresistible when it happens.

"So I was down below, enjoying my own station in life and the unusual luxury of perfect engines. You see, turbines were not common then. I had happened, during a spell ashore, to work in the yard where the Moira was engined and had become acquainted with such things while they were constructed. I had been with them on maneuvers. They had their own charm. They approach the ideal of a prime mover. The yacht slid swiftly through the Ionian Sea with no sound save a faint, continuous sigh far down below. Our ashes were discharged under the sea. Soundproof doors prevented even the noise of a shovel coming out of the boiler rooms. It was like playing with a fabulously expensive toy. Calabrian and Sicilian peasants, glancing down from their fields beyond Scylla and Charybdis, saw a white ship like a long, gold-tipped silver blade cleaving the blue sea. The fishermen, as we passed, would gaze up at the gilded Fate on our bows and all the splendor of the gleaming enamel sides and shout to one another as they pointed to the strange and unfamiliar Blue Ensign at our stern. 'Eccola!' I heard a bull-throated piratical person blare out, 'Eccola! Bandiera turchiniccia!' What a blue-looking flag! he was saying to shipmates, who knew our Red Ensign well enough and the White Ensign too. I couldn't help thinking what a good thing it would be if they had suddenly boarded us and seized the yacht. It would have evened the unbalance of things, don't you think?"

"Wait!" said Mrs. Kavanagh. "I guess I can use that." She caught sight of Mr. Spenlove's Puckish grimace and made a gesture towards him. "You knew I would," she said, taking out her pencil. "Yes, I could use pirates capturing a yacht. That could be the mystery when the yacht got back. A murder, but no one on board guilty. Now, what motive for keeping silent about the pirates?" She looked up in abstraction, unseeing.

"Why not pearls? Gun running? A diamond-smuggling ring? A secret radio station? The public eat secret radio stations. I don't know how they can believe in them, but they do. It's like believing in a secret lighthouse. But that's your business."

"Go on. Don't laugh at a poor author. It isn't as easy as you seem to think. It has to work out."

"True. I'll go on. Fiction has to work out. All I know is what has happened to me. I was with my toy engines, humming like enormous hives of bees, and in my sumptuous quarters two decks down, and the Moira, the ship of the fates, swam swiftly down the Ionian Sea. Lady Sternborough had no time for books, but I had. It was of no importance to me that my employers had their own way of amusing themselves. I became the perfect servant, efficient and invisible, an efficient eunuch, socially speaking, functioning as per contract."

"What were you reading?" demanded Mrs. Kavanagh.

"I was going to tell you. I was reading Donaldson's *Theater of the Greeks*. I'd picked it up, a perfect copy, in a Liverpool pawnshop, for sixpence. Like many another odd volume picked up by chance, it fitted in very well with where I was going. You want to know why? Curiosity. Old Donaldson has a lot of stuff we forget nowadays. He ought to be brought out by one of these modern publishers with a whooping advertising campaign, in a jazzy jacket. No need to say he lived a long while ago. There are plenty of agile professors of history who could stand on Donaldson's shoulders and scream that they are taller than he. It's done every day.

"And then I was reading Finlay. You wouldn't have heard of him, but I liked it because I spent part of my life in the Ægean on the old Manola and the people we came in contact with were not Hellenic Greeks. They were survivors of the Turkish conquest, and before that they had a Byzantine past. They had a past when the republic of Venice held them in bondage, or if you like, as colonies. There are a lot of Vene-

tians there now, among the islands and in the ports. Finlay
tells you about it. Finlay was a cantankerous Scotch savant
who hated Greeks and yet spent his life writing them up.
He even farmed land in Greece to find out what it was like.
But nobody who goes to Greece ever thinks anything about
that part of their history. Most of us fool ourselves. We look
at the Parthenon and have no curiosity as to the people in
the street and on the farms. The Greeks who killed Socrates
are as extinct as the Mayan priesthood who threw young
virgins into the sacred cenotes of Yucatan. Our Greeks, the
Greeks you find in New York City, are fish of another fry.
Elli Phalère was one of them. A hundred strains woven in one
slender body. That's why she was so modern, so very much
one of us, English or American. Ours are more tightly woven,
and that is all. The old Greeks had slaves. Elli Phalère's ancestors were slaves of the Ottomans and paid a yearly tax in
children sent to Istamboul. Imagine that for a sizzling melt-
ing pot! You remember the blond Anglo-Saxon kids on sale
in Rome? What the Levantines will become is more interesting to me than that meeting house on the Acropolis, or any
temple of Venus.

"Imagine my feelings when I was suddenly visited, off
Corfu, by the old gentleman who was the ostensible reason
for our trip to Nauplia. Sir Hector Digges came down with
the yacht surgeon, Lord Sternborough's personal physician,
who introduced us and then went on to see one of the firemen,
who was sick.

"I stood looking at that old bearded savant in astonishment. He was big framed, but bent. His hands were as large
and sinewy as a stone mason's. His face was gray and speck-
led, as if he had received a charge of birdshot full in the eyes.
He wore sun glasses with octagonal lenses, and they made
him look like a ferocious insect. He picked up Finlay, lying
on my table, threw a glance at me, and then, replacing the
sun glasses with gold-rimmed spectacles, he proceeded to
examine the bookshelves. He stood with his big shoulders

hunched, one hand grasping a chair, his linen suit hanging like a sack on him, his face close to the books. Then he grunted and lowered himself into a leather easy chair.

"I still didn't know what brought him down to see me, but aiming to be the perfect menial, I waited. He nodded towards the book. 'You read that?' he said. 'I didn't know anybody on this boat read things like that. Not upstairs! Disgusting.'

"He seemed to be talking in soliloquy. He sat shaking his head and swinging his spectacles by one bow. I said I didn't understand what he was talking about, as I never went upstairs.

"'You're lucky,' he told me. 'These people are emancipated, I suppose, but we used to have another name for it when I was in the army.' He'd been through the Sudan campaign as a young man, in the Royal Engineers. That was how he came to be an archæologist.

"'Well, we're all living exemplary lives down here,' I told him. 'I'm the only one who knows one Greek island from another, or who has ever heard of Missolonghi, or the Countess Guiccioli, or Mavrocordato. And I can keep my own counsel.'

"'I see you get my point,' he said. 'Love affairs are only tolerable at a distance of a century or so. Seen at close range, they fail to evoke admiration. If I saw Byron hugging his Italian lady I would be nauseated. But her memoirs are good stuff.'

"I said we would have to wait a few years and possibly some memoirs would come out of the love affairs on the Moira. Sir Hector snorted.

"'You read Fanny Hill? Well, never mind that. I ought to apologize to Fanny. She was only a cheerful victim of a man's lust. The up-to-date young woman can't be described as a victim.'

"'She's an experimentalist,' I suggested. 'But she's not very new.'

"'I fancy you're right,' he said. 'It's only because I am old and had all my jolly times before they were born. But it's damned dull up there, among the smart set, and you can give me a whisky-and-soda if you have such a thing.'

"We became friends. I fancy he would have been happier if he had declined the cruise on the yacht and had made his way to Nauplia by the old Pappayanni boat that called there. 'I'm only a performing dog,' he growled. 'The questions they ask! If I were a dentist or a watchmaker, they'd take the results of my labor and pay me for it and mind their own business.'

"'Yes,' I said, 'but they wouldn't honor a dentist or a watchmaker by taking him on a cruise in a yacht costing half a million pounds. They are doing the only thing left to them. They have no functions. Democracy has deprived aristocracy of all its pomp. You can't dedicate a book to a patron any more. A lord can't knight you as he could in Elizabethan days. You—and I—are both independent of him. The only power left is wealth, and that he has to share with the plutocrats, who may buy him up, unless he is a plutocrat himself.'

"Sir Hector liked that line of talk. He had written forty books on Archæology, and he had no respect for amateurs. He said I might be independent of plutocrats but he wasn't, for he needed their money to dig with. There was another tribe I had forgotten, he added, who had us all—Sir Hector used a vigorous masculine metaphor. He meant the bureaucrats. And you could never get a bureaucrat to find money for digging. All he wanted was to dig himself in, snug as a bug in a rug. A cocoon of red tape, the old man remarked, and poured himself more whisky.

"I asked him about the temple of Venus on the island we were heading for. He gave me a whimsical glance. 'Medieval!' he grunted. 'The whole country was Roman and Turkish for centuries. Some Fanariot hospodar had the fancy to build a summer residence in the design of a classical temple. He was probably rich, and patronized the arts at home in Byzantium.'"

"I never heard of them," said Mrs. Kavanagh. She made several hasty illegible notes. "Will you spell it?"

Mr. Spenlove did so, and shook his pipe at her.

"You have them, you have them, here in the United States! Peasants and kings at home, smooth politicians in America. Can't you see that Fanariot Greek from Constantinople making a great to-do over his Greek ancestry, boasting a name like Mavrocordatos or Dioscurides, and building himself a genuine bit of old Hellas on an island in his own bailiwick? Graft, you know!"

"Now!" said Mrs. Kavanagh. "You leave the Irish alone, once for all!"

"Well, I see you get my point," Mr. Spenlove resumed with great relish. "History repeats itself so marvelously I am never tired of contemplating America. But I am afraid there was something Byzantine about Lord Sternborough too, and Sir Hector Digges gave me some significant winks as he went on to describe the days of medieval Greece. He made allusions to the Honorable Maeve's Circean technique. This was after the fourth whisky-and-soda. He sat back in my easy chair, his noble and benign old head, the white beard stained with nicotine about the mouth to a rich amber, like an old meerschaum. He reminded me sometimes of Jove, and sometimes of God the Father in an Italian primitive. He knew so many things that I have always had a feeling I am pilfering from his basket. Upstairs, you see, they had not been listening to him, and he had his vanity. We all have, we who have the gift of communicating ideas by speech. His vanity had been hurt. They did not listen. They asked him this, that, and the other about his excavations and paid no attention to what he said. The young men laughed in that hollow public-school fashion which seems to be dying out in our time, a sort of resonant tremolo from the top of the windpipe. The girls uttered faint shrieks of protest when he said that many of his discoveries would make them blush. He flattered them. Especially Maeve, who was always with that young officer on the bridge.

"'Come,' I said, 'he isn't on watch all the time. Four to eight, with the chief officer.'

"'I mean she's with him. He was at dinner last night. That other chap's nose is out of joint. She goes up on the bridge.'

"'I am sorry to hear it,' I said. 'The fourth mate's a friend of mine. I like him. I've been at sea with him before we came here, and I don't see any future for him if what you say is true. I don't want him to be a rich girl's pet dog.'

"'What can you do?' he wanted to know. 'She's taken a fancy to him.'

"'He'll only lose his job. They'll put a stop to anything beyond a flirtation.'

"'Then why do you worry about it?' inquired Sir Hector dryly. 'I admit womanizing's no good when you're young. You have all the torment and none of the bliss. But interfering is the devil. Better leave him alone.'

"I said I would probably do that. I didn't want to lose my own job, now I had it. I was only feeling in loco parentis.

"'Well, let's have another drink,' he said, 'and you come up and see me. I'll show you some things I've found out about navigation in the time of the Byzantine occupation of Asia Minor. Magnesia, you know.'

"I went up, and he showed me the things he had found. It was extremely interesting, and his theory is to be found in one of his books. He reconstructed for me a sea battle and a myth arising from it. I don't know whether other archæologists accept his ingenious explanation of what he found. One German savant accused him of modeling the stone compass, throwing it secretly into the sea near Samos, and fishing it up years later. A German, and Sir Hector said this long before Sarajevo, can never believe you aren't exactly like himself and is always astounded when you hit back. There is nothing like tunneling into another man's obsession. It did me good. I met my owner, if you'll believe it, for the first time.

"That was shyness on his part. He had the idea that if he let us alone we would prefer it. The captain had tipped me off about this. He called Lord and Lady Sternborough 'the people.' He often told me how 'the people' regarded this and that. 'The people' were going to Constantinople later as guests of the Sultan. I got into the way of referring to 'the people' myself. I became aware of the constant preoccupation of 'the people' with the problem of their own status. They were extremely polite to us heads of departments, as though we might suddenly organize a mutiny and take possession of the yacht, while their dismembered corpses floated on the blue Ægean. I had a distinct impression that his lordship was not too convinced that the divine right of wealth protected him any more, now that he was a peer of the realm.

"He was a very quiet person, with a handle-bar mustache and gray hair parted in the middle, and he said he hoped I would visit Sir Hector at any time. And as there was a dance that evening, it being the last night before we anchored in the Gulf of Nauplia, he hoped I would dine in the saloon. He hoped everything was satisfactory in my department. He made himself extremely agreeable to me. It takes a long while to become adjusted to the rôle of a trusted retainer. I expressed myself as very appreciative of his kindness. And I put on my dress clothes, naval reserve style, very much what we have here, to attend the dinner."

"Tell me about that, please," said Mrs. Kavanagh. She had her notebook on her knee. She wore an intensely rapt expression. "I can see it coming out now," she went on. "Your remark, you know, about you starting a mutiny on board and the dismembered corpses in the blue Ægean."

Mr. Spenlove knocked out his pipe.

"You'll have to develop that yourself," he suggested, feeling for his pouch and regarding her with interest. "I don't believe you're listening. But of course you are. You merely want some local color. Are you sure you can transmit what you have only seen through my eyes? Can you reproduce the perfection of the scene in that dining saloon, paneled in ebony with silver sconces, with its illuminated hemispherical dome of colored glass depicting the loves of the nereids? Can you convey the exhausting impression that there was not a single member of what we call the middle class present? Don't imagine the captain and I came under that category. We were part of the show. A yacht like the Moira could raise us to a sort of professional peerage. Anyhow the captain was wearing the order of the Crescent, third class, which he had received when commanding the yacht of the Turkish Grand Vizier.

"Then can you bring out the clothes of the women? I can't possibly describe them or their jewelry. I learned later in the course of the voyage that a yacht at sea is one of the few places where those people really wear their gems. Another place is at court. Lady Sternborough had pearls as large as small cherries, which she wore day and night to improve their luster. So I was told. Are you interested? The Honorable Maeve and a dark girl, who smoked Russian cigarettes and wore a gown that looked like a snakeskin sheath, had bands of velvet, encrusted with stones, on their hair, and many bracelets on their arms. Their bags and shawls were so unusual and costly that I had no conception of their materials. I was abashed, as though I had inadvertently wandered into a sultan's seraglio."

Mrs. Kavanagh made a murmured protest as she looked up from her notebook. How, she wanted to know, would Mr. Spenlove know what a sultan's seraglio looked like?

"It's a fair question," said Mr. Spenlove, "and I dare say seraglios vary as much as bedrooms in king's palaces or even in Queens County, New York. I am merely trying to give you an impression of sensuous and slightly sensual splendor. As the dinner proceeded and the wines were passed, I had a sensation of being received into a mysterious communion of

godlike creatures who were graciously revealing themselves
to me by their more human qualities. I sat next to the dark
girl in the snakeskin creation. She was handsome, with her
dark hair in what we used to call the Lily Langtry fashion, on
her neck, and she was accomplished in the small arts by
which intelligent, wealthy people make us like them too well
to want to destroy their social system. And as the wine progressed her eyes sparkled and her smile became more en-
trancing, and she leaned closer to me as we talked, and I
realized for a while how very well I might succeed in that way
of life myself. There was a provocative tremolo in her laugh
when I made a daring retort to one of her sallies. I wouldn't
emphasize this bygone flirtation—I don't remember her
name, if I ever knew it—if it didn't illuminate for me how
young Nevile and the Honorable Maeve began the affair
that ultimately put him on the beach. I felt during that
glamorous meal that I might easily fall into those complex
and embarrassing toils that always await the man who steps
out of his own class into the one above him to meddle with
women. What? You don't have classes in America? If you
made a few voyages on this ship, dear lady, you would discover America much more completely than Columbus ever
did. It takes a European to discover America. No classes?
Well, that can wait. We have them, and the internal consciousness of our own class. I suppose that is what you mean
when you say you have no classes. That is what I shall never
know in my own experience. But I have learned that it is extremely difficult to discuss foreign social conditions with
Americans because they invariably see in imagination Royal-
ists, Cossacks, or Prussians with their jack boots thrust hard
against the necks of pure-minded, freedom-loving readers of
the *Saturday Evening Post*. In other words, they use their dim
memories of an imaginary French Revolution as the background for a romantic picture of wicked aristocrats riding
over the prostrate forms of peasants. I have never got anywhere in the discussion because you have no notion of an

actual social order in operation save that conveyed by the elevator telltale in one of your big buildings—a lot of individual lights going up and down endlessly. If they don't go up and down they are out of order and useless. . . .

"No, a sensitiveness to the social gradations, especially in sex, takes a lot of subconscious education. I was born in the lower middle class, and I can say I drew it in with my mother's milk. When I found myself basking in the light of that rich, aristocratic girl's smile, I was no more deceived than a third-class passenger is fooled when the barriers between him and the first class are taken down on the night of a ship's dance or concert in aid of Sailor's Snug Harbor. The third-class passenger knows it is only a gesture, and he will get a yellow landing ticket, instead of a green or red one, when he goes ashore. The only use the experience carried for me was to make me cautious and careful that the way back to my own social level was not closed against me. Most of us who have character do not want to rise in the social scale! Did you know that? Well, it is true, especially of us who have the entire social aquarium before our eyes all the time. It isn't worth the trouble. It means so much more time to achieve an entity of one's own, if one never has to agonize and strive to pull oneself up alongside of the Joneses. Ah, the Joneses! We carry them every voyage, with the families who are absorbed in arriving level with them.

"I was safe enough at any time. Out on the quarter deck, in the shadows between the colored-paper lanterns, with the huge loom of the crags of Eupopyle across the dark water, while the liveried servants brought us seventy-year-old brandy and Turkish coffee and superb Murias, I was able to remember that tomorrow was another day. Just for that evening I became a possible member of our British Samurai! I confess that the foundations of a romance were laid that evening, foundations that remain in my memory like mossy romantic ruins. Some streak of peasant caution inspired me to excuse myself for a moment. Only for a moment. I had no

intention of deserting that girl. I had a professional reason
for going below for a moment. The yacht had an electric organ, the nearest approximation a millionaire of those days
could achieve to our radio. I went below to see that the volt-
age was right for it.

"While I was away one of those sudden impulses had seized
the young people. The moon was coming up behind the hills
and someone had suggested a midnight visit to the island.
The launches were already in the water when I came up.
Servants were handing wraps and rugs. Young Nevile was in
command of the smaller launch. I looked down from the quarter deck and watched them. I remember being struck at the
time with the fact that they could all have gone in one launch.
Yes, the Honorable Maeve was in the smaller one with young
Nevile. I would like to tell you that she looked up at me, his
guardian angel, in triumph as they chuffed away into the
darkness. She didn't. She was absorbed in her own affairs.
She had to perfection that air some sensual women possess,
giving one the impression that they are reserved for the pleas-
ures of a particular god, whom they adore. Yes, I see it even
on this cruise steamer! It is the last residue of the Dionysiac
ecstasies. She had it. How she would have enjoyed being
young in our time! And how I shudder when I think of her as
she is, in the pages of the *Tatler*, a hard-mouthed woman of
forty, facing the extinction of her class, the destruction of
their wealth by taxation, and the insolence of the new subur-
ban rich who are surging up in London!

"They went. I didn't even go into the radiance of the
gangway lanterns. I saw the dark girl in the snakeskin
sheath, with whom I had been flirting. I saw her being as-
sisted tenderly into the large launch by one of the guests, a
young man of great possessions. Possibly he possesses her too
now, a plump matron who has to go to Homburg once a year.
All that were left on board were the seniors. I found Sir Hector Digges in the library, and joined him. I felt I could do
with some more of that seventy-year-old brandy and another

Muria. I found I was reluctant, after all, to step down again into the ranks of the employed!

"I would never have remembered that evening but for what happened to young Nevile. Sir Hector entertained me with the story of Euphemios, who stole a nun in Sicily and was sentenced to lose his nose. He invited Liadet Allah, a Saracen king with a strong fleet, to invade the island. The paynims conquered and settled in Sicily because Euphemios wanted to keep his nose. Sir Hector played with the notion of a history of mutilation. It had psychopathological significances. If, for instance, we could identify the impulses that lay behind the medieval machines for extracting information or the dismemberment of traitors . . . ! Books were no good. You read *Macbeth* or *The Faëry Queen* and remember that heads perched on pikes on the bridges, and quartered trunks stank all about London at that time. Books tell one nothing we don't already know about man. Think of the row Jenkins, a hundred and fifty years later, made about losing his ear! The war of Jenkins' ear. And the war of Euphemios' nose!

"So we conversed, and the brandy was lowered in the decanter. The electric organ droned away in the next room, *O Du! Mein Holder Abendstern!* I always think of the Moira when I hear that music. And eventually we went to bed. A perfect evening from my point of view and Sir Hector's. A perfect evening for anybody who was not deceived by that cunning little boy god, Love, with his leering promises of ecstasies that are largely fictitious. Even when they are real they last for no more than a moment.

"However, I must have had a little too much of the brandy. Next morning my mouth was dry and I got up early to get some cold water. The engineer on watch in the refrigerator room was in deep converse with our alert and communicative second officer. I surprised them, naturally, at such an hour. But the theme of their talk was too rich and juicy to be dismissed. They told me as I drank down some cold water thirstily. The third officer and the Honorable

Maeve were still ashore on the island, had been there all night! The launch had been to and from the beach several times, very quietly and slowly, so as not to alarm 'the people,' but nobody had come down to it. A vast powwow was going on in the executive quarters as to the best way of handling such an unheard-of situation. The captain had been ashore once but had returned. They were in a jam because of the girl. The captain was, the second mate said, between hell and high water. If he raised the alarm and started searching for the pair he might bring disaster upon us all. If he remained quiet and something terrible had happened to the girl, he was likely to lose his job at the least.

"I took several drinks of water before getting the whole of the story. It was a problem for the captain; but as captains always pride themselves on their sound executive genius, I wasn't worrying about him. I was concerned when I saw the implications in it for young Neville. He was in dutch, no matter how one looked at it. Of course, nobody was up yet, topside, said our second luff, and the Lady Maeve had disciplined them all so thoroughly by her outbursts in the past that until the fact crashed down upon them that she had been away with young Nevile all night nothing would happen. This was at five-thirty in the morning. The captain was going ashore in the dinghy, so as to make no noise, in another attempt to solve his problems.

"Back in my cabin I wanted very much to go with him, but it seemed to me that whatever was implied in this business was out of our hands. It was the girl who had been the person in charge, I knew that. I was filled with fury against her. I disliked her anyhow! One of those slender, rattlesnake girls, who are all sex where their desires are concentrated, and cold selfish bitches to the rest of us. But what sort of figure would I cut if I rushed ashore in a Greek island and ravished her of her lover because he was dear to me? Yet I would have done it if I had had any belief in achieving my object and could have been sure I wouldn't lose my own job.

I not only disliked Maeve, I was afraid of her. No humble retainer would stand in her way if she were ordering execu-
tions."

"But if she was in love with him!" protested Mrs.
Kavanagh.

"Love! Ah, possibly. I don't know. I can only tell you how
it fell out. The captain went ashore in the dinghy, and with
a pair of powerful glasses, from my porthole I saw him start
up the beach towards the ruined temple Sir Hector was going
to inspect when he felt able to go ashore. Ha! I thought.
He'll find the god Priapus still on the ground! He was the
son, you remember, of Dionysos and Aphrodite. I could just
see the gray-green entablature of the temple beyond the
rocks and above the vine-clad slopes of the valley.

"There was a village there, of course, which the captain
evidently hoped could afford him some assistance. Sound
executive genius isn't much use on a Greek island, however.
Especially if one is wearing expensive buckskin shoes with
thin soles while walking up a precipitous rocky gully. The
captain was obviously feeling his age as he toiled upwards.
He was a white speck in the center of my field of vision.
Then he vanished, and I sat down to think of my own affairs.

"You see, it might easily disrupt the lives of all of us.
Rich people are creatures of incalculable, invisible impulses
which they can instantly gratify. They are to us what a
speculative human is to an ant's nest when he drops a match
on it or stirs it up with a stick. We are flung hither and yon
by purely emotional eruptions. We scurry all over the place,
or are annihilated in absence of mind by a passionate boot.
Our lives, our savings, our families, are all suddenly imperilled by a tantrum on the part of some irresponsible being who
happens to have a lot of money. That was why I felt that
the situation deserved attention. And you'd be amazed how
quickly an appreciation of it flew around the ship in our lower
deck departments. Nobody save myself cared a curse whether
young Nevile was in dutch or not. What about us? was the

cry. What if we are ordered to lay the yacht up and all go home second class and start hunting a job again? We had a helpless feeling, very much what prehistoric man must have experienced when a herd of mastodons stampeded over his subterranean refuge and the stones rattled down around him in the shock of their passing. A blind insensate power begets a blind fatalism. We decided that what would be would be, and wished we were back in our old employ.

"By breakfast time, by which I mean our breakfast time, eight o'clock, we were all on the alert for the skipper's return. And he didn't return. There was no sign of anyone at all on the beach. The dinghy was back, of course, swinging at the gangway grating, and the crew were lowering the smaller launch for an expedition ashore. It looked as if nothing could save us from a crisis upstairs. I was having my own breakfast in my cabin when a message came down from Sir Hector Digges. Would I care to go ashore with him for a preliminary look-see? Ready at eight thirty?

"I was aware of the honor of such a proposal from him. He had taken to me, I suppose. I sent a message I'd be ready at the time he suggested and changed my clothes. I told the senior watch keeper I'd be ashore all the morning.

"Sir Hector was at the gangway, his huge curved back crossed by the straps of his high-power glasses and his camera. His big pockets contained notebooks and other paraphernalia. He showed me a steel tape measure that was like a satin ribbon and not much larger than a watch. He had a silver spirit level, and so forth. He was feeling much better, he said, and I could see the light of adventure in his eye as he tapped a heavy walking stick on the deck. I noticed the pockets of his billowing linen Norfolk jacket were torn, and his shirt was well worn too.

"He astonished me by saying he was poor. He said he worked most of the time for his expenses and was always piling up a deficit. What could anyone comment upon such a discovery? I didn't ask him why he did it. I knew that. I even envied him. Compared with the man whose guest he was and the other people on the Moira, he was a king among slaves.

"His talk! How can I give you any idea of it? He unrolled the centuries before my eyes like a scroll. I mean, he really knew. Even now I hear his rough baritone rolling out the words Mykenian, Menidi, Spata, Nauplia. I fancy he enjoyed my secret admiration of him. He told me he hated journalists because they were always making him talk rubbish, and sought without weariness for impossible 'discoveries.' 'Damn fools' he called them, unkindly. He was open with me because he knew I had no ulterior interest in making him talk. So we reached the village on the island of Eupopyle. And at the door of the wine shop, just inside where a yacht telescope couldn't reach them, were our captain and young Nevile.

"I was very much astonished. I suppose it shows my lack of experience, but I had had some notion that if our captain really did find those two, he would appear holding each of them by an ear, or possibly driving them, handcuffed, in front of him with a horsewhip. I had simply not considered anything rational as happening on such an occasion. But here were the two mariners, one of whom had been on a Greek island all night with a daughter of Circe. They ought both of them to have developed swinish characteristics. They were lifting glasses of what turned out to be coffee, however, and they saluted us by raising these glasses when we entered. Young Nevile stood up.

"He bore no marks at all, in his demeanor, of having done anything seriously disorganizing to us. He was neither insolent nor arrogant; on the other hand, I expected him to be much more embarrassed by our scrutiny. But he has rarely been embarrassed. It's one of his charms, that you don't have to feel contempt for him. He has never laid his burden on another person's unwilling shoulders, as so many of us do.

"He stood there, agreeably welcoming, while the captain, one hand on his knee, ordered coffee for us. Sir Hector stood in the doorway of that wine shop, his eyes screwed up behind the sun glasses he was wearing, as he contemplated young Nevile.

"'Ha!' he said. 'Did Ariadne give young Theseus the labyrinthine thread? You seem to be alive and undevoured, young man!'

"The captain looked from Sir Hector to young Nevile and back to me and smiled without understanding. 'I found him here,' he said to me; 'he was just coming on board.'

"'You been here all night?' I inquired. Young Nevile nodded and glanced towards the back room.

"'Lady Maeve is at the tribune's house,' said the captain. 'She'll be coming back to the ship too in about an hour.'

"'You see?' said Sir Hector, as he took his glass of coffee. 'They have kept the Roman terminology through all the conquests. So we have magistrates and consuls in England. Yes, well . . .' He seemed to be talking to ease the situation, and I made a remark about pro-consuls and procurators. I said to the captain, who thought we were a couple of lunatics, 'Are you going to wait for her?' 'No,' he said, getting up suddenly. 'We're going on board at once. This place is not safe. The pilot is coming with me. I came ashore to get the pilot, you understand. You'll watch the ship for a signal. This fine weather is treacherous, so close in. Come off at once if I signal.'

"They went away down the valley, and for a few moments I watched young Nevile, stepping lightly from side to side to avoid the rocks and butting goats, while the old man lumbered straight down, his shoulders shaking. I was upset. Young Nevile seemed unaware of anything having happened to him. And in front of me, of us, I believed, lay an encounter with that girl. We started up the hill again, and we saw, on the cedarwood door of a blue-and-white house, the brass plate of the tribune of Eupopyle. She's in there! we both thought. Well, I know I did. I thought of her, sleeping without tears or remorse, after working her will on a youth who would have escaped if there had been any chance for him."

Mrs. Kavanagh waved her hand derisively in Mr. Spenlove's face.

"That's it, blame her! As if he couldn't have escaped, as
you call it!"

"What? From the Lady Maeve, a predatory aristocrat of
his own race, while the moon rose over the Gulf of Argos
and she led him by the hand, through a veritable Vale of
Tempe, to a ruined shrine of Venus! That's what she did. I
got that out of him years later, and he only told me to explain
the extenuating circumstances. The mountains of Arachne
were visible beyond the further shore of Argolis. And you
say he could have escaped! It is a tradition of ours, to sur-
render under such circumstances."

"What was the temple like?"

"I don't remember much about that. Only that Sir Hector
told me the whole thing was part of a Byzantine gentleman's
estate; some retired tax collector, or oil merchant, who had
classical ideas. I remained outside. I sat on a carved stone
seat in a grove of ilex trees and watched Sir Hector's me-
thodical movements, pacing, measuring, gauging thicknesses,
and drawing sketches in his large notebook of squared paper.
He was absorbed in the chances of digging down and finding
the vestiges of some earlier building on the site. He called my
attention to the lay of the land. Look at the view, he said.
The yacht lay in the center of a medallion of blue sea enclosed by the dark arms of savage, rocky shore. Beyond her
the sun shone on the water. It made a background of dazzling
azure, and the distant peaks in Laconia rose faintly on the
horizon. Yes, I agreed, there would always be some sort of
building in a place like that. Nice location for anybody's
country villa. Sir Hector nodded. But he couldn't make me
go into that ruined and fraudulent temple. I was too much
occupied with the recent event that had taken place in there.

"The fact is, I had imagined that such things possess a
glamour of their own, a violence and drama that exist only
when some poet has been at work on them. I know better

now. It isn't a bit of good hanging around in the hopes of
seeing Jove descend through a brazen tower in a shower of
gold. Or trying to catch Circe transforming her guests into
swine. The quickness of the imagination deceives the eye.
We forget the one necessary ingredient, the artist. Somebody
like you, for instance. We may have an idyll or a tragedy here
on the ship, but we won't know it is an idyll or a tragedy
until you write a book about it."

"Now, don't you laugh at me." Mrs. Kavanagh put her
notebook into her big bag. She looked at her watch. "I must
go and find Terry," she said. "But what happened when you
got back to the yacht?"

"Whatever had happened was in the past already when
the launch came for us. I detected an unusual expression on
the face of the young coxswain in charge when he caught my
eye. He had an air of smug complacency. He was one whose
duties threw him most intimately into the company of young
Nevile. He was on young Nevile's watch as quartermaster.
He was aware of something tremendous going on which made
him feel cocksure and light-hearted. The lower classes are
very observant and sensitive when they are working for the
upper crust. So I concluded there had been no explosion
so far. And when we arrived on board I received orders to be
ready to move in an hour. We were going up the gulf to
Nauplia. The main expedition ashore was to Mykenae."

"You mean to say they had made no change in their plans?
They hadn't discovered . . ."

"I don't know what they had discovered. That the Lady
Maeve had spent the night ashore at the tribune's house,
possibly. That the engagement with young Copelin was
somewhat more tenuous. I didn't know what their plans were.
How should I? We took orders when they came. The whole
point of this adventure was the behavior of Lady Maeve,
who had made a clandestine visit across the no man's land
between her own social territory and ours. And while we all,
from the coxswain with his smug grin, to the captain with his

preoccupied air of gravity, had a conviction as to what had happened, we had precious little to go on. We left Eupopyle in that mood. We reached Nauplia in the same mood. There something took place which left us all in a daze because of the completeness with which it justified all our apprehensions.

"The second officer, bearing in his hand the bridge chits of distance run and speed—exactly as if it mattered how fast or how slow we steamed from Circe's isle—came into my cabin with the news. 'They've all gone, except the jane,' he said, meaning Lady Maeve. 'Now what do you know about that? She wouldn't go!' And then he put his finely chiseled lips close to my ear, and I heard the words, 'Dinner for two laid in the quarters—for her and him. I have it from the second butler. He comes from Waltham Cross, where my old lady still lives.' I said nothing.

"Can you imagine the hush that came over that yacht that night as we lay at anchor at the head of the gulf? I sat in my cabin looking out at the shores of storied Greece and feeling that I was bereaved of something, I hardly knew what. I fancy now I would have liked to go on shore with young Nevile and watch him take in the stories I could have told of Agamemnon and Menelaus. But at the time I was bereaved of more than that. It might have been a perverted class consciousness, a jealousy of all the powers that wealth and birth bestowed on a girl I disliked. I had fantastic visions of what was going on upstairs. At last, about ten o'clock, with the idea of spending half an hour with the captain, I went upstairs myself. And as I passed along the officers' passage I saw young Nevile in his cabin. He was in his bunk, reading by the light of a green-shaded lamp. He didn't hear me. I went in and closed the door gently. He looked at me and put his magazine down."

Mrs. Kavanagh stood up and gathered her belongings together. Mr. Spenlove slipped easily from the table he had been sitting on.

"I believe," she said hurriedly, "you are telling me all this

to arouse my distrust of him. To protect him! I believe you
have a perverted conception of women. I mean, what you
said about the girl seducing him. As if she would! What did
he have to say for himself?"

"Perverted? Not at all. Only realistic, and there's no need
to protect him any more. He has become immunized, so he
gives me to understand! No, I'm telling you what happened
to him and to me. He listened when I said he was playing a
risky game. I said he might jeopardize his whole career. He
said he wasn't playing a game at all. He said he had done
all a gentleman could to avoid embarrassing anybody. Then,
I said, what position are you in precisely? He said, 'I'm supposed to go and stay with them when we get home. She desires it.' 'What for?' I asked. And he said, 'Well, marriage.'"

"He said marriage!" said Mrs. Kavanagh in a faint voice.
"Was that a fact too? Had she broken that other engagement?"

"I doubt if she had—then. She'd sworn him to keep it
secret from 'the people.' But he told it to me in a casual tone
that made me feel the futility of arguing with him. He only
fingered his magazine and twitched his lips. I fancy he was
making use of me, seeing what effect it had upon me, so
as to get the hang of it. He wasn't—how shall I put it?—
completely aware, perhaps. That was the glamour of even
approaching a girl like the Honorable Maeve. The knowledge
that he had won her favor, had attracted her so that she had
carried him away to that ruined temple, was overshadowed
by the power such a liaison conferred on him. I know it made
him a little dizzy and afraid, for he told me so. He had been
so afraid, he had insisted on leaving her after dinner. He
couldn't bear the silent movements of the servants to and fro
in the dining saloon as he sat on the divan in the music room
or walked under the awnings aft with Maeve. He knew what
they were thinking—that he was one of those pretty boys who
try to become a rich woman's keep, and it braced him to
make her understand he had to go back to his quarters."

"And they, her parents and fiancé, didn't suspect?"

"I wasn't in their confidence. I don't know what they suspected at all. It wasn't as if young Nevile had been her first lover. He wasn't, in my opinion. Her first passion, if you like; but her passions were short flares that soon burned down and out. However, she wanted him very fiercely indeed at the time. When we reached Constantinople, it was obvious, from the uncertainty of our orders, that the people upstairs were changing their plans. Young Copelin didn't even wait to visit the Sultan. He took a train to Athens to rejoin Sir Hector Digges at Mykenae. The second officer, our eagle-eyed hearer of thrilling news, told us the launch was ordered. He called it 'a bust up.'

"The people visited the Sultan, and he came on board for a short visit. He was a very nervous person in a black frock coat and a tarbush. He was accompanied by a lot of fierce persons in uniforms and by a guard of janissaries. I saw them crowding the gunboat and swarming through the side doors into the Moira. There was a dinner and dance in honor of the Embassy people, and the yacht for once seemed worth the money she had cost. But we were told to stand by with steam up. Eyewitnesses brought us news of events. There was a family row on, we heard, but it was being conducted with a great deal of secrecy and a lack of what I might call ferocity. Handkerchiefs pressed to eyes, mustaches pulled by nervous fingers, and dead silence ensued on approach of servants. It seemed to me, from the descriptions, and a glimpse I had of Lord Sternborough, and young Copelin, just before he left, walking hard up and down the quarter deck, hands in pockets, pausing to face each other, and occasionally withdrawing a hand to stare at the knuckles—it all seemed to me very like a Pinero play. I used to be fond of Pinero. I'm afraid I'm fond of him still. A Pinero silent cinema!

"Yes, steam was up in several senses. The pressure on board became intense. And then, do you know what they ordered?

Copelin gone excavating Agamemnon's house, expecting to find something applicable to his own case; the dark girl, who had captured my fancy for an hour, leaving for a walking tour in the Austrian Tyrol. One by one and two by two the guests sensed the situation and departed. The yacht didn't seem worth the money she had cost after all. She had steam up, and we had the stupefaction of seeing the entire family, with their personal servants, go off in the launch to the Messageries Maritime steamer sailing for Alexandria."

"Why did they leave the yacht?" demanded Mrs. Kavanagh, turning at the door of the solarium.

"For no reason so far as I could ascertain," said Mr. Spenlove calmly, "except that they could afford to. You and I couldn't. We don't understand the psychology of those who have their Elysium on earth."

"The girl—she went too?"

Mr. Spenlove nodded. "Of course," he said, "and her personal attendants. She went to Shepheard's Hotel, with her parents."

"And you were left there, with steam up?"

"And orders to go home and lay the yacht up in Cowes. Which we did, and went home to our families, if we had families, on half pay. That's what happens when you work for plutocrats."

"And the young Captain Nevile, what became of him?"

"I'll tell you after dinner," said Mr. Spenlove, and he opened the door leading downstairs. "He was in great danger for a while."

V

THERE WAS A DANCE after dinner, and Mr. Spenlove, watching from his usual vantage point aft, saw young Nevile with a girl at the forward end. They were dancing and talking. He also saw Mrs. Kavanagh, in green, looking for someone,

and he divined that Mr. O'Relly was A.W.O.L. Mr. Spenlove was not entirely clear in his mind about that young man.
The lure of the bar was plain enough; but Mr. Spenlove, by
reason of his long contemplation of the floating fauna of the
United States, suspected Mr. O'Relly of other leanings which
would unfold themselves as he became more accustomed to
the life of the ship.

Mr. Spenlove watched young Nevile dancing. He did it
very well. He was wearing tails, and he kept to the fore part
of the deck. All Mr. Spenlove could see of the girl was a baby
blue frock, an orange shawl, and gold slippers. There were
twenty other couples gyrating in and out, obscuring his
vision.

Down in the bar there was no Mr. O'Relly. Mr. Spenlove
smiled as he glanced through a window and saw Mrs. Kavanagh sweep in and out in her search. To him, aware of her
instinctive tribal passion for her own kin, her progress among
the oblivious groups of drinkers, her flight along empty cor-
ridors in search of her brother, and her tireless return to the
deck of the dancers, were all part of a rhythmic biological
process. All other instincts were temporarily in abeyance, he
reflected, as he noted her abstracted glance and shake of the
head when young Nevile asked her for a dance.

Mr. Spenlove found himself glancing here and there in
search of the girl in baby blue, and he could see her nowhere.
It occurred to him idly that the girl who was still missing
from his table must be up and about on a fine night of smooth
warm sea. Unless she was an invalid. Or a tactician. Some
women shammed illness for several days and then came in
to dinner very late in a dress that vanquished every other
woman in the ship.

He wandered forward on the windward side, where only
a few in sheltered corners claimed privacy and silence, under
rugs and behind canvas windbreaks. In the social hall he
found Mrs. Kavanagh smiling, watching a bridge game beginning.

"You found him," he said and pulled his beard. She walked into the foyer with him.

"He's lying down, quite worn out, poor kid," she said. "I was so worried. I couldn't find him anywhere."

"You'll have no vacation if you worry," Mr. Spenlove suggested. "Let him enjoy himself."

"You don't understand!" she returned fiercely. "He's the baby! I have to look after him. And we're alone, exiles. . . . We have to hang together. Ah, you laugh!" She flung away from him.

"You ought to meet a few exiles," he said, and his eyes were as near twinkling as he considered safe. "What's the matter with him?"

"He has fits of depression," she said, and suddenly she uttered an exclamation. Mr. Spenlove looked around.

"He was with a girl," she explained. "Young Captain Nevile, I mean. He's awfully handsome in evening dress!"

"What causes your brother's fits of depression?" Mr. Spenlove continued. He could see no profit in discussing young Nevile's good looks. He resented Mrs. Kavanagh's exclamation. He had a curious reluctance to have her interested in young Nevile as he was. He wanted her to know the young Nevile of the old days as he himself remembered him.

"Oh, poor kid, he's had such a hard life. He's never had anyone to understand him except me. His brothers are all jealous of his ability. He's been very pathetic and unfortunate. People always misunderstand his motives."

"Except you. What are his motives now? I saw him following a girl."

"Where? When? What girl?"

"I couldn't identify her, Mrs. Kavanagh."

"I'll shoot her!"

"Well, that's out of my department. The master-at-arms has the armament of this ship. Perhaps your brother is in love with her."

"I'll shoot her!"

They walked away into the shadows on the windward deck. Mr. Spenlove tried to adjust his mind to the mood of his companion, but it was not easy. He could only imagine vaguely why she should feel this animosity towards an unknown woman. Probably the illusion of exile (with four million nationals and twenty million co-religionists around her at home) was a screen for passions she had never completely comprehended. Mr. Spenlove half wished he believed in some religion that would account for Mrs. Kavanagh's ferocious guardianship of a slightly alcoholic newspaperman. He heard her say that Terry would never finish his book if he began fooling around with the girls on the boat. Mr. Spenlove suggested the reins can be drawn too tight for safety.

"I don't care what you say!" she declared tensely. "He's not to run after them! I wish I'd seen him! He'd have heard from me. However, he's lying down now. I'm not sure this sort of thing is any good for people like us. We're better at home."

She sighed and gazed down into the dark water rushing past the ship. Mr. Spenlove was beginning to think she had quite forgotten her own affairs, when she said suddenly:

"I'm having an awful time with that yacht. I can't see how I'm going to make a real puzzle of the cruise. I mean, I can't connect the pirate crew who come on board and commit the crime with the theft of the diamonds in London."

"Why, I thought that was the elementary part of your profession!" Mr. Spenlove scoffed gently. They took a couple of vacant deck chairs. "I remember seeing William Gillette in *Sherlock Holmes*. When the gang of criminals have him in the gas chamber down in East London, they taunt him. How is he going to get out now? He says there are so many ways he doesn't know which one to choose. I've never forgotten it. I thought you detective people always had a dozen tricks up your sleeves."

"It's little you know about it," she sighed. "It's blood

and sweat, sometimes, to make it work out. Let me think now."

Mr. Spenlove lit a fresh cigar and allowed her to think. He saw couples, dim in the darkness, pass along and ascend to the boat deck. He saw one couple he thought he recognized. Young Nevile and the girl with the orange shawl. There was something distinctive about her figure and the shape of her head that was recognizable in the dark. Mr. Spenlove bit hard on his cigar. Then he shrugged the whole problem away. He thought of the changelessness of the leopard's spots and the trouble Ethiopians are supposed to have with their skins. Something distinctive and disturbing in her walk too, Mr. Spenlove reflected after they had gone up. The impression remained with him of a personality that might become a problem among the young men. A girl could walk in such a way that men would run, he announced to himself, and recalled some of them to memory. But this girl, who was only a sky-blue frock in the distance, an orange shawl and golden pumps clip-clopping up a winding stair in the semi darkness, was not quite the same as any of those. Later, when he became acquainted with her, he called this impression a premonition.

"I could change the Sultan to a pasha," said Mrs. Kavanagh suddenly, "and have him seized with a guilty desire for one of the white women of the yacht party. But where would that land me?"

Mr. Spenlove laughed silently. Mrs. Kavanagh was aware of him shaking in his chair beside her.

"Are you sure that doesn't constitute a red herring across the trail?" he inquired. "I have read somewhere that you mustn't do it in a detective yarn. The fans don't like it. The more bloody-minded they are, the more pure their ideals and home life. And besides, a pasha doesn't have guilty desires. He has concubines. Why don't you let him have a white concubine?"

"It's all very well to laugh," said Mrs. Kavanagh gloomily, "but you haven't told me enough to make it easy for me. What happened when you got back to England? It's all so inconclusive."

"You mean I'm a poor collaborator? I'll tell you what happened when we got back to England. We were put on board wages, like the rest of the staff belonging to the Sternborough ménage. We on the yacht were paid by the yacht brokers who handled the Moira. We were instructed to go home, but we had a month's notice given us, to take effect when we heard what decision would be received from Lord Sternborough as to his future cruises. So we went home. I went to London and saw young Nevile go off to Ipswich to see his people. Then I went down to Threxford and joined my own family circle for a week. They are all gone now except my sister, who tells me nothing can save England except a Mussolini. But there was a family circle then, and I had calculated from experience that we could endure each other for a week. They were rather impressed because I had been on a yacht.

"But I wasn't going on a yacht any more. I had decided that on the way home. It didn't suit my temperament after all. The captain made no comment when I confided to him my resolution. He is still captain of a yacht. I get a card from him at Christmas. It has a picture of the yacht on it, and a group photograph of the personnel inside, all wishing me the compliments of the season. It suits him. He has never had to go ashore in a Greek island again, to rescue a sailor from a Circean female.

"Well, I had written to several likely offices, and with the money I had in the bank I was going to wait and get me a job in a merchant steamer again. I kept such intentions to myself, of course. The yacht was so popular at home that I pretended I was going to be one of Lord Sternborough's life-long retainers. To the folks down in Hampshire, which is where Threxford lies, it was almost as good as my being in the navy. And then, as I was preparing to move up to London for a while, where I could see some shipping people and loaf

around a bit, I had a letter from young Nevile down at Ufford. He asked me to go down and visit his people.

"It simply put new life into me, to have this suggestion.
I had been unable to get anything out of him on the way
home. He kept his mouth resolutely shut even when we went
up to London together. He wasn't sulky, you know. What I
mean is, he simply evaded any allusion to what took place
on Eupopyle. In one way I had been glad, for it showed he
was aware of the importance of human dignity. There is
something almost shocking in the way the sea loosens men's
tongues so that they brag of their successes with women.
Aye, and even develop an astonishing gift for mendacity,
inventing triumphs for appropriating adventures they have
heard about. Young Nevile never did that. I have never
known him to do anything cheap or common in his life!"

"That's a most unusual thing for you to say, I suppose,"
said Mrs. Kavanagh sarcastically.

"It is! But that is the truth, paradoxical as it seems even
to me, for I have been so mad with him, sometimes, in the
course of my life, I could have thrown up my hands. Yet it
was never due to any cheapness or commonness on his part.
And he was young then. It must have been some instinct that
told him to keep quiet. You see, *he* had not been told to wait
for orders as we had. He was definitely out. They had 'accepted his resignation.' I mean the brokers who managed the
yacht. Orders, the captain told me, while we waited in a
Southampton hotel. He was gloomy because the episode
cast a shadow on his professional reputation. Young Nevile
never said a word. He went home. And now he wrote, en-
closing his mother's compliments and so forth, and would I
come down to Ufford for a few days? Take pot luck, he called
it. I wrote and said I would. I took leave of my family in
Threxford and went up to London. It was time I took a look
around for employment. For I was serious about not returning to yacht work. I wasn't cut out for the old retainer rôle.

"That was the year 1912, I fancy. My objective was to

get back into an employ I had years before, Gannet, Prawle
& Company. I had worked up with them, and only left with
their cordial good wishes and a promise of a billet if I applied again. I joined the Naval Reserve at that time. Gannet,
Prawle's offices were in Leadenhall Street, where the Baltic
Exchange stands now. It was up three flights of dark stone
stairs and through a heavy door whose ground-glass panel
was yellow with age. Half of the lettering was gone from the
glass, and you had to peer at a brass plate on the wall to find
out whose office it was. Inside you were in a long corridor with
a ground-glass partition and a mahogany peephole at the far
end. A boy of seventeen, in a very high collar, sat at a ledger
just inside the peephole and gazed at you with contempt if
you had the nerve to knock. It was an experience, to gaze
suddenly, as if you were in a dime show, at that pimple-faced
minion who had the power to keep you out of a job.

"The extraordinary thing about my visit was that it was
still Gannet, Prawle & Company. This company we are in
now is an accretion of many enterprises. I was in one of the
original lines—the Maracaibo Line. That was absorbed by
the Yucatan Steamship Company, and that again got swallowed by the Afro-Iberian interests. The same thing was
going on in England—consolidation; only over there they
let the lines run under their old house flags. Wilson, Furness,
Ellerman, and Runciman, smart business men, merged and
merged until mighty fleets were directed by men who might
never see the sea. But Gannet, Prawle were still hiding away
behind their ground-glass screens in Leadenhall Street.
More than that, they were building two new ships on the
Tyne. When I had persuaded the youth to take my name in
and had waited in a small anteroom in the company of two
half-models of steamers and a bookcase filled entirely with
nautical almanacs, I was admitted into a mahogany office
with a fireplace, where a coal fire was burning, and a Turkey
rug in front of it, on which my old boss was standing.

"I had arrived at an unusual moment. The chief engineer

of the ship already launched, which was having her engines installed, had committed the incredible folly of buying a steam laundry and had resigned to look after it. Anybody else's engaging in business, to the average shipowner, is incredible folly. My boss said this lunatic would lose his money and come back, hat in hand, for a job, by and by. He didn't. He retired years later with a comfortable fortune after turning his laundry into a limited liability corporation. I was asked if I knew about it. I did not. Then how did I happen to come in? I had come in, I said, because I didn't want any more yachts. Well, he said, when he had heard my story, he hadn't any yachts. Whatever Gannet, Prawle's ships might be, they were not yachts. The ship then fitting out was eight thousand tons and she was Gannet, Prawle's last word in reckless expenditure. They had never had a ship before with electric light, and they were frightened to death at the cost of it. But they were going into the long-run business, and their hands were being forced. Did I understand electric light? And mechanical draft? My good old boss was as innocent of the inside of warships as a baby in a perambulator. He had never been on board anything but tramps, and had forgotten what had happened to me. I reassured him about all these things, and he said he wanted a chief engineer to take the place of the lunatic who had bought a laundry. I told him I was on my way to spend a few days in the country and would accept the billet.

"He was rather struck by the insolence of an employee spending a few days in the country. You have no idea, now, of the delicate social mechanism of those days. If I had suddenly produced a checkbook and offered to write a check for a guinea for a charity, instead of offering a gold sovereign and a shilling, that boss of mine would have either fainted or sent for the police. If he had caught sight of me in the West End hailing a hansom, it would have constituted a grave defection from the behavior proper to my position in life. And a few days in the country, at that time, were the prerogative of the smart rich or the old aristocracy. I wasn't supposed to know there was a country to go to!"

"I should think it would have made you a socialist," said Mrs. Kavanagh.

"It might have if I hadn't been so interested in humanity as it is. I never want it changed!" Mr. Spenlove almost exclaimed. "Do you ever read Dostoieffsky? Well, do you remember the efficient engineer in one of his novels who had a passion for making people sensible? He proposed to cut off a hundred million heads in Europe in the cause of common sense. He was no confederate of mine. I wouldn't have one head removed in that cause. I want to see the show! I want a ringside seat at the battle of the century, the fight between Time and Man!"

"You win!" said Mrs. Kavanagh slyly.

"Well, I won that round, anyway. I explained I had a very frail invalid aunt in the country, and as her favorite nephew it was fitting that I go and see her. This struck a chord. I belonged to a social level in which a sick aunt was an acceptable feature and family solidarity approved. Away I went, with the understanding that the following week would find me on the Tyne watching the engines of the new ship. I put the letter to the captain, who was watching the hull, in my pocket.

"I had been lucky, remember. We don't always tumble over jobs like that. It improved my appreciation of the countryside. I took the old Great Eastern Railway to Ipswich, through East Anglia. I was looking about among the people on the platform, expecting young Nevile, as I had sent a telegram, when a girl who had exactly the same features, the same eyes, nose, mouth, and chin, came swinging through the crowd looking from side to side. When she saw me she smiled exactly as he did; as he does now in fact; only there was a subtle infusion of virginity as well.

"She held out her hand with the same gallant frankness I knew so well. You see, my beard—I suppose she had had me described to her, and there was nobody else filling the specifications. We shook hands, and the introduction was over. Where was my luggage? Only a week-end bag? There was a local to Ufford, but it didn't go for hours, so she'd driven in in the trap. It was at the Great White Horse. The family were down at Ufford.

"She meant a hotel in the town. Nobody dreamed then of taking a horse and trap into the excitement of a railway station unless one had a coachman, and a tiger to jump down and hold the animal's head. Miss Nevile had left her rig at the stable. We walked into the town and as it was about tea-time we had some in the commercial room of the Great White Horse.

"She explained why she had come instead of her brother. He was away on a visit. It had happened suddenly, she said. He was—and she hesitated a moment, gazing at me—he was at Boule Court.

"'You mean Lord Sternborough's place?' I said, and she nodded. I said, 'Good God!' and she colored deeply. You must remember this was twenty years ago, nearly. She would light another cigarette, nod and smile somewhat drearily now, I suppose. But at the time, which was 1912, she blushed. Yes, she said, he had been invited to go there for a short visit.

"I said I thought he had been dismissed in disgrace. I was aware of my clumsiness even when I said the words. I added, of course, I knew what she meant. But did they really intend to sacrifice . . .? She said, looking up at me again from her teacup, 'It isn't a sacrifice on her part. But they think she is going to have a child.'

"The blush hadn't prepared me for such a bald statement from Ursula Nevile. But then she was a lady. Down there they had preserved a straightforward acceptance of basic phenomena. No other explanation was possible when the Honorable Maeve Sternborough was involved with a boy like her brother.

"I asked Miss Nevile what she thought would come of it. She shook her head, to indicate that she thought nothing good would come of it. She said 'the family,' meaning her own family, did not believe her brother had been anything but unwise. He hadn't been despicable, she said. I agreed. I said I held the same view, and she looked at me gratefully. I asked her when she thought he would be back home.

"She said, 'It's only twelve miles from Ufford. But we hope he'll be back on Saturday.' That was two days away. She said, 'It would be madness to marry her, though the mater believes it might work. The mater has such faith in all of us!'

"I said I wasn't surprised at that, for she probably knew her own children. Miss Nevile gave me a strange look. She said, 'The mater doesn't know Sidney. I'm the only one of the family who knows Sidney, and I wish he had never gone on the yacht.' I said that was my fault. I had had the idea that it was just his style. 'Yes,' she said, 'it *is* his style; and I wish he had never gone, just the same. I know him,' she said. 'He is so susceptible.'

"'To what?' I said. 'To love?' She shook her head and touched her chin with her finger. 'To feminine influences,' she explained, and I said I wasn't sure I understood her. Well, I did understand her. I only wanted to make her go on talking. It was a queer sensation to have a sort of feminine double of the young fellow uttering magic phrases.

"She was wiser than I, though. She left me to puzzle out how she, a delicate young English virgin, buried deep in that ancient land, could know, or divine, so much about the character of her sailor brother. I had no doubt she knew what she was talking about, yet without yielding up any of her own sweet innocence, as it were.

"Soon we left. After walking down the great yard of the White Horse, we climbed into the dogcart and set out for Ufford, through Woodbridge and Melton. My bag and coat were in the back. Miss Nevile drove. She sat very erect, yet without haughtiness, the dogskin gloves with gauntlets and the brown felt hat with its pheasant feather giving her the appearance of a rather attractive young knight. The horse clip-clopped briskly and threw up his head occasionally as cyclists flew past with shrill bells. There was a crisis when we met a motorcar. It was standing still, but the engine was roaring under the sloping hood, and the driver was trying to make the driving belts catch. It was one of the early French cars. The horse put back his ears in an alarming way, but Miss Nevile was equal to the occasion. I heard her say something about 'those beastly things' after we were safely past. Her face was stern and beautiful, like the face of a classical statue in a museum, and for the same reason—she was oblivious of what was going on in the world. She was pre-occupied with principles—of honesty and truth and loving-kindness to the weak; and that other people were absorbed in pulling down the world in which she existed never occurred to her. This came out in her comments to me upon the recent upset in the family. Even the Sternboroughs, she thought, had been 'rather decent about it.' That was her ideal—to be rather decent about things. If you could, it was advisable to be jolly decent.

"No, she wasn't at all silly. It was her code. She was like a lot of English people of her class, she didn't believe in the existence of really evil people. It was all a mistake. She was more than half skeptical of those who are enslaved by their temporary passion, as the Honorable Maeve was. I am sure she wouldn't have let her brother go and stay at Boule Court if she had had any means of comprehending Maeve. That was a very curious thing about her virginal intuition. She was aware of her brother's susceptibility to feminine influences without having any clear notion of how different those influences were from her own! She said to me, as we drove down a deep lane into the very heart of rural Suffolk, as it were, 'I wish Sidney could get a situation in London. I'd go to London too, and keep house for him. It would be the best thing. I'm really keen on going to London. Nothing much doing in Ipswich.'

"'Don't you keep house here?' I said. 'Oh, Mother and the maids do all that!' she said. 'I'm nobody here, except that I'm rather useful with animals. But it's London I'd like to take up. I want to be a secretary, and if Sidney would give up the sea, it would just fit in.'

"'Won't he do that—now?' I said. She shook her head. 'He won't. I believe I know why too. He's restless. He wants to wander, you know.'

"'You mean you think men shouldn't be sailors?' I suggested. She gave me a quick grave look and then returned to the horse. 'He shouldn't,' she said. 'He needs someone to look after him.'

"I sat silent until we got past the squat church, with the old stocks just outside the wall. We were down in a secluded valley with cottages behind immemorial trees and box hedges. I began to wonder how this family I was visiting fitted in with such a scene. Suddenly Miss Nevile nodded toward a bright villa with a red-tiled roof and varnished gate opening upon a gravel drive. 'That's our place,' she said, and smiled with affection upon it. On the gate was the name of the house—Omdurman. I found out later that Mr. Nevile had just completed the place when Lord Kitchener destroyed the Mahdi's army in the Sudan. So he named the house after the battlefield. The children had all grown up in a house that commemorated a scene of horrible carnage, with machine guns and infantry volleys mowing down fanatical tribesmen. Those who stood steadfast received cavalry charges and were cut to pieces with swords."

"How could he do a thing like that?" said Mrs. Kavanagh, shuddering.

"Why, everybody did it. My sister's house is named Ladysmith, and it is close to the Pretoria Arms, a village pub. The Neviles were imperialists, I suppose. They believed in the Empire. Every good-sized town had a vaudeville hall

called the Empire. Imperialism corresponded to Americanism. When we called a fellow a Little Englander we burned
with the same fire that consumes you when you call somebody
un-American."

"What were you in those days?" inquired Mrs. Kavanagh.
"You seem very superior to all those human emotions."

"I was a Little Englander with a faith in the Empire,"
said Mr. Spenlove dryly. "I thought imperialism suffered
somewhat from the sort of people it attracted. But that's an
endless argument. I know better than to discuss my religion."

"You call it a religion?"

"One side of it. Mr. Nevile, Senior, wouldn't have hurt a
fly, yet he named his house after a bloody battle. And Ursula
Nevile thought it a perfectly decent sentiment. There isn't
any puzzle about it, really. I'm only telling you how things
were in those days. I admired Mr. Nevile. His house stood
where there had been a stockade east of the ford of the river.
It had been an outpost of another empire. Behind the stockade King Uffa had held the woad-stained savages at bay. I
dare say he named his wattle-and-daub residence after some
victory against the wild tribesmen of East Anglia."

"It's not a religion," insisted Mrs. Kavanagh. Mr. Spenlove could see only the sparkle in her eye. He missed the intense glow of blood on each cheek.

"Well, King Uffa no doubt didn't call it a religion either.
He worshiped Wodin and Thor, but he was too busy keeping
his little colony together and rescuing his men from the
human sacrifices the tribesmen were so fond of for their religion. We'll concede the phrase. Mr. Nevile was Low Church
of England. He was very much concerned, when he came
home from his Ipswich shop, about what he called 'mum-
mery.' He was a precise, quiet man of about forty-five with
an authoritative air, and he had given up going to church in
Ipswich when the parson installed a high altar and began
burning incense. We had several long talks about church

history, and I became well informed concerning some of the
heresies that were prevalent in England at the time. Well,
he called them heresies. I preserved an open, not to say vacant mind. I was more concerned with enjoying myself,
playing croquet—when the spring showers permitted—with
Ursula, and studying the parental attitude towards the young
fellow."

"Did he come home?"

"On Saturday afternoon. In a smart trap with a cockaded
coachman seated at least a foot higher than himself. As soon
as the rig stopped in front of the house he jumped down
smartly, lugged his raincoat and gladstone bag from the
back, nodded to the lackey, and came straight into the
house.

"We were having tea in the drawing room, which ran
from a bow window in front to French windows giving onto
the croquet lawn at the back. He came straight into the
drawing room, dropping his things in the hall. He kissed his
mother and said, 'Hullo, Mater.' He gave Ursula a hug, but
he was careful to avoid trouble with the silver teapot she
was carrying. He said something about 'old girl.' Then he
shook hands with me.

"He had a new air. Didn't I tell you, when we were on
the Manola together, there was a bloom? It isn't a perfect
description of what I mean, but it is as near as I can get.
Well, it was gone now. The new air seemed to signify that he
knew what it was all about. There was confidence in his
demeanor without pride. He said he was glad I could come
down, and sorry he hadn't been on hand to meet me. I said
Ursula had been a perfect substitute. He laughed, took a cup
of tea and said he supposed she was.

"As a prodigal, he didn't run true to type at all. He wasn't
even defiant, as so many young fellows are when they get
mixed up in an affair of sex. He was merely very glad to be
home after a visit. Not a word was said, in the family, about
the reasons for his visit to Boule Court. Not a word was said

to me as to the upshot of it. Only when he said I might like a walk over to Melton was there a chance to find out. I was curious."

"Oh!" said Mrs. Kavanagh. "Were you though?"

"I know it sounds perfectly imbecile to you," continued Mr. Spenlove, "but over there things aren't discussed. I gave you a sample of my conversation with his sister, and I give you my word, we were almost indecently loquacious. She was a very advanced young woman, and she was devoted to her brother, or she wouldn't have confided in anybody. I was his friend, she knew, and I was sufficiently reliable-looking as well."

"You! I wouldn't call you that. I don't believe you were —then."

"No? Well, Ursula trusted me, and I like to think the intuitions of British virgins are infallible! But when we set out for a brisk walk to Melton, he and I might be fairly compared with Damon and Pythias. I soon realized he had asked me down because he wanted someone to talk to. So I wasn't astonished when we sat in the bar parlor of a deserted pub and he told me about his recent experiences.

"'I was in a devil of a hole at first,' he said, 'because I felt as if I was being sold into slavery. You see,' he said' 'I'd be a sort of pensioner, a poor relation and so on, all my life, because Maeve couldn't live on anything I could make. It wouldn't buy her clothes. And with her money it would be impossible for me to feel independent.'

"I said lots of chaps married money and didn't go into a decline over it.

"'I know,' he said, 'but this is different. I feel trapped. I'm not in love with Maeve at all. I never was in love with her. I never wanted to see her again after that night on the island. But they appealed to me as a gentleman, and so . . .'

"'I see,' I said, 'and you find your instinct for self-preservation is stronger than your feelings as a gentleman. So are mine.'

"I told him he didn't know it but he had the beginnings, the embryo, of class consciousness in him. At that time it was a phrase creeping into circulation. We were beginning to use phrases like social solidarity and dictatorship of the proletariat. Young Nevile didn't understand me. He said he regarded it as a purely personal matter, but he wanted my advice what to do. He had left Boule Court after a brief farewell, and while they might think he was going back, he didn't want to.

"'Come with me,' I said. 'I've got a new ship. I'll get you a billet. Anyhow, even if the old man won't take you, you'll be on the spot for a job on the Tyne!'

"'Yes, I'd like to do that,' he said. 'I'm fed up with the country, to tell you the truth. And with this business.'

"I said nobody would ever believe him. Nobody we knew in our walk of life would credit that he wouldn't marry that girl.

"'I can't help that,' he said. 'I am in love with Elli Phalère. I thought of Elli, you know, on the island.'

"I protested when he told me that. We were sitting in a quiet bar parlor, the flies buzzing on the leaded panes, and a caster talking broad Suffolk out in the taproom. I protested!

"'Yes I did,' he said, 'and I thought, over at Boule Court, how, if only Elli had all that money, I'd stay. Yes, like a shot I would.'"

"Oh!" said Mrs. Kavanagh, in the darkness, apropos of nothing. Mr. Spenlove folded his arms and nodded to himself.

"I rather liked that frank confession. And when he went on to give me some idea of how he felt—on the island, you know—I was amused. No, not at his situation, but at his naïve notion he had discovered something unknown to the rest of mankind. He had never read Goethe, or he would have known it was all written down a hundred years before he was born. Elective affinities! It made me realize, too, how strongly he was held by that Greek girl's personality, when it overpowered the natural complacency a young man would feel over a love affair with a girl like the Honorable Maeve. It was so strong a personality it thrust Maeve out of her own body, out of her parents' house, almost. It banished her from the island of Eupopyle just when she seemed most in possession of it! A woman can do that, you know!"

Mrs. Kavanagh smoked fast, so that her cigarette glowed like fire in the shadow.

"Look," she said, and nudged Mr. Spenlove with her elbow. "Now they're coming this way after all. Who's that he's got?"

Mr. Spenlove, who had been absorbed in the contemplation of the sea by night as he explored his memory, came back to reality and gazed about him. He heard the steady thrill of the hull as her propellers thrust her through the Gulf Stream. The slow rise and fall of the deck in the swell, the medley of faint echoes that rose from the ship's interior, told him that everything was going well. And it pleased him, at such times, to explore with the flashlight of his intelligence the darkness of human destiny, to pass an appraising hand over the bright tinsel of human folly.

He saw young Captain Nevile with that girl again. They passed, he with his hand holding her arm, his head bent to hers. She, with her face raised in rapt pleasure, took one or two quick steps on tiny feet to reach the after rail, and there they were silhouetted, for the people in the two chairs, faintly against sea and sky. As they stood the girl raised her arms in a high wide embrace of something invisible, a gesture Mr. Spenlove learned to know very well in the future. There was something of ecstasy in it, even in the luminous darkness of the deck and the darkness, also luminous, of his mind concerning her.

To Mrs. Kavanagh the spectacle was sinister. The quick perception of the extreme smallness of those feet, the utter obliviousness of the girl to any passing woman's criticism (for she knew the girl had been aware of her) roused that antagonism which, for many women, is a substitute for moral courage. It struck her to silence, for she felt instinctively the immediate masculine interest the girl had inspired in Mr. Spenlove. Mrs. Kavanagh knew from experience the kind of women who inspire interest in philosophers and fools alike. She almost forgot to be glad that the creature hadn't got hold of her brother Terry, that it was that nice young Captain Nevile, in whom she had only a professional writer's interest, who was being caught in the toils.

A moment later the two figures at the rail had moved, had dissolved into the shadows, and other couples were moving past the rail to ascend the stairs behind the bulkhead.

"Now what?" said Mrs. Kavanagh, smiling. "He seems as susceptible as ever. Not immunized at all. I must say I thought he had more sense."

"You thought? No woman thinks at a time like this," Mr. Spenlove pointed out. "You only feel strongly, one way or the other."

"Well, you said he was through, didn't you? And now you see for yourself."

"I didn't mean it that way," said Mr. Spenlove. "In fact, I've no concern with what happens now. I fancy he's able to look after himself now. Wait till I tell you how he got on after that Boule Court business.

"He was lucky, you know, to be able to get away at the right moment. He was saved for even greater disasters! Yes, I am sure that it wouldn't have been any worse to marry a bitch like that Maeve than the woman he did marry."

"Who was it he married? You said she called herself Aïda."

"I will come to that. I say it would have been no worse, but on reflection it might have been better if he had lived with what are called the upper classes, because then Aïda would never have got hold of him. He would have seen through her shams."

"Did you see through them?"

"Not at first. She seemed an empty vessel to me and to give

out a hollow ring, but I didn't suspect the metal was base too. But that was long after our yacht experiences, after we came to America for good.

"He jumped at the chance to go to the Tyne with me. We traveled together on the old Doncaster express that ran through East Anglia every morning to the north of England. On the way up he gave me some more glimpses of his visit to Boule Court. I was curious to know what his relations had been with the parents. I couldn't see those two earnest converts to feudalism being very cordial to a young man who practically embodied a bend sinister on their scutcheon if they could not bring him to heel and who would be a mésalliance if they did. As a matter of fact, they didn't even try to be cordial. They remained in town, and an aunt, sister of Lady Sternborough, was duenna, if you can call a person who hardly ever left her own rooms a duenna. There were so many servants around, and workmen, who were finishing a new wing and laying out new gardens, that there seemed no more privacy than on a ship like this. He emphasized that lack of privacy because he wasn't sure whether, if he had been with Maeve in a quiet boarding house at the seaside, for instance, where they could have got to know something of each other, he might not have felt differently. But the atmosphere of the yacht Moira was even denser at Boule Court. He was a gentlemanly young fellow, and he couldn't bear it. I mean he couldn't bear feudalism. Even Maeve succumbed to it at home, and a superiority crept into her manner. Young people of her own age and tastes began to come down to Boule. They stood at the sideboard and squirted Apollinaris into brandy and drank it standing on the hearth rug. They had liaisons and talked of other liaisons. Maeve had reached a stage when she was ready for another experience, I suppose. The novelty of the good-looking sailor—I suppose you know this is a stock fantasy with English girls—was now safely preserved in her collection.

"I felt better every mile that was added to our distance

from that house. I wanted to get him to sea again, keeping a watch on a tramp steamer's bridge, eating our coarse food and forgetting all about broiled quails and vol-au-vent and so on. I wanted him, even if it meant a fresh lease of life for the Elli Phalère hallucination, to abandon the dreams that must have distracted him so long as there was any chance of Maeve making him marry her."

"Then there wasn't any child, of course?" said Mrs. Kavanagh. Mr. Spenlove laughed.

"I never heard of one. There never was any child in any of his complications. I don't think a child would make things any different for him."

"I would think it might have steadied him," said Mrs. Kavanagh uncertainly. "Taken his mind off girls."

"Does it?" inquired Mr. Spenlove with a rather obvious malice. "There was never any need to steady him, as you call it. He was and is the soul of steadiness. Do you suppose a man can command one of these ships and be an unreliable coxcomb? The point of his story is, he was always ready to leave them alone and mind his own business—if they would let him."

"As we saw just now—yes," murmured Mrs. Kavanagh, but as her antipathy to that girl made her withdraw the suggestion, she added, "I know what you mean, of course."

"Well," said Mr. Spenlove, smiling to himself, "that one is at our table, unless she is going to remain in seclusion all the way to Kingston. You can find out from her what her secret is."

"Ah!" Mrs. Kavanagh turned away and lit a fresh cigarette from her old one.

"It's plain she'll never pull the wool over your eyes," said Mr. Spenlove.

Mrs. Kavanagh said she could never understand what men saw in such creatures.

"Heaven, probably," said Mr. Spenlove calmly. "Timeless ecstasy, without responsibility or retribution! While they are together the man is dazzled and happy. It doesn't last, but while it does it's perfect. Later he finds a wife and settles down. That's my theory of the two kinds of women in our world, but like many other theories it is full of holes. How do we know what kind of girl it is he has picked up? I don't. He has picked up or been picked up by all kinds of women. I was going to tell you.

"I was not successful in getting young Nevile a job on my new ship. My captain had several friends of his own who wanted billets. But after a couple of weeks in the Newcastle boarding house where we put up, young Nevile came in and said he had shipped as second mate on a Glasgow tramp, the Cromarty Castle, they called her, which had been having a survey and her shaft lifted. It wasn't much of a job, for she was a typical short-run collier, but it was better than being a rich lady's pet dog, as we say, and I congratulated him. I didn't ask to see his new home. I could tell from his remarks he was rather ashamed of her dingy decks and not very tony quarters. I never saw that ship. She went away from there, young Nevile handling the mooring ropes aft, while we were out on our trials. It looked as if we had drifted apart again for good. I didn't even have any address to write to him. Of course, his sister Ursula would have forwarded a letter. But just then, with a new ship working herself into some sort of cohesion, I had no time for anything else. I was enjoying life enormously. We had a great deal to do on that ship. I had scores of emergency jobs in places you've never heard of, far down out of sight, behind boilers and under platforms. In those days they sent a ship out with plenty of unfinished business down below. But I had a good crowd and we worked together, knowing that the sooner she was fixed up the sooner we'd have a breather. We went to Rotterdam and took a cargo of coal to Nantes in France. Then we went up to Glasgow to get a cargo of general for the Black Sea. And we ran into the biggest coal strike in our history.

"We couldn't even get bunker coal to take us to some

other port. We couldn't have done anything there either, for
the strike spread in sympathy, and ships trekking to South
Wales or the North Sea were refused cargoes. There was
nothing to do but wait. The owners cut us down to a skeleton
crew and tied us up in the middle of the Queen's Dock.

"That was a familiar situation for us in those days. Business being good, a firm would build new ships, and business
would slump and leave the ships idle, eating their heads off
at some anchorage. Or a strike would start for higher wages
and throw us all on our beam ends. To hear the deep thinkers
nowadays you'd fancy we had no industrial maladjustments
in the world before the war. I've never had anything else in
my life. I've lived, like an active camp follower, in the rear of
industrial warfare ever since I began to serve my apprenticeship. Personally I've always enjoyed it. I remember being
laid off when freight to Genoa dropped to six shillings a ton
for Best Welsh coal, and I had a month without pay. I spent
the month reading Karl Marx in the old badly printed edition
of the 'nineties. He was nearly as bad as Kant to understand.
He evidently knew very little about work as I understood
it. He appeals irresistibly to the born clock watcher and sea
lawyer. Reading him was work, I grant you.

"So there we were in Glasgow, a brand-new ship, laid up
for lack of work. People in Italy needed coal, we needed a
cargo, but the miners wouldn't dig out the coal unless they
got more money. It was funny to see what they did with
money when the war came and brought them ten, fifteen,
eighteen pounds a week. Not that it was any of my business.
I had wasted five shillings of my own on *Das Kapital*. We
had to loaf in the Queen's Dock and hope for an end. The
Italians ordered coal from Russia, and ships passing Gibraltar
were flagged to turn around and go up the Black Sea.

"I didn't have much to do, once the hawsers were out, so
I would go ashore with my old man and sit in the Grosvenor
Bar for a while and take the air on Sauchiehall Street. We

were one of a line of idle ships, and there is nothing more subtly discouraging than an idle ship even with your pay going on. You cannot enjoy yourself in such circumstances unless you are an elderly watchman with a wooden leg and a clay pipe dozing over the galley fire. An idle ship saps one's vitality. It's like living in a corpse. I have seen fellows pretending to be glad they had a chance to read, or study Spanish, or learn to play the mandolin. Impossible! They give it up and mope. They cannot even drink—if they like drinking —with any comfort.

"So we always went ashore to get out of sight of our misery. And one day, as the strike dragged on and on, and we began to wonder whether our coal wouldn't give out altogether, I saw young Nevile coming towards me with a girl on his arm. I saw him first, and there was an expression of courteous condescension on his face as he listened to what she was saying. She was going wide open, too, telling him something intensely interesting to herself. A shop girl, I should say, from her rig and the lower middle-class cut of her jib.

"How can you say that?" demanded Mrs. Kavanagh indignantly. "Are all your aristocrats patricians?"

Mr. Spenlove laughed good-humoredly.

"I put it the wrong way. She was Fourteenth Street rather than Park Avenue.

"Anyhow, if I'd had any doubts about her, his expression when he recognized me would have told the story. From courteous, benignant patronage it changed to an almost pitiable boyish shame. He wasn't annoyed, you know. He was too glad to see me again. If only I hadn't found him at such a moment! He almost cast a look around in that crowded street as if to find some dustbin or trash basket where he could stow his companion while he reached his own social level again with me.

"This was really the beginning of what art critics would

call a period of temporary decline. He wouldn't have any interest for you in this period because, although he kept away from yachts, he developed no criminal tastes."

"Never mind me. I'm interested, just the same."

"I mean, he didn't proceed according to your rules in novels at all. He had a period of decline, as I call it. He became competent in his work, reticent about his affairs, and he developed a peculiar blindness to the nature of the women he went about with. That is why I mention this chance meeting when he had that shop girl in tow. She was short and overdressed, and she wore those loathsome lace gloves without fingers, and she disliked me at once."

"How could you blame her?" inquired Mrs. Kavanagh.

"I didn't. She was no more to be blamed than the flies on meat, or any other insect pest. It was my introduction to the first of a series of awful women young Nevile dallied with, or only associated with at odd hours, and I suppose some of my feelings showed in my face.

"He didn't introduce her. I doubt if he knew her name. Call her Miss Legion. She stood a few paces from us while we shook hands and exchanged news. He was caught too in the strike. Where were we lying? I told him. He said he'd come and see me. I watched him squirming quietly. I said, very low, 'Come now!' No, he said, he had to go with his friend. I'd have to excuse him.

"I didn't expect him to walk off and leave her. I merely wanted to see what he would do. He often did foolish things, but he couldn't do anything mean. It would have been merciful, of course, to do that, but it would have damaged him morally. So I approved."

"Didn't she count at all with you?" Mrs. Kavanagh raged without being entirely serious.

"Not an atom! She was merely a noxious organism momentarily infecting someone whom I regarded very highly. I regarded her as you would regard a diphtheria germ in your child's throat. Eliminate! If I could have lifted a sewer manhole and thrust her into it without incurring social ostracism and criminal action, I'd have done it! I felt quite strongly about it at the time, but of course later I realized I had been prejudiced against her."

"It looks that way," said Mrs. Kavanagh. "I'll have to go down and see how Terry's getting along. I want him to get a good sleep, for he's to start work on his book tomorrow."

She rose, and Mr. Spenlove helped her to her feet.

"That ought not to take long," he suggested. "I'm going down to my cabin now. You can bring him with you for a visit before you pack him off to bed. You know the way now."

"You come down and wait while I see if he's asleep," she said.

In the forward entrance hall Mrs. Kavanagh stepped through a doorway to glance into the library. She was about to explain that Terry might be there when she turned abruptly and walked out again, a grim smile on her sharp intelligent features.

She said nothing until they had descended the curved stairway to her deck, when she turned to Mr. Spenlove.

"Well, I've seen her," she said. "I mean that creature! I see he hasn't lost his taste for inferior women! They were in there!"

"Oh, come!" said Mr. Spenlove, smiling. "I haven't seen her so far, but that girl he was with upstairs tonight wasn't common."

Mrs. Kavanagh waved her hand at him.

"You men are all alike," she said. "You are taken in by a baby face and a silly simper."

She knocked at her brother's door and pushed it open a crack. He was not there.

"Some fool has given him drink," she said with a shrug.

"Let him enjoy himself," suggested Mr. Spenlove. Mrs. Kavanagh made a gesture of impatience.

"You've never seen him next morning," she said. "No, I'll

have to go and find him. He's the baby. I have to look after him."

Mr. Spenlove watched her trudge doggedly along on her extremely high heels towards the after stairway. He made no pretense of accompanying her or even of bidding her good-night. He watched her, entranced by the contemplation of her tribal instincts. If necessary, he reflected, she was prepared to drag her brother away single-handed, bearing him off on her back, out of danger, and mounting guard over him until he was safe in his own bed. In the morning she would make him start on his book. She would defend him with ferocity against the outside world, the barbarians who belonged to other tribes and who worshiped stranger gods than her own. They were marvelous, he thought, those women who shredded maternity down to a scarcely intelligent animal instinct.

He went downstairs and passed through the kitchens, which were silent and deserted now, the great electric ranges and receptacles shining in porcelain and nickel, the tables scrubbed and the tiled floors immaculate. He passed through a steel door and stood on gratings, through which came a resonant murmur and a hot acrid odor of burning petroleum. Far down below the tiers of gratings and staircases he saw the boilers fronting the white fireroom. The man on watch stood by a shining steel shelf reading an adventure magazine. Only the resonance, a sound, yet not a sound, indicated the pres-ence of enormous imprisoned energy. Mr. Spenlove enjoyed this spectacle almost as much as he enjoyed the sight of Mrs. Kavanagh revealing primitive instincts in protecting her brother from the onslaughts of alien influences. It was his philosophy to give each of these tremendous forces his rapt attention. They were, in his view, complementary, and afforded civilized man an adequate explanation of a confusing modern world.

Down in the engine room, between the quadruple-expansion, exquisitely balanced engines, he became even more convinced of the superiority of machines over men. For nearly a quarter of a century, he told himself, these same engines had revolved a hundred times a minute, which was nearly a million and a half times a day, for many days on end, performing their duty with a precision and fidelity that was a perfect reflection of the intelligence of their designers and of the long line of antecedent artificers whose toil had evolved them. Hence, he argued, they were superior to the common run of mankind as objects of devotion and sacrifice. They proved their quality, he believed, when they inspired the rabble with hatred and fear. By rabble, in addition to the proletariat, he meant also those who imagined that a world of sailing vessels was somehow more beautiful and humane than his own. He perceived a flaw in the logic of those whose humanitarian zeal concentrated upon the derelicts of humanity rather than upon the endowment of deserving machinery.

He did not reveal these sentiments to the readers of adventure stories, who he knew could be depended on in their minor rôles of junior priests in his temple. He saw that everything was running sweetly and climbed to his own cabin. He anticipated with pleasure the last rites of the day. He would get into his pajamas, switch on the green-shaded lamp over his bed-place, and he would open Mrs. Kavanagh's magnum opus *The Gilded Skull*. He still regarded this production as something miraculous when he thought of its author. Was it possible that an elemental tribeswoman could write a book? Mr. Spenlove was rather naïve about books. He liked to imagine that their inception implied gigantic intellectual labor. He found it impossible to throw off a solemn respect for the successors of Shakespeare and Milton, Whitman and Rabelais. But he had been talking to Mrs. Kavanagh, and he found it increasingly difficult to identify her with the sort of mind he imagined an author should possess.

He opened his door, full of anticipatory pleasure, and saw

young Captain Nevile on his settee, reading a magazine and smoking a pipe.

"Ha! The man of mystery!" he said lightly, but he was very pleased, nevertheless, that young Nevile had come to see him. "Mrs. Kavanagh thinks you have become entangled in the toils of an adventuress. She saw you in the library just now, and from the expression as she said it, you weren't reading."

Captain Nevile laid the magazine aside. He was smiling so that his face seemed to glow from within. The words came from his lips in a quick torrent.

"Fred, it's been marvelous to meet a girl like that on the way down! She's going to visit her father. He has a large estate in Jamaica. A planter. He's English too. So is she. And there never was anything less like an adventuress than Athalie."

"Athalie? You know her well enough to call her that already? I thought you were through, Sidney. I thought you were through. Forty-eight hours since that girl in New York was searching all over the ship for you, and you were taking vows of celibacy. And now—Athalie!"

"I know, but this is different. I think, Fred, I've met my destiny at last. She's wonderful!"

"And I am wonderfully pessimistic about it. Why doesn't she come to the meal table if she's so wonderful?"

"Well, the fact is, Fred, she's not like other girls at all. She's English, and terribly shy too. She'll come down soon. She hasn't been so very well, either."

"She's able to dance."

"She can dance, Fred, like a creature without any weight at all. She's a lovely dancer."

"Mrs. Kavanagh sized her up as a thoroughly disreputable vampire."

"She's nothing of the sort. She's virtuous and terribly particular about whom she associates with. She knows a lot of good people in New York. Plenty of men on the ship have tried to be fresh already. She's attractive. Men come around. That chap who's at our table, he wanted to get into her cabin."

"Is that so? Mrs. Kavanagh will tear her limb from limb if her brother is harmed."

"Let him keep away, then. Athalie Rhys doesn't want any of them."

"You mean Mr. O'Relly tried to get into her cabin without any provocation on her part?"

"Absolutely. She's not that sort of girl. She's very religious."

Mr. Spenlove heard eight bells, midnight, sound on the engine-room bar. He began to undress. He had no comment to make upon such a statement as that. Religious women he classified as incalculable, and no conclusion could be reached by discussion. He had been paying strict attention to the life of the Camotan since six o'clock in the morning, and he was tired. He was willing to believe Mrs. Kavanagh was prejudiced against that girl, but the case called for extreme caution. He said so at length as he stepped into his pajamas.

"Well, Fred, you have always been cynical. Athalie will change even you. Mrs. Kavanagh couldn't possibly understand an English girl of her type. I'll go and turn in. But I wanted to tell you. I believe I've met the real thing at last."

Mr. Spenlove did not answer. He climbed into his bed-place, and as the door closed behind young Nevile, he laid *The Gilded Skull* aside after all, and drew out from the book-shelf at the foot of his bunk a volume that had seen much wear. It was, he had sometimes remarked to smiling critics, a good book to fall asleep over, knowing they would never penetrate the true secret of his feeling for such a work. He opened it now.

". . . Philosophy portrays ideas, not realities: so is it with art: . . . art is a perpetual parody of itself. . . ." He read on, drowsing and hearkening always in the back of his brains to the rhythm of his ship. It was an excellent thing to have some lofty abstraction hovering above the earth and sea of his business as they faded into unconsciousness. Young Nevile, now, was disappointing him again. Mr. Spenlove felt as he did that day in Glasgow when he saw the young fellow with his shop girl in tow. He said he had met his destiny at last— that girl, who had raised her arms so theatrically to the luminous night, was destiny, of course. Any woman who appeared at such a moment would get the position of destiny to Sidney Nevile. So much for all the fine resolutions for the future. Men are perfect parodies of themselves! They see themselves as knights, hermits, warriors, and saints. They draw for us superb portraits of such characters, and then, in a flash you see the shabby real man behind the easel.

But Mr. Spenlove, as he lost hold of the book and dropped asleep, did have a faint doubt about that girl. She might be after all an exception. But what, he thought, will Mrs. Rossiter say?

VI

MRS. KAVANAGH, who had only been on a ship when she went to Europe by the northern route, was impressed by the sudden change of the ship's officers into white drill. It struck her as delightfully droll that men should have such an impulse, to bedeck themselves in white and gold against a background of blue sea. It struck her as an impulse because it never occurred to her that this apparently spontaneous change of fashion might be the result of an executive order. She thought it extremely attractive.

She lay on her deck chair beside her brother and wrote industriously in an exercise book. She was "drafting a scenario" as she called it, sketching tentatively the first shaky outlines of her new novel of a murder on a yacht. What she was doing might be compared with the work of those who mark out the plan of a building on the ground. Mr. O'Relly took no notice of his sister. Indeed, he never did take any more notice of her than domestic animals take of each other when undisturbed by anger or love. He stared at the sea, smoking innumerable cigarettes that seemed incapable of affording him any real solace, his black eyes full of a sort of alert animosity when other passengers walked within range of his vision or the three cut-up children on the ship came thundering past his chair. His sister had forgotten the scolding she had given him about the night before. She had forgotten, also, the briefcase containing the book he was supposed to be writing about the Administration. The briefcase lay on the deck under his chair. Mr. O'Relly himself regretted extremely his plunge into the literary life. He found it fatiguing to write more than fifteen hundred words at a time on any subject. His journalistic training had conditioned him to climb easily among facts and rumors, most of which were never printed. What was actually in a newspaper was like the visible portion of an iceberg. It changed from day to day in shape and color. The larger part, which remained submerged, was more dangerous. On it were wrecked reputations and governments. But to go into all this at length in a book, to hold his wind for three hundred pages, was fatiguing. What Mr. O'Relly really wanted to do was to get hold of that girl he had danced with and take her to the bar and give her a drink. It was a little early yet, but all his faculties were concentrated upon circumventing his sister's vigilance and slipping off to find that girl.

The sight of Captain Nevile in a suit of white flannels with an orange tie recalled to Mr. O'Relly the fact that that Miss Rhys had an unfortunate weakness for bringing Captain Nevile into the conversation. Mr. O'Relly supposed it was due to feminine fondness for titles, though this fellow seemed to be only a sort of captain by courtesy. Not that he, Terry O'Relly, had any intention of starting a fight with him over a lady passenger. The passion for fishing was never very far from the surface in Mr. O'Relly's nature, and he was certainly going to have a look at this new club. All he really wanted, next to several dry Martinis, was the society of that girl where his sister couldn't butt in and drag him off to work on his book. He was perfectly content to be a newspaperman, and he could never quite conceal his contempt for any writer who had a week or even a month to finish his stuff in.

Captain Nevile came up and said good-morning. He put his hand into his inside pocket and brought out a packet of folded papers held by a rubber band.

"How about a drink?" he said, smiling at Mrs. Kavanagh, to give her confidence in his discretion. Mrs. Kavanagh smiled back. Mr. O'Relly made a convulsive movement that brought him to his feet in a crouching position as though he were about to take Captain Nevile by the legs and hurl him overboard. But instead he straightened up and instinctively pulled himself together. He was still wearing the black shoes he had had on when he boarded the Camotan in New York, and (to tell the truth) the same suit. He had to the full that obliviousness to what he wore that is observable in scarecrows, geniuses, and the less predatory Milesians. He stared for an instant at Captain Nevile's classy white buckskin shoes and clocked silk socks. A faint ray of light penetrated his intelligence, filtering through the reticulated classconsciousness which renders the Fourth Estate immune from either irony or sarcasm. It did occur to Mr. O'Relly at this moment that Captain Nevile might have a more powerful attraction for that girl than a brilliant newspaperman who nevertheless looked as if he had spent the night, without taking off his clothes, in a sailor's flop house. He sternly repressed this idea at once and picked a dead flower from his buttonhole to equalize matters.

He heard Captain Nevile explaining to Norah Kavanagh that he had some business to discuss with her brother and they could do it over a highball in the lounge. The thought of

a week's fishing off a tropic isle for big fish that would need
a tarpon rod, all free, no expense, suddenly made Terry
O'Relly feel rather faint. He turned almost savagely on the
steward with a tray loaded with bouillon cups. He wanted—
just for a moment—to take the tray and throw it into the sea.
Instead he said, "Let's go!" to Captain Nevile. The idea of
drinking bouillon with the bar a few yards away struck him
as shocking. He wanted to get away from it.

At the door of the lounge he halted as if he had just
thought of something. He had. Why not, he said, ask that
Miss Rhys to join them? She was at their table.

"She doesn't drink," said Captain Nevile, and there was a
sort of exultation in his voice which Mr. O'Relly failed to
understand. "She doesn't take anything at all."

Mr. O'Relly's reaction to this was confusing to a superficial
observer. He became genial as he took his seat in the lounge
and shook the dice in the leather cup. He had once had a
vague feeling, before the altar-boy period had completely
evaporated, of a vocation for the priesthood. What interested him, even now, was applied psychology. He had a professional pride in reading the true motives of men and women
behind their actions and utterances. He had formulated some
axioms, and one of them was that a woman who did not drink,
smoke, or otherwise act in the manner normal among his own
acquaintances was preoccupied with thoughts of sex and
might be more easily seduced than the standardized emancipated creatures who bragged of their freedom from inhibitions. He did not proceed from this to the assumption that
such women invariably experienced a violent passion for
himself, but he found it sufficiently accurate in his daily work
as a basis for character analysis and in those cynical sketches
of Washington lesser lights for which he was becoming celebrated among his fellow craftsmen. It was they, the fellow
craftsmen, who had told him that he ought to write a book,
for it is one of the paradoxes of our time that those newspapermen who are most sensitive of their professional dignity

and resent alien intrusions most bitterly, cherish the desire
to become the authors of books.

Hence the news that that girl did not drink, or—as it
transpired—smoke, and even had a prayer book in her possession, caused Mr. O'Relly to place her in a certain category
in his mind, and he cheerfully disposed of several cocktails
and listened to Captain Nevile's program for bringing a party
of newspapermen down to the new fishing ground for the
purpose of introductory publicity. Mr. Rossiter, son of the
Wall Street Rossiter, was "the moving spirit," he learned.
Rossiter, Jr., had "arranged the financing." Mr. O'Relly
was familiar with these phrases. He was also familiar with
young Mr. Rossiter's public relations counsel in Washington,
a gentleman who had the care of young Mr. Rossiter's political ambitions on his mind. Mr. O'Relly said nothing of this.
He wanted to go fishing in style, for nothing. He wanted a
teak and mahogany motorboat with a two-hundred-horse-
power engine, an ice chest, and a skipper who knew how to
cut bait. He wanted a fishing seat with deep leather cushions
and a rod such as he had not yet possessed. He wanted to sit
back and pull the peak of his fishing hat well over his eyes
and squint along the bubbling wake to where his bait was
making a silver feather on the blue water. He wanted to do
all this and forget Washington, forget the wife who had left
him, and even his family, for a week or two. He did not want
to forget his religion. Indeed, he had a secret illusion that he
always recovered much of his religious feeling when he went
fishing, and he might become a devotee if he could abandon
his profession and live far away from the haunts of men, in
some rocky cove where he could fish and lie in the sun and
invite his soul. The latter phrase was always used by those
poetical fellows in the newspaper game who wrote nature
stuff.

He wanted to go fishing, and he was willing to do his part
in getting the fellows to come. If it went through, Captain
Nevile said, Mr. O'Relly could accept an honorary vice

presidency of the club, and he could write to his professional brethren from the Press Club at Washington. That had the advantage of being the central focus, as it were, of publicity. It was the central focus of a good many things, Mr. O'Relly mused as he sank another Martini. And he tried to remember just how this fellow had got him away from the subject of that girl.

The lounge was filling up. The table, spread with enough food to save a starving garrison, was surounded by passengers who would go down presently and consume in addition a luncheon of several heavy courses. They had already had morning tea, a large breakfast, bouillon and crackers. They would have afternoon tea, and later a heavy dinner. With the exception of sandwiches and olives at 11 P.M. this would comprise their provender for the day—unless they had candies and fruit of their own in their cabins.

The lounge filled up. Young men and girls in sweaters, who had been playing deck tennis, crowed to each other as they raided the food table and drank cocktails to encourage an appetite. They were an unconscious response to the suggestion of millions of advertisements that happiness could only be expressed by opening their mouths wide and revealing all their teeth. They were so completely at ease that their manners disintegrated into the collisions and scuffles of young animals at play. Sudden explosions of cackling laughter over secret jokes evoked strained smiles from other parts of the lounge. Some of the more sensitive outsiders sat with mask-like grins on their faces, contemplating their drinks and waiting the signal for another explosion.

Mr. O'Relly followed Captain Nevile into the corridor. He wanted to suggest that they go in search of that girl and take her down to lunch. Captain Nevile stopped. He seemed to be seriously considering the subject.

"You don't want me to come, do you?" he said good-naturedly. Mr. O'Relly said he didn't know where her cabin was.

"Neither do I. It's somewhere on the deck below this, but I don't know the number. I do know she won't be down to lunch."

"How do you know that?" said Mr. O'Relly.

"Because we had a swim together at six o'clock this morning, and she told me she never takes lunch."

"Doesn't drink, doesn't smoke, doesn't lunch?" mused Mr. O'Relly. "And says her prayers, you say?"

"And doesn't pet either, I can tell you," said Captain Nevile gravely. "It's just as well to know that in advance."

"Did she tell you she didn't?"

"Indirectly, of course. She's English, which may account for everything, you know."

Mr. O'Relly stepped over the doorway onto the promenade deck. He made no further allusion to the girl, who had loomed through an alcoholic haze as he danced with her and who had left a mysterious and puzzling impression upon his mind. She had fallen into no classification, being neither blond nor brunet, neither tall nor short, neither flapperish nor sedate. He had cut in, and they had danced but she had said nothing at all. When the orchestra ceased, somehow, without his knowing just how it had come about, Mr. O'Relly found her vanished. He had wandered around the ship looking for her, but it may be doubted whether he would have been able to identify her in her wrap. All that was left was a vague impression of something unusual in quality, something he ought to make some sort of effort to possess, though he was far from clear what it was all about. Perhaps it was a glimpse of that shadowy region of a happy marriage, an existence in which neither his church nor his family could by any chance butt in and spoil it. He had no real animosity towards either, but he felt they were both singularly unfitted to manage his private life for him.

He saw his sister talking to that fellow with the beard. He too was in a white uniform. Mrs. Kavanagh had her brother's briefcase on her lap under her own papers, and she was listening to the chief engineer's conversation. Mr. O'Relly felt a faint gratitude towards Mr. Spenlove for keeping Norah interested, though what they found to talk about was beyond him. He was slightly afraid of the man. He couldn't place him, with his talk about yachts, and that sarcastic lift of the heavy black eyebrows. Mr. Spenlove had the expression about the eyes of a chief of police Mr. O'Relly had once known, a chief of police who now ran a successful private detective agency. But identifying that particular expression didn't result in placing Mr. Spenlove, for he didn't talk in the least like the owner of a private detective agency. There was nothing of the yo-heave-ho boys about him either, the ship officers who brought in the sea-serpent tales or the news that the Gulf Stream was now running backwards into Montevideo.

"You've not started on your book since we left New York," said his sister in a low voice as he halted in front of them.

"I'm collecting material," he said, lighting a cigarette. He never looked directly at his sister Norah. He stared at Mr. Spenlove.

Mrs. Kavanagh made no reply. Mr. Spenlove, watching them, suspected more strongly than ever that this worry about her brother's book merely indicated a desire to have him under her eye.

"Local color," he suggested kindly. "A book without local color is bound to be a tame business." He watched Mr. O'Relly drift towards the forward stairway as the luncheon gong thundered faintly down below. "He ought to dedicate his book to you, if he ever finishes it."

"If he ever does!" she said, getting up briskly and holding her belongings in her arms. Mr. Spenlove accompanied. He was going down to lunch. He had a desire to see this new friend of Sidney Nevile's. With such perfect weather there could be no reason for her failing to come to the table at last.

But she was not there. Mr. Spenlove found the one empty
chair an unexpected embarrassment to each person at his
table. There was no conversation until he called the head
waiter and asked if the lady was still suffering from mal-de-
mer.

"No, I don't think so, Chief. She doesn't take lunch, the
stewardess says. On a diet, I fancy."

There was nothing more to say after that. He listened to
young Nevile talking to Mr. O'Relly about the fishing club.
It was the first time that new job became real to Mr. Spenlove. He had half believed the club was a mere figment of
Captain Nevile's imagination, a scheme for which he hoped
to find backing. Now, with the reading matter young Nevile
had given him, it took on the aspect of an authentic enterprise. And Mr. O'Relly's interest was authentic too. He had
one of the booklets in his hand. He had drawn it from his
pocket. Mr. Spenlove realized that in the past few years he
had seen so little of young Nevile that he might be unac-
quainted with some of the young man's mature qualifications.
It might be that he knew what he was doing and the professional dislike Mr. Spenlove had for anyone in a ticket
office was blinding him to real qualities. Unlike most seafaring
men, Mr. Spenlove was not only aware of this prejudice but
could see all around it without being able to destroy it. So
he said nothing. But he became so absorbed in the problem
that Mrs. Kavanagh imagined he was in a bad humor and
contented herself with watching the other passengers.

But Mr. Spenlove was not in a bad humor. He made
this plain as they reached the deck again. He invited
Mrs. Kavanagh to come to his cabin to tea, and she accepted.

"I want to know about that girl you found him with in
some place," she said.

"Glasgow. You could fill that in yourself."

"Not in love with the shop girl?"

"No. That was always his problem. He used to go with

that kind, and they were always falling in love with him, but not he with them."

"I can't recognize him in what you say," she protested. "He's such a perfect gentleman. Why did he have to go around with . . . ?"

She left Mr. Spenlove to pursue his way and sought her cabin. She knew her brother was going to have a nap, and it was useless to suggest any work until the following morning. And as she lay in the darkened cabin the scene of the previous night came back to her. She recalled that glance around the library. Young Neville had been leaning forward to speak, and the girl, whose reddish-brown bobbed hair was visible over the back of her chair, had her head averted and a flush was staining the white neck and shoulders. Mrs. Kavanagh refused to face the implications of such a scene. She wanted to believe the girl was a scheming adventuress luring a handsome young fellow to make love to her. Some women had the knack of making themselves mysterious, of making people wonder about them. Looking back along the perfectly straight course of her life since she had left the school kept by the nuns, and almost at once had married Michael, who had been altar boy before Terry's time, Mrs. Kavanagh remembered several women who had revealed to her a technique with men that involved them in a great many innocent deceits of no consequence at all. The results, however, were often important in getting a man to believe them. But that wasn't quite the same thing as getting all men to dream about them, as she knew Terry was dreaming about this creature who got herself up in a frock of baby blue, like a flapper, with gold shoes too small for her into the bargain. She might well blush, even at her age, which must be twenty-five if it was a day!

Mrs. Kavanagh's foot twitched. Even if that were true, the creature had the odds on herself by ten years, she thought. Suddenly she smiled to herself. She was behaving like a lunatic. Her portable typewriter stood on a small table by her wardrobe. She got up and went to it. She really knew well enough from experience how the first two chapters should go. The first two chapters of any book were the same, she felt. It was the chapters that followed which made the literary life so arduous.

VII

"IT MUST BE a wonderful life, the way you live," she said, as Mr. Spenlove's steward brought in the tea. "Nobody deserves such an absolutely perfect existence as you seem to have invented for yourself."

"That's rather shrewd on your part," he admitted, "but the question of deserts doesn't enter into it. It implies that the existence is open to competition, so to speak. Well, it is, but the people who might compete don't exist. At least, they don't exist in such a form that they could avail themselves of the life you are good enough to praise."

"I know you don't mean nobody exists who could hold your job," Mrs. Kavanagh muttered, "but that's as far as I understand you."

"You want me to reveal the secret, the magic formula? There isn't any. I have colleagues, you know, who are in charge of other ships in the line. To them this life is an atrocity. It's a mockery of human existence. They want to get home to Sea Cliff, Long Island, or one of those interminable avenues in Brooklyn, and live the lives of civilized bourgeois citizens. They want to go out to some unpronounceable region in New Jersey where they can have a Ford, a couple of beehives, three children, dogs and chickens. And they never want to set eyes on a passenger again! Yet you say I have an existence so ideal nobody could ever deserve it! Tell some of the others that! See what they say!"

Mrs. Kavanagh did not reply. She was squeezing lemon juice into her tea. Mr. Spenlove's pretense that he did not know what she meant was flagrant, but she enjoyed his conversation. She remarked finally that she supposed it was being a bachelor that made it attractive.

"Anyhow," she added, "I bet even you look forward to retiring. You won't go on living on this ship forever."

"Not for more than a few months," he said. "I shall go to England and bring out a new ship. I would prefer to stay where I am, but that's what will happen. As for retiring, why should I wish to do that, if it is all you seem to think?"

Mrs. Kavanagh waved a hand.

"We'll come and visit with you when you retire," she said. "Will you invite us?"

"I'll tell you about that," he said. "I have the place already. I don't go there much, but it has a future. When I get my vacation I'll go there. But retiring is too much like dying for a seafaring person to think about it in advance. I agree with you. It is a good life. I tell my juniors that, and they think I am stringing them. They think I am a capitalist in disguise trying to fool them with honeyed words. They dream of government jobs with pensions. They hear of all sorts of juicy opportunities ashore in America now socialism is abroad in the land, and all the things they've heard in their youth come back to haunt them. Things like Opportunity, Democracy, Freedom Out West, High Wages, and so on. Moreover, do you suppose they don't know all about young Captain Nevile getting this marvelous job down in the West Indies? They do. They talk about it all the time. They know a lot about his career since he commanded a ship. Some of them think they wouldn't muff the chance to marry into a well-cushioned executive position in the States. Oh no!"

"I want to know about that marriage of his. Why do you seem to dislike his wife so much?"

"I'm prejudiced, I suppose. Mind you, she's a remarkable girl, Ada is. She'd make her way in any kind of society. I was coming to her. But I told you we met in Glasgow that time, during the strike that paralyzed everything. And he was wasting his time walking out with a well-meaning little trollop he'd picked up in Renfrew Street on her night off. There were two reasons for that. First, he was still in a very complicated state of mind about that Elli Phalère. He couldn't understand why he had a passion for a girl like that, a girl who was the mistress of some foreigner and whom he would never see again unless he inherited a fortune and went traveling on his own. Even then, when he got to Malta, he might find she had gone away again to some unknown town.

"And he had a reaction from the yacht. Men never regret scenes of social grandeur, but a woman never ceases to regret them, if she drops in the social scale."

"I dare say that's true," said Mrs. Kavanagh.

"It was true for him. Possibly one of the attractions women discover in him lies in his unawareness of any class but his own. It's quite different from being democratic, as we say. It isn't being consciously aristocratic or benevolently plutocratic. It's being unconscious of one's own existence, I should say. He had no need to excuse himself to that poor kid I saw him with in Glasgow. She was perfectly happy until I hove into view and he had to explain her to me. It is we others who are the trouble—friends, husbands, brothers, and so forth. The women ask nothing better than to be left alone with him.

"That was why he refused to give her the push and walk off with me, though he wanted to. He was genuinely glad to see me again, and he came over to my ship the next day. The fact was, he had no idea, after we sailed for Rotterdam, where we might have to go to, and a ship tied up to the buoys slips out of the daily shipping movements in the papers. He was rather at a loose end too, for the rest of the mates and the engineers were extremely Scotch on the Cromarty Castle. They cultivated an attitude of reserve towards a mere Englishman and spent a great deal of time at home with their families. That, young Nevile remarked, smiling, was all they did spend. They brought their wives on board, and they all seemed equally thrifty, he said.

"I gathered he had taken up with the girl I saw him with in sheer boredom, for he knew nobody in Glasgow. Now, he said, he hoped the strike would last a little longer, so we could see each other. And so did I.

"But it wasn't necessary. Our captain was far from satisfied with one of his protégés, the third mate, who had been coming back next morning after a night of it along the pubs of Renfield and Sauchiehall streets and lying in bed all day with a hangover. The old man came to my room while young Nevile was there, and I introduced him. After four or five warnings our captain sacked our third mate. He then came to me and asked whether I thought young Nevile would care to accept a step down for a voyage or two. He was second on the Cromarty Castle. I said I thought he would, but I could find out for sure. The miners' unions were coming to a decision, and the government was toiling night and day to arbitrate, and we might load any day. I got a messenger to go over to Clydebank and tell young Nevile to pack his bag. I knew he was getting less there as second than he would have on the Brandeston as third. We were on what was called the London scale of wages.

"He came over in a taxi at once and was very glad to join as third. And a couple of days later we went under the tips and got our bunkers filled. We had rain, of course, and we were all in a mess, but young Nevile was as pleased as a dog with two tails. The Brandeston was new off the stocks, he had a nice room to himself behind the bridge, and we were bound for Buenos Aires to get a cargo of hides and grain. We took a load of coal from South Wales to St. Vincent, which had sold all its coal at sky-high prices to tramps. Of course, the liners had contracts.

"There we were, together again. I had the idea he would stay with us now, get engaged to be married, work up with us and marry, and worry along until he got a command. He was definitely finished with high life and low life, and gave me to understand he could be as sensible as anybody else about his future. He was going to save his wages, too. On the way out he showed me a savings-bank book with seventeen pounds something shillings on deposit at two and a half per cent, which was highly creditable. And he said he did not expect to go back to his family when he was on leave in England. It transpired that it had at last penetrated his parents' heads that the Honorable Maeve was a bad egg. She had appeared in the Nevile's Sunday paper in connection with a divorce in high society, the fast set. He had heard about that from his mother, and even an awfully decent and understanding letter from his sister Ursula did not make the dose much sweeter. It was as if those two Protestant Low Church East Anglians, comfortable bourgeois folk, had suddenly realized the horrible risk their boy Sidney was running while out on the ocean. It was as if they had come to believe in sirens who lured nice young sailors onto rocky promontories and destroyed them. He had a letter from a brother who was in business at Norwich, I remember, a chap who had a touch of his own. He suggested—he was in a bank—that young Nevile let him invest his savings and hold them in trust. A fine big-brotherly loyal scout sort of letter, full of 'old fellow' and 'old chap' and 'don't be a silly ass now' and that kind of talk. It worked too, later on. I'll tell you about it. He still has the money, on loan. It's perfectly safe. I mean it's safe with him. Young Nevile tried to get it when he married that Ah-ee-dah as she calls herself, but he has it still to come.

"Well, he was through and all his wild oats sown and garnered. We got into the trade wind, and there's no finer voyage in the world for the merchant seaman. Fine weather, tropics, good breeze, long run without a chance to spend money, and B.A. at the end of it. We'd had too long a spell in Glasgow to take any pleasure in the beach at the Cape Verde Islands. Buenos Aires was something special in those days. We had pay coming—a whole five weeks' pay—and so we went ashore."

"You mean . . ." said Mrs. Kavanagh.

"Oh no. Not in my case or young Nevile's. He never did. Our captain said to me, when the thing happened, 'So that's your wonderful young man of good principles!' He was one of these sarcastic skippers, who made a great to do about not being a hypocrite himself and having no patience with others who were hypocrites.

"What happened was that the night before we sailed young Nevile had an experience up at the Bier Konvent. Our chaps called it the Beer Convent, and I dare say some of them thought the girls were supposed to be nuns in that convent. The German population had brought the phrase with them to Buenos Aires. As you might say, a beer convention. We convened to drink beer in a large hall with an orchestra and a concert platform. We sat at little tables, and waiters brought the beer.

"Now it was well known that the girls who performed on the platform as well as the girls who sat at the tables were far from reluctant to break the monotony of their exile by meeting new friends. In fact, it was an accepted custom of the place: if a patron desired to see more of a lady artist, he gave the waiter his card with a couple of pesos. The lady artist would write her address on it and send it back; or she would shrug her shoulders and tear it up. The waiter would then return and shrug his shoulders, and the customer, resigned, would shrug his. No harm done. If he received an assignation he would proceed to the address at the time mentioned. It was all cut and dried for those who patronized that sort of sport. Most of our chaps were either too shy or too short of pesos to try it on. They enjoyed going there for the show and the gayety.

"Well, young Nevile was there, a bier-stein in front of him, and the second mate was throwing the dice in the leather cup, when the waiter came up and, laying a card on the table under young Nevile's nose, went away.

"For a moment he was unable to understand what had happened. He had applauded the last two turns by a very handsome girl who was singing risky songs in Spanish. The second mate said she called herself La Campanula, or the Snowdrop. She had, he said, hair so blond it was almost white, so I suppose she would be called a platinum blonde now. The funny thing was that, apart from impersonally clapping at the end of her songs, neither of the young fellows had indicated any interest. But when young Nevile found a large square card, with 'La Campanula' on it and an address in the corner, he was seized with a violent excitement. He told me, long after, when we met again, that he grew hot all over and he thought everybody in the place was looking at him. He didn't know how unusual it was for the process to be reversed. He didn't know anything at all except that the girl he had seen on the stage, a girl with amazing eyes and white arms with long black gloves, and whose voice still rang in his ears, had been looking at him and had singled him out among all those scores of men of all nations and had sent him her card.

"When he showed it to the second mate—another artist was singing by then—they had a short debate. 'Go on,' said the second mate. 'Why, of course! By golly, wish I had your luck! What you afraid of?' So he told us. He had no jealousy about it. Perhaps he wasn't sorry, at heart, afterwards, that it hadn't happened to him. It was the first time he had been ashore with Nevile, for they usually took turns in keeping harbor watch, but the chief mate had let them go off because they had been doing long hours tallying. The second mate had been as surprised as anyone else at what happened. He himself had drunk up his beer and drifted out to go down to the ship. He had seen young Nevile, the card in his hand, walk off towards the Avenida de Mayo. And that was the last we saw of him."

"You mean to say he didn't join the ship again?" said Mrs. Kavanagh.

"Just that. We sailed next day as soon as the captain got his papers, bound for Antwerp, and we naturally couldn't keep seven thousand tons of cargo waiting for one young third mate. That was why the captain made his sarcastic allusion to my young friend of good principles. It didn't seem much use arguing, either."

"What had happened to him?"

"For one thing, he lost his discharge book, because the captain had it in his safe and impounded it. Theoretically all his sea time vanished, and he would have to begin again.

"That was what made me feel so utterly dejected on the voyage home. Even when I received a letter from him, long afterwards, I was very much upset. He had falsified all the hopes and affections I had lavished upon him and had become a beachcomber. Nobody on board had any sympathy for him. The other mates kept watch and watch and damned his eyes all the way to the Tyne, where we went to load for Santos. I didn't damn his eyes. I had received a wound that wasn't mortal, of course—we can survive the casualties of any number of our friends—but very deep. It had a partially paralyzing effect on my feelings for humanity.

"Yes, when his letter arrived, I had lost my own job owing to the ship and her new sister the Bramblewood being sold under us. A German firm bought them all standing, to use on a colonial charter they had secured, and we were on the beach ourselves for a while. It took the heart out of me, because I had contemplated remaining on that nice new ship, the Brandeston, for a decade at least. Of course we were promised jobs; but the strike of the seamen came along and dished us completely. Small owners lost a lot of money at that time. The competition for freight was a war to the death. One of our ships took kerosene from New York to Vladivostok for eighteen cents a case.

"I had a lean time. Memories of that time come back to me occasionally, and I pinch myself to make sure I'm not dreaming. I had temporary jobs on all kinds of shabby steamers. I dropped down as far as third engineer of one of old Bandy's horrible workhouse ships. But never mind.

What has happened once can happen again. I had a bit of luck in Liverpool and got into this line that's taking you to see the West Indies—the Afro-Iberian. That brought me to New York, and I have been here ever since except during the war. And I met young Nevile on South Street.

"Yes, I had got a letter while I was hunting a job. It came by a roundabout route—agents—owners—my home in Hampshire, and so forth. He wrote from Panama, where he had a job running a tug on the new canal that was being excavated. He told me he had had a very good job on construction, handling a gang of riggers who fixed stages and derricks, and so on. He said he was a gold employee, of course, which meant he was paid in gold certificates. At the very end of his letter he added a postscript. I suppose, he said, I've lost caste with you for missing my passage, but I could not have done anything but what I did under the circumstances. Something like that, he wrote on the last page of his letter, almost as though he had nearly forgotten to mention how he left us.

"It wasn't just for a handful of silver, however, or even a ribbon to stick in his coat. I heard the story when he turned up again in New York. I had been in low water, as I told you, and finally connected with this company by joining one of their ships out of the builder's yard in Belfast. I began to be in funds again, and the war found me in America. I had joined the small army of expatriates, taking bread out of the mouths of native-born Americans and settling down with New York as my home port. And one day in 1913, about a year before the war began, I was informed that somebody on the dock was signaling to me. I was watching the stores coming on board and did not notice young Nevile. He came up the crew gangway, the same as ever, very eager, smiling, and looking fairly prosperous too.

"He had been looking for a ship to get back to Liverpool, he said, and he had noticed the Red Ensign on our poop, so he had come aboard with the idea of getting an able seaman's job. To save the fare. He had some money, several hundred dollars, in fact, but he didn't want to waste a hundred of them just to get home. While he was casting about for somebody to ask, he caught sight of me. Well, it was a surprise.

"I had him into my cabin, and we enjoyed a talk about our times together. I gave him a drink and found out what he was up to. He had been paid off in Colon as the canal was being opened soon, and he was merely giving way to homesickness when he tried to go to England. What would he do? I said. He had no discharge book, and if he tried to get a new one he might hear about what happened in Buenos Aires. He said he still had his certificate and he had discharges from an American ship he had worked on down the coast.

"'So you're all right, then,' I said in sarcasm. He said he wanted to start under the Red Ensign again, now he had a stake. He said he reported his discharge book as lost with the consul in Panama, and he got a temporary one. The consul was satisfied from the papers young Nevile had on him that he was what he pretended to be.

"The fact is, he couldn't have come to us at a more opportune time. We needed men for the ships, men with certificates who would take any position. I said I thought the port captain could put him on a ship. Everybody knew that the men we found on the spot had wandered about a good deal. America was still the land of opportunity. There was a diplomatic conspiracy of silence about our pasts. I am speaking of the pre-war days, of course. The men in the big lines looked down on us, and they might well do so because our ships carried fellows who had been in big lines and had been fired or run off, as young Nevile had run off in B. A. That was no obstacle in those days. We had men from all over the world in our messrooms: men of the wanderlust. The man who relieved me at eight o'clock on one ship had been in a salmon cannery in Alaska. Another of our chaps knew more about gold mining in Malay rivers than he did about ships. So I knew young Nevile could get a job.

"We had a day together before I sailed. He sailed on another ship as third officer before I got back, and it was a year before we happened to be in port together again. But we had that day and evening, and when I reached his room in the West Seventies, a quiet room on the fourth-floor back of a brownstone mansion gone to seed, I asked him where he had run to in Buenos Aires. Why had he risked his whole career for some foreign trollop? I pitched it strong. I never set eyes on her, but I called her a trollop.

"He said, in the first place, he had had no intention of losing his passage. He had been 'drawn into' an affair, another person's affair, and it was just fate. He arrived back at the dock a few hours after we had sailed. Finding we had sailed, he 'saw his goose was cooked' and went back to carry out what he had been asked to do, and had 'rather funked doing, as a matter of fact.'

"In the second place, he said that Miss Phillips was neither a trollop nor a foreigner. That was her name. Well, it might not be her name actually, but she called herself that in private life. La Campanula was just a stage name because she was a blonde and the South American men were crazy about fair girls. Alma Phillips was the name on her passport.

"He had gone off in a sort of trance when he left the Bier Konvent. The card in his hand; the memory of the girl singing 'My Girl's a High-born Lady' in a throaty contralto; the romantic notion of meeting an actress; the beer he had been drinking, and all the intoxication of one of the gayest cities on earth—all combined to make him a little dizzy. She had scribbled a note on the back of the card, that she would be home at one o'clock. In the morning. He had three quarters of an hour to wait before going to Calle Guido.

"I said, 'You might have fallen into one of these traps for foreigners. You should have torn the card up and come back to the ship. What did she want? What made her pick on you?'

"He said she had seen him come in and saw he was English. He was coming in, quietly looking about for a table while she was singing her first song, and I suppose he had captured her imagination. She was an English girl in a particularly alien environment. She had been brought out there, or had come out, to work for a concert bureau. As far as I could make out from young Nevile's description and the picture he had of her in tights, with gauze wings behind her shoulders and a small bow and arrow in her hands, she had character. She was English, and she had seen he was English. Of course there were other Englishmen there, but not his sort. She had been a judge of character, and she wanted somebody who was a gentleman. That was the reason she gave him. It's all very well, as I tell myself, to smile cynically at the way men fall for a woman's wiles, but I doubt whether I wouldn't tumble for that one myself. To be mistaken for a gentleman—what a dream!

"However, I think he was the real thing. What she wanted was a husband. I don't mean she wanted to marry young Nevile, though I dare say she would have taken that up too, but she had a chance to work in Montevideo, which is across the Plate River from Buenos Aires. If she went over by herself they would send her back as an undesirable. The police would come to where she lived and not only would they want about half her salary in graft, but she would have to receive the police chief and his friends. So she wanted a husband. If she had a husband she could achieve a different status altogether, for she happened to have a personality on the stage. She was able to arouse the generous feelings of humanity, evoke smiles and memories of other days. She could sing 'Sweet Dreamland Faces' so that men swallowed hard and avoided each other's gaze. Most girls who answered the advertisements for concert artistes for South America were either fools or merely daughters of joy. This girl was clever and she was an artiste. She had made a name for herself, raised her price, and paid her way clear of the bureau who had signed her up in London. And when she wanted to get out of the country she knew what to do.

"It sounds crude to tell it. It sounded fantastic to hear young Nevile say he was carried away by her voice. He said he had never heard anyone with a voice like hers. Well, she was an actress as well, I suppose. Her voice was a contralto that vibrated like a harp string as she talked to him. She was much older than he, I believe, and the fact that she had taken a liking to him made her all the more seductive. To miss a ship meant nothing to her compared with helping an English girl in a hole. He could get another ship. There were a couple of score of steamship lines running into B. A. What was a ship? She had a friend—oh, never mind how it had happened —but she had a friend,. a lawyer, who would get her a cedula, a carte d'identité which would include the two of them as husband and wife and would enable her to accept the engagement she had offered her in Montevideo.

"What she was relying on was young Nevile's intelligence and love of adventure. She took a chance in sending him that invitation as if she were a mere piece of soiled goods trying to increase her clientele. Quite possibly she had made the gesture before and found someone who drew back quickly and hurried off to his ship or his office, rather scared of the danger he had been in.

"Young Nevile himself had hesitated. He had hesitated because of his career. She had failed utterly to understand that. As the time drew near when the Brandeston was due to leave, he said she opened another bottle of German champagne. Champagne was rather unusual with us in those days. He wouldn't say if he believed the wine had anything in it or not. He didn't feel afterwards as if he had been drugged. He remembered looking out of the window of her apartment on Guido and seeing a high convent wall across the street. The chapel bell was tolling for early morning service.

"He told me this in that quiet exemplary room at the back of a brownstone boarding house in the West Seventies. He said he had not been in love with Alma Phillips, nothing of that at all. On the other hand, he had a feeling of extraordinary affection for a girl who had singled him out to help her. She was, he said, the most attractive girl he had ever been intimate with. There had been a concatenation of influences, qualities, attractions, elective affinities, whatever you want to call them, that overturned the balance and sent him in her direction. She had possessed an ability to take care of herself, and she revealed a kind of maternal craving for a young man, hardly more than a boy, with the same background as her own. Compared with the average young Argentino, he was just a nice child.

"When he found the Brandeston gone he felt, he said, as if he had burned his boats. He had even played with the idea of settling in Uruguay or on the pampas. He said nothing at all about his life in Montevideo, and apart from the fact that he had not done anything criminal, it was his own affair. He got a job easily enough on a river steamer going to Rosario. He found, as a lot of young fellows have found, that keeping house with a theatrical woman is the most disillusioning experience of a lifetime. Even if one is married to an entertainer, there can never be any real peace unless the man is a nonentity, a colorless dummy. But young Nevile got a job as second mate of a river steamer. He did tell me, as though he had gained some knowledge of other aspects of his adventure, that he never took a penny from Alma. He happened to have several pounds in gold on him when he went to her house. He never took a penny, and paid his share of the apartment rent in Montevideo.

"She was very successful there. She was so successful that she got an offer to go to Rio, which was what she was after. Rio is like Paris to a girl in South America. And while young Nevile was coming down from Rosario she left for Rio on the German mail boat and left word for him to follow.

"I could get no clear reason from him why he did not do so. I suppose he was not easy in his mind, now he had a chance to think things over, as to his status in the world of men. Adventure is not invariably a bright road illumined by romance. You can sink into a state of quiet emotional sloth, but it doesn't last. You either have fresh experiences or become a conventional, acquisitive Anglo-Saxon. Young Nevile hesitated. He stuck to his job for several more trips. And then he met a man who was going to the Panama Canal. This man said conditions were excellent at Colon. Plenty of work of all kinds at high wages. Young Nevile went with him, second class, up the coast, to try his luck. He had not been away more than a few months from us, but he already felt that he ought to make a move towards civilization, as he called it. It was a halfway house to getting back into harness again.

"I fancy the real reason why he didn't follow his Alma Phillips was that he didn't find in himself any talent for living with a woman older than himself, especially one who was so competent as she was. It is a talent, you know, a very rare one. It is a talent I've studied right here on the ship, and I've never understood it. Young Nevile was satisfied he had done nothing to tarnish his honor, but he was becoming experienced. I said that when he was a young cadet there was a sort of virginal bloom on his character. After the affair on the island he became harder, more tolerant yet complacent about women. Now that I saw him again, as he told me of his life in the Canal Zone, and since he arrived in New York on his way to England, he was amused and watchful. He had become aware of the fact that women were attracted to him, and in the early stages of that awareness he was a shade cynical. As he expressed it to me, 'I don't take any notice of them. Find them, fool them, and forget them, is my motto. I'm going to take care of myself.'

"So he did. He joined one of our smaller ships as third officer. He was second of this ship when war started in 1914, and he was appointed chief officer of her a short time later. I came here when she was made a troopship, and by that time he had a command. Promotion was fast in those days. Ships and men were in demand. I met him in Brest one day in naval uniform, and it struck me he had taken to it like a duck to water. I never heard him make any allusion to the war in the sense of being patriotic. I fancy his life ashore in North and South America had driven his private emotions so far down inside him that he was no longer able to bring them to the surface. He had developed a protective shell. When others spoke of Huns and Boches, of fighting for the Old Country, he would say, 'Yes, well . . .' or 'That's very true,' or even, if he were a little bored, 'Well, what do you want me to do about it?'

"As far as he could, he avoided all argument, not because he was not patriotic, but because he was marking time in his soul. Some men found themselves in the war. They were caught up in a wave of emotion. A girl, a job, a war were merely three phases of one tremendous exaltation of spirit, lifting them to a higher plane. They were the lucky ones— if they died for their country. Those who lived through it, and experienced the awful let-down to the tempo of civilian existence, are very noisy about it. Young Nevile went through the war very much as a job of work. He did not have, so far as I am able to discover, any love affairs. He sailed to and from France, commanding ships loaded with stores, munitions, troops, and even nurses. He simply stayed where he happened to be when war broke—on the bridge of his ship. It was not his business to decide on the rights and wrongs of it. He must have had opinions, but he went on with his job. I had gone to the Mediterranean, and until the Armistice let me out I only heard at long intervals that Captain Nevile was on the So-and-so or the Such-and-such. Auxiliary cruisers and transports.

"In my private opinion, it was an incredible thing for him to be in command. I still thought of him as a boy. I was half disposed to attribute his rise to the top to the confusion of the war, which threw up some very astonishing freaks, I may tell you. But when the war ended and we straggled back to our old routine over here, young Nevile held his job. He got command of one of the older ships, and as the new ones began to leave the yards in Scotland he got one of them, and it was on the Aramaya, making a cruise to the Mediterranean, that he met his wife Ada. Ah-ee-dah! she calls herself."

"And how you do love that woman!" said Mrs. Kavanagh.

"So would you, if you'd ever met her and stood for her effrontery. That's the only thing inside that lovely shell of hers—I grant you she's a handsome creature at ten paces—there is nothing except an adoration of her own magnificence. I don't believe she has the slightest interest in any human being except as he or she contributes to Ada's own ease and glory. He's well rid of her. Any man who has been married to her ought to have experience enough to keep him safe for life. I say, ought to. I don't go bail for him.

"Yes, she was a passenger, Mrs. Kavanagh. She was on a cruise after having secured a divorce. I believe it was her second husband whom she had divorced that time. She was that kind of girl. She was like an expert craftsman with a complete line of tools for opening the locks on many different doors, but she didn't stay anywhere very long. It is the thrill of getting in and then getting out that really attracts her. She nailed Captain Nevile as soon as she found he was unmarried. She passed up all the shore excursions, except the Parthenon by moonlight, and he went with her on that occasion."

Mrs. Kavanagh moved and stood up so that she could gaze out upon the circle of sea and sky, both unbelievably blue to her eyes, bisected by the sharp straight line of the horizon.

"I don't understand why you dislike her so," she said. "What has she ever done to justify the way you think of her? Wouldn't it make any marriage a failure, to have the man's friend so antagonistic?"

"I wasn't antagonistic! I didn't even know he had met her, or fallen in love with her or was going to marry her! I was on another ship. I am innocent of all occult powers over their marriage. You have to remember that in real life we can endure the follies of others and we can forget our friends when they are out of sight without much remorse. When I met him again he was already married. We happened to be in port together, and he came to see me. He had an apartment in the East Forties, and he took me up there to dinner. It was a ritual, expressing his final abandonment of his native land. He was married to an American girl, earning American wages, and paying rent in an American city. He wanted me to see the progress he had made in the world. He had a sort of shy pride in capturing such a brilliant creature—though as a matter of fact it was she who had captured him.

"Oh yes, she was in love with him at the time. She is always in love with the man at the time. And he was in love with her, perhaps. But it was not long before I gathered how stupefied she was when she discovered how small a salary a ship captain received. She had told him she had money, and she had convinced herself that he had money too. Hence the extravagant apartment in a residential hotel, the dinners ordered in from the restaurant downstairs, the maid and the valet service, and the taxis she took so lavishly instead of walking a few blocks."

"You mean he couldn't afford it?" said Mrs. Kavanagh anxiously.

"Have you ever lived in one of those places? Two hundred a month for two rooms and bath with a cupboard six feet square they call a kitchenette? How does a captain with three hundred and fifty a month look in such a place? It took every cent he had saved to pay the bills to furnish it and buy her clothes. More! His brother had a lot of his savings. He owed for things like fur coats and shoes. I don't suppose he realizes

it even now, for he never had any sense of money at all, that
he had a prize gold-digger on his hands.

"Of course, that wasn't all there was to Ah-ee-dah. She
had a line of her own. She had such a tremendous conviction
of her own personality that she practically acquired a personality. She was, and is, in my opinion, nothing at all. But
she impressed herself on men of quality with such force that
I seem to be a voice crying in the wilderness. . . . She still
impresses! I saw her not so very long ago. I'll tell you about
that. She was just going to be married again, triumphantly."

"What's she like?"

"The same as the day I first saw her in that apartment on
East Forty-seventh Street, a radiant shell. She's really very
like what I imagine they used to call a 'professional beauty.'
She has all the attributes we attribute to Helen of Troy. In
fact, when I try to imagine Argive Helen, I think of Ada
Nevile, whose face might not launch a thousand ships, but
who could certainly disorganize a shipmaster's life."

"But you said she wasn't so much a gold-digger as ambitious," said Mrs. Kavanagh.

"I know I did, and I meant it. But you must understand
that women like Ada have to have the environment first,
or their ambition cannot get started. To travel the road she
desires, she must have shoes at twenty-eight dollars and
stockings at ten dollars a pair. She has to have a practically
continuous supply of expensive cigarettes. She has a costly
hairdresser. In her mind Ada is always going to pay for all
these things herself out of the huge salary she will command
some day in the profession she is working at."

"What profession?" insisted Mrs. Kavanagh. Mr. Spenlove chuckled.

"I was afraid you'd ask that," he admitted. "It all depends, you see. It changes. When she was married before, to
a fellow who did miniature painting for Park Avenue parents,
she was a photographer. She had a studio near Beekman
Place. Number One, a professor with some private income,

really financed that, though she claimed to have started it on a shoe string. That shoe string is always coming up in her conversation. It's a magical affair, that shoe string! Then, when she got young Nevile, she became overnight an interior decorator. She started that on a shoe string, and it set young Captain Nevile back twenty-seven hundred dollars. About all he had, outside of his salary and the money in his brother's bank. Does she know anything about interior decorating? I am not in a position to say. It is a very modern kind of decorating and includes chairs made of polished steel rods and black carpets with chromium-plated floor lamps. It doesn't matter, because she gave it all up suddenly when she had found Number Four and decided being married to a sailor was depressing her personality. She is a screen star now, in her own mind, I mean. Success will come later. Number Four seems determined to 'put her over,' and he has more money than the others.

"She is very lovely, I assure you. She is one of these statuesque blond creatures with hair like a cap of hammered gold, eyes that are violet rather than blue, and a nose that thousands of prettier women would give their eye teeth for. I'll be open with you. I wouldn't be surprised if she made good where she is now, if she is where she said she was. The trouble with Ada rests in the fact that you can never be sure she hasn't added a few frills to the story. She is the sort of girl who gets a curt letter making an appointment for a screen test, and tells you, over a nine-dollar luncheon at the Ritz, she has just refused seven hundred a week. It makes one cautious in discussing her future. But at the time I first met her she was an interior decorator. She could fix you a stunning boudoir for seventy-five hundred dollars, I believe.

"When I walked into that residential hotel foyer, with an office like a confessional on one side, a doorman like an admiral, and an elevator door made of carved bronze that reminded me of Babylonian mausoleums, I felt as if I were in the orange-lighted crypt of a travertine cathedral in one of

H. G. Wells' fantasies. Wells always forgets that there will be religion in the future, and he could find the makings of it in the apartments inhabited by interior decorators. That is the religion of modern women. They no longer fuss around church altars. Their ambition is to serve cocktails on altar cloths from Russian chapels. The elevator door slid open, and I was carried up, up, up to the umpteenth floor, and cast adrift in a corridor of closed doors. I can never get over a regret that I have not brought a sledge hammer with me to batter those blind portals down and establish a community spirit among the inhabitants. Even the grille and peephole of the speakeasy, the convent, and the house of fair reception seem more human than those catacombs in New York apartment houses.

"However, young Captain Nevile, in a velvet smoking jacket that took the place of a tuxedo, was standing at one of the doors to welcome me, and I went in to meet his wife. Was I jealous? No, I wasn't jealous, but I was faintly alarmed at the splendor of the apartment. You see, I knew his salary quite as well as he did, and the moment Ada set eyes on me I had a very definite sensation of antagonism streaming forth in my direction from those violet orbs. It was so sweet of me to come, she said. She had heard so much about me from Sidney; she was crazy to meet me.

"Altogether it was a fairly successful evening. I thought it out as I walked to the subway to take a train back to the ship. I laid aside all my sentimental notions about him marrying a nice English girl and bringing her out to live in decent comfort near my rose-bowered cottage by the sea when I had retired and could no longer work. All that went overboard! He was a modern shipmaster, young and successful, and he had to live the way people did nowadays. It gave me the shivers rather, though, the notion of coming back from a voyage, to that collection of brittle furniture and even more brittle emotions, and calling it home. It seemed to me the Brooklyn boarding house where he had been staying between voyages, a red-brick house with a glimpse of the East River from the bedroom balcony and the sound of tug whistles faintly heard at night, was more human and suitable.

"But I was not a skipper. I had simple tastes. You must remember we were living in boom times. Our firemen wore silk shirts in the fire room. It was the golden age for labor and capital too, an age that may never return. We had passengers who were dizzy with alcohol and others who were dizzy with new money. They used to pass thousand-dollar bills around in the smoke room as guarantees of their substance. Our wages rose, and our wives, if we had wives, entertained delusions of grandeur. We all bought stock, and insured our lives; and the stock rose, and the lives became—in our own opinions—increasingly valuable. Our passengers came back from bankrupt Europe and gave out statements which showed how good and great they were and how silly Europeans were. Dividends and profits had been piling up for these gentlemen while they were in Europe. They bought Rolls-Royces for their children and fifty-thousand-dollar pearl necklaces for their wives. They took suites on our ships and brought their servants with them, their cars and their dogs. So you can understand, the commander of a ship had to keep up appearances. He had to be in the swim. Captain Nevile had married a perfectly stunning interior decorator, and he was living in the style to which she had been—to hear her tell it—accustomed. There was only one fly in the ointment. When the bills were paid at the end of the month he had very little in his pocket beyond subway fare down to the ship."

"But why did he do that? Why didn't he tell his wife?"

"I imagine because he was a gentleman. He had no equipment for matrimony, even if he hadn't been a seaman and away on an average twenty-eight days every five weeks. He had given hostages to fortune, which in America means he had to pay for all the harebrained obligations his wife happened to incur. But he had no experience of living with a woman. I doubt whether he visualized the life a seaman's wife has while her husband is away, especially when she lives in New York. And I don't suppose the apartment seemed so extravagant to him because it only carried on the style to which he was accustomed on the ship. Anyhow, I doubt if he ever alluded to the fact that they were living somewhat beyond their means. Whenever she bought something expensive, like the nine-hundred-dollar piano-player or the period radio, she always added it to the list of things she was going to pay for out of the profits of the interior decorating studio. Meanwhile, another thirty a month would be added to Captain Nevile's expenses."

"Did she make a success of her studio?"

"She would have, but she had a serious illness. A breakdown. She told me she was in the hospital for a month, but I believe it was less than that. Anyhow, the place had to be shut up and the stock sold off, at a considerable loss, of course. It was when she was convalescent that I called to see her at the request of her husband, who was away on a cruise in the Mediterranean. I happened to be in port during the week he was due back. I was curious to know how it was working. I did not know then just how strapped he was. I learned about that by accident later.

"I confess the atmosphere of that apartment, the costly furnishings, the stench of ambar cigarettes, the riot of superfluous junk she had bought, made an almost panicky impression on me. I looked at that lovely creature sitting up in her elegant bed, arrayed in an oriental coat of peacock-blue silk with gold dragons writhing up the sleeves. I looked at her imbecile patrician face, crowned with that marvelous burnished gold cap of close-curled hair, and I was frightened to death at the thought of any Englishman getting himself into such a fix. Because she hadn't an idea in her head concerning his welfare! She talked in a high-pitched yet musical warble, of how hard up they were and why didn't he have a larger salary? I asked her, bluntly, why she had to live that way? I told her that most shipmasters' wives lived in forty- or fifty-dollar a month apartments over in Brooklyn, near where I lived myself, in lodgings.

"She said, 'I can't live that way! How can you expect me to? I'd be making all kinds of money now if I hadn't had this awful breakdown.'"

"What was the matter with her?" asked Mrs. Kavanagh.

"Nothing! All she needed was a horsewhip, expertly applied where it would do most good. Do you know what she told me, her cultivated Park Avenue voice coming out from a cloud of cigarette smoke? She said, 'Father is going to get me a divorce.'

"It was the first I had heard of her family. From what young Nevile had told me, she was one of those wonderful girls who are sturdily self-supporting. 'She's done it all herself!' he chanted happily to me, when he showed me some of the photographs she had taken. When a man is in that mood you can get no information worth anything. I inquired about her father when she made this statement, and I wondered how long she would keep her husband in ignorance of her intentions.

"She said, 'Father's a darling!' which didn't get me anywhere. I watched the smoke ascending, as from altar fires. I saw the antique ash trays all over the room piled high with gilded stubs and the fine gray ash that always reminds me of the contents of funeral urns. I had an unfortunate impression—just for a moment, you know—that my young friend had married the daughter of Lamia. Absurd, of course. She had just said her father was a darling, and how could Lamia be married to a darling? But the utter impenetrability of those large violet eyes, or rather an entire lack of anything behind them, daunted me, and put all sorts of fantastic notions into my head.

"She considered her father a darling because she could get anything out of him. I saw him once; a worried architect of

Long Island palaces. This girl was all he had since his wife had run off with one of his clients. I never had the story clear because Ada never told it twice in the same way. Her parents had met when her father had gone to Egypt to build, for a rich American patron, a winter villa at Heliopolis. She said her mother was an Egyptian princess, or a Circassian princess divorced from an Egyptian pasha. I forget the exact tinge of royalty she insisted upon. I didn't verify it because I didn't believe a word of it. I mean, she had no doubt some trivial fact to build on, of course, but it meant nothing to me. A Circassian princess is like an Irish king or the dukes of Edom. She corresponds to the social arbiter of a small American town. But the illusion of royalty was enough for Ada, and she called herself Ah-ee-dah.

"At that time, I fancy, her father wasn't doing any too well, but he wanted his little girl to be happy, and if she wanted a divorce, his little girl should have it. The trim maid, in black and white, brought me a Scotch-and-soda, and I received Ada's request to speak to her husband before he came home. She had no gift for expressing herself in writing, and she dreaded a scene, she said.

"I looked at her. I suppose she would be classified by every judge of beauty as 'easy to look at'; but I looked at her, not with ease, but with the sort of curiosity I would feel on looking through the glass window of a coffin and peeping at a dead person. I want you to note she used the word 'home' without being struck dead for blasphemy. She didn't even know she was blaspheming. She had never been alive, I imagine, in the sense of straining passionately towards another human being.

"I said, 'I'll speak to him if you like. I take it you want me to head him off, keep him from coming here any more? Tell him you don't wish to live with him?' She began to weep. At any rate, she put her lovely hands to her face. Then she buried her face in the pillow. She said he had never really understood her, and she had been totally misled as to what they had to live on. Nothing could be gained by trying to do the impossible. Since her breakdown she had realized it was all a mistake.

"So there I was with a very peculiar mission. I assure you I agreed with her. I could see nothing but rocks, shoals, rapids, and quicksands ahead for them. I saw her side. I saw it better than she ever imagined! What she needs is a man always close at hand to ride her with a check rein that he isn't afraid to use, and to ply the spurs as well. It may be that her wealthy Number Four, with his Motion Picture Finance Corporation, will succeed in the job. Three other men, young Nevile and his two predecessors, have failed. The miniature painter and the professor of English at a small Southern university, who was Number One, were hopelessly incompetent. Young Nevile refused to give up so easily as that. But he was beaten in the end. Or if you prefer it, he saw better game ahead."

"That's awfully malicious of you."

"No! I am trying to show you how it came about. I said he never did anything mean or shameful, and I can prove it in this matter. I also say he was not passive either. He did noble things to make Ada stick to him. He had numberless inducements and temptations to be faithless to her. You can have no conception of the state our passengers got into during those cruises unless you were there. It was a time of almost bacchanalian release from the home-town conventions. In the classic days seamen had only to contend with sirens on the rocks, and the sacred courtesans of the myrtle groves as they passed from their ships to the wine taverns of the town. Nowadays the sirens come on board as passengers, and I think we had sacred courtesans too, priapic females who left their inhibitions like garments behind them and flung themselves with naked souls upon astonished seafarers. Ulysses had to land upon Circe's isle before she could work her magic arts. The modern Circes take double suites, and try to turn us into swine beyond the twelve-mile limit!"

"And you want me to believe they receive no encouragement?" said Mrs. Kavanagh. She was amused, for all that. What she had noticed at odd moments convinced her that even now, with a Depression reducing the speed and spending power of her countrywomen, there were some of those creatures on board the Camotan.

"It all depends on what you call encouragement," said Mr. Spenlove. "They needed precious little, I can assure you. A ship's officer is between hell and high water when women run after him. He has to exercise an extreme circumspection. Many girls, of course, are merely giving way to a passion for a uniform, like a slavey yearning after a sergeant in the Horse Guards. It's a common enough weakness, and afflicts the most exemplary virgins, as I shall tell you. But the vogue among wealthy women of older growth was like nothing in history since the days of the Roman emperors, when noble dames entered the sacred groves of Aphrodite, and Tyrian sailors took home uproarious tales of Sidonian revels on the warm beaches below the moonlit snows of Lebanon!

"Even extreme circumspection does not always work, however. It didn't in his case. But that came later. The suggestion that I act as an ambassador to him did not appeal to me, although I flatter myself I have many of the qualifications that make ambassadors successful, if not great. I suspected Ada of ulterior motives in asking me to do it. I know she exerted her arts, and for such a beautiful woman she has only the most obvious and elementary arsenal of arts, to make me feel I was her true knight whose sword should shield her from harm in a world full of base knaves.

"But see what happened. Young Nevile had been away on a cruise, and the star passenger had been a Miss Spottiswood, daughter of the man who had assembled half-a-dozen shipping companies and merged them into the Afro-Iberian Line. He is dead now, but he was a great man in our organization. He had the genius to see that just as it is more economical to have a fleet of taxis or trucks or hot-dog stands under one ownership, so it pays the manager of ships to have a hundred all operated from a central office, instead of a hundred competitors cutting each other's jugulars. So you may say he had vision as well as genius. I read many biographies of American business men, and that is what it all boils down to. They have a genius for eliminating competitors. They have the vision of an ever expanding market accompanied by an ever augmenting personal accumulation of money. Old Spottiswood had all the good and some of the evil of such men. He was a wonderful man to work for because he knew so well what he wanted and what the ships could do. He was ruthless and kind. He would spend half a million to break a strike, and give half a million to a college where young men studied the causes of social unrest and compiled works of reference that showed him up for a benevolent autocrat, an economic anachronism in any sane scheme of living.

"Well, it was his daughter—the one who was afterwards married to a prince and had a lot of trouble getting a divorce —who was the unconscious agent of bringing Captain Nevile and his wife to a reconciliation. She was a nice enough girl, but the daughters of benevolent autocrats who are millionaires have a tendency to become autocrats on their own account. She knew she could make or break anybody she disliked, I suppose. She fell in love with Captain Nevile, just as, I dare say, she fell in love with her phony prince, whose principality probably consisted of a dozen goats on a savage hillside in the Caucasus.

"You see, as the star guest, sitting at the captain's right hand at table, using his launch in shore trips, escorted by him, as by command, to the houses of the great on the Riviera and on the shores of the Adriatic, she had a rare chance to gratify her desires. And he, as the employee of her father, could not take offense, or avoid her without giving offense. She was about thirty then, and a reasonably personable young woman, but nothing to rave over. She might have won the affections of a worthy sales manager or pump draftsman if she had had no money. Young Nevile had found it difficult to preserve the exact balance of enthusiasm and frigidity for six weeks, because all the time he wanted his wife. The breakdown, the hysterical annoyance at having to give up her interior decoration atelier, had drawn him to her more than ever, had created in his mind a delicate tenderness that was even better—for her—than love, because it was entirely independent of the spurious passion she had inspired in him when he married her.

"Indeed, at this time it might easily have worked out so that they would have understood each other, grown to interpret each other's minds and established a marriage. I am not sure. I doubt if she has it in her because she is so preoccupied with her own needs, material and spiritual. She really is a spiritual gold-digger. She wants so much! The wasted frames of men's ambitions and fortunes will lie behind her as she climbs into the hills of security and plenty. So possibly I am only sentimentalizing when I say that when Virginia Spottiswood had Captain Nevile demoted, as we all believe she did, Ada Nevile had a chance to become a wife.

"She had a chance to become a poor man's wife, anyhow. So far from agreeing to the suggestion that he let his wife get a divorce, he took the initiative at once. The management said he had to go chief officer for a while, as several skippers had come back from the naval reserve and were senior to young Captain Nevile. Well, he made no complaint. When Miss Spottiswood, on her way to her father's ranch in Wyoming, called him up by long distance from Chicago, he refused to talk to her. He hung up gently and walked past the stupefied cadet who was in charge of the ship-to-shore telephone and who had dashed into the captain's cabin with the news: 'Chicago on the wire, sir! Miss Spottiswood calling, sir.'"

"But she wouldn't have done that if he hadn't given her some sort of encouragement—some response," said Mrs. Kavanagh quickly.

"You may be right; but who is to define encouragement as a woman recognizes it? I can't. I have a fumbling, embryonic theory that if only our rich young women had some secret groves of myrtle and ilex into which they could plunge, to discover temples wherein gods awaited them, they would behave much more rationally on their return to the everyday world. As it is, they are the victims of illusion when dealing with mortal men. They imagine a man means all he says, that he controls his emotions, and is therefore responsible for what he says and does during those thrilling moments that a woman knows how to evoke. He may be only waiting for her to make an end!"

"You talk as if you knew a lot about women," said Mrs. Kavanagh grimly.

"Only an humble student," said Mr. Spenlove, smiling; "a lay reader of hearts! A janitor in the House of Life, who sees the lovelorn pass in and out. I am the spectator who sees most of the game.

"Young Nevile was perfectly clear at this time. He wanted to keep his job, of course, even if it had become only a mate's job temporarily. He knew the office would hear of him being on long distance with the Spottiswood girl, and that they would get a garbled version of the story. And he wanted to keep his wife. When I went to see him he was packing his gear to move over to another ship as Number One, and he had his line of action ready. He could not prevent Ada getting a divorce, but he was going up to see her. He was going to make her come with him to an apartment suitable to his new salary —about a couple of hundred a month. She would have to do that or he would refuse to be responsible.

"He showed a quiet efficiency about it, too. He had been figuring things out and had written his brother to send him the money, about four hundred pounds, he had over there. There had to be an end of all this extravagance, not because he grudged Ada anything, but because they had to live on his salary. I sat on his settee while he stowed his dunnage, and

enjoyed a lecture on thrift! It was a rather queer line for him
to take, but I understood him all right. It was a subtle reaction from the experience he had had with Virginia Spottiswood, whose old man gave her a couple of thousand a month
for clothes. He had had a dizzy glimpse of an unfamiliar country, and it had sent him scurrying back to something he
understood.

"The joke of this is that Ada fell for it like a shot. Or perhaps it would be more honest to say that after further talks
with her darling father, who had probably suggested she wait
a bit before starting proceedings, she broke out in a fresh
place. She went Greenwich Village. It was all the rage at
that time. I have seen a Rolls-Royce waiting outside con-
verted stables to take some young thing home after a party
in her Village studio. I was once taken by a passenger to a
party on Christopher Street in an upper chamber, like that
other gathering where the Holy Spirit descended upon them.
I remember, as a precious souvenir of those days, a policeman
and a West Pointer asleep in each other's arms, and a guest,
attired in royal robes, singing the Marseillaise. Art was long
and skirts were short, and the best people were going down
below Fourteenth Street to get rid of their inhibitions. I think
it was Freud who sent Ada down there. She had just discovered the new vocabulary from Vienna. A psychoanalyst who
had treated her told her she ought to release her inhibitions
in some artistic activity. I'm not sure of the exact nature of
his advice. Ada was a perfect receiving set for the new gospel.
It fitted perfectly her vigorous yet infantile mentality. It
flattered her ego enormously to have a pseudo-scientific explanation of her dislike of sustained regular work and the
responsibilities of marriage. She kept a libido very much as
my sister in England keeps a yellow tomcat.

"Even her husband, Captain Nevile, now chief officer, was
startled by the sudden change. I fancy her father had not
been doing too well that year. Building palaces for plutocrats
with paper profits sometimes leaves an architect suddenly

with a lot of unsalable blueprints and specifications. And she had sensed the rising boom for slumming in the Village. Women she knew were doing well in tea rooms with astonishing names. Others were making money out of batiks and Russian hardware. So, when young Nevile issued his ultimatum, she almost took the words out of his mouth. She wanted to live in the Village. She was going to do caricatures. She had been playing around, during her convalescence, with crayons. Yes, she can draw, a little. She can paint, a little. She can model, a little. She can sing, a little. So now it was caricatures and long-legged French dolls, of which she had a large number. She was going to design them and sell them and make lots of money. Dolls as caricatures of celebrated persons. Dolls as portrait studies for the smart world at fifty dollars each. Dolls in group formation, expressing Armistice Night in Paris, or the Russian Revolution. Things like that.

"So down they went. They even sold all the stuff in the apartment because it wasn't in tune with a Village studio. It was a week or two before his new ship came in, so he was able to go around with her to the junk shops and watch her collect Armenian hammered brass trays and Algerian camel bells and a prayer rug like an old sack that had been left out in the wind and dried in a lime kiln. They had a place up four flights of stairs with a flat roof outside the back room. There were a concrete urn and a black iron seat out there. Ada took possession and began to produce another of her peculiar conceptions of a home for a man. It had one advantage. It was within his income for a while. It gave him a breathing spell, as a man might find a precarious foothold on the edge of a cliff before going over. . . .

"Because the novelty soon wore off the new life for Ada. She hadn't the resources of the Village belles. She might smoke a hundred cigarettes a day, but she disliked liquor, and she had an aversion to the sexual divagations of the young people who sprawled on her studio floor and dragged the cushions out onto the roof on summer nights. It sounds strange possibly, but she wasn't that sort at all. She found she was, to use her own expression to me, 'in the wrong pew.' Painters who wanted to paint her portrait and then sleep with her; dealers who were willing to place a nice order for dolls if she would join a party to Atlantic City, were evaded and fobbed off with vague hypocritical promises of future assignations. She hadn't any morals of that sort at all, if you know what I mean. She remained faithful in that sense just as she never drank gin or ate caviare. She disliked all three luxuries. What Ada was interested in was Ada: her face, her figure, her future, her ambition. A lover was as superfluous as an extra ten pounds added through eating pastry.

"When she slumped, she slumped in her own way. She lost heart, as we say. She became slack in the apartment. She got the habit of not getting up until noon, or later. She would leave the dishes in the sink and go out for the day. I think her real dislike of me began the afternoon I called at the Fourth Street studio and found her still in bed.

"The place hadn't been cleaned for a week. The dust lay on the tables, and the painted floor was littered with matches and glasses. There had been a party, I suppose, some recent evening. The sink was full of dishes. Cups and saucers were on the mantelpiece, and there were glass rings all over the place. Some oranges and a glass of milk were on a tray by her bed. She had sprung up and pulled on a peignoir as she came to open the door.

"'You!' she said. 'I thought it was Sidney. You'll have to excuse the condition the place is in. I haven't been well to-day.'

"She looked well enough. She was taking the utmost care of herself. Although she was not dressed or made up to receive visitors I could see she was in as good condition as ever. Nothing ever deflected her from the essentials of her ambition. When I say she slumped, she was still living on fruit and milk, keeping her weight down and her skin miraculously smooth and clear.

"Young Nevile's ship was over in drydock, and he had been getting away to dinner each evening for several evenings. And he was coming home to this? I said, before I could stop myself. She gave me a blank violet stare and carried a cup and saucer into the kitchenette. The cup was stuck fast to the saucer. She said they went out to dinner. What else did I expect with a salary like Sidney's? She had to do everything on a hundred and eighty a month. Everything! So he had five dollars a week for himself, I thought. I noticed her stockings were as expensive as ever, and her mules were new, with osprey feathers on the instep. Not five dollars a week for himself, I thought! She looked at me with that blank violet stare and dropped another cigarette stub on the pile. She didn't offer me tea, though it was tea-time. She was absorbed in her own problem, of how to get out of the mess she had got herself into by marrying a sailor.

"I did a little missionary work. I felt I owed it to myself to make her see I didn't regard this horrible dust heap as a home for a man. I might as well have preached to the heathen. She never budged from her conviction that she ought to have great possessions. I tried to make her see this present situation wouldn't last long, that young Nevile would have a command again and four hundred a month possibly. She gave me a straight look and said it wasn't enough. She had had to ask her father for money. She had bills Sidney didn't know about, for clothes. She couldn't go on like this, anyway. I might have saved my breath. My suggestion that this period was a test of her fortitude she didn't even hear. I even mentioned the pioneer women, the heroic mothers who went West and nursed their children in the wilderness and endured hardships; but Ada wasn't having any of my blarney. She said she had to have money or she would die. This place was getting on her nerves.

"I agreed with her about that. I said that if I came back from a clean ship to a place like theirs I didn't know what I would do. Commit suicide probably. I said, 'You aren't really a married woman at all, Ada. And you'll never make a sailor's wife. It's a highly specialized, skilled trade, being married to a shipmaster.'

"I expanded this theme until young Nevile came in. He was slightly embarrassed when he saw me, but I could ignore that because I knew he was glad of a third person present when he came home. That is the most critical period in such cases, when a man who is striving to fulfill his ideal of a husband dreads being alone with his wife. The fact which was plain to me was that these two had no community of interests. Ada couldn't even concentrate for a moment on the profession by which her husband earned his living. If he had made twenty thousand a year by it she might have made an effort. And he couldn't understand that the source of her misery was her lack of background, of tradition, and a lack of confidence in her own personal existence. He took too much for granted, like most Englishmen and all sailors. Of course, in the sense you understand it, no seaman can be married unless he takes his wife to sea and lives with her all over the watery globe. I'm not sure that is a solution either, because she is out of her element then. It's like expecting an oyster to take up bicycling, to demand domestic qualities of a woman while sailing about. No, that's not a solution; and anyway, shipmasters don't have the chance nowadays to carry their wives. Young Nevile and Ada were becoming strangers to each other again. The bright crystals of their passion were breaking down into dusty dross. Their illusions were dissolving before their eyes. They were really so grateful to have a third person with them that they were almost drawn into a fresh friendship for each other!

"So the crisis was tided over again! They turned over a new leaf. Before his ship sailed Ada pulled suddenly out of that dreadful smelly walk-up place and found an apartment on Twelfth Street, in one of the old houses, with high ceilings and tall windows. She was going back into photography, she said. The front room, with a bedroom off it, was an ideal studio, and there was a kitchen and living room at the back. Young Nevile was delighted at the change. He believed it was a move in the right direction. When I saw them, the night before I sailed, they had their arms around each other as they said good-bye. They believed! And I believed too that it might work out after all. Lay readers of hearts are almost as often mistaken as the hearts themselves!

"I remembered that night because I did not see young Nevile again until a couple of voyages later, when he was moved to my ship as mate. No command in sight after all. He had to wait his turn. Or was it something the Spottiswood girl was doing, all unknown to us? I was sure of it. Now I don't think so. It was merely the routine of the office, and he had to wait until all the other senior skippers were provided for. He wasn't the only young man in the company who had to stand back for a while. The trouble with him was he had no money. He couldn't save a cent with Ada dependent upon him, and he couldn't get that money out of his brother. It was 'safely invested.' So safely, in fact, he has never seen it since.

"There was every chance that he was about to settle down into a failure, a dependable chief officer, ignored by the office. The sort of chap whose place is instantly filled by another exactly like him and who is as instantly forgotten. The temptation lay in the chances to make good ashore so that he would quit the sea. The big boom was on. Money was being made by everybody, apparently. One of my engineers quit us suddenly, to sell bonds, of all things in the world. He sold some of his bonds to the fellows on the ships, and they would like to get hold of him now! They hung on too long and lost all their money. Even skippers quit, to get good jobs ashore. They became executives . . . ah well!

"Young Nevile might have been one of the first to succumb, you would have thought, but he did not. He did not even when it was almost a threat. He refused all the agreeable prospects passengers held out for him because, so he told me,

'I am a ship's officer. I know nothing about business, and would only feel a fool in an office. I'll wait. I'll have a ship soon.'

"He was justified. He was ordered to Scotland to bring out a new ship. Old Spottiswood, with one bark over the telephone, settled that. Whether he knew what had happened between young Nevile and his daughter I can't say. He simply designated him to go and bring out that ship.

"Sidney came across to see me in Havana Harbor. He was on the way back to New York, his last voyage as mate. He had just had a letter instructing him to go to Glasgow. I congratulated him.

"'Now,' I said, 'it will stick. You have a ship. She'll be yours until you get a better one. That's the style! Ada will be able to hold up her head again! I'm very pleased!'

"'No,' he said slowly, 'Ada has left me. She wants a separation. She says I am trying to dominate her in making her live on my pay, and she cannot develop her personality. She has left me. The place was locked up when I got home last time. She wants a separation.'

"'What does she want to do now?' I inquired. He said she had written some free verse, but her interest was now in motion pictures. 'She's had a screen test,' he said.

"I did a few minutes' thinking. It is a dangerous thing to advise anyone in a case like that. I temporized. 'How long are you going on like this?' I said. 'You'll have a heavy stone around your neck all your life. You'll never have a good bank account at this rate. You won't be able to face a day's unemployment. Why don't you make a clean cut of it and start afresh? She'll be back, you know,' I said. 'Free-verse writers always come back.' I didn't know this for a fact, but I had never heard of a free-verse writer who didn't need financial support, so I took a chance.

"He said, 'I can't desert Ada so long as she needs me. I've written to her asking if she wants to come with me. They say I can take my wife if I want to.'

"'Has she accepted?' I said. 'No, she won't go,' he told me. 'But I'll have to leave her provided for.'

"He did, too. He left her half pay, and although I believe she was then going around with the fellow she is now engaged to marry she accepted it. I don't mean she was unfaithful in the adulterous sense. Ada has never done that. Never! She is too calculating, and there is a touch of Mrs. Grundy deep down under all the froth and blather of her Freudian posturings. That isn't her line. I suppose she knows instinctively that you can't get a man that way. She's fond of telling you, with a blank violet stare and her head raised, to hide a faint suspicion of double chin: 'I have no inhibitions.' Hasn't she? She's nothing else but inhibitions. What she means is, she has no prudish objections to discussing other women's lack of inhibitions. She's a lovely creature! In her own way a gifted creature, and she has no inhibitions against letting a man give her all kinds of costly things and even pay her bills, without conceding him an inch of real intimacy."

Mrs. Kavanagh, after glancing at the clock, attempted a sneer at Mr. Spenlove's lack of Christian charity.

"She has the gift of keeping a man as long as she wants him, anyhow," she added, though she knew it was a poor retort.

"That I grant you, and it is a great gift too. It is the one essential quality of American womanhood that, for her, chastity is no longer identical with virtue. It is her contribution to the spiritual life of our day."

"That isn't what I meant," said Mrs. Kavanagh. She got up, for it was time to prepare for dinner. The warning gong was roaring and droning in a distant corridor. Mr. Spenlove pretended surprise.

"Well, what did you mean? That Mrs. Nevile was fighting with the weapons with which nature had provided her? I could have said that, but I recognize the spark of intelligence in Ada that differentiates her from her jungle sisters. She——"

Mrs. Kavanagh waved her hand in derision.

"She certainly made you fall in love with her!" she said as she passed out.

Mr. Spenlove escorted her to the upper decks.

VIII

MR. SPENLOVE, because of his extensive and peculiar familiarity with the world, never suffered from stage fright. But he came near it when he approached his table in the saloon that evening and saw all the seats save his own occupied. He had a remarkable momentary sensation of confronting four people, complete strangers, who had mysteriously purloined the bodies of his acquaintances for the evening and sat, not quite certain of the success of their experiment, waiting to see what he might do about it.

The second steward, who was near at hand for a reason Mr. Spenlove failed to divine immediately, held the latter's chair ready. Mr. Spenlove bowed as he sat down and cast another glance at the four faces. This time he became aware of the girl on his right. She was wearing black tulle out of which rose very white shoulders and throat, and he noticed a fine gold chain around her neck, which held suspended a small gold locket in the deep cleft of her bosom as she leaned forward to eat. There was a white arm near him, too, on whose wrist was an antique gold bracelet. And then Mr. Spenlove looked for the first time into the eyes of Athalie Rhys, the owner of the arm and the bracelet.

He heard himself making a number of jocular remarks. He said he had begun to doubt her existence, and had even cross-examined the purser as to whether she had actually come on board. He called Mrs. Kavanagh to witness that he and she were planning to write a thriller called *The Missing Heiress*. He said Mr. O'Relly had been sending radio messages to his paper about the new sea mystery, and Captain Nevile had

been walking up and down for hours with binoculars trying to
sight a passenger overboard.

The girl colored deeply and showed teeth so extraordinarily
lovely, so obviously genuine, in a momentary charming smile
that impressed Mr. Spenlove as something unfamiliar and
seductive. It indicated, it seemed to him, that she understood
his teasing as well as the seclusion which had inspired it, and
also that she was extremely virtuous and good. He said to
her, in a slightly mocking tone:

"You see you have set us all by the ears. Finally we were
convinced you were on board but hiding. We have all been
unhappy because we thought you had something against us.
We sent out ambassadors. I mean, Captain Nevile volun-
teered. He brought back word that if we were very good indeed you might relent and mingle with us mortals."

While he kept his smile upon the girl Mr. Spenlove was well
aware of Mrs. Kavanagh's restlessness under this neglect.
Miss Rhys colored even more deeply and turned her head
from side to side as though seeking a way of escape.

"You embarrass me," she whispered in a sweet childish
voice.

There was something mysteriously alluring in the conjunc-
tion of her woman's body, the face resembling Rossetti's
Lilith, though the hair was bobbed and tawny, like a bronze
helmet, and the childish voice. Mr. Spenlove had no time to
meditate upon the origins of love. He became aware of something like hate on his left. He saw Mrs. Kavanagh vibrate as
she kicked her brother under the table. He saw Mr. O'Relly's
rapt features harden for a moment as his shin encountered a
sharp, furious heel. Yet what was he doing, Mr. Spenlove
demanded of himself? He did not believe that Miss Rhys was
permitting any of those advances under cover which are so
large a part of the alcoholic amorism of these days. He associated correctly the expression on Mrs. Kavanagh's face with
the concentrated feminism on his right. It was beginning to
dawn upon Mr. Spenlove that he had hitherto underesti-

mated the hatred some women have for others, and this girl
seemed to be one of the others. The discovery, which took
place while he was disposing of his mulligatawny, gave him a
great deal of pleasure. What might happen after the Camotan
left Kingston nobody knew, but in the meantime he felt life
would be full of interest.

He was sure, now that he saw the attitude of the two men
facing him, two men so utterly different in race, tradition,
training, and profession, that Mrs. Kavanagh was guided by
an infallible instinct. To women like her, sequestered as they
were in domestic forts all over the world, and protected by
their men, the problem consisted in preventing those men
from going over to the enemy. It was a situation after his own
heart, he decided. He took another glance at the girl on his
right.

They were talking of a kidnaping case in the radio news
that morning. A young woman had been kidnaped out of a
wealthy home. A large sum was demanded of the husband for
her safe return. The newspapers were successfully hindering
officials from doing anything by publishing every move in
advance. Mr. Spenlove heard the sweet childish voice, like
the melodious twitter of a bird, tell of how she had been
"almost" kidnaped. Gangsters had entered her apartment in
New York. She had been in bed. The barking of her "dear
little dog" had frightened them, and she had just strength
to reach for the telephone and call the police before she
fainted.

Mr. Spenlove hardly dared to look at Mrs. Kavanagh. He
managed to remark, over his fish, that this was right up her
street. She could get the impressions of a lady about to be
kidnaped at first hand, straight from the stable, as they say
in racing circles. Mr. O'Relly was not listening to this. He
was taking advantage of his sister's stunned expression to
get information. Where was this? he was inquiring. And did
Miss Rhys live alone in New York. The Village? What street?
And so on.

He did not get that, Mr. Spenlove noted with a quite illogical satisfaction. He was sure young Nevile had it, though.
The girl's eyes, greenish hazel they seemed, in the one glimpse
Mr. Spenlove had of them, were rarely raised from her food,
and when they were, rested on young Nevile for an instant.
That instant showed Mr. Spenlove that she had an interest
there. A definite interest.

Mention of the Village, however, roused Mrs. Kavanagh.
Terry's wife, the creature who had never realized the enormous privilege conferred on her in becoming Mrs. Terry
O'Relly, who had deserted Terry without ever even trying
to understand him, had come from Greenwich Village, and
Mrs. Kavanagh had no use for the goings-on down there. It
was what she would have expected, to learn that this Miss
Whatshername had an apartment in the Village and lived
there alone. Terry received another sharp one on the shin,
and it roused him enough to glance away from the magical
girl at his side and say "Hey!" to no one in particular. He
also drew his feet under his chair so that the head waiter,
from his post near by, marveled again at a passenger who
wore holes in his shoes near the toes and had run-over heels
as well.

It had its effect, however, unexpectedly, and Mr. O'Relly's
ejaculation seemed to frighten the girl into a close attention
to her dinner. If, Mr. Spenlove said to himself, one could call
some spinach and a poached egg, a few crackers and a glass
of milk, a dinner. And she did not explain where she did
live.

Mr. Spenlove found himself as much at sea as his companions, and wondered whether he would ever again feel as
natural as he was accustomed. There was a peculiar feeling in
the air, augmented by the expression of extraordinary happiness and pride on the face of young Captain Nevile as he
talked to Mrs. Kavanagh, who was on his right. Doing this,
he tacitly left Miss Rhys to Mr. O'Relly, and for that Mrs.
Kavanagh was furious. It showed up Terry's weak point. He

was awfully clever, of course, but he could not make small talk with a strange woman without flirting in a crude way that suggested a city slicker dating up the bathing beauty at a local beach opening. For a while Mr. Spenlove, left out of the conversation, was able to contemplate the cause of this situation at his table, but he was unable to diagnose the trouble.

Because, he thought, she is not beautiful in any conventional style. There was a defect in her nose or on one nostril that eluded definition. She had, truly, a miraculously clear skin, yet it was freckled on the shoulders and under the greenish-hazel eyes, which were narrow and almond-like. Slowly it dawned on Mr. Spenlove that while Mrs. Kavanagh was rouged and had used an orange lipstick, the other had no make-up at all. Or had she? She gave him occasional momentary illusions of a milkmaid who had just left a prudish high school after living all her life with a vegetarian maiden aunt. She had a trick of dropping into what seemed a chaste dream, of years spent in a hygienic convent, and awaking, when addressed, with the movement of an extremely well-bred but startled fawn.

Mr. Spenlove reproached himself at the very moment of arriving at these conclusions. It was, he insisted hypocritically, the ancient antagonism of the veteran, virtuous married woman for the girl who has her chances ahead. Nothing more. Mrs. Kavanagh was human, and why not? He himself seemed to be human too, for this girl fitted into no pigeonhole in his extensive knowledge of women. She was no pigeon, for that matter, and he could think of no bird, whether eagle, wild duck, or barnyard fowl, that she resembled. Even when he heard again the sweet childish treble telling Mr. O'Relly "Never mind!" as that gentleman returned to the matter of her address in New York. "Never mind! I may not be back for ages!" and something about "an estate"—not even then did it occur to Mr. Spenlove that this was as natural to her as breathing and not artifice at all.

"I understand," he said, when he had a chance, "that you are going to visit your people in Jamaica."

She said "Oh!" as though stricken and then, coloring deeply, bowed her head. "My father," she whispered, and gave Mr. Spenlove a scared glance from the long greenish-hazel eyes, "has estates there. Yes, English, you know."

"Well, we are celebrated all over the world for our filial feelings," he told her, "but you can't expect us in America to think of you in the same way as we would if you were going to see your mother. You know how Mother's Day affects us."

"My mother," she said in the same low tone, "is in heaven. She died when I was born."

It was like the sound of temple bells far away, he thought, as he said he was sorry. The deep blush on her cheek faded slowly, and she raised her eyes to smile divinely at him and tell him it was quite all right. The anniversary of her mother's death was her own birthday, and she had her mother's portrait and a lock of her hair in . . . she laid a finger on the locket that dangled between her swelling breasts.

Merciful heaven! Mr. Spenlove thought, what have we here? I shall begin to snuffle myself soon, if this goes on.

He was disturbed beyond his own imaginings, and he saw young Nevile smile as though he understood perfectly how confusing everyone must find this girl whom he had marked for his own. Mr. Spenlove saw Mrs. Kavanagh smiling also, but her smile was less reassuring than young Nevile's. Mrs. Kavanagh was holding herself in nobly. For a woman struggling to repress a desire to tear her opponent limb from limb and to scatter those limbs upon the surface of the blue sea outside, she was behaving with singular politeness. But why should she? complained Mr. Spenlove to himself, as he removed the foil from his two pieces of Roquefort. Why should this kind of girl set up these cataclysms in a married woman's soul? Mr. Spenlove had heard matrons trumpeting against the boom-time flappers who sat in the smoke room yelling stridently at young men and calling for highballs. But this girl was refusing a cigarette while Mrs. Kavanagh was lighting what was doubtless the fiftieth cigarette of the day. The girl was declining dessert, timidly asking the steward to bring her—what was it she wanted? Mr. Spenlove speculated. He was gratified a few minutes later, to see an apple arrive. Eve! He wondered whether Mrs. Kavanagh would hold that as evidence of guile. It was possible, he decided, because her animosity was merely a residual instinct in operation and had no basis in reason at all. And then, catching sight of the abyss of conjecture opening before him as he pursued this train of thought, he drew back and endeavored to find out whether Miss Rhys might be dieting for some special ordeal in sport. But he knew she was not. She had the wrists neither of a tennis player nor a golfer. She had, he was able to declare to himself, with almost mystical enthusiasm, the wrists of a lady of the eighteenth century, who was always carried in a sedan chair, and for whom doors were opened by powdered footmen.

He had a chance, while securing a cigar in his cabin and lighting it, to reflect upon the whole business. He had had nothing to drink all day, yet he felt as if the conclusions he had reached about that girl were the result of an indulgence in heady liquor. She had an atmosphere, he told himself, and immediately dismissed the word atmosphere as grotesquely inadequate. He drew in the first superb inhalations from his Havana. A woman is only a woman, he remembered, but even that whiskered old bromide failed him. Not in this case! he was compelled to confess. She seemed to be something a shade more mysterious than the ordinary passenger, at any rate. He understood now Mrs. Kavanagh's peculiar maneuvers since the Camotan left New York. She had felt it in the air! She had had premonitions. She had been instantly sensitive to warnings which had eluded his own coarser masculine intelligence.

When the cigar was drawing properly he turned to go out.

He wanted to discover Mrs. Kavanagh's opinion. He saw Captain Nevile at the door and beckoned him in.

"What do you think of her? Isn't she everything I said she was?"

Mr. Spenlove remained leaning against his desk, looking down at the young man who now sat on the settee, his evening clothes remarkable in the dun-colored surroundings of a chief engineer's cabin. The clothes were new and very modish, and the handsome head with the close-curled hair touched at the ears with gray, the mobile mouth smiling in confidence and the steady gray eyes fixed upon his old friend, were all reflected in the mirror across the room. Mr. Spenlove grunted.

"For a man who was through with women and looking forward to a life of celibacy only a few hours ago, practically, you have staged a most remarkable recovery," he said.

"I know, Fred. I know it seems awfully inconsistent. But am I not justified? Did you ever meet a girl as marvelous as she is?"

"You're bewitched, Sidney. Now's the time to keep a double watch and look out for danger. What do you know about her? I mean factually."

"Well, she's English . . ."

"Well, good God! And because she's English you swallow everything, hook, line, and sinker! You wouldn't make such an imbecile mistake if we were at home in England, would you? How, may I ask, do you know she's English? Her voice might be Oklahoma or plain Tennessee."

"Well, she's been a long while in the States."

"Doing what? Living in an apartment by herself? While her father lives in Jamaica by himself? Come alive, Sidney!"

"I don't pretend to know all about her, Fred, but I'll go bail she's genuine. She has her own money, I fancy, and coming down to visit her father is, well, rather decent of her, I would say. They are a very old family from Central Wales."

"I've never heard of Central Wales, Sidney, and it sounds like London, England, Paris, France, and the social column in a small Texas City. You haven't heard of Central Wales either, except from Miss Rhys. I grant you it's Welsh, unless it's from New South Wales."

"Fred, you're prejudiced."

"I certainly am prejudiced, but not against her. What I'm prejudiced against is the folly of offering me all this problematical stuff before you have any sound earth under your feet. I admit she's unusual. But wait, wait!"

"Fred, I'm afraid I'm in love at last!"

"At last! Io, Hymenæe! Are you going to ask Wensley to splice you on the ship? He wouldn't do it."

"Oh, of course not. You bet I'm not asking anybody in the Line to butt into my affairs any more. I'm coming back under my own power."

"What do you mean, coming back?"

"I mean I'm going to get my command back some day, and not a very distant day. Now I've got Athalie to work for."

"This is the most astounding lunacy I ever heard from a supposedly sane man," said Mr. Spenlove calmly. He waved his hand at young Nevile, who faced him steadily. "Think, man, think! How do you . . . Why, you don't know she isn't married already!"

A stubborn expression appeared on Captain Nevile's face. He shrugged his shoulders.

"You can't be a very good judge, Fred, if you think she would act the way she has—with me—while she was married. Of course, there's an obstacle. But I've given my word of honor to say nothing."

"I'll bet you have! Well, it's not my funeral, Sidney. Only I'm sorry. I want you to be happy, but you need a little sense in going into a new affair. Won't you ever learn any? Won't you ever get hold of the fact that the women who attract you are always what are called 'attractive'? That they are never the kind of women who would be any use to you as wives?"

"What possible objection could you have to Athalie as a

wife, Fred? She's good! I mean she's good as well as attractive."

"She may be too good to be true."

"That's not so! If I don't know, how can you be so dogmatic?"

"Well, what makes that Mrs. Kavanagh so hostile? She wants to kill that girl. She says she's vamping Mr. O'Relly, giving him encouragement."

"Is that so? Well, Fred, I'll give Mr. O'Relly all the rope he wants to hang himself. If Mrs. Kavanagh says that, all she's got is her own suspicions. We—Athalie and I—have both been decent to him because I'm getting him interested in this club. He can handle our publicity in New York and Washington, and he's simply mad about fishing. It's an ideal combination. But as for Athalie—well, I'm afraid she has given Mrs. Kavanagh an unfortunate impression."

"That's a very mild description of what she's given Mrs. Kavanagh," said Mr. Spenlove, looking at his cigar. "You talk as if you'd known this girl all your life."

"I feel as if I had," said young Nevile gravely, "I feel as if she was my dream woman. Yes, I know it sounds rot to you, but you are too cynical about girls, Fred."

"Dear, dear! Why, she must be all of twenty-five or twenty-six, Sidney."

"What's the odds if she is? Could she keep that complexion if she was anything but genuine?"

"There you have me. I don't take bets of that kind. But why isn't this lovely creature married long before you heave to alongside? You aren't asking me to believe in elective affinities, are you? Not again!"

"I don't know what you mean."

"I know you don't. I'm taking too much for granted in assuming you know how to take care of yourself now you are out of your element. Because that is what you are, Sidney. You haven't any charts for the course you're on now. Complexion! Does she say her prayers?"

"As it happens, she does."

"Then all I can say is, be careful! I see danger ahead for you, my boy. I don't know what the danger is. I don't know your inamorata any better than you do, but I have a premonition, only a premonition, that things are not what they seem. Think of Mrs. Kavanagh. She's a Celt. She has second sight. She doesn't like your Miss Rhys at all."

"Mrs. Kavanagh seems a very decent middle-class middle-aged person to me," said young Nevile, getting up, "but nothing to write home about in intelligence."

"So that's your opinion! I can tell you she's extremely gifted," said Mr. Spenlove, but he laughed reminiscently. "Go on, Sidney. Go on to your new life. Don't chuck your hat over the moon. Wait."

"I've waited too long," said the young man. "Too long for my own good. Now I have found the real thing, you want me to wait—and lose it!"

Mr. Spenlove counted on his fingers the exact number of hours since young Nevile had sat in this cabin declaring that he had done with all women.

"I admit that. I'm inconsistent. But I hadn't met Athalie then. You'll change, Fred, when you know her better. She's wonderful. She's—how shall I put it?—well, she's a lady of quality. Awfully old-fashioned, too. Do you know where she was born? In Berkeley Square! It's a fact. And she's been presented at court too. Yes, you can laugh! She has everything."

"Sidney, do you remember the yacht? The Honorable Maeve, daughter of Baron Sternborough of Boule Court?"

"Those people! They were just new-rich snobs. This is the real thing, man."

"Well, you have the advantage of me. You hold the world's record for self-delusion, I fancy."

"Wait till you know her. Wait till you know what I know. I'm sorry, Fred, but this is jolly important to me. I've got to go now. I promised to walk around top side. The moon is magnificent tonight."

"Very suitable, Sidney. You are a lunatic. You're moon-struck."

"No, Fred. Saner than ever in my life. Fancy comparing her with Maeve! Why, Athalie's people have been in Debrett since the seventeenth century!"

"Go on, Sidney. Don't keep her waiting. I never thought you'd backslide like this."

"We'll come and see you, Fred, in the country."

"And bring a copy of Debrett with you, with the references marked."

The door closed and was held by the short hook. Mr. Spenlove sat down for a moment, drawing on his cigar. Now that he had relieved himself of his own forebodings he felt better. It was one of his favorite philosophic axioms that a man's preoccupation with the affairs of another was never altruistic, no matter how disinterested they might seem. He was forced to the conclusion that his criticism of that girl's credentials was really a doubt of his own ability to remain calmly observant. If she was an impostor she stood every chance, he told himself, of arousing his own interest. And he had no wish to have it aroused. He had had his follies, heaven knew (though no one else did), and he dreaded any more at his time of life. He suspected also that there was a streak of truth behind young Nevile's infatuation. She was, beyond all peradventure, something new. History, Mr. Spenlove reminded himself, held no record of any man successfully resisting that particular temptation.

IX

HE FOUND MRS. KAVANAGH in her chair, which she had had moved to the seclusion of the after promenade. She was alone, and she pointed to the knot of shadows on the forward port rail gazing eastward, where a faint light glowed at intervals.

"They are looking at Watling Island. It is one of the thrills we offer you Americans. They say Watling Island is the San Salvador of Columbus, his first sight of American land."

"Don't you believe it?"

"Professionally, yes. Just as I believe Dr. Johnson sat in the Cheshire Cheese. We don't know he didn't. We don't know Watling Island was not the navigator's landfall. It was possible, for he wasn't a navigator at all, only a great illusionist."

"Now you're just trying to be clever."

"I am serious, Mrs. Kavanagh. Wasn't it characteristic of America to be discovered by an illusionist? I have read a book which tried to make him out a Jew. I have read another book in which, standing on the deck of the Santa Maria, he could see the towers of Manhattan. The author of that book said America was the grave of Europe. He was an American, and his intentions were not entirely clear to me. I fancy he meant one had to be born again, rise from the dead, in a way, if one wished to put on immortality in America. Or perhaps he was disdainful of America's interest in materialism and regarded her as a mere mausoleum of dead ideals. Take your choice."

"All that about Columbus! Well, he came, anyway. You aren't trying to prove he never existed, I suppose. Or that America doesn't?"

"No. Only suggesting he was looking for China and died believing he had found India. They were so sure in those days America didn't exist that they called it something else. Imagine the risk you all ran of being known today as West Indians! It's a perfectly easy thesis to maintain. America is a much more suitable name, though. God's country, but bearing the name of a wop who never even set eyes on it, and who stole the fame of Cristoforo Colombo."

"Well, I don't care! You're only trying to make me mad.

Unless an Englishman does it you think it's nothing. You certainly have a sublime contempt for everybody else. Is it a big island?"

"Quite small. It hasn't any real significance. Even Columbus, poor navigator as he was, could hardly help running into one of these islands. There are scores of them around here. It isn't lighted up in honor of Columbus, but for the guidance of our navigators. Captain Wensley is now gazing at it. He knows he has two days more before he docks when he sees that faint light on his beam."

"Did Captain Nevile do all this when he was commanding a ship?"

"Of course. Very well too. He always raises his lights just where he expects them. It seems to be a sort of natural aptitude in some men. Others are less confident. It is a professional mystery to me."

"It seems a pity, having to quit and take up something else, the way he had to do."

"He wasn't at all eager to do it, I assure you. He suffered from the fact that he had offended a woman who had the power to strike him down."

"I want to hear about that. I thought you said he had escaped Miss Spottiswood."

"It wasn't Miss Spottiswood. It was because he was doing the right thing for Miss Spottiswood that he offended another girl on the ship. That was Esther Davidge. She hadn't any intention of doing him any harm either. She only wanted him for herself.

"I told you how he had to step back to chief officer for a while and finally received orders, confirmed by old Mr. Spottiswood himself, to go over to Glasgow and bring out a new ship, the Santander. It was a new start for him. He had been in double jeopardy for some time. When a man has to take a lower rank and domestic disaster as well, he is a bad spiritual risk. On the other hand, if he comes through without damage to his character, he receives a high rating."

"He went off while I was down South, and he left his half pay to Ada, who accepted it as merely her right. What? Well, it may have been, from your standpoint as a married woman, but you'll never get me to agree to it. She had gradually built up in her mind a conviction that her husband had fooled her. She nursed the grievance that he had led her to believe he had money, or a large salary. It varied when she talked to me about it. I paid her several visits because she fascinated me as well as repelled me. I was also curious to know how she passed the time.

"She was glad to see me, too, in spite of her suspicion that I saw through her. I was obliged to admit that she looked very well in her new rôle, or rather her old rôle, as a photographer. She seemed to know something about it too. She developed a line of her own. She would take pictures of two, or perhaps a group, of her extraordinary dolls, posed as lovers, or in some easily recognizable imitation, with strong lights and cunning shadows, and sell them to advertising firms."

"Then she *was* clever," said Mrs. Kavanagh.

"Undoubtedly. She had a cleverness all her own. I don't remember denying it. Every woman has. The trouble with Ada is twofold. Her cleverness needs a rich soil in which to grow, and it is of no use to her husband."

"It was perfectly easy to see that her new establishment on West Twelfth Street wasn't being paid for out of that half pay. And the second time I called she introduced me to her friend who was an executive in motion pictures. At that time he was making a lot of money out of a small studio up in Yonkers, which he sold to a large combine that took him in as a vice president.

"She will be Mrs. Aubry Gainsborough when she marries him. It is curious how sure I feel that this time it will stick. Abraham Gunzbarth he was born, in Upper Silesia, and he is devoted to her. He was excessively formal and courteous to me when I met him, and it wasn't long before I was in possession of what he called 'our side of it.'

"Their side of it was that the marriage with young Nevile was a mistake which ought to be corrected in a perfectly civilized, legal way. He, Aubry Gainsborough, was in a position to 'straighten the matter out.' A separation, then a divorce through a Mexican lawyer he knew on Park Avenue. There would be no publicity, none of 'this dirty New York business,' as he called it; nothing unpleasant at all. He was careful to insist on this for my benefit as an ambassador, though I might not see Captain Nevile for a long while, now we were on different ships. I accepted the commission provisionally with a few reservations, for with the ground firm under his feet again, I warned them, he might be difficult to handle. I told them we in England did not have the same attitude towards divorce. Especially a fixed-up thing from a provincial city in Mexico—Morelos, I fancy.

"They were not much impressed by my words. Ada said, 'He can't refuse now. He knows everything is over between us. I couldn't go back to him. He can't stand between me and my happiness, my career. He never tried to understand me.'

"That was probably true. Very few Englishmen have the idea of setting to work to understand a woman in the sense of letting her walk over them. I didn't argue that. I only wanted to see for myself how she looked at the impasse. She was in no hurry about it because she sensed how strong this new attachment was. Mr. Gainsborough knew exactly what he was looking for, and Ada filled the bill. She had the looks, the blond, statuesque, slightly frosty beauty that men like him are ravenous to possess. To him she was a most cultured creature, though it was no thicker than gilt on a statue, and she conveyed an impression of being extremely well born. He was going up in his world, and he saw Ada as an asset as well as a passion. Neither of them would defy any convention for love. Convention, in fact, was the breath of their nostrils. So far from taking advantage of her unprotected situation, Mr. Gainsborough was surrounding her with defenses, a maid and an elderly companion whom he paid to live with

Ada. The way he looked around at the apartment which
Captain Nevile had provided indicated how deplorable he
thought it for a girl like Ada to be shackled to such a poor
meal ticket. He made no comment. He was too concerned
with the correctness of his behavior. He was correct in everything. I saw him glance at my clothes. His were correct
to the last stitch, modish to the day before you set eyes on
him. He had one of those small British-officer mustaches, and
he wore a plain but very expensive wrist watch with a snakeskin strap. His shirts were silk, very stylish dark blue, with a
tie that probably cost eight or nine dollars. Ada used to adore
him with her eyes as he talked to me and held his highball
in a hand that bore a ring of price. I fancy he sent her cases
of liquor, for we did very well in that line. She hardly touched
it, and he adored that streak of sense in her. Oh yes, she's
clever, and now she has a divorce at last, she will never look
back. She knew."

"What do you mean? What did she know?"

"That her husband was never in love with her. He dreamed
of Elli Phalère, but a sort of English Elli, an Elli without
Elli's strange background. Ada only divined the hallucination, but she had a woman's unerring sagacity in such matters. The way she put it to me was: 'Sidney was only trying
to forget when he married me, the same as I was. It was all a
mistake.'

"Yes, she was honest in her fashion, I agree. But do you
like the fashion? She was being, in a very definite way, an
American woman. Then what, exactly, did she bind herself
to do, when she married Captain Nevile? I suppose for you
she wasn't married at all because it wasn't a sacrament to
either of them and she made the best of a bad bargain. But
wasn't it a sacrament for him? I am perfectly convinced that
he wanted desperately to make a go of it and believed in its
permanence. He was proud of Ada too, in his way, but it
wasn't the way of that Upper Silesian who prefers to be
called Gainsborough. Can you see young Nevile changing his

name? Or his race? Yet he had the honest desire to sink his origins so that an American wife would find herself eventually with an American husband. Gainsborough is proud because Ada will be a symbol of his success as a Western Aryan. I doubt whether the most wonderful brunette would make much impression on him personally, though he could gauge her box-office value at a glance."

"But Captain Nevile could never sink his origins, as you call it. It sticks out all over. I like it—in him—but even if it was disagreeable he couldn't hide it."

"I dare say. All I meant was, he had the emotion of fusing his fortunes and dreams with hers. He was striving for that. What do you suppose occupied his mind during the voyages, when he was beset on all sides by the distractions of the lady tourist? He had reached a state of spiritual equilibrium so that all he needed to become a normal and rather uninteresting shipmaster was a little comprehension and coöperation at home. He didn't get it, and so never became uninteresting.

"At first, mind you, while he was over in Glasgow, with a trip down country to visit his people, he was still loaded with the momentum of his early married days. He might believe Ada would never return. He might even begin to admit to himself that he could get used to it. But he had not begun to feel his own bonds were loosened. I think, from one or two remarks he dropped to me at that time, that he was more careful than ever to leave the onus on her. You can, you know. A feeling of virtue sometimes begets virtue. And there was his sister Ursula.

"We met, he and I, nearly a year later. I walked on board a fine new ship, very sleek and modern, in the Canal Zone. She was on her way down the coast with a full complement of vacationists. The Santander was as fine a looking ship as you would find anywhere. She was so beautifully modeled, and the new docks were so vast, that she seemed small, until you walked up the gangway and saw the seventy-foot beam of her and the height of the bridge. I was very pleased to think, as I walked along the concrete pier, that a young fellow I had known and liked for so long had reached the command of her.

"Of course, nobody took any notice of me when I walked aboard. I was in uniform and known by sight to several men who were about. I went on upstairs. Most of the passengers were ashore after dinner. I went up to the bridge. I wanted to give him a surprise, but it was he who gave me one. He had a girl up there.

"I happened to be on the wrong side of the ship, so I stepped through the thwartship officers' passage and knocking at the door marked 'Captain,' turned the handle. It was locked. I saw a light under it and decided he was using the outer door while in the tropics. I walked around the bridge, and the screen door with louvers, giving onto the captain's private deck, was just closing. I knocked. After a considerable pause, Captain Nevile asked, 'Who is it?' I said, 'I give you three guesses, Captain.' There was another pause, longer than the first, and I rattled the handle. I said, 'Well, Spenlove's the name, Sidney, if you are so particular.' And then the door opened.

"He was glad to see me, but he was so restrained about it and his uniform coat had been so recently buttoned, two of the buttons only just sticking into the holes, that I glanced around as I entered. He had a fine room paneled in walnut, and in a fine deep armchair, upholstered in red leather, a very pretty girl was sitting holding a magazine. I bowed, and he introduced me to a Miss Davidge as an old friend. Miss Davidge bowed to me and, after glancing at her magazine, gave me a sudden second scrutiny. She was a shade disconcerted, and she was breathing faster than I believed necessary unless the magazine were very exciting indeed.

"Yes, I know you want to know what she was like, and it is easier to ask than to answer because she belonged to a period and a class which seemed to turn out thousands of girls like her so very much alike that one had a vision of some factory assembly line, off which, every minute, another girl stepped complete, varnished, enameled, shod, stockinged, gowned, mink coated, and Paris hatted, complete. We had a crowd of them on this ship once, going on a vacation tour of England, France, and the Low Countries. They came from an expensive Mid-West college, and to us they seemed absolutely alike for a few days. I fancy they *were* alike inside, and my metaphor of the assembly line isn't so grotesque as you might imagine.

"Miss Davidge was still in that stage. She was about twenty-two, with soft brown hair in a tight bob, liquid brown eyes, a snub nose, a rosebud mouth, and a white skin without any color at all save her two red lips, which she had painted dark red. Her eyebrows were plucked a little but not much. She was in black, and I believe it was her way of asserting her personality that she always wore black or deep orange. I noticed a platinum chain on her ankle under the stocking. She wore no rings, but her necklace I could see had cost more than Captain Nevile was earning in a year. Her clothes too, for that matter, for she afterwards picked up an ermine cape that made me feel faint as I thought of what it had cost.

"She picked it up because it was decided we should go ashore and see life. But first of all, after being presented, I sat down while young Nevile got his old friend a drink. They had not been drinking. He never had anything to do with a woman who drank much; but that means very little. Or doesn't it? Perhaps some innate fineness in him deflects him from the grosser cravings. Esther Davidge took a little wine sometimes, she said, but without gusto.

"It appeared she was traveling with her father, and he was dining with an admiral. Her father is president of a concern that made either carburetors or magnetos. I forget now. He had patents, and he made these things for a dozen automobile firms, several makers of agricultural machinery and a lot of airplane builders. So I learned later. And she is his only daughter. Looking back, young Nevile seems always to have become entangled with only daughters. No, once he was nearly roped by one of two sisters. A solitary exception. The amusing thing to me was that the other sister disliked him with a cold, intellectual animosity. She wouldn't even look at him if she could help it. And she roused her parents against him too, so that they were like three furies descending upon him. But that was a later adventure.

"The suggestion that we go ashore was the captain's, and it arose from the fact that he could not take her ashore alone. She seemed to have the usual enormous liberty such girls do possess, but he couldn't take her to the places she wanted to see without some third person in the party. And he changed into mufti. While he was doing it in his bedroom I drank my Scotch and had some conversation with Miss Davidge. I discovered almost at once that she was in love with him.

"I'm not going into that. I can't explain why she gave me that impression, because it does no particular credit to me. I wouldn't even undertake to say it about any woman. It isn't that girls like Esther Davidge are any less 'maidenly' than others. It's rather that they live in an age and environment which makes them independent of the usual feminine secretiveness. They know too much to be Victorian, and they know too little to hide their desires.

"She didn't know, of course, that I had any interest in Captain Nevile. Only when I said I'd known him since he went to sea did she regard me otherwise than as an intruder. She became friendly and said they had had a wonderful time since leaving New York.

"They had been together almost the whole voyage. Old Mr. Davidge, the wealthy widower of the cruise, either played poker or slept in his deck chair. Captain Nevile and Esther Davidge had a joke between them and the theme of the joke was a Mrs. Sneeder, a lone eagle trying to make Mr. Davidge. By the time we were ashore and seated in a cabaret, I had gathered that old Mr. Davidge was immune from wan-

dering females and discussed them with Esther in the privacy
of their suite. It was part of Esther's responsibility to chaperon her father when he required her services. Mrs. Sneeder
had been under the impression that Mr. Davidge would take
her ashore that evening and had been seen carrying out a
man hunt all over the ship long after the admiral's launch had
wafted Mr. Davidge away to dinner on a warship at anchor
a mile off shore. The joke was, Mrs. Sneeder couldn't swim.

"You can solve for yourself the conundrum, that a rich
and lovely girl a couple of years out of college would go to the
captain's quarters, yet would on no account go ashore with
him to a cabaret. She had very definite standards, Esther had,
and I dare say that was the basis of her father's confidence in
her. There was another aspect of it. Captain Nevile wouldn't
want to be seen with her at a cabaret, alone. Now I had wandered into the affair, they felt free to enjoy themselves."

"Was he in love with her?" said Mrs. Kavanagh.

"Not in the sense that she was in love with him. That is
why I mention the affair. I watched them dancing and
through the episode that ensued. There was a scene, you
know. Some Panamanian official, a politico in uniform, was
standing near our table with some henchmen. I saw him
combing his black mustache with a long finger nail and eyeing
Esther Davidge as she danced with Captain Nevile, who was
in a suit of plain white drill. I saw him speak to one of his
friends, obviously inquiring who Esther's escort might be.
And I saw him seize the moment when the couple came near
him to step forward and cut in.

"The change in that girl was electrical. If anyone had imagined, from her rapt expression of bliss in Captain Nevile's
arms, that she was a college girl at a fraternity dance at home,
they would have been deceived when she turned and saw that
half-breed Latin American trying to take hold of her and
draw her away. He was a sallow specimen, and the shape of
his cheek bones indicated a trace of mongoloid among his
other diverse ancestral strains. She gave one horrified glance

at Nevile and then, wrenching her arm from the intruder's grasp, she swung her hand hard against his jaw.

"It was so sudden it took effect. His face became even less attractive, and I saw him look around as if he actually thought of calling on his bodyguard. Young Nevile by that time had stepped in front of the girl and was speaking with a very tense face to the official. One of this fellow's epaulettes had been caught by Esther's right arm swing and dangled from its button. The music was stopping but the conductor, seeing the affair, began again. Nobody heard what was being said. The look on the Panamanian's face became homicidal. There was a moment when I expected those two to be arrested. He followed them to the table where I was sitting, and I rose.

"In those days I wore ribbons. I mean war medal ribbons. It was our custom, and for those who still like it I have no criticism. I suppose I presented to that illiterate and untraveled Panamanian politician a formidable aspect. The four gold stripes, the ribbons, the beard which in some parts of the world is regarded with reverence, had their effect. Possibly too I wasn't looking any too benign anyway. I knew too much about him to feel anything but nausea when he laid hands on a white girl. What I did was to wave my forefinger very rapidly in front of my nose and address him in Spanish as the illegitimate offspring of a negro cab driver. Which he might easily be, with a Chinese great-uncle in the background.

"Of course, after that, Esther Davidge's thirst for Canal Zone night life was assuaged. She didn't want any more of that. I suggested we go to a hotel I knew where we would be unmolested over a supper which I felt able to order. It was a few blocks down the street. You ought to have seen the queer contrast that girl, with her ermine cape and gold shoes, made with the cabaret girls and the sort of unearthly blonde type the Canal Zone gets from God knows where. The bleached females who seem to be created especially for the petty officers of navies all over the world! I think young Nevile realized it too.

"We had a pleasant evening after all. He was enjoying himself. I'll tell you why in a word. He had begun to live, but he no longer fell in love. Now that Ada had definitely left him and he found himself in command again, he was becoming aware of his opportunities. Up to this time he had accepted as a definite convention that men made their choice of a woman and pursued her either legally or illegally. He had not believed that his own experience was anything but very exceptional. Now he was able to see that the modern woman does her own pursuing. Mrs. Sneeder was only one of dozens who haunt cruises trying to capture a husband. And it was perfectly in tune with our modern mores that his simple statement, 'my wife has left me,' gave him a special freedom that Esther Davidge found congenial enough. He probably fulfilled some dream of her college years, for the basis of all the culture she possessed was neither American nor French nor German, but English. He possessed unconsciously qualities she had imagined necessary to her happiness, or perhaps only to her vanity. Much of the animosity of American men towards Englishmen is inspired by this peculiar admiration American women have of English characteristics. I don't blame the men at all. I would react with even more vigor than they do in similar circumstances.

"I admit it! Yes, it is intolerable, this complacency, but there is nothing fraudulent about it, nothing presumptuous. Most Englishmen feel as young Nevile did when he retorted to me a little later in New York, 'I didn't create the situation, Fred. All I have done is to take advantage of it.'

"I had been spending the evening with him and he had spoken enigmatically of this Davidge business. What, I wanted to know, was the impediment? There had been a fresh alignment after that escapade at Panama. Old Davidge had heard the story from Esther, with Captain Nevile present. What he had said was, 'Well, if you fly with crows, you must expect to be shot at,' and lit another cigar. It brought Captain Nevile into a new intimacy. He was invited to dine in New York. So what was the impediment?

"It was really that Captain Nevile was logical enough to see where he was in the economic scheme. In his situation, and it is the situation of all of us, he couldn't be a married man at all in your sense. He had no bent that way anyhow. He saw he was a highly paid servant of the public, and for him home life had no existence so long as he practised his profession. He therefore was inclined to abandon the pretense and find his own diversion and social life. Can you blame him?

"There was another thing. He had very little money, and the disparity between his own resources and the sort of people who took him up was too obvious to miss. The Davidges had a place at Greenwich, in Connecticut, a vast white Colonial pile with lawns, shrubberies, rose gardens, and pergolas that sloped down to a huge boathouse, and a seventy-foot cabin cruiser on the Sound. He was invited there, and Esther met him at the station in a long lemon-colored convertible of enormous horsepower and European origin. He told me he had done some intensive thinking while coming back to town from that place. Esther wanted him to get a real American divorce, and she let him understand that 'Poppa' would take care of it.

"When it was denuded of its American verbiage it meant that old Mr. Davidge was willing to buy his daughter anything she wanted. Young Nevile said to me, 'I don't care much about it.' And it was a real problem, for his salary of less than a hundred dollars a week was so grotesque to old Davidge that I doubt if it ever really reached his intelligence. Esther had more than that for her clothes. Young Nevile had a chance.

"On the other hand, she wouldn't let him go. She was mad about him. The story goes she was on the dock more than once when the Santander came in, ostensibly to meet friends.

She was there to meet Captain Nevile. You can blame him
if you like. But I don't. I see his dilemma. I admit I advised
him he ought to make up his mind one way or the other, if
she would let him, but I saw too much of the American Girl
during the twenties to expect he could do it. He was with her
all the time in New York. She could only go to places like the
Plaza and Sherry's, and it cost him a lot of money to run
around with her. I pointed out to him he was not displaying
any sagacity, but he said he was. He said, with a faint smile,
'She's enjoying the experience. Why shouldn't I let her have
it? It's wonderful for me, I can tell you. But it wouldn't be
wonderful if I let myself be drawn into their life. I don't like
the position of poor relation. I'd rather pull out altogether.'

"He made an effort to, as I shall tell you. While he was at
sea he was discovering other interesting friendships. He was
changing. He was becoming more sure of himself. He was
coming to regard women as experimentalists and not very
scrupulous where their own instincts were concerned. He
adopted the position that he was justified in looking after
himself. It's no use criticizing any man for that. He can only
judge women by the women who like him well enough to seek
him. Women have an unerring instinct in this, as you have
shown me."

"Why? In what way? Because of that creature?"

"Exactly. She's a young woman, and she possesses that
quality that appeals as strongly to Captain Nevile as it repels
you. Well, that's what happens every time. When you hear
an elderly man, with shell-rim glasses and a gray business
suit that seems to be cut out of sheet iron, speak austerely
of young women who make men do crazy things for love, you
are probably right in assuming that when he was young he
lacked the gift of the gods. Only virtuous females of unim-
peachable propriety were attracted to him. The others, the
nymphs, fled from his presence by instinct. Every now and
then we read in the papers of some elderly hunks who makes
a frantic snatch at paphian joys by buying them. Too late!

And one cannot buy them. All one can buy is pity and light laughter.

"Young Nevile knew, however, that he must not 'get in too deep,' as he called it to me. He had reached the stage when he could 'pull out' if he wanted to, without remorse. He saw, with perfect clarity, the difficulties he would face if he let Esther Davidge make him give up his sea job. Old Davidge would find him a job, of course, and he had no stomach for such an arrangement. Yet Esther wanted as much of him as she could get. She had a great many social distractions naturally, but she wanted him as well. And it was a mistake on her part, if she wanted him that badly, to go off to Paris for a month or two. It gave Captain Nevile the chance he wanted to 'ease out a bit.' And while Esther was out of the way he had another experience which made a profound change in his attitude towards American women. It made him believe they will stop at nothing to get a man they want. Of course he was mistaken. He was only generalizing from the women he knew. Esther imagined he had been lured away from her by another girl, that Virginia Spottiswood I told you about. It wasn't so simple as that. He had changed in his attitude. He was discovering America, feminine America. What illuminated the whole country for him was the Wyatte family.

"I was responsible, mind you, for introducing him to the Wyattes. I know them now, very well indeed. It was Mr. Wyatte who first told me about the shack I own on the shore of Long Island Sound where I am expecting to end my days. I have the highest esteem, even affection, for Mr. Wyatte. He doesn't know quite what to make of me, because he is a business man, one of the most perfect examples of the working ant I have ever known. All his activities take place inside his cage. Perhaps he ought to be compared with a highly intelligent rodent born in a cage with a revolving wheel which is called Real Estate. He never gets away from where he is, but he makes the wheel revolve. He toils without ceasing and regards himself as the fine flower of our financial culture. You ought to hear him on the Future of Ashridge, which is the place he is trying to develop. My place is on the border of his territory. He thinks I am a queer bird because I want it left just as it is, a shack in a dense thicket of oak and hickory. He says I need 'more land.' That is his cry, 'more land.' He would have made a splendid baron in the days of the Norman invasion.

"But you can't see Wyatte in any real perspective apart from his family. They were on a cruise with me some years ago, during that boom in the twenties. Mrs. Wyatte had been in grand opera. She has the physique and the voice of a diva. That mighty soprano used to hurtle out of our music room across the moonlit Caribbean. I can hear it now and tremble: 'Ahh—vee—Mah—ree—yah! Heah my—ee cr—r—y!' It was a great experience to sit under that megaphonic voice and watch Mr. Wyatte shining with simple pride. The two girls sat as if stunned. They were nice quiet creatures then, about fifteen and sixteen, with their hair in large plaited ropes down their backs. They were dressed much younger than their years, and I soon found out a strange fear of growing old in those two parents. They were so much in love with each other that they wanted to stay immortally youthful. That was why she sang with such—well, such élan! Time stopped while Mrs. Wyatte was sending her trumpet tones across the sea and making our rigging hum!

"No, they were not old. They were in the early forties, and very ambitious. She was ambitious on his account and they are both ambitious now on the girls' account. You see, they are descended from colonial stock, and they have an ancestral chart showing a tree growing out of the loins of a gentleman in medieval armor of the time of the Plantagenets. On a microscopic twig in the top right-hand corner you can find Clarice and Juanita Wyatte. I was shown it when I went to dine with them in New York. Mr. Wyatte owned a couple of houses on Washington Square, and they lived in the top apartment of one of them, with a garden on the roof.

"As I told you, I like them. I'm not concerned with their indignation over young Nevile because I think they are to blame. In fact, I know they are. It was the sudden clash of two conceptions of life, but the Wyattes were too naïve.

"The way of it was this. I found that Mrs. Wyatte was very interested in social work for sailors. I don't mean Poor Jack the Able Seaman, or Bill Bunker the stoker, but the officers of the ships that lay in New York. A friend of hers had a club for officers and apprentices. Midshipmen, she called these. It was a very mild affair in a cellar in the West Twenties. There was a clubroom where the lads could write home, some shelves of nice books, a sort of cafeteria, and once a week there was a dance. The daughters of the ladies who ran it would turn up in force and act as hostesses. Would I go down and shed the light of my countenance on this worthy enterprise?

"Of course I said I would, but on the afternoon of the day, the Santander docked, and young Nevile came over to see me. He wanted to discuss his vacation, which was due after the following voyage. I suggested he come with me to the Wyattes and go with us to the dance at the Watch Below Club.

"At the time I'm speaking of, Juanita, the younger girl, was in her eighteenth year and full of a sort of suppressed vehemence about life. She would interrogate me so intensely about my experiences that I mentally labeled her 'Rosa Dartle' though she was less like Miss Dartle than any character in fiction. She was magnificent! Mrs. Wyatte was magnificent. They were almost the same size and style— superb grand opera brunettes. For that matter the other girl was magnificent too, but in a pinched, statuesque edition. Clarice was the brilliant student of languages at college. She wrote free verse, but it was better than Ada's, I fancy. She took courses in Romance literature and Provençal Folk Songs. She eyed me with a speculative appraisal at times as I conversed with Juanita and hurriedly bowdlerized my reminiscences to suit the Wyatte conventions.

"I must mention those conventions. They were the most conventional beings I have ever known, and that includes all the supposedly conventional English I have known. The elder Wyattes were not as we say 'slaves to convention.' They were devout believers in it. If conventionality had not existed they would have invented it. They assumed it appealed to everybody else as it did to them. They moved easily and enjoyed life, or what they called life, within its circling walls and bastions, and the drawbridge was never lowered save to usher out some moral leper. I have to harp on this or you won't understand the explosion that took place when young Captain Nevile withdrew, when he spurned their superb offers of an alliance with a colonial family with a coat of arms and a lot of illegible ancient deeds in frames, besides plenty of modern cash.

"So everything had to be done in form. When the Wyattes get to know anybody he or she receives cards, formal invitations, and so on and so forth. In fact, I believe they are 'in society' and about to get into the Social Register, but I don't keep up that side of my education. Mrs. Wyatte made it very clear to me once, in her coloratura tones, that it was all essential to civilization, but it escapes me now. It always does, as soon as I am out of the presence of that stunning woman. Don't imagine I am derisive. She is stunning. She has a presence. She would make a gorgeous empress if America ever becomes an empire. Clarice would make a fine grand duchess. Juanita I am not so sure of. I fancy Juanita would elope with the imperial chamberlain and live in exile. She wants to know too much. She has a heart and viscera, and would fling her hat over the moon for love, and then she would sob out the whole story on her mother's majestic bosom. Clarice would stand by with downcast eyes and even pulse, sorry for her tempestuous sister and devoted to her daddy when he rushes in to play the lordly male, paterfamilias in excelsis, storming along about family honor, American womanhood, self-respect, and modern looseness. I had it all from him and his wife, booming away on each side of me, when young Nevile walked out on them. I didn't get a word in edgeways for quite a while.

"Captain Nevile made an instantaneous and highly favorable impression in Washington Square. Mrs. Wyatte was delighted. She told me when she had a chance that he was just the kind of young man they wanted 'down there.' I could see Juanita was smitten, but I didn't understand what she was like at the time. They had always been held back and treated as if they were still children, and I was yet to behold some of the more intricate ramifications of American psychology, that perplexing blend of prudery and jungle freedom which makes us Englishmen suddenly scared of the whole pack of you!"

"Protestants you mean, of course," snapped Mrs. Kavanagh.

"Ha! I might reveal all! But this is Captain Nevile's story. He seems to have had no other experiences so far as I know. Yes, Protestants, of course. The Wyattes, as you might expect, were communicants of the Episcopalian sect. They attended St. Giles' Church on Seventeenth Street en famille, in a black limousine with a coal-black chauffeur. It was impressive. It made me feel the solidity and virtue of their ideals. For they had ideals, make no mistake about it. They knew the world, in a way, for Mrs. Wyatte had been a professional songbird, and he had once been connected with the theater too in some vague executive position. But they found it was not possible to live virtuous lives in that milieu, and withdrew. As Mr. Wyatte put it to me, 'It was too sticky.' Financing real estate, turning tumbledown buildings into refined apartment houses with a fountain playing in the courtyard and a doorman dressed as a British Lifeguardsman, red coat, busby, and sword, was much nicer. Much more profitable too, I imagine. Mr. Wyatte couldn't see a humble tenement without wanting to buy it, pull it down and put up an apartment house that only rich people could afford to live in. It didn't matter a hoot to him where the poor went after eviction. He took care of them when he contributed to the offertory at St. Giles' on Sunday. The solidarity of the Wyatte family was impressive. They all thought exactly alike about things like that. They had a way of assuming every other respectable person thought as they did.

"We dined en famille, and Mr. Wyatte gave young Nevile a lot of questioning, openings as it were, to show his genuineness as a conservative member of society. He did very well, because where his own feelings are not concerned he can reflect almost any prejudices he finds around. What is the use of arguing? is his attitude. Juanita's liking for him grew rapidly in such a favorable climate. Captain Nevile! She hadn't been acquainted with a captain before. The young fellows at the Watch Below Club were more often grubby third and fourth officers and tongue-tied into the bargain. They were mostly off British ships, and these girls were hard for young Britishers to identify in the social microcosm. It was a mild form of slumming for the girls, going to that cellar in the West Twenties, dressed rather expensively, and dancing with young ship's officers. Juanita only regretted that we were not in uniform, she told us as we prepared to depart in the long black limousine with the rose-shaded lights in each corner. She loved uniforms, she told us, and her youth and genuineness carried it off. Mr. and Mrs. Wyatte smiled indulgently at Juanita's ingenuous warmth. She was the child of their first trip to Europe. They had had a second honeymoon in sunny southern Spain and named her Juanita in memory of fragrant nights on the balcony of a moonlit patio, when Mrs. Wyatte had sung wild Spanish gipsy songs and startled the quiet Spanish inhabitants out of their wits. Wonderful time they had there, Mr. Wyatte boomed at me, so long ago. Even their unconventionality was conventional and tinged with Episcopalian rectitude.

"Before we reached the club I had to explain to Juanita why the young Britishers were hard to thaw out when she introduced them to French, German, and Dutch officers. I said we were suffering from an inferiority complex as a result of the war. She said the foreign lads were much more willing to wear their uniforms than the Englishmen. I said that was due to the same complex. We had been brought up to hide ourselves in civilian clothes. She asked Captain Nevile if he would wear his uniform next time, and he said he might, if it hadn't gone to the cleaners. Ah, of course we were teasing her! Mr. Wyatte laughed with a mirthless resonance that put us all at ease, except perhaps Captain Nevile, who took the chance when no one was noticing to give me a surprised and pleased glance.

"That was the beginning of the affaire Wyatte, as I think of it. Juanita learned from Captain Nevile that he was taking his vacation in five or six weeks and Mr. Wyatte invited him to come to dinner again. Mrs. Wyatte followed this up by suggesting he come down for a long week-end to their place at Ashridge. He was, I could see, effectually launched with the Wyattes and I wasn't surprised when Mrs. Wyatte took me into her confidence and asked what Captain Nevile's prospects were.

"I wonder what she thought they were. I wonder what women like that think about when they are alone. Because her own husband had capital and was making probably twenty thousand a year she imagined anybody else worth anything at all could do the same. I swear to you, it is easier to bear the insolence and patronage of the English rich than the naïve assumption of well-to-do Americans that everybody they meet has a five-figure income. I told Mrs. Wyatte that Captain Nevile had a fine future behind him, as the Irish say, and he was as far ahead in prospects as he could ever hope to be. I warned her we did not have large salaries, and she said at once it didn't matter, if he was a gentleman. I refused to say whether he was or not. I pretended I didn't know what she was up to anyway, and she said: 'Isn't he married? We would like so much to have him as a house guest for Juanita, but he's married, isn't he?'

"'I think that's pretty well finished,' I said. 'His wife is releasing him.'

"'Releasing? Oh, yes? Then of course that would alter the situation.'

"Anyhow, they got him. I gave him the key of my shack, which Mr. Wyatte had found for me and which was about two miles from their own Ashridge place. I thought he would feel more free if he didn't have to depend on them all the time. I would be at sea, anyhow. He was very thoughtful when I gave him the keys. 'That's awfully decent of you,' he said. 'I'd like to have a few days in the country. It will be simply great to get away from everybody for a time!'

"I didn't know it at the time, but he meant the women on the Santander. He had been carrying heavy lists of winter cruise passengers and the women had included some predatory females from Texas and New Mexico who had almost flung themselves on him in a flying wedge. Very fine young women, but the sea acts upon fine young women from those parts in a very peculiar way. When a man is in command of a ship and is like young Nevile as he was then, they are a problem in transportation. So, although he played their game so that they went home full of glamorous memories, he was glad to be shut of them for a while. And two miles off, with a couple of cars in the garage, was Juanita.

"Mrs. Wyatte kept an alert eye on the cars, however, and probably rested easier for that. But Juanita had the bit in her teeth when she had Sidney Nevile so close and so secluded from those horrible women on the ships. She would walk to Ashridge Corners to get the mail and order the groceries. Clarice was taking a special course in Old French in New York and commuted daily. I often wondered, when she was calmly reading Villon, or even the antique story of Amis and Amile, what Clarice would do if François Villon had suddenly leapt through the window. Juanita had a dozen ways of reaching Captain Nevile that her mother did not know of. But nobody knew of it at the time. I was the unlucky means of discovering their assignations.

"When my vacation time arrived, I thought it a good idea, instead of spending most of it crossing the Atlantic to visit people who seemed able to get on splendidly without me, to go to Ashridge and rusticate. I took plenty of cigars and books and reached my shack. The woman who cleaned it told me the Wyattes had been over while I was away. I found their cards showered over the hook rug inside the door. My simple evening meal was barely over before they arrived again.

"I made them welcome, of course. The girls were away. Clarice had joined a study group and was in Paris. Juanita was staying with a girl friend in the Maine woods. The Wyattes themselves were in the pink of condition. They were in flannels and white sweaters and Mrs. Wyatte's voice thrilled and tremoloed among my rafters, and her magnificent bust was like one of those old figureheads of sailing ships, that literally breasted the waves, which we used to see, near the London Docks, in old wood yards. Her face was raised like theirs too, as if waiting for a heavenly radiance to shine.

"I made them welcome. My elderly Abigail made some more coffee, while I solaced myself with whisky. The Wyattes never drink anything stronger than claret cup. We were conversing amicably on various topics, and we moved around when the coffee came in. And I heard a sudden exclamation from Mrs. Wyatte. She had stooped down and lifted a snakeskin pocketbook from the bookshelf behind where she had pushed her chair.

"She held it up, and her eyes met her husband's. They were both speechless for a second, and as the old woman hobbled out through the green baize door they wheeled upon me and came forward.

"'Juanita's!' they chorused. 'She's been here!'

"I was at a loss for a moment. They meant, she had been there while young Nevile had been there. I shrugged a bit. I hadn't any ammunition ready for such an attack. They stood facing me, aghast. They had grown pale and stern.

"I said, 'I'm afraid I haven't any jurisdiction.' It started them. Jurisdiction! But they had trusted Captain Nevile like a son. They had never dreamed he could bring Juanita into his house unchaperoned. How many times had she come? If once, then three, five, ten times, while she pretended to be hiking over the country or in the village. And she had lied to her mother. Said she had dropped her pocketbook while coming back from New York. Had she gone to New York that time? Good God! Mr. Wyatte sprang up from the chair he had sat on, and walked to and fro, his hands behind his back. He stopped in front of me and shook his finger in front of my nose. 'Damned gate crasher!' he said. 'That's what we get for receiving him. Juanita's absolutely impossible! What a situation! Neither of them here. Oh damn, damn!'

"Mrs. Wyatte had slumped on my sofa, her hands clenched on one of her imperial knees, staring at nothing. She said it was her fault, and he agreed that it was. She had not suspected such treachery in her own daughter, but there it was—she had been hoodwinked. She looked around in a horrified way as she imagined the meetings of those two, in a secluded love nest in the woods. Mr. Wyatte had been staring out of the window, and he wheeled suddenly upon me. 'He'll have to marry her now, that's all!' And he sat down, a broken man.

"I didn't know how to touch the subject without getting an electric shock. Or perhaps I dreaded the moment when nature would be able to bear no more and I would collapse on the hearth rug shrieking with laughter. If I didn't keep a strangle hold on myself, I knew I would carry away. And they did nothing to lessen the tension. I saw Mrs. Wyatte gaze at me for a moment speculatively and then shake her head slightly. She was in the grip of complicated and titanic forces. But it was no use expecting me to offer to marry

Juanita, if that was what she had in mind. I was sufficiently in possession of my faculties to evade that dire result of my hospitable instincts.

"You see, it was the hopelessness of getting hold of Captain Nevile that struck them down. He was somewhere on the Spanish Main, like a pirate, with their daughter's honor below hatches, as it were. And what could they do, even if they had him right there in Ashridge? The fortuitousness of their discovery dismayed them. They had come into my house like a roaring lion and lioness full of the benevolent good-humor of financially, socially, and morally successful Americans. And now you should have seen them, deflated and forlorn, picking up books and putting them down again as though no book could afford them any comfort or counsel in such an abyss of misfortune.

"Mr. Wyatte pulled himself together and said, 'Well. Of course, it's not your fault. It's our fault. I take the blame. I ought to be more careful about gate crashers.' It was funny how that hallucination stuck to him and still sticks. He had the conviction that somehow, when they weren't looking, young Nevile sneaked into their house and stole their daughter's affections. I said nothing. He had given me a clean bill of health, and I wasn't going to jeopardize it. Mrs. Wyatte made a sudden tragic gesture as she picked up the unfortunate snakeskin pocketbook and gazed around. 'We never dreamed!' she almost shrilled at me.

"'Why not wait till he comes home?' I suggested. 'He may have an explanation.'

"'He can never explain how he allowed a young girl to visit him here, alone!' boomed Mr. Wyatte.

"'Well, maybe she wasn't alone,' I said.

"I might have saved my breath. They lived in their own world like fish in the sea, and when you tried to bring them up into our element they gaped and goggled like fish out of water. They had nothing to conceal, so long as the economic element, in which they existed, did not subside. You know how deep-sea fishes die even before they reach the surface. The Wyattes are like that. They will never need to worry over red ruin and the breaking up of laws. They will never live to see it. And so I treasure them and feel the present system has its virtues. They are really good people. But they don't understand a man like Captain Nevile—as he was then, I mean—at all. They simply mistook him for something else.

"I had to excuse them. They were too broken up to enjoy my company, and I saw them into their station wagon. 'Anything I can do, command me,' I said hypocritically, but of course there was nothing I could do. They scuttered away down the lane in the darkness. So two Roman parents might have gone back to their lonely villa to open a vein and bleed stoically to death as expiation for their daughter's dishonor.

"The daughter made a sudden descent on me a week later. A glittering runabout stood in front of my door where I could look right down into it from the window. A girl I didn't know was at the wheel, and Juanita sat beside her. They seemed uncertain whether to come in or not. I went to the door, and they came up to me slowly.

"I was introduced. Miss So-and-so. They came in. Juanita looked around. It was a nice autumn day, and I had a fire of sticks for company. She seemed bigger and more of a person than ever before. I mean she seemed more important, more sure of herself. They sat down, and I offered refreshment. Juanita, like all the Wyattes, did not indulge, so I didn't offer her either cocktail or cigarettes. She said, 'I'll take one too, please,' and she did. She smoked unhandily, defiantly, everlastingly flicking the ash from it and drawing too hard on it. She took too big a gulp of the drink and put it down hurriedly while the tears came into her eyes. And finally she said, while the other girl, a cool ash-blond customer with rolled stockings and a bare knee showing, gazed into the fire, 'My parents have been to see you, haven't they?'

"That was true, I said. It was about something they found

here. 'Yes,' she said, 'my pocketbook. I left it here when we were here before.' 'We'? I said. 'Yes, Tuppy and I were here one day, and I forgot my bag.' 'Oh,' I said, 'so it was all a mistake. Your parents will be so glad.' She said, 'It's none of their business. I happened to have Tuppy with me. Tuppy told them so when she arrived. But I can call on Captain Nevile if I want, can't I?'

"I said she certainly could if she wanted. I wasn't quite clear what she did want, to tell you the truth. I waited. They looked at each other. I waited again. Then she said, 'You don't understand, I can see.' I said no, I probably didn't, but I was making every effort. 'My parents are awfully conventional,' she said. 'They don't understand us at all. We— Tuppy and I—have to humor them. Tuppy insisted on coming with me because she said she'd go mad if she didn't have a cigarette and a drink soon. You see, Mother and Father hate girls to drink and smoke. And they don't understand about anything else either. They ought to be psychoanalyzed, both of them. They're hopeless extroverts.'

"I thought, Whee! I am in for it now. And I was. Juanita had been studying psychology at college and other things from Tuppy, who seemed to me to know all there was to know on earth, her eyes were so unfathomable as she gazed into my fire.

"'Then,' I said, 'you don't think so badly of Captain Nevile?' 'Why should I?' she said. 'It wasn't my fault he preferred me.' 'You mean to your sister?' I said. 'No,' she said. 'I knew you didn't understand. Mother wanted him for herself. To stick around and be a friend of the family.' 'Oh,' I said, and felt quite faint. 'Mother's always doing that when we have men friends come to the house. So Tuppy and I . . . You see?'

"I suppose I said I saw, though it was still dim enough to me. Or perhaps I should say that I saw too plainly. Tuppy's long green eyes had slid in my direction, and without moving her head she was examining me. She seemed to be studying me attentively. I gave her another drink, filling her glass as she rested it on her own bare knee, which was like polished ivory. Her lips had reddened the edge of the glass. She had gobs of mascara on her eyelashes. It was only later, when I found Tuppy's father was an important business associate of Mr. Wyatte's, that I understood why they had her around.

"She did not speak at all until they rose to go. She extracted a card from her bag and gave it to me. There was an address in Barrow Street in Greenwich Village. She said it was the studio of a girl friend, where they went to tea. Would I bring Captain Nevile, maybe? I said I couldn't be sure because he might not be in port. I would give him the card.

"I did give him the card, when I had a chance, but all he did was to twist it into a spiral and drop it in the cuspidor in his cabin. He said, 'That's out. I had a letter from old Wyatte. I don't want to go there again. They seem to think I'm some sort of bandit.'

"He was rather warm about it. I asked him what he had been doing up there anyway. He said he particularly resented the suggestion he had run after them. Juanita had come to see him. She had brought that other girl, Tuppy, they called her. There was some sort of strained relations at first because Tuppy tried to make him, and Juanita thought it was unsporting. Then Tuppy, who had only come down for an overnight visit, faded out. She had written him, but he hadn't answered. Juanita was lovely; but he wasn't going to mix in with a pair like her parents. I laughed. 'Mrs. Wyatte adores you!' I said. 'Secretly, of course.' He stared hard at me as if astounded at my penetration, and shrugged his shoulders. He said, 'I haven't the time to follow up.'

"I said, 'The real reason is, you have so many other interests now, you want to welsh.'

"'No,' he said. 'I'm not welshing. Juanita knew there was never anything in it. She knew what she wanted, too. It isn't that. It's Esther Davidge. She's back from Paris. She's coming on the cruise next voyage.'

"'You'd better clear your decks, then,' I said. 'She's the goods, Sidney.'

"'Yes, but,' he said. I knew what he meant. He didn't dread marrying her so much as he dreaded being a family retainer. Like me, since that time on the yacht he looked askance at golden chains.

"But he couldn't get out of the crisis that was coming. He couldn't ask Esther Davidge and her girl chum not to sail on the Santander.

"'Don't you want her to come?' I asked, rather amused. In my opinion he had had great luck in getting away from the Wyattes. He said, of course; but he wished people wouldn't assume that he hadn't any eyes in his head, or that he could play their game all the time. He had to be nice to a lot of people recommended by the office, and it wasn't always easy to avoid giving offense.

"'You'd better tell her not to come if you aren't going on with it,' I warned him. He said he wasn't a bit afraid of her coming, or even of 'going on with it.' What he wanted to avoid was 'complications.' People, he said, and especially women, were sensitive. Didn't I know it? I had had sensitive people offer me tips at the end of the voyage, but I would have been less sensitive myself if the largesse had been larger. Yes, passengers are sensitive. We study them, you know, and we learn in time to maneuver among them so that they remember us with smiles of pity and sometimes of affection. Young Nevile's problem was more complicated. He was very popular. The company had a lot of nice letters from people who had liked Captain Nevile so much. Make no mistake, he was a successful shipmaster. His love affairs were so dexterously subordinated to his professional duties that everybody seems to have been satisfied. He had nothing really to complain about when he was talking to me. His dilemma arrived on the morning of sailing day. He received the information from the office that Miss Virginia Spottiswood was making the Mediterranean cruise with him this time and would have

Suite A on the promenade deck. He would of course make special efforts to make her trip as enjoyable as possible, etc.

"I only heard about it afterwards, when it was all over and he was out of the Company. I heard scandalous and garbled versions that I won't mention. They needn't detain us, Mrs. Kavanagh. Yes, I know you want to hear them, but they have nothing to do with the case. They are merely reflections of the souls of those who go to sea. Sentimentalists love to imagine seafaring men as having a pellucid simplicity and clarity of soul. Sea fiction represents us as honest illiterates who have an elemental probity of spirit. I'm sorry to disillusion you, but envy, hatred, and all uncharitableness are abroad upon the ocean. You'll never understand us until you remember we are human.

"No, no scandal. Here is the truth, without malice or even embroidery. Virginia Spottiswood had not forgotten young Nevile. She had, indeed, made a number of maneuvers to get in touch with him, but he had been evading them. I take it that she was in love with him. Or perhaps love is not the right word. You are a woman and can supply that word in your heart. Anyhow, she was going to Europe, and she could do as she pleased, so she was going on the Santander as far as Naples, where she would leave on the train for Vienna and join some friends to go overland to London. No harm in sailing with a skipper she knew and liked, surely! If she had ulterior motives, who could criticize? Her old man was the big shot in our organization then. So she came, and Captain Nevile was aware, as he took his ship out, that Virginia and her maid were on board.

"Now take Esther Davidge. She didn't even know Virginia existed. She was, compared with Virginia, who was intelligent and aware of all her father's financial affairs in our company, a mere butterfly on the wheel. Esther's responsibility for chaperoning her father was a mere sinecure. The old chap was as hard as nails and as smart as a whip. He only pretended to be afraid of widows, and his apparent neglect of his daughter was a blind. He honestly believed it would be a good thing for Esther to marry young Nevile, for he liked him, and he knew she would have to marry somebody. As for what had happened, if it had happened, he didn't know, I think. He was a realist in his way, and possibly he would have regarded it as no business of his. He wouldn't have made an ass of himself as my dear friend Wyatte did.

"The fact to remember is that Esther, who had come back from Europe more in love with Sidney Nevile than ever, and had seen him at her home, was romantic about him. She had not the sophistication to envisage anybody like Virginia. So the stage was set to give Captain Nevile a bad voyage.

"There was the captain's table. Virginia, of course, had to sit beside him, and it would have seemed strange to Esther if she hadn't had the other seat on his left. Fortunately there were four other people at the table, married couples who were rich enough and important enough not to care a damn where they sat so long as they were fed. It is the Middle Westerner and his wife, we find, who raise the worst and most useless hell about sitting at the captain's table. Especially his wife, who makes the management hold their heads in anguish when she demands precedence of plenipotentiaries and potentates. Our captains sometimes envy the driver of the Twentieth Century Limited who doesn't have to entertain his passengers at all. Captain Wensley won't go down to the saloon for anybody,

"Captain Nevile sat between those two girls as seldom as possible during the first days at sea. He had some fog and remained on the bridge. He had to explain Virginia to Esther and Esther to Virginia. He knew he was only staving off the inevitable complications. For Virginia, innocently assuming that, while he had not been too ardent before, he belonged to her for the voyage, would never understand that since then Esther had been very much in his life, had faded out, and was now resuming the place she felt belonged to her. Esther had been planning this rapprochement. She had spent a lot of money in Paris on clothes, and she was a dazzling person when she gave her mind to it. They say women do not dress to attract men. Not in the obvious way the unintelligent use the phrase, perhaps. A girl like Esther is much more subtle. When she sailed that time she had everything, as we say, except perhaps a certain worldliness which would have explained the power and prestige of Virginia Spottiswood, who had smashed a bottle of champagne against the stem of the Santander when she was launched and who owned 30 percent of her in stock. It was bad luck that Esther should have run up against the one combination that was sure to wreck her plans.

"Because Captain Nevile had no intention of losing his job by neglecting Virginia. He had then and never has had the slightest remorse, because he never gave her any encouragement. If he flinched from being absorbed into the Davidge ménage, think what it would have been if he had married the woman who became the Princess Abajoli! He would have become either a social parasite or a cipher in one of our executive offices. He was never deluded into thinking he could make money in the American manner. Even now he would go back to sea if he could get his job again. He was never in doubt for a minute about that. But he was never in doubt either about Esther. He once confided in me that if she had only been a working professional girl in New York, a secretary or something like that, with her own apartment, he would probably never have left her for anyone else."

"You mean he would have married her?" said Mrs. Kavanagh.

"I don't think so; no," said Mr. Spenlove. "He had had enough of that. He was, as I said, a realist about marriage while he was at sea, and he had no desire to leave the sea. Esther's error lay primarily in supposing he wanted her around while he was engaged in his profession of commanding a ship. She wanted to have her wonderful first time all over

again, and this is always impossible. She wanted him to for
get she was living in an utterly different world from his. S⟨
she didn't see that instead of emphasizing that difference b⟩
walking about in clothes that cost as much as he made in ⟨
year or two she ought to have been austerely simple an⟨
understudied a hard-working soubrette. She could have kep⟨
all her magnificence for Greenwich and Newport. She cam⟨
instead with the intention of knocking all the other wome⟨
cold.

"Of course, the fact that she was considerably younge⟨
than Virginia made it all the more tragic. She was prettie⟨
and more attractive too, though you mustn't run away wit⟨
the idea that the ex-Princess Abajoli is not attractive. She i⟨
much too interesting, informed, and intelligent to fear com⟨
parison with any woman. She lacked one thing. Captai⟨
Nevile was not very interested in her. She knew that, bu⟨
expected him to change as the voyage proceeded. She wa⟨
aware that prolonged propinquity works wonders on a man'⟨
outlook. I dare say she has a streak of irony in her make-up⟨
She knows that you can't have everything.

"But Esther was not aware of any of these truths. Sh⟨
was an innocent, and I suppose she suffered more than any⟨
body at the time. When she found Captain Nevile makin⟨
a fuss over Virginia and going off with her and the cruis⟨
authorities in Madeira, the bottom fell out of the whol⟨
thing for her. It was no use the captain explaining to her tha⟨
he *had* to do all that, that Miss Spottiswood was the owner'⟨
daughter and *had* to be waited on hand and foot, on bende⟨
knee and even with the forehead pressed to the earth befor⟨
her footstool. If Esther had been awake, she would have see⟨
everybody on the Santander in the same state of professiona⟨
genuflection towards Miss Spottiswood. But she wasn'⟨
awake. She was dreaming of a fabulous voyage through th⟨
realms of her own fancy.

"The chief purser of the Santander was an old shipmat⟨
of mine, and he was a good mimic. He saw some of the scene⟨

between Captain Nevile and Esther, and once he heard her say something. She was standing close to the captain, and her eyes were very bright indeed. This was when they were getting close to Gibraltar and the purser had come up in a hurry with some papers. 'Make up your mind!' she said, 'make up your mind!'

"Which was possibly what he couldn't do, for he wished them both to hell! He told me so, with the only bitterness I've ever known him to express.

"Esther Davidge did not appear again except to go to the purser's office and tell him she and her chum would leave at Gibraltar and go overland to Paris and back on the Île de France. They had that option, I fancy. That was how the purser came to remember what she said: 'Make up your mind!' She left without a word to Captain Nevile. He's never seen her since. She went to Paris, and as a rule that assuages an American girl's grief over anything. But Esther must have poured out a rare story to her father over the transatlantic telephone. I fancy she must have talked him into her plans, and he had been indulgent towards her choice of a man. And she had simply told him all about it when she called him up to explain the change in her life.

"The way old Davidge got it must have made him mad, or at any rate irate. He probably thought modern girls a bit crazy, the way they ran after men, but he wasn't going to have his girl given the run around, and he took action. He complained. He said his daughter had been slighted, insulted, and forced to leave the ship to avoid further humiliation. He wanted a head on a charger, and as he was—and is—a very wealthy, influential, and forceful person, he got it. Captain Nevile, who had been occasionally on the wrong side of Virginia Spottiswood before he reached Naples, was asked to resign.

"He wrote me a letter which I received on arrival, and asked me to go up and see him. He had taken a room in a midtown hotel, quiet and unfashionable, until he could find his feet. I went up there, and we had dinner. He looked strange in a very new and expensive double-breasted blue suit with a light gray fedora and spats.

"'What's the idea?' I said. 'Are you going on the stage, Sidney?'

"'Something like that,' he said, smiling. 'All the world's a stage, they say. No. Uptown ticket office, Fred. I was only kicked off the ships. I have a new billet now. I don't know whether I can swing it, but I'm going to have a jolly good try.' And then he made a remark which I remember now. He said, 'I'm done with women, Fred. They've used me and made me lose my job. Now I'll use them when I get a chance, to make money.'

"I was astonished. For a moment I thought he contemplated going into the uptown gigolo business. What he meant was he intended to use the social lever to sell tickets. He had a card index which he had been keeping ever since he had taken command of the Santander. All his passengers with whom he had made contacts, with the data from Who's Who and any other information. He had proposed a trip to the traffic manager, and he was going off in a week's time.

"When I understand the scheme, I hardly knew how to classify it. Young Nevile said, 'It's a cad's game, but I'm going to do it. They all do it over here.' 'What?' I said. 'Why, use their friends to cadge business,' he said. I suggested he wasn't making it better by giving alibis. But he was determined to capitalize what he had, and he went.

"He must have been away from New York a couple of months. He had written a lot of letters to his passengers, said he was coming to their part of the country on business and would call. In many cases he had invitations wired him to come and stay with them. He met lots of other people in their homes and moved along doing missionary work for our cruises. He came back to New York with a reputation. It even came to Spottiswood's ears, and he had laughed, but he wasn't going to have Captain Nevile on a ship again. That held until old Spottiswood died and his daughter married her Prince Abajoli from a village in the mountains of Erzeroum.

"Yes, he had laughed, which disposes of the story that his daughter had Captain Nevile demoted on that former occasion. But I did not laugh. I was thoroughly disillusioned. The abyss between being Captain Nevile of the Santander and our Mister Nevile of the uptown ticket office was so unpleasant I couldn't bear to look into it. I had to suffer the complacent comments of men who would never be in his place. They would say, 'I wouldn't like to be in his shoes.' They were in no danger of that, and I reminded them of the fact. They were very virtuous because they had never been dismissed on account of a lady passenger. They knew nothing of the inside story. The story that went around was conventional. Miss Davidge had complained to the company because Captain Nevile had forced unwelcome attentions on her. One junior officer told me he had it from the bell-hop on the Santander that the captain had tried to go to her room. Well, they were all far enough from the truth, I fancy.

"For a long while after this happened I didn't see him at all. I was at sea, of course, and his work didn't bring him near the ships any more. He dropped out of our life altogether. In fact, my vacation came round again before I had a word from him. He telephoned me when the ship docked. He asked if I was going to Ashridge. I said yes, after I had been to visit some friends in the White Mountains. He said he supposed he couldn't use the place until I came back. I said, of course. What did he suppose, anyway? And where had he been keeping himself? He said he had been very busy with the winter cruise business about to open—this was in late August, and he meant the campaign for the cruises—but he was able to get off a few days at a time now. So he could use my place?

"I said, 'I suppose you mean you want to bring a friend?' He said that was about the size of it, and he didn't want to bother me if I felt I'd rather not. . . . I said, 'The postmaster has the key. I'll write him to let you have it. Who is it now?'

"He said it was a very special friend indeed and I would like her very much when I met her. I said I might and I might not. I knew the sort he ran after. He said, 'Quite the contrary. Wait till you meet Mrs. Fawcett. She's a splendid person!' I said I knew the sort he ran after. Well, he said, he couldn't argue about it. I would see for myself. A really splendid person. And he hung up.

"I admit my curiosity was aroused. He was over thirty, I told myself, and he surely knew enough now to keep away from the sort of rich young woman who had lost him his job. When I got back to New York from Lake George, where I stopped over for a week-end, I called him up in the office on Park Avenue. He said he hadn't expected me quite so soon, but it was all right. I said he could stay on at my place if he wanted, he and his special friend. 'Why,' he said, 'she's out there now, writing a book.'

"I suppose I might have known he would have that sort of experience. Most of the women he had run around with carried very little top hamper. Now this one was writing a book. I think my curiosity was increased. I said we could go down together and surprise his Egeria at her literary labors. And he said, 'Right ho.'

"There was a definite change in him when I went to his apartment. He had a small two room and bath place on West Fiftieth, with a thing in the corner that looked like a piano organ but which opened out into an electric buffet, so that he could cook himself breakfast. He rented it furnished, and the only personal things in view were his trunk, the suitcase open on the bed, and a couple of books on a side table. The bookcase was half full of magazine and filing envelopes. A large commercial photograph of the Santander was leaning against the wall, not very clean, I'm afraid. It looked as if he hadn't moved it since he came into the place. The rooms were dark, the furniture was pretty well worn, but I was obliged to admit that it was good enough.

"'I said, 'What about Ada? Don't you hear from her at all?' He said, 'She's got a Mexican divorce, but it's no good. That friend of hers, the Jew fellow, wants me to play the game and let her get what she wants in New York. He says it is only a matter of form.'

"'And are you going to do that?' I said. He said, 'Of course. Why not? She wants to marry him. She says she loves him. He is awfully fond of Ada, too. I don't want to be a crab.'

"I asked him what he had to do. He said it had all been done. They hired a professional co-respondent and he brought her to this bachelor apartment of his. She put on a kimono and he gave her a few drinks and talked and they waited until some of Mr. Gainsborough's friends called and surprised them in flagrante delicto. They all had another drink, the co-respondent dressed herself, and he never saw her again. The case, he told me, was uncontested, and in another month or two Ada could marry anybody she liked. 'What are you going to do?' I asked him. 'I'm going to stay as I am,' he said. 'Once bitten, twice shy. Wait till you meet Mrs. Fawcett. She's a splendid person!'

"'You've used that expression several times about Mrs. Fawcett,' I said. 'How old is she?' 'I don't think it matters in her case,' he said. 'She married very young, and has a son married, but it doesn't really matter. She's very intelligent. She writes things. She was a passenger on the Santander once, you know, and although I spoke to her, of course, and all that, I don't think I really noticed her. She's rather a quiet person. Her husband has a big job in Washington, but they haven't lived together for years. She's on this street, just across the Avenue.'

"So here he was, running around with a grandmother! I put it that way to myself because I was depressed by the deterioration, as it seemed to me, in his moral fiber. I'm not clear in my own mind why it should seem a deterioration for him to do this. It sounds illogical, in retrospect, for he had incurred my unspoken censure for running around with young girls. We oldsters are hard to please. I suppose I would not have been completely content with any woman for him, after Ada had slipped away. I was disappointed.

"We went down to Ashridge, and Mrs. Fawcett met us at the station in an old Ford touring car. It was raining, and she was wearing a yellow oiled silk coat and a brown felt hat that looked expensive in spite of its obvious age. All I could see was a healthy pink face and gray eyes. It was the least romantic meeting in the world. She said, 'Hello dear!' and he said nothing; just climbed in beside her and smiled. I was in the back with the bags. We drove off in the rain to my place, passing the Wyatte estate on the way, and I wondered whether that perfect flower of modern capitalism knew about his neighbors. I reminded Captain Nevile of it, and he said, without turning his head, 'They're in Europe.' He was conversing easily and pleasurably with Mrs. Fawcett. She was older than he, probably a little over forty, but she was extremely vigorous and capable. She had the figure of a well-built dairymaid and the healthy, ruddy complexion of a young naval officer. She looked back at me for a moment when I said I hoped they had made themselves at home, and she smiled as she said they certainly had.

"I remember the moment. We had come to a grade crossing, a track that ran a few miles to serve a village with a hat factory. It's a branch line. Mrs. Fawcett ran her Ford up the slight incline onto the track, and as she started it forward again, the engine stalled. She smiled as she pressed the starter, and we rolled away down the lane and up the hill to my place. There were so few trains, now the factory used trucks, that nobody worried about them.

"It was a very delightful week-end for me. A table had been moved to the window in the living room and on it were a typewriter, a number of books on sex that didn't belong to me, and a lot of yellow files, scratch blocks, press clippings, and notebooks. I asked Mrs. Fawcett what she was writing.

She said, 'It's a secret,' but she smiled. I liked her very much. She had evidently had a lot of worldly experience and did not expect too much of anybody. She had, I learned, done her duty and now intended to have a little fun.

"We decided to cook supper instead of going to a road-house some miles away, and young Nevile went off to the village for a few things. Mrs. Fawcett sat in a rocking chair on my porch and smoked a cigarette and told me they had had a wonderful time.

"'What's the situation?' I inquired. 'Merely temporary, I suppose.' She shrugged.

"'I'm an old woman,' she said. 'I'm not fooled by love any more. But I'm crazy about him. I don't mean I'd shoot myself if he ran away, but I do feel more alive and happier when he's around. He's a peach, you know. Did you know he's one of the nicest men I've ever known in my life? And I've been around a lot. I've lived in Europe and the Philippines too, and I know what I'm talking about.'

"'How do you mean, nice?' I said. She said, 'Well, ninety-nine men out of a hundred are so damn selfish. He isn't. He's thoughtful. He's like that statesman in English history —never in the way, never out of the way. I've lived with several men, and the trouble with lots of them is they're under foot or in a rage about something most of the time. They are either fussing or trying to excuse themselves. Sid's not like that. He's always willing to oblige, and you never know he's in the house.'

"I told her I'd known him for years. 'He's told me all about you,' she said. 'He thinks you're sore because he quit going to sea.'

"'Something in that,' I admitted 'but not very much. He got into trouble with a girl on his ship. He was off his course.'

"She said she'd heard something of that, but what of it? He hadn't done anything a gentleman could be ashamed of, had he? Girls were fools. They made a mess of nice men.

What did I mean by being off his course? What was his course?

"I told her. I said, 'Mrs. Fawcett, it's the very quality you seem to think so attractive. Do you imagine you are the only woman who has been crazy about him?'

"She said, 'Good God, no! I told you I am an old woman. I am! I'll never see thirty-nine again. I wouldn't be such a fool. And I never said he was in love with me, did I?'

"'No,' I said, 'but there it is. There's the whole thing in a nutshell. When he was in love he wasn't anything like the tame angel you find him. I've seen him when he was in love. He was in love with his wife—until she destroyed his love by neglect and he let her go. And I say he's off his course because he can make such a magical impression on you. I'd rather he was still with his wife and quarreling with her.'

"'You're a sentimentalist, Mr. Spenlove,' she said. 'One of the worst I've ever met, but I don't blame you. He told me what a friend you'd been to him when he was a kid. But you don't grudge me the little happiness we have out here, do you?'

"'Not in the least,' I assured her. 'I never interfere any more. I am only telling you what you wanted to know. And I dare say you'll do him good. The job he has now is not so good for a man who has commanded his own ship! I don't mean it is disreputable or even unprofitable. But the ethics are not ours.'

"Mrs. Fawcett said, 'If he makes money at it . . .?' Then she pulled herself up. 'It's a subtle distinction,' she said, and sat staring out into the green shadows of the wood."

Mr. Spenlove stood up and walked to the rail. The promenade deck was no longer illuminated save by a few shaded lights. He himself stared for a moment into the mystery of the tropic night. Mrs. Kavanagh joined him at the rail.

"What was she writing?" she asked, trying to see the time on her wrist watch.

"Seven bells just gone. That's eleven-thirty. We are prob-ably the only passengers awake except those who play poker in the smoke room. What was she writing?" Mr. Spenlove smiled as he fingered his beard.

"Tell me about the book you said she was writing," begged Mrs. Kavanagh.

"I didn't say she was writing a book. Young Nevile said that. He regards a woman who can read with a certain degree of reverence. Think of the impression made on him by a woman who was writing before his very eyes!"

"I haven't had any luck like that," Mrs. Kavanagh pointed out.

"Because he hasn't really been aware of your existence," Mr. Spenlove said, not very happily. "He never sees any woman except the one he is occupied with. That accounts for his success, and the occasional blast of hatred that descends upon him. No, she wasn't writing a book. It was a story. She made a great deal of money writing true confessions for the magazines you see on the newsstands with rousing, exciting covers. I could see she didn't want to discuss the way she made a living, and I would never have discovered it if she hadn't resented my assumption that she was cheating, in a ladylike way. She said she didn't take a penny from any-body, and her husband had not supported her for years."

"Hadn't he?" said Mrs. Kavanagh.

"Ah! There you show yourself a woman of the world. I don't know. She wanted me to believe he hadn't, just as young Nevile wanted me to believe he hid in his heart a quenchless pure love for Elli Phalère and his affairs with women were only a sort of drug with which he dulled the ache. He invoked that alibi more for himself than for me. He could not abandon the ancient costume that generations of English gentlemen had handed down to him, though he knew it was moth-eaten and falling to pieces and he had almost for-gotten how to put it on. Only a day or two ago he said Elli Phalère was the only girl he had ever loved."

"Does that creature know that?" inquired Mrs. Kavanagh. "And are you sure you aren't idealizing your Mrs. Fawcett? She sounds like a man eater to me, and as if she was resting comfortably, after a full meal, when you met her."

Mr. Spenlove laughed. He prepared to go below as one bell sounded.

"That's rather more than I intended to convey. She was no vegetarian, I grant you. A splendid person, young Nevile called her, and I know what he meant now. So long as you don't introduce the vampire motive, I don't mind. She was to me more like a handsome, intelligent American earth-goddess, a modern version of Ceres. She destroyed nothing valuable in his character. He might have stayed with her from indolence and inertia if fate hadn't been so unkind. They say it never works, for a man who has been a wanderer to settle with a woman older than himself. But that never came up with them."

"But what happened?"

"Well, I had my three weeks' vacation and went to sea again, and as I wouldn't be using my place I left it in Captain Nevile's charge. I heard he had gone to Chicago on traffic business, but that didn't worry me. And then, who should come down to see me on my return from the voyage but Mr. Wyatte. It was a highly unconventional thing for him to do, but I made him welcome. The captain was in my room at the time and I introduced them. That was Wensley, the one we have here. Then, when we were alone and the door closed, Wyatte leaned forward and said: 'Have you heard the news?' I said 'No'; for I had no idea what he meant. 'Not from Ashridge? From that lady you rented your place to?' I said 'No.' I had to think fast at that moment, and I decided that Mrs. Fawcett had found the place congenial for the writing of confession stories and had remained there. Also it flashed through my mind that young Nevile would not want to meet Juanita or her parents, so he would keep away. I said 'No.' Mr. Wyatte said, 'Why, my God, man, you don't know she was killed? Her car stalled on the track at the level crossing, just as a freight train came around the curve. She hadn't a chance. Our Chinaman came flying back to the house on his bicycle and told us. He'd seen the whole thing. Ghastly! We'd just come down for the week-end. It was a terrible shock for my wife. We didn't know how to communicate, you see. Finally we located her husband. He was making a speech in New York at some dinner by the time we got hold of him. He hadn't known exactly where his wife was. She had had her letters forwarded from East Fiftieth. Separated for years—you know how it is with these people. Well, you'll have to go down and see if your place is all right.'

"And of course I had to. I received a letter from Mr. Fawcett about the rent, and I told him that was all paid up. It seemed the simplest solution. But he called me up and asked me to see him at East Fiftieth. He was a tall, executive sort of man, gray-haired and formal, as though he had been cast in some special American metal, or perhaps an alloy, of brass and tin. He asked me if I knew Mrs. Fawcett at all well. I said I'd met her when she had friends down at Ashridge. He said she'd written him announcing she wanted the money to go to Reno for a divorce, as she wished to marry again. A Captain Nevile. Did I know him?

"I said yes, I know him, but I also said, which was the truth, that I knew nothing of their affairs. Well, he said, that was their intention apparently, and he had raised no objection. What sort of man was this Nevile? Would he have made her happy, if this hadn't happened? I said, yes, for it was as near as anyone could approach to truth. Well, he said, he regretted causing everyone so much inconvenience. He had written to this Captain Nevile at his office but had received no reply. It was just a tragic mishap, like a heart failure, or being struck by lightning, or a railroad collision. He had so little realized what had happened, never seeing anything of it, that he compared it with what it was!

"There was no sign of any tragedy when I reached that grade crossing, on foot. My place is about two miles from the station. Mr. Wyatte had got a man to go over and obliterate all traces. The car had been hurled fifty feet. All I saw was the track, a bit rusty, and a pheasant running in the way pheasants run, as though they have some big news for the other pheasants at home.

"When young Nevile came back from Chicago he gave me a ring. When I reached home again, I mean. He asked me to come up to his diggings. I went up, and the first thing that met my eye on entering his apartment was a girl sitting in front of the electric stove he had going and making herself very much at home. Young Nevile came out of the bedroom to greet me. He wasn't in the least perturbed. He introduced me to Miss Whoever-it-was. Her name escaped me then as it does now. She was one of those hangers-on of advertising who are so much alike one cannot recall them. I mean she was a publicity contacter for a large furnishing firm. Perhaps press agent is the right word. I'm not sure. These people are as touchy as capitalists. They leave it in the air as to who they are and what they do. The program for that evening was to go to this girl's apartment down in the Village, and another girl was coming to make four for dinner.

"I enjoyed myself very much. I always have done when I am with him, and the women were smart, intelligent, and interesting. I even forgot for the time being what had so recently happened in his life. When we reached his apartment again he did not mention Mrs. Fawcett at all. He did not even mention Miss Whats-her-name. He brought out some whisky and lit a pipe. Finally I said:

"'So you were going to marry Mrs. Fawcett?' He nodded, filling his pipe. 'I *was*,' he said, and the implication seemed that he had given up the idea before he went to Chicago. I asked him about that. He said she wanted it, and he had no objection, but he felt he ought to have more money. He didn't want to live on a woman. I said, 'You mean you hadn't any feeling for her?' He said, 'She was a splendid person. But women want so much. She was always wanting me to say more than I could possibly feel for anybody again in the world.' I said, 'Well, you seem to feel you're well out of it.' He said, 'I probably am. I haven't anything to reproach myself for.'

"And he hadn't. He seemed to have set himself a mark— to be independent. He once quoted Kipling's 'If' to me as his ideal—'Where all men count with you, but none too much,' amd he added 'All women too, Fred. But I leave you out. You count more than anyone.' I said, 'You are sure?' And he said, 'Fred, nothing matters a damn to me until I get my job back. I'm not a man at all, only a beachcomber. I get pretty sick of it all at times, and as for women, it's find 'em, fool 'em, and forget 'em.' And he stared at me in a very dismal way.

"I went away back to my ship, and I didn't see him again until he came down to us the day we sailed. I couldn't let him go on making a confidant of me and trying to get me to bear the responsibility. I have no messianic complex. I accept the burden of my own sins, but not those of others. I thought I could do him more good by staying away—if he was a beachcomber." He paused a moment. "And here he is, going to start a new life."

"And a new foolish love affair," said Mrs. Kavanagh. She allowed Mr. Spenlove to escort her to the forward entry.

"Yes, and possibly he has taken on more than he realizes," said Mr. Spenlove. "Charming, very charming, and mysterious. He has been sworn to secrecy."

"Ah—h—h! You men make me sick!" Mrs. Kavanagh hurried down the stairway smiling and waving good-night. Eight bells clinked deliberately from the bridge and was answered by the man on the forecastle head.

X

IN AN OLD double-breasted blue jacket, whose purple and
gold bars were dim with age, and a white muffler around his
neck, Mr. Spenlove smoked a black briar pipe in the hour
before the dawn. The Camotan had just passed the lighthouse at Morant Bay, and the east was lightening behind the
enormous indigo masses of the Blue Mountains. Orange and
blue rays, like spokes of a phantom wheel, struck up from the
summits, and in the intense shadow of the shore the lights
glittered jewel-like across the calm sea that reflected the
stars. Mr. Spenlove walked back and forth quickly abaft the
palm court, listening to the sounds that arose here and there
about the ship and meditating upon the events of the past
days. He heard the warning gongs and noted the time on his
wrist watch. He saw the deck hands moving about the
hatches preparing to raise them. A winch suddenly burst into
activity as a boom rose like a warning finger in the blue night
already luminous with the dawn beyond the mountains.

It had been amusing, telling Mrs. Kavanagh what she
wanted to know. And how much she wanted to know! Last
night, for instance, after watching young Nevile dancing
with that girl, that Athalie Rhys, Mrs. Kavanagh had said
that she would never understand men, but it had given her
an idea for her new thriller, hearing about him and that
woman who was killed at the grade crossing. There would
have to be a section of the book that covered the period of
the yacht's cruise and brought in what happened at home.
The widow who was suspected of being the accomplice of the
pirates (who seized the yacht on a moonlight night in the
Ægean while a dance was taking place on the quarter deck)
had to get in touch with her lover, the Wall Street clubman
who was financing the whole scheme. When he got the news
he would drive from his Long Island home at breakneck
speed to New York. And at a grade crossing . . .

Mr. Spenlove saw the incredible green of the eastern sky above Blue Mountain Peak turn paler and paler. The color seemed to be mounting like a long-drawn musical note. Even now, as the light of dawn spread over the sea and the stars paled, the shore was in darkness, the lights glittered with an intense hard brilliance that Mr. Spenlove never tired of contemplating. The blend of tropical odors that came from the island aroused in him a nostalgia for the days of his youth, when he had been in tramp steamers that lay long weeks in such places and he had awakened in some jalousied chamber at dawn to go back to the ship. What perfect days they seemed, at this distance of time! Well, they were very good even then, he told himself, smiling, and in the smile was a trace of benevolent compassion for passengers who wanted so deeply to achieve romance and were permitted to purchase only an expensive imitation of it. They were waking up now, coming timidly to the doors and gazing apprehensively at the wet decks and rank of folded chairs. They had missed it again, he told himself, smiling. They had missed that magic half hour before the dawn. They would appear presently, correctly garbed in white suits, and with expensive movie cameras and binoculars; but no camera could catch that miracle of color beyond Blue Mountain, no binocular could reach the romance he had known. Already the hard early morning light had come. The mystery of the shore was gone. Mr. Spenlove experienced a faint glow at the thought that nobody had seen what he had seen. Old Wensley never saw anything except the pilot in the canoe and Plum Point, where the voyage technically ended.

He heard the gongs once more and took his way down to his own domain. Nor did he appear on deck again until the Camotan was alongside and the gangways thronged with shore people, the hot sunlight pouring down upon them, the mountains beyond shimmering in the heat haze. The passengers were clustered at the rail, and Mr. Spenlove saw Captain Nevile, in a white suit and panama hat, standing beside a girl in bisque linen, whose feet were encased in extremely small shoes of green leather with high heels. Why green? Mr. Spenlove meditated. They were looking down at the dock, and she was making slightly dramatic gestures to someone down there. Mr. Spenlove wondered to himself, as he took up a discreet position, what the secret was about some women, who had sturdy bodies and were not even petite, yet conveyed the impression that they could sit, like a Tanagra statuette, on a man's hand.

He went down to the deck below and saw the person on the dock. That, then, was the parent whom she had come to visit. Mr. Spenlove saw a tall lean figure whose sun-reddened face seemed to be squinting up at the funnel rather than at his daughter. Over his arm he carried an old raincoat, and his walking stick supported his hip. He was wearing an immense planter's hat, stained like the khaki suit, but clean. The old buckskin shoes, Mr. Spenlove noted, had an unmistakable air of having come from London a long time ago. They went, somehow, with the dangling monocle.

Sometimes he walked a few steps, nodded to someone he knew in the crowd, and looked up again, squintingly, towards the people on the ship. He would wave his hand tolerantly, and presently Mr. Spenlove saw him put his monocle in his eye and his thin, almost transparent features assumed an expression of blank hauteur as the glass disk reflected the sun. He became a cyclops leaning on a cane, as though he had come down from the Blue Mountains seeking a human being to devour. So Mr. Spenlove fancied for the brief moment before that tall composed person suddenly took long strides to the gangway.

The passengers were going ashore. Mr. Spenlove had a few hours before he would sail south with the Camotan. He saw Mrs. Kavanagh and her brother disembarking. She was looking about in a quick nervous way. Mr. O'Relly was being shepherded in spite of his apparent care of his sister. And Mr. Spenlove took his way towards them. He wanted to say good-bye, or rather au revoir, to Mrs. Kavanagh. He felt a tender interest in her new thriller about a yacht.

So he was a down-looking spectator of the meeting between Athalie Rhys and her tall father. She was not tiny either, he reflected, smiling. How did she come to give one that impression? No doubt it was the small feet, the delicate blue-veined wrists, and the sweet, gurgling baby voice. Perhaps also that theatric way she had of standing, feet together, one wrist pressed to a rosebud mouth, and then tripping forward into her father's arms. Oh, very theatric! thought Mr. Spenlove, and watched Sidney Nevile entranced by it. He too went forward from the gangway, hat in hand, to be presented by a girl who was blushing deeply under her large hat with its ribbon and bow of baby blue.

Mr. Spenlove swung down the gangway to go to Mrs. Kavanagh. Captain Wensley, leaning over his bridge rail, a placid pink moon from which protruded a cheroot, was watching his former shipmate, whom he did not like, Captain Nevile and that piece the office had commended to his, Captain Wensley's care. He had not spoken to her. She had wangled a letter out of the head of the Company's legal department, and Captain Wensley had a hunch she was just a sweetie that lawyer wanted to favor. Anyhow, she'd hooked Nevile, who had always been a skirt hunter, Captain Wensley suspected, or he wouldn't have been fired by old Spottiswood.

Mr. Spenlove, glancing upward, although he saw only that pink moon with its cheroot and the hunched shoulders of his commander, could read all this behind that face. He saw Wensley, as the girl made another theatric gesture, clinging to her father's arm and smiling ravishingly at Captain Nevile, give a single wink and incline the cheroot towards the group. Mr. Spenlove winked back, but he told himself that human beings were a damned sight more interesting than fat, successful skippers with twenty thousand in War Loan. And he went across to Mrs. Kavanagh and Mr. O'Relly.

"Ah, we're sorry to leave ye!" she said sincerely. Mr.

O'Relly agreed in his own way, which was partly west of Ireland peasant and partly Park Row newspaperman. He stood with one foot on the other and lit a match with one hand for his cigarette. Mr. Spenlove said it was not allowed, and Mr. O'Relly contemplated an enormous black dock policeman with a sudden shattering realization he was no longer in the United States.

"We're going to the Antrim House," Mrs. Kavanagh went on. "Do you know it? Can you not come and see us for a while?"

"Yes, I've been out there for a drink," he said. "They have a nice garden, and it's very quiet. You'll have time to write, out there. I can come out for an hour. I'll follow you."

"Terry's going to rent a car. Do you think he can?"

Mr. Spenlove gave her some information. He saw the other party moving, and he followed them. Captain Nevile, once he was out of sight of the ship, turned and beckoned. Mr. Spenlove heard himself introduced to "my father." He heard a low refined voice murmur, "How do? How do? Delighted, what!" To his daughter Major Rhys said, "Who's this? Who? Oh! quite! Well, have to toddle."

He seemed, Mr. Spenlove observed to Sidney Nevile, afraid somebody might get near enough to pick his pocket, which had the weekly London *Times* sticking out.

"She says he was shell-shocked and coming into a crowd makes him a bit absent-minded. I say, I'll come over and see you when you call back. I'll have to go now. It's pretty marvelous, isn't it? Having her here, I mean!"

"I don't know, Sidney, I don't know. You've had a lot of marvelous things like that happen to you. Have you forgotten that woman—Mrs. what was the name? In New York?"

"Absolutely. All finished. This is the real thing, Fred. Can't you see? I'm going to get married as soon as . . . Well, I am. I have to make good on this thing, of course. I'll be able to see her. That's the main thing. There's a car at the club. It's to be here after lunch. You lunch with me at the hotel?"

"Will she be there?"

"Oh no. Her father always goes straight back to his place. He hates towns. It's hard to explain. We said good-bye on the ship. I'm going up there as soon as I've had a look-see at the club. Why, don't you like her?"

"She's too mysterious for me, Sidney. I prefer Mrs. Kavanagh."

"There's a reason for that mystery, Fred. I told you I had to respect her confidence. . . ."

"And for God's sake do, Sidney. Don't bring me into it. I'll see you at lunch. We'll have a drink to your success."

"Fred, I tell you she's the most marvelous person! She's the real thing. Beauty, breeding, youth, everything so just what I've always wanted and never found."

"See you at lunch, Sidney. What an enchanted fool you are!"

"You're absolutely right, Fred. Enchanted is the word. I don't believe there's another chap in the world who has what I have now. You think I'm off my nut, but I'm sane enough. You know, Fred, she has estates in Wales. . . . Well, I'll see you at lunch."

Mr. Spenlove, who was going to the office with the purser, stood watching Captain Nevile follow his baggage to the customs shed. There was an expression of Puckish mockery on his face, his cap askew on his head, his hands in his pockets, his feet planted firmly on the plank flooring. The purser came up to him with his classy briefcase in his hand.

"What's the joke, Chief?" said that gentleman as they fell into step.

"I was thinking of something Captain Nevile said just now. He must have gone a little queer in the head, being ashore so long."

"Queer in the head! I wish I had his speed and some of his luck," said the purser. They turned out of the gate together, walking smartly. "That skirt he's with wouldn't look at anybody else. And he's got that swank job, too. Chief, I wish I could get queer in the head. If I was nuts maybe I'd get me a rich passenger want to marry me, and give me a swell job lookin' after her pekinese. And listen. You know who gave that girl her pass? You do? Whee! And Captain Nevile's got her dated up from now on. And you say he's queer in the head! It hasn't affected his nerve, Chief!"

"He doesn't know anything about that," argued Mr. Spenlove bleakly.

"Oh yes he does. Old Wensley mentioned it. He said— ha-ha!—he said to me, 'Tip off that beachcomber who it was who gave the Follies girl her pass. Tell him he'll have to fight the whole legal department of the Afro-Iberian Mail Line.' You know his way when he gets sarcastic. But it didn't work. Captain Nevile says, 'They didn't give me a pass, mister. And besides,' he says, 'her pass came from a very old friend. I know all about it. She told me,' he says."

"You're only jealous because he's got him a crack billet ashore and can thumb his nose at all of you," suggested Mr. Spenlove. The purser nodded.

"Something in that," he admitted. "Who wouldn't be? We aren't like you, single and with a nice roll. God! Some men have all the luck! Look at Nevile. Divorced and no alimony to pay! And gets a swell job. He's going to be paid to go fishing! Can you beat it?"

"He's going to get married again," said Mr. Spenlove. "So where's your argument?"

"Says you! To the Follies girl? Whee! Then I guess you're right, Chief. He's queer in the head."

"We all are," said Mr. Spenlove in a hollow tone. Their two bright figures, in fresh white uniforms, dazzling in the Jamaica sunlight, turned suddenly into the shadows of an office entrance and vanished.

END OF BOOK ONE

BOOK TWO

Fog lay in the valley below the wooded slopes where Mr. Spenlove's squat screened shack looked towards a distant, dim gray sea. It was October, and the long twilight of land that faced eastward under a hill was in progress. A fire of oak logs burned quietly and with clear flames in the rough stone fireplace, and in the kitchen out back the curved, draped form of an elderly female person could be discerned moving without fuss to and fro on a series of short journeys from dresser to sink and from refrigerator to the oil range, where she was preparing a meal. One corner of the large front room was occupied by a table, laid for supper with a coarse check cloth and homely utensils. And on the porch, on the low settee where he slept during his vacations from the ship, Mr. Spenlove was smoking and watching the narrow track that led up the hill. He was wearing unpressed gray flannel slacks, a khaki shirt, and a very ancient Norfolk jacket of rust-brown Harris tweed, the pockets torn and the elbows no longer in good repair. He was waiting for someone to come into view. His friend Mrs. Kavanagh was bringing her husband Michael over from Briarcliff.

He was grayer, now, than when the Camotan had docked in Kingston two years earlier and had disembarked Mrs.

Kavanagh and her brother for their vacation at Antrim House. How characteristic, he reflected, to patronize a place because it had an Irish name! And Norah Kavanagh's luggage had been marked with a green band of paint around each trunk and suitcase. And yet those quaint residues of tribalism did not tarnish her real quality, her capacity, and her perception of character. She seemed to keep her intelligence and her prejudices in separate compartments, with an airtight wall between them. It was very enjoyable, he remembered, and often wished, when things were slow and stodgy, that she had been on board.

He knew what inspired this visit, however, and how much she wanted to know. She had sent him a clipping from a New York newspaper. There had been neither date nor the name of the paper to guide him, but he had needed no more than was in the item. He knew Mrs. Kavanagh would take no denial now. Once when he and she, with Mr. Kavanagh, had dined in New York (at a place where Irish stew and Dublin stout could be had) she had given him no peace until she heard the latest news of "that creature" who had infatuated Captain Nevile, and even fooled him into quitting his splendid job at the Turtle Bay Anglers Club and coming home to New York to go on a ship again. That was six months ago, nearly, and Mr. Spenlove had had precious little to say about it. Mrs. Kavanagh had had her suspicions. "You're on her side, I believe," she had announced.

He had been, of course, but he could not have explained it to Norah Kavanagh, who believed everybody had a motive for every act of their lives. Her artistic creed was that life was a pattern, whereas to Mr. Spenlove it was a phantasmograph, a divine comic strip that was always to be continued. It wasn't a pattern, he reflected now, as he waited for Mrs. Kavanagh's not very new flivver to appear. She had to make her books to a pattern, she had told him, with characters like the scenery in Elizabethan theaters or in the penny gaffs in the fairs of his childhood in the country. One character was labeled a hero, another a heroine. There was a criminal who murdered, and a nemesis called a detective. There was a half-witted maiden aunt or an Irish house boy for comic relief. A pattern, or a puzzle, which you put together yourself. She wanted Sidney Nevile to marry an heiress who comes to the club to fish. Mr. Spenlove had the faintest suspicion, born of his extensive knowledge of the subconscious world, that she wouldn't mind becoming miraculously an heiress herself, a mysteriously and extravagantly wealthy widow, possibly, who would appear rejuvenated at the Turtle Bay Anglers Club and infatuate him herself. That being impossible, she had to invent an imaginary heiress for him.

Mr. Spenlove had tried to show her, without undue emphasis, how defective her understanding of Captain Nevile really was. It merely showed, he suggested, that she had thought a lot about him after meeting him on the Camotan and had gradually invented a Captain Nevile of her own, bearing only a superficial resemblance to the manager of that Anglers Club in the Caribbean. He himself had paid the club a visit as guest of the manager, and he assured her she would have been surprised at the change in the young man if she had seen him there. And he would never marry an heiress, as Mrs. Kavanagh phrased it. Oh never! It was a quirk in his character, to make women with money keep their distance. Possibly, Mr. Spenlove suggested wickedly, there was a thrill in doing it, besides the genuine sagacity that kept him from putting his head through a golden horse collar. That phrase had aroused the tigress in Mrs. Kavanagh, or rather the American lioness. She had been brought up in an age and atmosphere which accepted as axiomatic that all Englishmen, especially those of title, wanted to marry the beautiful daughters of Chicago packers and Pittsburgh steel magnates. It ranked with the myths of the Revolution and was treasured by the same kind of people. Mrs. Kavanagh's intelligence had informed her long ago that myths gave her no lasting comfort, and she defended them with all the more ferocity. And as an American woman she could not tolerate the theory that there was anything shameful in a man without money marrying a woman who had a fortune. But Mr. Spenlove could be a lion on some occasions, too, and this was one of them. There could never be any palliation of such an act, he said, and Captain Nevile was entirely right in his ethics, whatever he might be in his morals. The distinction had deflected the argument, as Mr. Spenlove knew it would.

The clipping had upset him more than Mrs. Kavanagh could possibly have expected. He had it in his wallet even now, though it was useless, and Mr. Spenlove did not believe in relics of the past. And he remembered all it said, it was so brief. Every day the papers carried items exactly like it unnoticed by all save friends and relatives.

Athalie Rhys, former Follies girl, was found dead late last night in her gas-filled apartment on East Eighth Street. Police listed the death as suicide. A note addressed to Floyd Wroot, attorney, of Shap, Va., was found, police said.

That was all. A dead leaf spinning for a moment in the swift dark current of city life, and then it had vanished. He had the dead leaf in his wallet and the story behind it in his heart. Yes, his heart. The brain had no use for such folly as hers. He, and all the others, were still alive; even her father still lived, after his own fashion, on a far plantation in a tropic isle; but she herself was no more. No more! The question Mr. Spenlove often put to himself now was, had she ever lived in this world, on his plane or on Norah Kavanagh's? Had she not always had some shreds of unearthly brightness about her? The trouble was, they seemed no more than tinsel to many, those shreds. Or perhaps it was nothing supernatural. Perhaps it was only, as Mr. Spenlove imagined, and kept it to himself, that she was an anachronism. Born in the wrong century, she had never been able to make herself at home in ours.

Was she no more? That question too was insistent when he thought of her children, especially of Ginevra, the brilliant girl, spinning on her toes, bending and straightening like a rapier of flesh, her ice-green eyes fixed enigmatically on her mother's lover! Was not Athalie there in that fifteen-year-old body now? Mr. Spenlove, as he remembered Ginevra dancing before them, recalled the expression in her eyes and on her thin lips, told himself that time would show. Nor was he malicious. Time had shown him many things about love, and he was rather afraid of the god. He was certainly afraid of Athalie's daughter.

Just now, however, he awaited Mrs. Kavanagh and her agreeable spouse with a very genuine pleasure. Hospitality, in Mr. Spenlove's opinion, was easily corrupted by pride, avarice, and a mere aversion to solitude. Nine tenths of the hospitality he had experienced from Americans seemed to be no more than a sort of frictionless and impersonal benignity. The hosts and hostesses of these impeccable Roman villas and Florentine palazzi were merely performing sacred feudal rites handed down from a mythical antiquity. You established, he felt, more intimate and human relations with the Polish maid who took your coat and hat than with the rest of them. He thought hospitality, like an etching, could be effective in its small size and in what it omitted. He believed one only had so much of it available and it should be restricted to the few. It should be inspired by a definite longing to see and talk with those few, a longing unadulterated by the desire to show off material possessions. Mr. Spenlove kept these heresies to himself; but he held them none the less strongly. And he felt they would have full play when that antique flivver in which the Kavanaghs transported themselves came up the sunken road from the valley.

II

"WHAT I HAVE NEVER been able to understand," said Mrs. Kavanagh, "was, how she ever got into such a fix. Why, Terry would have done something. You know, he used to call her up, and once or twice he got her to go to dinner with him. It must have been something else besides money."

"It was. It was." Mr. Spenlove responded. He sat by his fire after dinner with Mrs. Kavanagh smoking a cigarette on a squat hassock. Mr. Kavanagh's benign bald head could be seen above a chair by a bookshelf where he was smoking one of Mr. Spenlove's Havanas and reading, in a state of mellowed amazement, a book he had never seen before, *The Anatomy of Melancholy*. Mr. Spenlove wondered what that devout papist was making of old Burton.

"It was, of course," he went on, "but even if it had only been money she lacked, I doubt if your brother would have been able to understand the situation."

"He's convinced she was crazy," said Mrs. Kavanagh. "He never knew what to make of her. He said she scared him, and he didn't call her up any more. It was just as well, too, after what happened."

"I could see you were glad, when you sent that clipping from the paper," Mr. Spenlove said equably, pouring out three glasses of Scotch whisky. Mrs. Kavanagh exclaimed:

"That's not so!" but she stared into the fire as she inhaled deeply. "What was behind it all?" she muttered. "There he is, on a ship again, captain of that ship we went down on, the Camotan, and she's—gone! Why didn't he marry her if he wanted to sacrifice his new work for her? Or why didn't she marry him?"

"Well, it's complicated," admitted Mr. Spenlove as he walked over and supplied Mr. Kavanagh with a highball. "Did you know," he continued, "that I went over to England to bring out the new ship? I had a few days in London too."

"What's that got to do with it?"

"Nothing much. But I had a piece of paper in my pocket and an address on a card. I'll tell you about it from the beginning of the trouble. You remember we did not see the girl again. She traveled north on a Royal Mail ship that called at Kingston three weeks later. And young Nevile did not get over to see me on the way up. I had to wait until we went south next voyage. We stayed there overnight, and I had an invitation to go to Turtle Bay Anglers Club. Young Nevile was waiting for me in a new fast English two-seater at the dock gate.

"It was the first time, really, that I rid myself of the notion that his job and his club were only a dream, something he had thought up to explain his presence in the island. I said so to him, and he laughed as he spun the big steering wheel to dodge the nigger children in the road. 'You wait, Fred,' he said. 'We have a rattling good place out there. Give the customers no end of a good time.' 'What about you?' I inquired. 'Are you having no end of a good time? Would you rather do this than go to sea?' He shook his head very emphatically at that. 'No,' he said. 'I want to command a ship again. I'll do it, too, by Jove!'

"That was the tone of all his allusions to what he was doing. But don't imagine he wasn't doing it well. He was working like a horse. Your brother can tell you about the club, the island in the lagoon behind the mangroves, the clubhouse and all the modern double-screened cabins in a semicircle among the trees, the concrete tennis courts, the bathhouse, the dock with the six fast launches for the fishing. He showed me everything. They had word that a steady stream of people would be coming down soon, and there were others from England promised. Gangs of men were improving the road from Spanish Town, and there was a scheme afoot to have a small steamer bring stores and guests right from the big ships in Kingston to the club. I could see there was money behind the enterprise, and an intelligent fellow at the New York end directing it. Young Nevile was very enthusiastic, in spite of his words to me about getting a ship again. I was half inclined to put them down to a conventional attitude of mind that covered no real intention. I was wrong there; he meant what he said.

"There was a party in a boat anchoring a double line of buoys through the entrance to the lagoon, and he took me out in a fast speedboat he had for his own use. It was one of those diminutive things with a large engine that lifted most of the hull clean out of the water when he opened the throttle. The noise was extravagant. It was just what I imagine being in a rocket ship must be, for he had no muffler. He shot through the water in front of a deafening uproar and just behind a fan-shaped curtain of spray. It was like sitting with a battery of machine guns under a cataract. It was the ultimate folly of speed, for you couldn't see anything except the upreared bow, you couldn't hear anything except the exhaust, and there was no particular need for haste. We had the whole afternoon to go a mile or so to the buoys. But to young Nevile I could see that speedboat was becoming an extension of his personality, a means of expression. He stood up as he drove it, shirt open at the throat and blown taut with the wind of our passage, a look of supreme confidence and delight on his features, which seemed to be sharpened with speed. One hand he kept on the wheel, the other drew the flying hair from his eyes. Sometimes he sent the helm over, so that we swooped hither and yon in a dizzy way that made me wonder whether we weren't going to turn clear over. There was an unpredictable lurch in the thing that made me think of an animated and demented razor blade cutting frantically through dark blue satin. We created beauty in our madness and abandoned it instantly. I will not pretend to you that I was happy in that boat. But it explained something of young Nevile I hadn't known before. When he slowed down to a

blessed six knots among the cays outside, and the boat
floated instead of rearing on end, and the engine made only a
sort of threatening hiccup, he sat down beside me and
laughed. When I asked him why he seemed so pleased, he
said:

"'Why, I've got an object in life now, Fred. I'm not going
to be a blasted beachcomber for long. The news you brought
me helps, too.' I said, 'What news?' and then I remembered I
had told him of the change in the office. The resident marine
manager had retired, gone home to a farm in the Chiltern
Hills, and a man we all liked, Captain Sylvester, had the job.
I remember Sylvester had been privately indignant when
young Captain Nevile was fired because some skirt had
squawked, as he put it. He had been known to remark that
girls know perfectly well what's in store for them when they
play around on board of a ship, and if they want to be left
alone they need never run any risks. I saw what young Nevile
meant, but I could not see that he was any nearer rein-
statement.

"'Old Spottiswood will never let him put you on a ship
again,' I said. 'He has been heard to say you're out and you're
going to stay out. Especially now you've quit the employ
altogether.'

"'Yes,' he said, 'but the venerable Spottiswood won't last
forever. Did you hear Virginia is a princess, now? Some
swank, eh?'

"I said I had heard it, but I was one of those who look
down on princes who marry commoners. He laughed. 'Good
luck to her!' he said. 'She has so much money I suppose she
wants to buy something very high class indeed. A good-
hearted girl, Virginia. Make him a fine wife.'

"He was loafing along, throwing out the clutch, so that the
boat's speed dropped to a crawl, and lighting his pipe he told
me he had seen Athalie a lot while she was on the island.
He had been up to their place, Caerleon Park, and he had
brought her down to the club for a day.

"'So it's going strong, eh? You mean you are going to marry her?'

"A very intense look came into his face. 'You don't know Athalie if you think anything else could happen,' he said. 'Why, Fred, there's something saint-like about her. You may laugh at me, but I tell you she is a saint!'

"I didn't laugh at him. I had seen him only a moment before with the wind of our speed in his face, and he had looked like a conqueror, a paladin, anything you like that is superhumanly attractive. But the word 'saint' was disturbing. And when he said they went to church together on Sunday and she had persuaded him to start saying his prayers again, I was temporarily at a loss. Wouldn't you be?"

"That creature!" Mrs. Kavanagh said in a sort of low, crying voice.

"No, no!" said Mr. Spenlove. "I can't go on with the story if you insist on looking on her as the embodiment of Kipling's Vampire. She wasn't that! You haven't even grasped the problem. . . ."

"Oh, haven't I?" said Mrs. Kavanagh, nodding at the flames that shot up as the logs fell apart. Mr. Spenlove thrust them together with an old harpoon he had bought for the purpose. "Haven't I?"

"No! For once, your woman's matchless intuition is miles off the track," said Mr. Spenlove with an emotion hard to distinguish from satisfaction. "All wet, as you say! I suppose, as a devout communicant, you are all ready to tell me you know what a saint is and I don't. Are you as certain as you'd like to make out? A saint has a genius for goodness that saturates the immediately surrounding human material. We are aware of that genius when we are in touch with the possessor of it. Beyond that area saints don't have any power, which would account for their innocuousness in the history of the world. Of course, there are holes in my theory. I have known so few saints! There is, for instance, the baffling difficulty that you didn't like her. I almost sensed a feeling of, well, resignation when you sent me that little clipping from the newspaper that told you she wasn't here any more. Am I right? Were you really shocked with grief or with relief when you knew she was gone? Your brother was safe again."

"He's never safe," said Mrs. Kavanagh, with a sigh. "He's been running around with a Greenwich Village poetess since he came back from Washington. But I wasn't worrying about him at the time. He had become convinced that girl was crazy because she told him she had once worked on the *Globe* under the society editor, and Terry had it straight from Mrs. Bozer, who's been on the *Globe* for years, that the young lady was making a mistake. Besides, can you see her, that Miss Rhys, in a newspaper office? I can't. Terry couldn't. He got scared of going near her. And now you say she's a saint!"

"Well, it's one mark in her favor that she can't pretend to be a newspaper woman. As for your brother being scared . . . But why can't you see her there?"

"Don't you try to get me into an argument, now!" said Mrs. Kavanagh, with a distinctly serious air. "You know as well as I do what I mean when I say I can't see her there! I can't say it in so many words. But a saint!"

"It's still possible we are both of us right about her," admitted Mr. Spenlove. "And that's a concession to your intelligence, because I know the story and you don't—yet."

"When Terry asked her why Mrs. Bozer didn't remember her, she said she had worked outside the office, going to really fashionable affairs of the really old families ordinary newspaper women couldn't reach! Can you beat that?"

"I can confirm it. It did happen—once! Wait till I tell you how I found out who she was. The affair was the Long Island visit of a very royal highness, not one of those princes that endorse cigarettes or sell champagne, but the heir presumptive of a throne. Well, by a trick, I suppose we must call it, she received an invitation. She happened to be eligible, for she had been presented at court when a girl. And her family was known to the hostess."

"Then why didn't Mrs. Bozer know about that?"

"Because, as a matter of fact, the girl couldn't remember anything. She was carried away by the splendor of the affair and forgot what she had to do. So the city editor, who had suggested the scheme and who has his own reasons for saying nothing about it, let it drop. Mrs. Bozer had no hand in it. He let it drop. Like your brother, he was suddenly scared and abandoned the whole thing. I mean he didn't see her very much eventually. I suppose you aren't going to maintain that he and your brother were frightened because she was so wicked, are you?"

"You mean she was carrying on a flirtation with the city editor?"

"I don't suggest such a thing. I'm trying to get you to see that your analysis of her character just fails everywhere. Do you suppose, or argue, that with her equipment she couldn't have made a killing whenever she wanted to, if she'd been what you imagine her? No. The reasons why her life ended in tragedy went far back."

"But how did you come to discover them?"

"Because young Nevile asked me to. Wait. I'll go on where I left off. I had to make you see that the ideas you had of her didn't explain anything except that you and she had led very different lives. So, when he said she was a saint and that she wanted him to go to church with her, I waited to hear more. After all, I reflected, he had gone to church when he was a boy. He and she belonged, he said, to the same church, so she wasn't proselytizing. And neither was she trying to compromise him, for he said she couldn't marry him, or even be engaged to him.

"He was not very communicative about this part of it, and I couldn't discover much about the place that strange father of hers had in the hills above. He said it was an estate, and it was mostly coffee. What he did was to go up there in this car of his and take her over to Montego Bay or up in the mountains to Moneague with a half-caste girl, who lived on the estate, as a chaperon. Mr. Rhys is an Englishman of the old school, and Athalie explained how he hated American manners, especially American girls and their freedom. Which is odd, for he married an American. The girl's mother came from Virginia. I learned all about it from the family lawyer, a remarkable person. He sat right here in this room and told me the story of her marriage and her children."

"I knew she was married," said Mrs. Kavanagh. "I was sure of it. But children . . ."

"Two. In fact, I believe another one died, but I'm not sure. She would idealize imaginary events, you know. I grant you that. But is that ever more than the bright plumage of the soul? Some people are always truthful. Men have a subconscious passion for truth in women. I doubt whether the passion is genuine. I think it arises from a misunderstanding of the nature of sex. We love mystery and are never happy until we have dissipated it.

"I am certain that in the beginning of this love affair young Nevile was entranced by the mystery in which she surrounded herself. She fulfilled all his unquenched thirst for a romantic attachment. She was a glorious reincarnation of Elli Phalère. She had Elli's glamour and a patrician background. Oh yes, she had! I am going to tell you what I discovered in London when I went over to get my new ship. She had it, all right. That was what sent your brother and that city editor, and several more perfectly genuine unpretentious males, scurrying away from her. She spoke to them, I have no doubt, of ancestral acres and noble Welsh lineage and an unwavering faith in the Church of England. The thoughts of a man who is essentially simple and unpretentious in his mental processes, like your brother, for instance, rarely reach beyond the sensuous images evoked by that sort of girl. They like her background to reveal a familiar landscape. If she had come from Middletown to the big city with perhaps a year at Columbia, all would have been well, even if she had refused to be as emancipated as some. But with her they found themselves sailing uncharted seas. They could get nothing out of her about herself save these vague adumbrations of former grandeur. They were confused that, though she had been on the stage, she evidently had resources that made her independent of a job. And they were alarmed by her casual allusions to well-known persons."

Mrs. Kavanagh nodded gravely at this.

"Terry told me," she said, "that she told him the vice president of your company was a very old friend of hers, which was how she could go to Jamaica on a pass. Mr. Wilmarth, she said. You see Terry knows Senator Wilmarth, the older brother at Washington, and he got us a complimentary passage too. When Terry heard her say she knew Mr. Wilmarth, he thought he'd better not interfere. But he wasn't sure she was telling the truth. He said you couldn't ever be sure of that."

"Stout fellow, Terry! I understand his dilemma. But at the time of which I am now speaking, down in Jamaica in that speedboat, all these puzzling features of her character were so much fascination for young Nevile. He reveled in them. She was a mystery, but she had sworn him to secrecy about herself. He didn't know her secrets then. I'm not sure he knows all of them now. He did know she was married and therefore could not marry him.

"But the fantastic habiliments in which Athalie Rhys concealed the realities of her situation don't constitute a crime. There was a subtle comprehension, through her love for him, of the best way to hold him. It was a fluke, if you like, that he should have met her, for he was made, emotionally, to appreciate her peculiar destiny and all the aristocratic trappings of her past. Think how he was fitted to be the lover of a girl whose father was Mortimer Justin St. Cyr Rhys, late of His Majesty's Welsh Borderers, a descendant of a collateral branch of the earls of Caerleon. That was what he meant when he said he had found 'the real thing at last.' I'm not approving of this state of mind. I'm only reporting it, and I am not convinced that such ideals are bad for us. Or perhaps I had better say, for him. We stand on our own feet, and those feet are in the trough of democracy. Young Nevile had a profound instinct for his own race. She must have known that, for she was English to him."

"Terry said she was an American in spite of her talk about her ancestors. He's sure of it."

"Terry's right, of course, but Captain Nevile believed what he wanted to believe. And she had the wit to encourage him. They were both in such an exalted sphere of feeling that what might seem fictitious to us was golden truth to them. She *became* what he believed her to be! Perhaps you have been married so long you have forgotten that. Or perhaps you never had any need to act a fairy tale."

"Why should anybody?" Mrs. Kavanagh flared suddenly. "You're only condoning . . ."

"There are those who have that need," said Mr. Spenlove mildly. "They are not the most fortunate beings in the world, possibly. They create an atmosphere in which they can live and dream. When they meet kinship of spirit and are in love, each believes the other, and everything becomes true. But the other kind of person, you and I, for instance, can never understand them, and call them fakers. . . ."

"And her children, were they fakes?"

"Oh no! They are very genuine. I'm coming to that. You see only the boy, Morty, is the child of his father. Ginevra, the girl, is the problem, because she knows what it's all about. Ginevra's only fifteen, but she has the future in her hands.

"It wasn't only the fascination of her father being English and an aristocrat. She had been on the stage, and for a young man of Captain Nevile's origins there was a double magnetism in that. There was the magic of the stage and the traditional connection, in England, between the stage and the aristocracy. I could see it in his face, even if he hadn't said it in so many words. 'She's the perfect mate for me, Fred. Why, I'll work like a crazy man to get her!'

"I said 'but how? if she can't marry you? Why doesn't she get a divorce?'

"His face grew very grave at this. 'I'm not at liberty to explain that,' he said. 'There are reasons why she can't get a divorce, on her children's account. It would be against their interests.'

"'Oh come!' I said, 'you mean to tell me you believe that? It isn't reasonable.'

"'Well, Fred,' he said, 'you ask her yourself when you go to New York. I want you to go and see her. She's marvelous. Here's the address.'

"'You say she was on the stage?' I said. I was looking at the sheet of paper. There was a crest—a visored helmet with plumes and a motto in Latin, *Dum spero, vivamus* or some such tag—heavily embossed in blue wax on white paper. The date was not written as we write it, but as the third Sunday in Lent, in green ink. That was another habit she had, of writing in green ink. He did not show me the letter, of course, because it was, I imagine, a love letter, and that sort of literature is distasteful to me. I'm not sure, if I had known then what she was like, that I wouldn't have asked to see it. Not that I wanted to pry, but because I think she often wrote what would strike the reader with wonder.

"'Yes,' he said, 'she was on the stage. But she could not keep on with it. She has a beautiful soul as well as a beautiful body.'

"'And you think a beautiful soul is out of place on the stage?' I said.

"'In a chorus, yes,' he said. He told me she was a dancer. It was there, you see, that she met our Mr. Wilmarth, the Senator's brother and vice president of the Afro-Iberian Line."

Mr. Spenlove took a drink of his whisky and gazed into the fire for a few moments.

"I haven't any data about their friendship," he went on

slowly. "We keep out of our own people's goings on. But I can put this and that together, after having known her. It began while she was in the chorus and probably a successful legal luminary was contemplating one of those delicate relaxations sacred to the tired business man. I say it probably arose from such a scheme. And Athalie Rhys had a histrionic streak in her. She would never act in a prudish way with such a man. When he had taken her out to dinner she probably invited him in to her apartment. She had an apartment on lower Park Avenue at that time, three high and ancient rooms at the top of a dark stair lighted at the landings. She could stand at the top after pressing the front-door release and watch who was coming up, and when you reached the top she was prepared to make the impression she desired. It was up four flights, and she could change a dress before the guest could reach her. Well . . .

"Whatever Mr. Wilmarth had in mind when he became acquainted with the third girl in the back row of that chorus, he probably had a change of heart when he reached that apartment. He was over fifty, and there is nothing like a walk-up to make a man think. Wafted aloft in a swift elevator, you become a fatalist. What will be, will be. And the apartment made him think too. It wasn't a chorus girl's home, I would say. There was something confusing in the mingling of dim lamp shades, the framed copies of primitives, the gold triptych with sacred figures, the prayer book on the table near the door, and the dark portrait in oils of an eighteenth-century ancestor over the white marble fireplace.

"Yes, recalling my own impressions, I would conjecture Mr. Wilmarth did a lot of thinking. And the upshot of his thinking seems to have been that, while she was very far from being the sort of girl he anticipated before he took her up to the Arrowhead Inn in Yonkers for dinner, he thought it an agreeable change! He accepted the rôle of virtuous counselor with which she had credited him, and enjoyed the sensation of being received by what seemed to be a sort of recluse. It was another of her habitudes to ask her men friends to escort her to St. Giles' Church, where she probably sat not far away from the impressive Wyatte family when they were in town."

"She didn't ask Terry," said Mrs. Kavanagh.

"No, she probably smelt him out at once. But most men who find themselves in a chorus girl's apartment on Sunday morning, expecting to take her for a spin out to Jones Beach or Dobbs Ferry, and find themselves holding her prayer book and New Testament, are too frightened to back out. Mr. Wilmarth was too solidly successful to be perturbed. I fancy he liked the novelty of it. He gradually became what girls call 'a very good friend.' He sent her a tremendous box of Easter lilies, a really good pair of etchings for Christmas, and a great many books. I imagine he did a lot of quiet thinking about her, being a man of wide legal experience, and while he never suspected what lay in the shadows of her life, he knew something was there and didn't try to lift the curtain. He knew that if it were merely a legal trouble she would accept his aid. As she didn't mention it, he was convinced she was in a real clutch of circumstance.

"I'm conjecturing now, remember; but it fits in this way with what I learned from her, and with the hints young Nevile dropped when he lost sight of her.

"Sitting in that speedboat and listening to his plans, the suggestion he made to me to go and see her when I was back in New York, I became aware of those shadows I have spoken of. 'You mustn't be surprised if she doesn't seem entirely frank, Fred,' he warned me. 'You see, she's in a queer position, being English and living in New York and married as well, yet not having a husband. It's political, I think. I can't be too explicit, old man. I see your side of it. I see hers too. She's so honorable, one has to—well, one has to be considerate and so forth.'

"'Political!' I said. I admit this bowled me out. 'Well,' he said, 'I'll trust you, Fred, not to breathe a word about it.

Her husband, you know, had enemies. They framed him. He was put in an impossible position. And he couldn't get back at them. His hands were tied. You know how it was with Mooney and Billings. And she doesn't love him any more.'

"'Here!' I said. 'Did you think that up?'

"'Of course not,' he said. 'She told me. And mind, Fred, she put me on my honor. Only you are so old a friend. She knows about you, and me, in the Mediterranean.'

"'You don't know her married name then?' I said. 'No,' he answered. 'How can I cross-examine her?' 'Well,' I suggested, 'you want to know a bit more than you seem to before you jump in with both feet.'

"He wouldn't see it that way then. He said they were in love. He said he hadn't believed that any love like hers existed anywhere in the world, even in poetry books. They were, he said she insisted, made for each other. So I said to him: 'Then what? Are you going to wait, like Jacob, seven years? Or for how long? What's the program?' He said some way out would open for them, he was sure. Of course, they couldn't live together. 'No!' he said, 'that's just blasphemy.' The very idea of suggesting it to her, a lovely sainted girl like her, was enough to make a fellow sick. I said, 'Ha!' and, I fancy, 'Humph.' I had, for a moment, the malicious desire to use an Americanism on him. I wanted to say she had evidently sold herself to him, which shows you how different American is from English, for it would have hurt him profoundly. Yet, in American, she had certainly done that, and it made me want to know more about her than he was ever likely to know in his present rarefied condition.

"'Well, in God's name, what are you going to do?' I inquired.

"'Why,' he said, 'I'm going to get my job back on the ship, and I'll devote my life to her and—' here he looked at me as if he was not sure he could trust me so far—'Fred, she's got a child!'"

Mr. Spenlove glanced at Mrs. Kavanagh as she flung a cigarette stub into the glowing embers and took up her glass. There was a bright carmine spot on each of the lady's cheek bones, and Mr. Spenlove saw she was trying to conceal her failure to discern anything maternal about that girl on the ship.

"I'll confess," said Mr. Spenlove, "that she hadn't given me any such impression, and when young Nevile went on to say she had a son nearly fourteen, I was incredulous. I remembered what you told me of women nowadays rejuvenating, or rather remaining always young, yet I remained, myself, incredulous. I did my best to get her chronology straightened out in my head, and I didn't succeed. This, I felt, was becoming one of those problems with a dénouement. My mind flew one way and another. I thought of our Mr. Wilmarth for a while. In fact, I came to the definite conclusion that our Mr. Wilmarth was the man, when it darted into my head that it was the Senator. I did some mental arithmetic. Go back thirteen—fourteen years and the war was on. Senator Wilmarth was over the other side on government business; yes! I made a fine, watertight legend of it.

"But I was wrong. I wasn't anywhere near being on the track of her story. Because in that case, I reflected later, why such a mystery? The Senator wouldn't have had any objection to her getting married, and if she was married to him . . . well, he happens to be married, with married daughters, and he never set eyes on Athalie. Never heard of her."

"Never," said Mrs. Kavanagh. "Terry knows him well and told me nobody has anything on Senator Wilmarth. He isn't that kind."

"I believe you. He was out of the question. So was our Mr. Wilmarth, I decided after a while. I was left with the extraordinary yarn she had unloaded on Captain Nevile. After darting about and alighting on a number of fantastic possibilities, my mind came to rest. I decided to wait until

I had seen her myself, since he was so eager to have me call on her.

"He wanted me to gain her confidence, he said. I told him he was the fellow to do that. No, he said, he meant that she was in need of real friends in whom she could trust. She had to know a person very well before she could confide in him. What about women? I asked him. Hasn't she any women friends. He said, 'She has . . .' and he looked at me without completing the sentence. Instead he let the engine out with a roar, and away we flew, back to the Turtle Bay Anglers Club, at forty knots.

"As we drew near to the city again, in his new fast two-seater, I asked him what he meant by that sudden dismay in his face and the unfinished statement about this wonderfully perplexing person. 'Oh,' he said, 'I just remembered she didn't want me to mention her daughter.'

"'Her daughter!' I said faintly. 'Has she a daughter? You mean grown up?'

"'Well, she's fourteen, Athalie says. I only tell you, Fred, because I need a friend who knows her and, well, something about her. It's rather a responsibility. If I could only get my job back!' he said savagely. 'God damn those women!'

"'You mean Esther Davidge?' I said.

"'I mean the whole damned crowd of them!' he told me. 'All they think of is their own tin-can personalities and gratifying their own miserable fancies! And what does it amount to? A fellow would be nothing but a girl's keep if he went on playing with them. They are tripe, if you ask me. Athalie's worth the whole shoot of them. Yes, she has a daughter as well. The boy is a year younger. That's the devil of it. It's frightfully complicated. Now, Fred, don't let me down. Go and see her. Find out all you can on your own. You make people confide in you. I'll come over when you arrive back.'

"I said I might not arrive back very soon, as I was scheduled to go to England but I would drop him a line. He said, 'Well, look here, I wish you'd take this and find out what it's all about.' He tore the top from the letter he had shown me and gave it to me. 'What do you want me to do?' I said. 'Find out about it,' he said, not looking at me. We were stopped at the side of the road near Tom Cringle's tree and I thought of that other young Britisher and how delightfully simple life was—if we believe the books—in those days. Young Nevile did not look at me. I came to the conclusion later that he was ashamed of his own weakness. He had discovered a shadow on the bright mirror of his passion! He believed, oh yes, he believed; but he did want a little confirmation from someone else. I sailed back to New York with that commission. I often took that piece of paper out to study the armorial bearings in the top left-hand corner. Not that I knew anything about armorial bearings, but I seemed to have before me, in that helmet with its barred visor and the shield with one small bird fluttering, a symbol of the magic that girl had wrought upon young Nevile. The face of the person inside the helmet, if I could have got in touch with him, would have revealed the secret.

"That was the situation at that time. She did, she didn't; she would, yet she wouldn't; and not a single definite fact had she divulged to anybody. On the other hand, I was struck by the remark of a passenger I had at my table that voyage. She was an invalid. Something the matter with her heart that imposed an avoidance of all excitement. She had been quoting from some novel she was reading, that we all lead incommunicable lives. She said that was true. And as she lay in her deck chair with her eyes concealed behind large dark glasses, I told her the outlines of this problem that was occupying my mind. No details, no names. Just the mystery and the significance of it in a man's life. 'I don't believe it matters at all,' she said, 'if they love each other.'

"How delightful! My invalid companion disposed of everything like that. It didn't matter at all to their happiness. Or did she, being a married woman, with husband, wealth, children, relatives, and intelligence—did she mean that it didn't matter because young Nevile and his girl would be unhappy anyhow? Did she mean that anything we can ever find out about each other, factual data, is so impersonal that it cannot affect our relations? I swear sometimes I think that is a fact. The happiest women are those who never ask questions at all. And the happiest men probably are those who never answer!

"Well, we cannot get anywhere by arguing whether he was unwise to want to know more about her. I had hinted pretty broadly to him that it was a large order, and he had taken me at my word. I was to go and see her; call her up first and say who I was—he was particular about that—and then gain her confidence. As I began to imagine what she might be like in her own place, I wasn't so certain about my success. How was I to know? His version of her character might be out of drawing.

"I had her number, and when I was free I gave her a ring. I had to wait a while. Then a faint, far-away, dying sort of voice came over the wire, 'Who—who is it?' I repeated my name and style, and after a wait the same faint tones said she didn't know any engineers. Did I have any business in the apartment? I began again, patiently outlining my more recent history and emphasizing that I had just come back from visiting Captain Sidney Nevile. The voice after a long pause said, 'Oh!' I seized this sign of intelligence to ask if I could call, and she said, 'Who?'

"I began again, leaving out nonessentials and trying to hold myself to a good-humored baritone. She suddenly cut in with, 'I don't hold conversations over the telephone with people I don't know.' I said she had met me. I was the chief engineer of the ship she went to Jamaica in. She said, 'Who?' again. I gave her my name, and she said, 'Oh yes!'

"Well, that was a distinct advance. I asked her if she would be in that evening. I suggested six o'clock. Would that be convenient, Miss Rhys? There was another of those long silences which to me are mentally paralyzing. They make me want to yell into the receiver. I waited. I said, 'Did you hear what I said?' She said, in a faint voice, 'Quite.' I said I had a lot to tell her from Captain Nevile. She would have a letter from him in the morning. Would I have the pleasure of seeing her at six o'clock? The wait was not so long this time. She said, 'I'll probably be in then.' I was going to get something a shade more definite when I found she was gone. Hung up!

"I was calling her from the ship, and as I turned away from the instrument our purser, who came over with me from the Camotan, was waiting to use it. He looked at me and shook his head. 'At your age, Chief!' he said; 'makin' dates at your age!'

"He might well think so. But I wanted to know one thing very much indeed. She'd told young Nevile she had estates in Wales. Or he had so construed something she had said. I wanted to know about that. I had my private reasons for linking her father's place, Caerleon Park in Jamaica, with her story. I wasn't going to let an eccentric telephone technique keep me from this mystery. And if you insist on the whole truth, I wanted to see her again for herself. She was a change from most of the girls who were running around on the cruises of my new ship.

"The house was an elderly 'walk-up' on lower Park Avenue. As I glanced at the row of brass buttons and letter boxes, and found hers, I saw there were two names on the same box, Rhys and Wilkerson. I noticed a letter stuck in her box. I mention it because it might have explained part of the puzzling features of her ménage, if I had known.

"I pressed and pressed. After a long wait the latch clicked so feebly I could hardly get the door open before it ceased. In fact, I think the lady with a fox terrier in a harness of red leather and brass studs, who had her hand on the door inside, saved the situation. I fancy the girl upstairs had been in a mood to keep me out after all! I walked slowly

up the dim carpeted stairs, pausing to get my wind and to
study the closed doors on the landing. I looked up and saw
a white arm and a burnished shingled head at the top of the
well. I reached the landing below hers and coughed gently
to indicate my proximity. I then took the last lap with fair
speed and reached an empty landing with both doors closed.
I knocked at 4B and waited.

"It might have seemed longer than it really was before
the door opened half an inch and I saw an eye, a cheek, and
a shoulder that was very white indeed. Then the door opened,
but she kept behind it to a certain extent, as though I were
carrying a piano or some bulky object and she was keeping
out of my way.

"I could hardly believe that I was actually in her presence.
She closed the door slowly, looking at me with a mysterious
and very alluring smile, yet giving me a queer impression
that she was placing herself in my power by letting me in.

"The room was large. I have mentioned the main features
of it: the subdued lights, the prayer book and Bible on the
table by the door, a faint odor of incense still in the air,
and the portrait in oils over the white marble mantel. There
was a large doll's house too, which attracted me, and a
colored copy of Burne-Jones' Light of the World just above
a small shelf and a red hassock that looked exactly like those
in a church.

"She said, 'I'm so sorry! I couldn't think who it could be,
and I've had a lot of trouble with men calling up and trying
to make dates. I don't make dates. Now I remember you,
of course.'

"I said I'd come as a special envoy from Captain Nevile.

"I have never been able to decide about her, whether she
possessed the power of some great actresses, of causing the
blood to flow at will through the cheeks, or whether she really
was so sensitive. Anyhow, her face and neck became tinged
with a deep blush, and she turned her head away.

"I thought to myself, What century are we in now? I

asked myself the question peremptorily. This couldn't go on! I would have to come to see her in silk stockings, knee breeches and a sword, with possibly a gold-and-enamel snuff-box of Rappee!

"I realized anyhow that it was important for me to make a favorable impression. I had to establish myself definitely as part of her conception of young Nevile. I did this by beginning to speak of our times together in the Mediterranean, and of my visit to his people in Suffolk. While I did this she never interrupted. She listened with downcast eyes, and they were such beautiful eyes. Or didn't you think so? They were like long, narrow aquamarines. She rose and laid a cigarette box at my elbow, with matches and an ash tray of bronze fixed to a red leather shield. She listened attentively, her eyes fixed on her own extremely small feet. I became expansive. Very soon she rose again and, placing a long-necked English decanter with a wineglass beside me, she poured a glass of sherry. And sat down again. The whiteness of her arms, neck, and bosom was to me something to marvel at, for I suffer very much from the passengers who insist on revealing large areas of what seems parboiled flesh. I believe they have a conviction that a woman who is virtuous can affront the world with impunity by exposing a blotched unlovely body. So I was all the more ready to appreciate this girl's beauty, which was, if you remember, devoid of cosmetics. Sometimes, as I spoke of early days and how attractive young Nevile had been as a youth, the color would come and go in her face and neck. . . .

"Well, I paused after a while, and noted that half an hour had passed. I heard her say, in her low, far-away voice:

"'Please go on. I love to hear you. You bring him so near to me!'

"Who could resist an appeal like that? I said possibly she had an engagement. Oh no, she said, no engagement. Then, I suggested, perhaps she would dine with me, and I'd tell her some more. She said she would be so pleased. She wanted so much to hear me talk. 'I am,' she said, letting me see those long aquamarine eyes for a single moment, 'having such a good time with you!'

"Well, I was beginning to understand how your brother didn't have such a good time with her. Behind all this sensuous softness, this gentle eighteenth-century female with the superb body and incredibly pure whiteness of texture, this timid creature with the long, cat eyes and tawny shingle, there was something watchful and secretive, something that might bite and scratch. I don't believe she ever did do that, but I am ready to swear she could give a carnal-minded man of simple tastes, like your brother Terry, an uncomfortable feeling that he was being played with by an adventuress. I could even imagine the grave caution with which our Mr. Wilmarth might comport himself with her. While you were pondering the imponderable—the strange difference between what you imagined she might be and the actual presence before your eyes, you found yourself studying the delicacy of the texture of her skin, the parted lips, uncolored, and moist like a child's, the eyebrows like thin pencil curves, and the hair as thick and lustrous as a tomboy's mane.

"You may say that hers was the art that conceals art. You may dismiss it either as artifice or artfulness . . ."

"Terry isn't carnal, as you call it," said Mrs. Kavanagh with spirit. "The poor kid has been badly treated by that wife of his. And it didn't do him any good to be moved to New York, either. He's looking for someone who understands him!"

"Well, my impression is that Athalie Rhys understood him so far as he revealed himself," said Mr. Spenlove. "She was the wrong sort for him. He is a simple organism, whereas she was so complex I doubt if anybody ever penetrated to her secret.

"Whatever it was, and now I'm speaking of men, it made a profound impression on me. When I looked around, while she was getting ready for dinner, I tried to imagine myself a detective of the Sherlock Holmes school. What would such a man conclude? I looked at her books and was no nearer a solution, for she had a scratch dozen of novels that indicated no particular taste. It was the same with the pictures; they told nothing. I felt I was no good as an amateur detective. A bag of golf sticks, a tennis racquet, a guitar with a blue ribbon, a pile of magazines, and a Harvard pennant tacked on the wall by the door of the kitchenette led me nowhere. Except that the racquet was not in a press and the guts were slack and dusty. No, I was not getting anywhere.

"When she came out, dressed charmingly, I took a plunge. I said, kindly, you know, in a voice that I tried to make absolutely sincere, 'You'll make a friend of me, Miss Rhys, won't you? Captain Nevile told me something about you.' She went very white, almost as white as the gloves she was putting on, and sank to the davenport by the fireplace. 'About me?' she whispered. 'That you are married,' I explained. She held her hands to her face for a moment. 'Oh!' she said, 'I can't talk about that. I have been so terribly hurt.' She looked up at me for an instant. 'Will you be my friend? I am so alone!' She paused. 'I don't mean I live here alone,' she said hurriedly. 'I have a woman friend.' She smiled up at me again. 'She ought to be in now. Mrs. Wilkerson.' 'Oh yes,' I said. I recalled the business letter in the box downstairs. It had been addressed to Mrs. Henry Wilkerson. She rose to go out with me, switching off the lights except one with a rose-tinted shade that illuminated a colored picture of St. Cecilia. Very effective.

"I dare say you think I had a pretty dumb evening. On the contrary. You have such a prejudice against her that I almost despair of explaining how completely she filled a man's definition of a perfect female companion. That sounds crude, but the word 'feminine' has a different meaning. We went to a place with which I was familiar, a discreet and highly select dive in the East Fifties to which I had been

given a card by one of my passengers. It was very quiet,
and for reasons best known to themselves the occupants of
the loges showed no curiosity about any of the other customers. There was a small bar in a room beyond, but those who
wanted hilarity did not patronize that speakeasy. Most of
the men were considerably older than their companions.
I suppose I fitted into that category. Which reminds me that
early in our conversation I took another plunge. I said I
had been astonished to hear she was married because she
seemed hardly old enough. How old was she? I promised to
keep it a secret locked forever in my breast.

"I said, 'You must be about twenty-three.' In that dim
place, in the light of a lemon-shaded lamp on the table, I
felt I was perjuring myself. She seemed more like sixteen.
Yet she had two half-grown children! Her face was without
color, yet it was not pallor, but the animated dewy freshness
of a young girl who washed her face with soap and water.
What really made her seem so young, though, was her
manner. She seemed ready to shrink back out of sight with
modesty, shyness, and pleasure when I said she must be
twenty-three. She wore a large black hat that made her face
smaller, and when she smiled I understood the utter and
inevitable captivity into which Sidney Nevile had fallen.
It was not a classical face, and it wasn't even a magazine-
cover face, yet it expressed a female type that was not really
new but old. I was reminded of the portraits of great ladies
of the eighteenth century. Over and over again I had that
impression.

"She said timidly, 'Oh, I am more than that.' I maintained I would pretend she was, well, twenty-four, then.
She blushed. I said, 'Tell me about yourself. Sidney has been
something like a son to me, you know. He is in love with you,
so I feel I must take you under my wing.'

"She said, 'If you only would, or if you could! I would be
the happiest girl in the world!' I said, 'Well, what's to prevent? What's the obstruction? Can't you get your freedom?'

"She shook her head slowly. She said, 'Only death can give me my freedom.'

"I wanted to know why. 'Surely you can trust me. Are you sure that's true? Think of what depends on it. He is very much in love. He has never spoken of any girl the way he speaks of you.' 'Oh, I know!' she said. 'And I adore him. But I am not free! And I cannot be free. It is so difficult to explain.'

"I said I would try to understand if she would try to explain. I said, 'You know Sidney always trusted me when he was a young fellow in the Mediterranean.' She shook her head again.

"'You see,' she said, 'it is a question of honor! I do not look at things from the modern point of view. I am a lady of quality! And honor comes first.'"

There was a silence in Mr. Spenlove's house, broken only by the faint noises of the fire.

"Did she say that?" said Mrs. Kavanagh. "Did she call herself a lady of quality?"

"Those very words," said Mr. Spenlove. "It struck me just as it strikes you, or anyone else who lives in our commercial world. For the first time I had a feeling that behind all her artifice and femaleness there might be a lady of quality. It seemed impossible for a girl to go to such lengths of pretense for nothing at all. The point, I suppose, was a fine one. Young Nevile had said she no longer loved her husband, and the inference from her words was that honor forbade her to desert him in view of his misfortunes. I was trying, you see, to construct something that would bear a little weight. It didn't amount to much because the notion of a man being politically railroaded into prison was not easily assimilated in real life. And even so, the mystery she was making of herself didn't help a man in prison. If she no longer loved him it made no difference if she left him. Or did it? That's the fine point of honor. To her, I believe, to a certain extent, it was important. I suppose that is all honor amounts to—to be faithful when fidelity doesn't matter in a practical sense. We have lost our feeling for it.

"So what I did was to put the matter in a plain way. I asked her then, what could she and he do? What could I do to help them? I confess I wanted the job. Next to loving her, to be within her orbit, to feel she trusted me and would allow me to direct her movements, was something, I felt, desirable indeed."

"You mean," Mrs. Kavanagh interrupted, "you had fallen in love with her yourself, but you hadn't any intention of running any risks with her!"

"Probably you are right," said Mr. Spenlove, and he gazed for a moment at the end of his cigar. "I think that's true of most women I meet."

Mrs. Kavanagh shook her head and stared into the fire. "I dare say!" she said. "I dare say! If I were in love with you," she added, "I'd kill you!" And she smiled at the fire.

"Well, it would be a glorious death," Mr. Spenlove conceded, but without enthusiasm. "Think of the loss to mankind, and to Mr. Kavanagh, who has found *The Anatomy of Melancholy!* Athalie Rhys could never have said anything like that to me! She was too much of the eighteenth-century woman. You have to keep this all the time in mind, that she irradiated sex so intensely that a pretty waitress in a tea room would suddenly gaze at her and withdraw to make some caustic remark to another waitress. Or she would be a long time bringing our order. I've seen it. I've seen what you used to feel, rising in women in the subway—women who have had to look round to see who was having that psychic effect upon them!

"That, I think, is the chief feature of her character, and it explains her queer little evasions as well as her superb sense of honor, that she was untouched by the modern epicene spirit, by which women lose their spiritual virginity almost before they leave school. They imagine they are changing what is known as 'a man's world' by becoming masculine themselves, earning their livings alongside of men, claiming civil rights and political privileges—claiming even the single standard under which to fight, and wearing hermaphrodite clothing. Well, they are easier to get on with, as you say. That is probably the reason why they are becoming so common. It makes marriage easier if the woman is half a man intellectually and spiritually, but in the same proportion you lose the ecstasy and torment of love. You have seen them, the girls struggling to get the reputation of being good fellows, of having no female characteristics, even denying their right to be spiteful and deceitful and evasive! I hear girls on the ship use carefully obscene language to impress men with their liberal attitude and their complete emancipation from sex.

"Yes, eighteenth century was what she made me think of. She had called herself a lady of quality, and perhaps she was. She had what they called 'sensibility,' and she expressed herself often in an ornate fashion that went with powder on the hair, dress swords and an admiration for *The Sorrows of Werther*. Living in New York in our time she had developed a protective coloring, as it were."

"You defend her anyhow!" said Mrs. Kavanagh. "How do you explain her killing herself when he wanted to marry her?"

"I can even explain that, because, as I told you, I happened to learn all about her. Yes, all there is to know. I know more than Captain Nevile, sailing triumphantly to and fro about the world, without a care. To the superficial eye he seems one of the most successful men in his profession, and he may be. But it is his destiny to seek a new perfection in the next woman he meets. He has a lofty ideal of his own. He thought, he believed that Athalie was the embodiment of that ideal, and although he no longer believes it, she was. She had, as he once said, everything. It was not her fault that he could not understand why she did not confide in him. He would never have believed the truth.

"That evening laid the foundation, anyhow. I had her confidence as far as I could hope to gain it. I began to be familiar with her character. She ate next to nothing, some fish and spinach, and drank only a glass of milk, which I suspect had to be sent out for. My excellent Chambertin I had to drink myself. It was not that she had any high moral views, for when we reached her apartment she produced a flask of Benedictine which had been given her by a friend.

"There I was, comfortably ensconced with a cigar before a small log fire she had lighted, and faintly aware of my unworthiness, with young Nevile toiling away down in the tropics, to sit talking to his girl. More than that, I felt I was as far away as ever of making her out. I gazed at the dark portrait in oils over the white mantel, the head and shoulders of a ruddy-faced, handsome man in some sort of uniform. It struck me it was an uncommonly good job. I said, pointing, 'Who painted that?' 'Oh,' she said, 'that's a Lawrence. It's my great-grandfather.' 'It's a good job,' I repeated. And I began to recognize some of the features; the long, beautifully shaped eyes, the clear skin and the wide smooth brow. 'Who was he?' I said. 'I told you,' she said, 'my great-grandfather. We are people of quality.' 'And do you come from over there?' I went on. She bowed her head in assent and gazed at her two hands on her knees. Those were the days of absurdly short skirts, and she was drawing the stuff down a little, very gently and without much success. 'He was a nephew of the Earl of Caerleon.'

"My mind went at once to the crest which had made young Nevile both proud and puzzled. She had evidently fitted so perfectly into his conception of the ideal woman that he had been jolted, ever so little, into wondering how much of her was genuine. So he had given me that piece of paper, in case I had a chance, as he said, to 'find out about it.'

"'Why,' I said, 'I thought you were American.'

"She made me wait a few moments before she said, 'I

don't feel that way at all. I was born in the West End.' Her
voice died away. When I said, 'You were?' she added faintly
'Berkeley Square.'

"Well, this either was so or it wasn't. Here was a clear-cut
issue, and upon my soul I was unable to make up my mind
whether to believe her or not. I had to assume that for impenetrable reasons she had a fake ancestor by Lawrence and
a fake crest on her notepaper. . . . I didn't know what to think
because it seemed improbable a girl should invent all this
when it served no particular purpose. Moreover, it had no
bearing on her reluctance to tell us why she couldn't get a
divorce. It didn't explain her living in decent comfort in New
York while her father lived in what I discovered was a sort of
poverty on his estate in the West Indies.

"I said, 'And you live here alone in New York? You never
see any of your—husband's people?' I had forgotten the Mrs
Wilkerson she had spoken of, whose letter she had put in her
pocketbook as we went out to dinner. I went on to be a shade
more candid. I was in a mood of benevolent candor. She was
intensely attractive in repose, sitting there by her fire, like
a high-school girl in a brown study. Mention of her husband
made her look up, and a most peculiar expression came into
those long narrow green eyes. Then she put up her round
white arms above her head in a dramatic gesture and clutched
her tawny mop of hair. And let her hands drop to her knees
once more.

"'Then,' I said, 'why don't you make a clean break for
your own sake and Sidney's? Have it over. He wanted me to
tell you that. He wants you.' 'Oh!' she said, 'and *I* want
him too! But I can't! I can't! It's impossible!'

"I asked her, 'Why is it impossible? You tell me that—
you're too good to waste like this. I'm sure something can be
done.'

"She made an astonishing reply. I mean it was astonishing
after her timidity and evasiveness during our telephone
conversation. She said, 'I would go to him if he wants. I

would give myself to him, though it is a sin. But we would have to go away, far away, India, China or some place.'

"'Why?' I asked. I had an idea, born of her exaltation. She had a really unearthly loveliness as she slid to a stool by the davenport and laid her white arms along the cushions, and her hair tumbled over her face. Yes, I had an idea. 'Why not go down to your father's place?'

"'My father!' she said. 'He does not know. He thinks I am with—him. My husband. No, no! I can't leave New York. There are reasons. Did Sidney tell you I was married? Did he say anything more?'

"'Just the bare fact,' I said. 'Naturally, I asked what separated you.'

"'I have a child!' she said. 'I was married when I was so young, you'd not believe! I was sixteen. And there is a huge black shadow over my life. My—my child must never know. My father must never know. It would kill him. He is very proud of his line. And now this wonderful love has come into my life, I cannot reach out my hand and take it.' She stretched out one hand towards the fire, 'Like that, and I mustn't take it. Nobody must ever know. Not even Sidney! Never that. He's English, and he would leave me. I know how they feel about such things.'

"'I think you ought to confide in him,' I said firmly. 'Yes, you ought! It will be the first step in the solution of your trouble.' She rose and knelt on the stool, clasping her hands under her chin and gazing into the fire.

"'Yes, you think so!' She gave a little shrug. 'Once I thought that, too. Once before, happiness was in my grasp . . . someone who was dear to me learned my secret, and left me.'

"'Then he didn't amount to much,' I said. 'I'm quite sure Sidney Nevile wouldn't do that. Anyhow, he wants to marry you. You know, he's never had a wife really. He's had lots of love affairs, of course, and he was married, but he hasn't been wedded, if you know the difference.' She nodded. 'We are wedded now, in that sense,' she said. 'But I am afraid. Men are cruel, cruel!'

"'Then you won't?' I said. 'Well, perhaps you know best. But what's to come of it? He knows you have a child. I fancy he would be all the more attached because of that. He's reached the age, you know, when a man wants something depending upon him. You ought to be as utterly frank with him as you can. He is very chivalrous.'

"'Is he?' she said. 'Are any men chivalrous? I haven't found them so—to me. They are chivalrous to girls who have a background because they jolly well have to be!' Her voice became clear and strong suddenly as she leaned her elbows on the cushions and threw her head back to stare at the Lawrence portrait over the mantel. 'They think I am their lawful prey,' she added and gave me a brief glance. 'They talk about me. They telephone, and stop me, follow me in the street. They think I have no thoughts or personality, no life of my own! I suppose you are like all the rest of them. You think if a girl has enough looks to get by and a body she can show on the stage, everything is easy. It's not so. It's terribly hard work. I couldn't stand it. I couldn't stand eighteen hours of rehearsals every day. I couldn't stand the lights. I had to sit all day Sunday, after church, in darkness to rest my eyes. And all the time it's the other thing too. They never let me alone. As if I hadn't my own life!'

"'Why couldn't you try something else?' I said.

"'I have. It's just the same. I've worked in stores and offices. I suppose I just don't speak their language.'

"'That's the reason,' I agreed. She looked at me for another fleeting instant out of the corners of her eyes.

"'I thought I could earn money now I have more expenses,' she went on. 'My—my boy's at school, you see. It's an expensive school. I have to give him what he has a right to from me. Yes, there are expenses. Father thinks my husband ought to support me. He doesn't know my husband hasn't given me a cent for the last five years. I can't tell him because of what happened. I can't tell anybody. It would ruin my chil—my son, if he ever knew or anybody else ever knew. I thought I'd earn more money, but it's not so easy for me. Somehow I—well, I give men a wrong impression.'

"Looking at her at the moment, I was very well able to believe that. I was wondering whether, if anyone came suddenly upon us just then, he or she wouldn't gather a wrong impression of me. I thought of her friend Mrs. Wilkerson using her key without warning. I even mentioned Mrs. Wilkerson, hoping I wasn't intruding too long. Athalie came slowly out of her languorous pose before the fire and seated herself near me on the davenport.

"'That's my name,' she said, smiling faintly, with one of her fugitive glances. She laid a forefinger on her chin, and I was reminded of some eighteenth-century drawing by Fragonard, in which, under the formal clothing, one is aware intensely of a vital woman's body. 'That's my name. You see, I wasn't sure you weren't one of these—well, I pretend there's a girl lives with me. It's safer for me, if I have men callers, isn't it?'

"'Ah,' I said, rather startled, you know. 'You have men callers?' I thought to myself, rather miserably, I am a fool to think otherwise. How could it be otherwise? Girls like her are surrounded by invisible battalions of men. She sank to her knees in front of the fire, her fingers touching the rug lightly. 'Oh, I have sometimes,' she said. 'In the future . . . no more!'

"I wish I could give you the changes in her voice, her manner, as she talked, because it was in that infinite variety that she conveyed the impression of a woman escaped, not from another world, but another age. She lacked completely the camaraderie, the good-fellowship, the instinct for what the American men around her wanted to know. The more she confessed the less one knew or could comprehend. When I left her that night I had a lot of information that I could have made up for myself, but she remained as much a mystery as ever.

"So I said, 'Won't you have dinner with me again before I sail? Say Friday?' This was Wednesday. She said, 'Oh, I'm going away.' 'You mean from New York?' I said. 'Oh yes, I'm going to see a friend.' 'Well,' I said, 'if you won't be home on Friday, say next voyage. You'll give me a message to take down, won't you?'

"'Oh, I may be back!' she said uncertainly, looking at me for a moment. She clasped her hands under her chin and raised her face to mine. 'You are so good, so kind!' she said. 'I've had *such* a good time!'

"'And you won't take my advice, to confide completely in Captain Nevile?' I said. 'I am speaking now as a man of the world as well as your friend. It's the best thing.'

"'No, I can't!' she cried softly. 'If you knew, if you had any idea, you wouldn't expect it. Please! I will do anything you ask but that.'"

Mr. Kavanagh came forward to have his glass replenished, *The Anatomy of Melancholy* under his arm. He was an industrious newspaperman whose work took him up and down the country in search of local political opinion. As Mr. Spenlove prepared the drinks, Mr. Kavanagh said:

"Did I understand you to say her name was Wilkerson? I've heard the name in connection with something, but it's a long while back. It was in the news, anyway."

Mr. Spenlove nodded as they sat down.

"It was. I can refresh your memory. But wait a bit. That comes later. I was coming down here on the following day and was stepping up to a ticket window in Grand Central when I saw a familiar woman's shape just moving off, her head bent over her purse as she put in the change. It was Athalie Rhys. I saw several men take long glances at her, but she was alone, and without haste she walked towards the train gates. I got my ticket and followed, but she had disappeared. There were two trains on that platform, and I couldn't run to and fro looking for her. I walked along musing to myself, following the redcap who had my bag, and as I halted behind him to pass into a car, there she was just seating herself next the window where I was standing.

"The effect of seeing me there was alarming. She struck her hand to her mouth, staring at me with her body suddenly thrust away from the window. For a moment I saw terrified dislike in her eyes. I raised my hat and gave her a bow and smiled, but she sat there in that pose, her brows contracted, absorbed (I know now) in trying to figure out to herself how I had managed to track her.

"I realized that if I went on into the smoking car ahead and gave no explanation of myself she would be lost to me as a friend. I would never regain her confidence. So I told the darkie to take my bag into her car. The seat beside her was still vacant. She was wearing a smart blue serge suit and a black hat, with beige stockings and black pumps, and she had a huge fur around her shoulders. And men were looking at her. And so were women, but with a difference. I don't know just why. I have only a vague theory. I tried my best to see in her only an attractive girl seated in a train; but the line of her cheek, the curve of her almost colorless lips, the angle of her nose, the shoulder she kept turned to the world as she gazed out of the window, all these things conveyed a sense of tragic enslavement! It was as though she expressed with unconscious art the pathos of sex—which most women have forgotten and behold again in one of their number with curiosity and amazement.

"I opened the paper I had bought and waited a while. I became aware of the fact that she was trembling, and her face had gone very white. I put the paper down and was meditating some sort of opening when the train moved. We glided quietly through those gloomy caverns of steel and concrete, and I wondered why so many people had to travel so early in the day. When we came out into the open air I said:

"'I didn't know you would be on this train. I'm going to Norbury. And you?'

"She started again at this. How was I to know why? She looked round at me with scared eyes. 'Why should you ask that? What do you know about me?' 'Nothing but what you've told me,' I said. 'You going to visit your friend?' She looked down at her white kid gloves and nodded.

"I went on to explain that I had this place in the country near Norbury and was coming down for a couple of days, and so forth. I made conversation to give her a chance to recover her poise.

"'I thought you were following me about,' she said.

"'Then you must be in a most unwholesome state of mind,' I said. 'It was only because we were talking about you so much that I didn't mention my summer shack last night. Are you going far?'

"'Not far,' she said. 'Not very far.'

"She tried to keep me from seeing her ticket when the conductor came through. She took the ticket from where he stuck it in the back of the seat in front of her and put it in her purse.

"I said, 'We aren't getting anywhere. What am I to tell Sidney Nevile, when you think I'm a detective following you around? It's preposterous!'

"She said, 'You've no idea how I felt just now. I wanted to get out of the train and throw myself under the wheels. I thought you were trying to find out about me and tell Sidney, so that it would be all over between us.'

"I said, 'You talk as if he was a damned fool. What could he possibly learn that would make him leave you? One would think he was a duke in disguise, to hear you, instead of a sailor who has lost his job and been divorced.'

"'Don't!' she said. 'He is a younger son.'

"'A younger son!' I was confounded.

"'He was once going to contract a loveless marriage with a peer's daughter. He told me.'

"'Ah!' I said. I was a shade overwhelmed by her interpretation of what he had told her. Or perhaps they had both soared together into that region closed to you and me, the region of Lover's Lies, which are only truth in a new and splendid raiment. 'Ah! but you ought to confide in him in return.'

"She smiled as she looked away, out of the window, shaking her head slightly. It was a very faint movement, and there was nothing but frightened misery in the smile, but it was more emphatic than a shouted negative. I said she didn't seem very happy at going to see her friend. She turned to me with her eyes closed and her hand to her mouth. 'Oh please!' she said, in a low voice.

"Well, I dried up. I read my paper. The train gathered speed, and the motion and vibration had a sort of toxic effect on our relations. I was conscious of being unusually close to something I couldn't define or discuss, just as I was that evening on the ship (you remember) when those two walked past us and she stood at the rail and raised her arms to the stars, as though she were making a silent supplication to an inexorable fate. For the remainder of the journey we sat as though we were strangers, she looking out of the window or straight in front at the green-plush seat back. When the train slowed down I wrote our telephone number on a piece of paper and laid it on her lap. 'Call me up if you're free,' I said. 'That connects with the ship.' She took it and held it and slowly put it into her purse. 'Keep cheerful,' I said as I got my bag off the rack. It was a banality, but I had no inspiration at the moment. She gave me her hand as we parted.

"Once I had got away by myself, with a chance to reflect upon my adventures, I began to see a little daylight, but I had so little to confirm my conjectures that I was in a dozen different moods. It was strange that although she had told her lover her secret it was obviously not the secret she had feared to give to me. Supposing what she said was true, why had she shown such genuine panic when I happened to take the same train as she did? And why did she allude so freely to her son but not to her daughter?

"I thought of all sorts of solutions. Then I dismissed her from my mind. I was only getting morbid. I found I was asking myself improper questions. There was that apartment, not fashionable, but discreet, and on Park Avenue. There was her income, which seemed adequate. There was her shadowy aristocratic background. And there was the even more shadowy domestic life that had been hers when very young with a person who was now no more than a shade himself, if what young Nevile said was true."

"Wilkerson," said Mr. Kavanagh again, frowning. "Give me time. I'm ready to swear I've heard of him in connection with some piece of news."

"You have. I'm coming to it. I only wanted you to see how poor a private detective I was. You'll understand that I didn't even use the natural intelligence of a man who might have fallen in love with her and wanted for his own reasons to get hold of her secret. What I did use was a sort of inverted wisdom which we call for convenience instinct. I didn't want to fall in love with her."

"Are you really sure you didn't?" said Mrs. Kavanagh again, making a face. "You've given her the breaks all along. I'm not vindictive enough to feel any real pleasure at what happened to her, but didn't she bring it on herself?"

"Oh no! She had no breaks at all in the end. Certainly, if she'd told young Nevile everything when they were in Jamaica together . . . But to do that she would have had to be somebody else. And he might have welshed on her at the time. Nobody would have blamed him if he, a man who had been through quite a peck of his own troubles, had withdrawn from taking over what she had to offer him.

"Friday I was back on board and pretty busy. We sailed next day at noon. I was having a sandwich and some beer in my cabin with the foreman from the yard when our purser put his head in at the door. 'Say, Chief,' he said, 'there's a lady on the wire. Wants to make a date with you. Say, Chief, it isn't that one we had on the Camotan, is it? You know the one I mean. She says her name's Rees. Wasn't that her name? The one the old man warned Captain Nevile about. Yeah, Rees.'

"I said, 'You must be a liar, you have such a long nose and a long memory, Pay.' He said, 'Well, Chief, for an old bull o' the woods, you got us all beat! Tell her to dig up a friend for me.'

"When I reached the phone I was a little surprised to find she answered my Hello at once. I said I was as pleased as punch to have her call up. I said I had kept the evening free, in case. Yes, I would call. Not before six, eh? She wouldn't be free before six. Righto!'

"A curious thing happened on my way to her apartment. I was early, so I had been up into the Forties to have some tea at a place I favored. About five-thirty I walked slowly down Madison Avenue and then east along Thirty-sixth Street. I was passing where she lived but on the opposite side of the street, and at the curb, in front of her door, stood one of those dark glossy limousines that indicate professional affluence and prestige. A sober-looking fellow of middle age was the chauffeur. Getting out of the car and entering the building, which meant going down two steps from the street, were Athalie Rhys and a man. As she hunted for her key, he took a deliberate yet casual look up and down the Avenue. Then he followed her into the hallway. It was our Mr. Wilmarth.

"I walked on downtown for two more blocks and crossed over. Of course, I said 'Ho-hum' to myself several times. Mr. Wilmarth and his chauffeur knew nothing of me, so I walked up on the east side without any precautions. I was passing the car when Mr. Wilmarth came out and made straight across to it. He sank into the corner seat and looked out of the rear window as if to see if anyone were noting his departure. He is a grave, middle-aged lawyer with a gray toothbrush mustache and a steady gaze. No Lothario, you know. I don't believe, really, he was ever a Lothario since he was a young law student. No, he was obviously puzzled as he sat there and was carried swiftly and smoothly uptown to his ornate duplex apartment in the East Sixties. I think he is still puzzled, and if he knows she is gone he has a blend of anger that she should have failed to seek him out for help, and relief that she does not puzzle him any more.

"I waited another five minutes, going north two or three blocks, and then I returned to ring the bell. The latch clicked at once.

"When I reached her door I noted it was open an inch or so. On the wall outside was a tiny framed text I remembered but had not looked at. It was a pious, gentle invocation to those about to enter what she called her house. Peace to all who pass my door, no evil thoughts are here. God grant repose to rich and poor, tum-tum, tum-tum, tum-tum. Something like that, in church gothic type with a design of holly foliage. I forget the exact words. The idea is what matters. She did that sort of thing naturally. It served the double purpose of confusing the carnal-minded male and convincing women, if any ever came to her door, that she was a faker. She wasn't. That's the chief thing I discovered about her, that she wasn't a faker. That was her ultimate secret.

"There was her door, ajar. The old hymn came to my mind, 'The Gate ajar for me,' and the fun we used to have in Sunday school with the word 'ajar.' I knocked. I looked obliquely through the opening and saw her in a pose, finger on lip, that might have been modeled from an eighteenth-century French print. She had the same clear, transparent complexion, the same arms and wide-set breasts that you see in those drawings of Chloe and Dido. She was not looking towards the door either. She was sitting by the window gazing down into the street, quietly absorbed in her thoughts. So it seemed. I opened the door, and she started up, alarmed, laying a hand on her bosom.

"I can see now that all this camouflage, as it were, had to be gone through with. She had to do it, and anyone who gained her confidence had to put up with it until she could dispense with it and reveal her real nature. It arose from the life she had led. But at the time I felt it was just a silly stunt. It made me suspicious, and I stood inside her door, closing it behind me, convinced that she was playing a complicated game with any number of men, that Sidney Nevile, down in Jamaica, was a besotted young fool.

"Because she made no allusion to having just been out in the limousine of a well-to-do lawyer whose relations with a girl who lived alone on Park Avenue could have only one significance. She made no allusion to her trip into the country 'to visit a friend' with no baggage or traveling clothes. When I made a remark: 'You are quite sure you are free this evening? I don't want to butt in, you know,' she inclined her head gently and smiled. 'Let us forget the world outside,' she said in a faint voice; 'the world that always thinks ill of us and puts the worst construction on everything one does—if one is a girl without a background.'

"And you know, that complete and stunning description of the world, including myself, was so quietly uttered that I didn't appreciate its full force. It was true. And when I mentioned casually, during our dinner at the Plaza, where she asked me to take her, that our purser on the Camotan told me she had gone to Jamaica on a complimentary ticket from the legal department she said, without any confusion, 'Mr. Wilmarth is an old friend. He is very good and noble-hearted. He wanted to—to marry me, you know.'

"I said, 'He *is* married! We had his daughter on her honeymoon last year. And her mother came down to see them off. You don't mean he would have got a divorce?'

"She inclined her head again. 'I respect him and admire him and all that. But I could never marry a man I did not love. And besides, it was impossible. I am not free. Only death can . . . I have told him I can never love him.'

"I wondered if it were true. But you wouldn't believe I spent our time together merely talking of other men. Oh no! In that chaste oval dining room at the Plaza I enjoyed myself. It was like telling stories to a child, a smiling, very sensitive and refined child just back from boarding school. 'Oh! that's wonderful!' she would say when I spoke of distant places like Japan and Java. 'Oh, I'm having *such* a good time!' she said, in a sort of gay chant.

"What fascinated me as I watched her was that this ageless creature who clapped her hands when she was suddenly happy, who kept her aquamarine eyes always half closed and downcast and her transparent skin so clear of make-up and lipstick, had twice gone through pangs of childbirth while we were in the war, while she herself was a child, the wife of a man who had vanished, leaving her alone. I struggled with this problem without getting anywhere. What was he like, the man who had had this fairy creature in her teens as a bride? And her son at school, what thoughts had he of childhood and his phantom father? And the daughter, of whom she did not speak. And there was that quiet elderly Englishman in the soil-stained khaki suit and planter's hat on the dock at Kingston, the descendant of the earls of Caerleon!

"I said, 'So am I having a good time. I wish Sidney were here to have it instead of me.' She put her hand to her face in a stricken way. 'Yes,' she said. 'I write to him every mail.' I said, 'Why don't you go down and stay with your father? You could see Captain Nevile constantly then!' She said— and it was exactly as though a cloud had passed, leaving her heart in the shade—'I cannot do that. My duty keeps me here. Please don't go over that again. I am a prisoner of fate. I live only for the future. Some of my ancestors lived for years in dungeons.'

"There it was again, that theatrical note which made one skeptical of everything she did and said. Why on earth did I keep thinking of her walking from that glossy limousine to the door of her house? Merely it was my badly disciplined imagination. I envied, perhaps, the owner of the limousine. I credited him with privileges I think he had never enjoyed. She read my thoughts, some of them. She smiled, a particular smile with a gleam of teeth, a slow raising of the head, and a sidelong glance from half-closed green-blue eyes. I got to know that smile very well, and so has young Nevile. It has him in its thrall even now, that smile. Ginevra has it, I mean. And Athalie said, 'I suppose you think every girl who has been on the stage is easy, especially if she lives alone.' I said I had no such thoughts. I said I found her a perfect companion, but a man in love was sometimes very intolerant, and I wanted her to keep the love of a man I was very fond of.

"She did not cease to smile in the same way. She said, 'It's for him to go on believing in me. I have the heavier load. It's easy for him, comparatively. He can swallow his pride while he is a beachcomber.'

"I said, 'Did he call himself that?'

"'Yes,' she said, a far-away look in her eyes, 'a beachcomber. And what's more, he doesn't even think being a captain, out here, is so much. He thinks himself a failure, but with me by his side, he would go home and make a name for himself.'

"'What would that be for you?' I said. 'Aren't you English too?' 'Yes, in heart,' she said. 'And I was born there, in Berkeley Square.'

"'And is that what you will do?' I asked. She nodded vaguely. 'Some day. I may get the release I pray for,' she said. 'You mean if your husband died?' 'I didn't say that,' she said hurriedly and in some distress. 'I never said that, even in my thoughts.' 'Well,' I said, 'you're beyond me, Athalie.' 'Yes, I know,' she answered, 'only God knows my heart.' She let her glance rest a moment on my face. 'My grandmother was the only human being to whom I ever told everything. In that house in Berkeley Square. I was so happy! And then my mother died and granny too. Then a great love came to me . . .'

"'Your husband?' I said. I hardly knew how to talk to a girl who dropped such phrases so naturally and as a matter of course. She shuddered and shook her head. 'No,' she said faintly. 'The war . . . I was in Paris . . . he was an officer.' 'Who? The great love?' I felt I had to get this straight, for it seemed she had begun at last. 'No,' she said, and a look came into her clear face that seemed to harden it to old alabaster, polished and transparent. I tried to figure her as she was at fifteen, and it came to me with the suddenness of a blow that she might now be thirty or more. 'No. My husband. He found me . . .' She turned her head away and looked across the dining room. 'I was unprotected,' she concluded.

"What could one make of such a story? I found that all one could do was to believe it. I thought of Perdita, that other lovely creature who was lodged in Berkeley Square. One was given the choice of either understanding Athalie's position or showing oneself an unintelligent fool. She invoked all the fine conventional conceptions of the days when women were classed with children and idiots. She had a good intelligence, but she used it in an unusual way. She used it to hide in. She spoke of a great love as if she expected me to know exactly what a great love—at fourteen or fifteen—might imply. But what did it imply? I was brute enough to ask her, thinking still of Perdita:

"'Did he—the man you loved—desert you?' I said. 'It wasn't his fault,' she said, and as if to herself she added, 'no matter what anyone may say.' 'What sort of man was he?' I went on.

"I didn't expect to get any answer to such a blunt question but she told me at once. A look of melancholy pride stole over her face as she glanced up at me for an instant. 'A genius!' she said, 'one of the greatest. . . .' 'Perhaps I've heard of him, then,' I said. She shrugged her shoulders slightly. 'Not unless you know the Chelsea crowd. I didn't

say he had the world's recognition,' she told me warningly.
'He doesn't cringe.'

"'You defend him, although he left you unprotected,' I
said. 'I told you he couldn't help himself. The war called
him,' she broke out. 'What did you say his name was?' I said.
'Harold Fakenham,' she said proudly.

"'Why,' I said, 'I *have* heard of him. The name's familiar.'
'You mean his brother Gerald,' she corrected me. 'Gerald's
the society painter.' 'Weren't they alien born?' I said
vaguely. I had a dim notion they had changed their name
from Falkenheimer or some such Teutonic form. 'Yes, I believe so,' she said, 'but it was a long while before the war.
Their father, I think.'

"So I was getting somewhere after all, but it was taking
me away from the main problem instead of towards it. If
her husband was a shadow, how tenuous to me and young
Nevile was the figure of the great love that came before she
was married, during the war or just as it came . . .! And he
was a genius she said, one of the greatest. That was important, I reflected, as I went back to the ship, because it implied
something very definite in her life. The fellow had her loyalty
somehow, even now that another great love had come into
her life. And she had hinted at a second great love too, who
had turned craven and left her when she had recklessly revealed her secret.

"Back in her apartment, where she again placed the flask
of liqueur at my elbow, she went into the bedroom and came
out with a miniature. 'My grandmother when she was a
girl,' she explained.

"It was a delicate piece of work, on ivory in an enamel
case. The figure had ringlets and beautiful shoulders. The
important thing was that I was gaining her confidence as she
talked of her childhood 'on our estates in Wales.' She began
to tell me of her family estates near Caermawddy.

"Mind you," said Mr. Spenlove quietly, "I am telling
you what she told me. I'm not maintaining she ever saw her

family estates, or that the family had owned them since the
time of William the Fourth. But she spoke of them as if they
were in residence there. She spoke of ancient Caerleon, that
marvelous city of towers, and temples and hot baths, of
palaces with golden roofs for Roman patricians and pro-
consuls, as if her ancestors had lived there. Maybe they had,
though the place was a ruin before Doomsday Book. While
she talked I was thinking of her father's place in Jamaica,
Caerleon Park. 'Yes,' she said, 'one of my ancestors was
Governor of Jamaica.'

"Further and further away, you see, from what I wanted
to know. But how pleasant it was, to be closeted with a beautiful creature whose family was a cadet of an ancient earl-
dom, with coats-of-arms and estates and so on! Did she by
any chance, knowing I was English, use the unfailing un-
guent for my soul? I'm not even sure she knew I was English.
And how tragic it seemed, too, much more tragic than if she
had been merely the daughter of a lowly East Side immigrant,
that she should have this shadow over her life! I think I penetrated to the core of that conundrum. Our instinct is right,
and so was Athalie's when she built up that marvelous background of Welsh mountains and ancient castles, where her
branch of the Mortimers rode out against the hillmen and
raided the neighboring valleys. And if it thrilled me to imagine her the daughter of a hundred earls, as it were, think how
young Nevile, hungry for what he called 'the real thing,'
must have felt!

"Genuine, you say? Was it genuine? Of course their love
was genuine. It wasn't any the less genuine because they pretended they had what Athalie called 'noble blood.' Whatever
they believed became true. Comfortably married people forget that! She had been married—yes, but of that I must tell
you in good time. It was, she told me, 'a dreadful mistake, a
loveless union,' even if the horrible thing hadn't happened
afterwards. It certainly wasn't comfortable."

"What?" said Mrs. Kavanagh sharply.

"Wilkerson," said Mr. Spenlove. "The affair Mr. Kavanagh is trying to remember. I know all about it."

He filled the glasses again and threw on some logs, so that the fire blazed up in the wide chimney.

III

"AND DIDN'T YOU ever see her again?" said Mrs. Kavanagh.

"Yes, but not for a long time." Mr. Spenlove stared speculatively into the sudden flames. "I was away in the Camotan for a three months' South American cruise. It was my last voyage in the old ship. We took in Havana and Trinidad, but not Jamaica, so I did not get a chance to look up Captain Nevile. I had no letters either, of course. We were moving pretty fast to make all the calls advertised in our cruise literature. I was preoccupied with having the Camotan do her best while I was with her—she's nearly eighteen years old, you know—and also I had a new ship to bring out from England. I was really looking forward to that. Wensley and I were going over by Cunard. I liked Wensley because you never knew he was on the ship he was commanding. I liked him because he never went on the rampage and always accepted responsibility. He backed you up, but invisibly and inaudibly except in the office. I know a lot of passengers thought he was pompous, and the younger generation disliked him because he saw through their pretensions. And he had the name of being high-hat because he wouldn't eat in the saloon with passengers. He used to say the saloon was for passengers and he wouldn't intrude. When he is a passenger he never goes near the officers. Wensley was all right, in spite of the fact that he had strong antipathies. He never liked Captain Nevile. They couldn't look at each other. They are as different as chalk and cheese, or oil and water."

"Mr. Spenlove means the captain of the Camotan when

Terry and I went to Jamaica," said Mrs. Kavanagh to her husband. "I didn't like him."

"That's why I am speaking of him now," said Mr. Spenlove. "He never had any use for Nevile. He called him 'that beachcomber' when young Nevile went into the uptown ticket office. Wensley never had any arguments with anybody. He lived alone on his bridge, and the most he and I ever had at sea was a few minutes' conversation. When he knew Captain Nevile was on board as a passenger he ignored him except to tell the purser that that beachcomber had better keep away from old Wilmarth's bit of skirt. Wensley had one of those powerfully pervasive personalities that reached to the uttermost part of his ship. He was aware of all that went on in what seemed sometimes to be a supernatural way, for he hardly ever appeared in the flesh.

"Wensley's argument was that Nevile being fired could be blamed on nobody but himself. He had no business to get into such a jam. Wensley would say to me in a bass growl, 'You leave the skirts alone, they'll leave you alone.' It wasn't true, although it might be true for Wensley. He and I get on very well. He's so big and solid and competent he makes me think what an ideal tutelary deity he would be. I'm not sure Wensley doesn't half believe a sea captain *is* a deity of some sort when he knows his job as Wensley does. He enjoys assuming omniscience if not omnipotence. He used to read a great deal and he liked the reputation he had of being 'the best educated skipper on the North Atlantic.' Perhaps he was. It isn't saying much, if you ask me. He had a great deal of information, and he could tell a story impressively. He sits perfectly still, never moving his head, and his enormously solid body and rather bloodshot eyes gave him a distinct resemblance to some highly educated ju-ju or Indian idol. He expected you to listen attentively, and when he gave the signal, to laugh. He was a most restful commander because you knew exactly what he would do and say under given circumstances. He hadn't any imagination at all. He was a safe shipmaster. He was the exact antithesis of Captain Nevile, who always has a touch of skillful daring in him when he is navigating. Wensley was so safe that he was unaware of being so. He was known never to have taken any chances in his life. Nevile has. He knows just what taking the chance involves, and then he takes it and goes on as before. They both use judgment; but it isn't the same kind of judgment.

"Those two were quite unable to look at each other. The fact that I was a friend of Sidney Nevile did not prevent Wensley giving me his opinion of him. He thought Nevile ought to have 'cleared out' when he was fired. I said he hadn't really done anything. 'Never mind!' said Wensley, 'as a matter of dignity he shouldn't have gone on the beach selling tickets like a tram conductor.' I asked him where he and I would be if somebody didn't sell tickets to passengers. 'That's entirely beside the point,' said Wensley. 'We're talking of a shipmaster. He's a cut above a ticket clerk, isn't he? He ought to have gone home, or gone West, or to the South Sea Islands. If a chap wants to be a beachcomber he shouldn't stick around where people know him.'

"He was the same when young Nevile went to run that club. He was skeptical about its being so grand a job. Wensley is quite unable to believe another skipper has any qualities he himself lacks. He is not quite able to believe in the existence of the qualities themselves sometimes. He thinks music and pictures and statues grow like frost on a windowpane, or toadstools in the night. He's that sort of character. And so he had a slender chance of knowing what sort of talent it was that came into action in running a club of rich men and making them over into a congenial, homogeneous yet ever changing body of good fellows. Wensley would expect them to obey his orders, you see. Young Nevile had to make them believe he was following their orders, yet keep command of them without their becoming aware of the fact. Which is quite different from commanding men. As for Athalie Rhys, Wensley is constitutionally incapable of understanding her at all. The fact that he had given orders that she was not to be put at his table shows Wensley's character. He was solid enough at all times to ignore even a man like Wilmarth when the legal vice president 'sent his pick-ups on board for a free ride.' That was Wensley's crude way of putting it to me when we were discussing it, going over to England. Yet he had the sagacity to send a warning to Nevile by the purser to 'keep off the grass,' which was another of his phrases. He is a happy man, because most of the things that break the hearts of men and women are either invisible or incomprehensible to him."

"He has no imagination, then," said Mrs. Kavanagh. "He looked like a retired contractor to me when he was going on shore."

"He would like nothing better than to be a retired contractor," said Mr. Spenlove, smiling. "He bemoaned to me the fact that he couldn't retire for another fifteen years. 'And by that time,' I told him, 'the revolution will be here and you'll have nothing to retire on!' Like my sister, he thinks only a Mussolini can save England. By England he means his own social order. Wensley was very severe on me for granting common humanity to liberals. They ought to be exterminated like rats and other vermin, he thinks. He feels that a lethal chamber would solve a lot of our problems. 'Put the poor beggars out of their misery,' as he expressed it. The war, though he does not say so, was a jolly good thing, in his philosophy."

"How can you like a man who thinks such things?" Mrs. Kavanagh protested.

"Well, he graciously includes me in his scheme of an orderly and thoroughly reconditioned universe," Mr. Spenlove explained. "He is organic. He doesn't go home and enjoy England, as I did. He becomes a part of England. He is the embodiment of unconscious British well-being. He has an instinctive apprehension of our social structure, and he is aware of the hierarchy of divine beings in which he is a tutelary deity. One of the real reasons why he disliked young Nevile was the feeling that the fellow was an interloper in our ranks and was dodging his destiny by not being in the navy or some government billet. I don't say Wensley ever put that feeling into words, but he has made remarks which bear me out. I say has made. He isn't here any more. He has been translated, as they say of bishops. So I speak freely and with affection, although he tried to kill young Nevile's ambition to 'stage a come-back,' as you put it. But that was after we went to England to get the new ship.

"I have said that I knew all about that extraordinary episode in the life of that girl, but to explain it, I have to go back into the past, when she married Captain Wilkerson in Paris, fifteen or more years ago. Why, I ought to go back even beyond that, to the beginning of our century, when young Mortimer Justin St. Cyr Rhys quarreled with his father and was cut off with a shilling! That's the customary euphemism. I imagine he had some sort of allowance. You remember him on the dock in Kingston, Athalie's father. I'm speaking of him as he was thirty or more years ago. The old man was rich. He was a rich Welsh draper in London. For some dark reason the Welsh used to be good at it. We in England said it was because they could live on less than anyone else. Old Rhys was head of Rhys and Robinson, and his son seems to have hated both the old man and the business. I don't blame him about the business. His mother was a Mortimer, and her father had been a nephew of the earls of Caerleon. Old Rhys had been born in their part of the country and had contracted this high alliance in the 'sixties through what we would call nowadays 'personality.' He put himself over. He was an assistant in a haberdashery or some such house in Haymarket, and the girl fell in love with him. To use another euphemism, she threw herself at his head. This is worth noting because it is part of a hereditary strain. A romantic streak, if you like. It's the easiest thing in the world to misunderstand. It explains Athalie—and her daughter too.

"She threw herself at his head, and so he captured the daughter of an ancient house. He made a fortune and bought the town residence of the ancient house in Berkeley Square. How did I find out that interesting historical fact? Well, I happened upon a person who has a professional interest in the family affairs. He is what we call in England a family solicitor, the repository of ancestral secrets, only he lives in a hill town in Virginia. He came to New York when the daughter of his former client, Martha Rayne Rhys, took her own life. He found that Captain Sidney Nevile, then at sea on a voyage, was the legally appointed guardian of the two children. When he reached the captain by radio he was referred to me as being on the spot and knowing the circumstances. And so," said Mr. Spenlove, taking up his glass, "he spent a night or two down here, and his account of his client's adventures in English matrimony, before she tried the American kind, rounded out what I learned in London.

"Yes, that girl's grandmother threw herself at his head, the head of a clever, ruthless Celtic trader, than which there is nothing more vain and egocentric in the world. For Rhys trade was a mystical frenzy, and he and his kind will go to the stake for their business faith. And the result of finding such a girl crazy enough to marry a counterjumper was to make his pride in himself engender a contempt for her and her family. When his son, Athalie's father, took after the mother, in looks and shape and disposition, with nothing of himself to show, not even ordinary business ability, the contempt evolved into scorn. He was in the forefront of the nonconformist renaissance in England of that day, the renaissance that culminated in the Methodist Cathedral in Westminster. Old Rhys, the successful Methodist draper, took a radical nouveau-riche delight in living in Berkeley Square and trampling financially on the old order. He enjoyed helping to get hold of Lily Langtry's Imperial Theater and pulling it down to build a vast noncomformist vatican in the heart of the West End. He was a Little Englander and anti-imperialist anyhow, and his son showed his hatred of his father's politics by going out to the war in the Imperial Yeomanry.

"But previous to that, after emerging from Winchester, which is the most ancient and the haughtiest school in England, the break between the wealthy draper and his son came when Mortimer Justin St. Cyr Rhys refused to follow in his father's footsteps and start at the ribbon counter in Rhys and Robinson's. And where? In Hackney Downs, or in Putney or in West Ham. Rhys was smart in his day. He knew the West End wasn't London. He knew London was growing, so he started his drapery stores out at the far end of tram car and bus routes. One and eleven pence three farthings was his favorite price card, which seems less than two shillings. He started the custom of giving away some rubbishy article (which cost him nothing as he got them as bonuses from the wholesale dealers) instead of change out of a shilling. He bought rubbishy cartloads of cheap books in flashy bindings and gave away one with every purchase of ten shillings. He was clever at merchandising, which consists of making people buy things they don't need by giving them something they have no use for. His shops were crowded. It was the thing to do in the suburbs—shop at Rhys and Robinson's.

"Young Rhys refused. Of course, he had his mother backing him up. She had her own money. Not much, from old Rhys' scornful standpoint. He would have called it a mere pittance. But for those who didn't want to build Methodist vaticans or contest a seat in Parliament in the Liberal Nonconformist interest, it had its merits. And she could do as she liked with it. She had a plantation in Jamaica, and a considerable amount of stock in American railways. She also had the house in Berkeley Square, with the brass name plate of Mortimer polished into illegibility by a century of house-

maids' toil. Old Rhys had bought it and made over the title
to her. So when young Mortimer Justin St. Cyr broke with
his father she gave him the plantation and some of her
shares in a railway, long since consolidated, that went
through the western part of Virginia, serving rich coal
regions.

"That is important because it was due to this that he
met Martha Rayne. He had an introduction to the New
York traffic manager of the line, and he was a fellow named
Rayne who came from a place called Shap, in the mountains.
He lived in New York, and he had a daughter Martha. He
didn't know much about it, but 'supposed' he was Welsh.
It was, he knew, 'way back,' and of small consequence to
one who had been born in that distant hill town in the northern Appalachian ranges. He was as preoccupied with getting
ahead in the railway business as old Rhys was with drapery.
They would have understood each other. But Martha, as
they say, was avid of life. She was bored to tears with talk of
stocks and transportation and bank loans. She and the young
Englishman were instantly in love. I call him an Englishman
because that is what he was. Being an Englishman is a state
of mind. It is the forty-ninth state of this country, and it is
useless to glare at me, for I am only describing a condition
that existed long before I arrived."

"There was never in the world such complacency as
yours," said Mrs. Kavanagh, but her husband only laughed
as if at some remembered diversion.

"But I am stating an important fact in the social history
of America," insisted Mr. Spenlove. "What have I to gain
by inventing imaginary species? It used to be assumed that
all American women were after titles, which was as untrue
as it was superficial. Girls like Virginia Spottiswood, who
got her Georgian prince, go after titles, and always will because they are covetous of glittering power. But when
Martha Rayne met young Mortimer Justin St. Cyr Rhys and
they fell in love instantaneously in the house on Lexington

Avenue, she regarded him as something unprocurable in her
own world. She was, so my informant the family solicitor
told me, a 'Southern belle.' which to me has such an old-
world flavor I accused him, Mr. Floyd Wroot, counselor-
at-law, with a law office upstairs opposite the county jail in
Shap, of being romantic and quoting something he had read
from the pen of Lilian Bell. I used to read a lot of Lilian
Bell's works when I was in the Liverpool–Savannah cotton
trade, and Counselor Wroot's allusions to Martha Rayne's
girlhood as a Southern belle in Shap were romantic. He was
a lad there, and he remembers Martha bringing her Englishman to that town lying in the fold of those immense dark
green and black ranges. She brought him, not to live there—
she knew there was precious little chance of that even if
she had wanted it, which she didn't. No, she brought him
to show him off, as something extraordinarily valuable she
had found and acquired. She knew instinctively that the
other girls in Shap wanted exactly the same luck, whatever
they might pretend.

"Mr. Wroot remembered their arrival at the railroad
depot and the reception at the Rayne place. Shap is at the
junction of two mountain rivers, the Strid and a smaller one
called the Blackhoof. They come lunging and crashing over
beetling ledges, cutting through canyons that look like the
dumping grounds for the ruins of a shattered world. They
slide under black cliffs that are horrible with damp and
fungoid excrescences and they come together under a black
trestle bridge that is like the dolorous way over to oblivion.
I spent a week in those parts, for Mr. Wroot is by way of
being a fisherman, and I took him fishing while he was here.
I had the curiosity to follow him down there when I had a
chance. Well, it was a legitimate curiosity. I am always being
told by Americans that I have a lopsided view of them,
because I am always on the Atlantic seaboard. They pay
themselves a poor compliment. They are, in themselves, living sculptures carved from their native rock! I can dispense

with America so long as I can have Americans! In fact, I dislike the country and would never dream of living in it if it were full of Chinamen or Indians, or even Negroes. We are so blinded by the agreeable qualities of the inhabitants that we fail to notice the unpleasantness of the country itself. The average American never realizes this paradox. He is proud of going places faster than anyone else, of having superb hotels and artificial entertainment, but he never sees that all these things are forced upon him because otherwise he would go mad in such a savage land! They do go mad when they are shackled to some definite section. American native literature consists of case histories in lunacy. Only a certain type can survive in such surroundings. Mr. Wroot says he couldn't live anywhere else but amongst his mountains. He said he tried to enjoy Florida while fishing, but he gets seasick in a boat, and the flatness of the land nearly drove him insane.

"I said curiosity took me down there to Shap. And possibly a desire to improve my knowledge of the world. Then there was the picture I had in my mind, from what Mr. Wroot had told me, of Mortimer Justin St. Cyr Rhys, Esq., stepping off the train in that place, stared at by the local folks who hang around to see the train come in, and also by the inmates of the county jail across the square, who chew tobacco behind the bars and converse with the citizens who chew tobacco on the sidewalk below. I was fascinated by the picture! It seemed to me that if I knew how he took it, and what impression the house up the Blackhoof Valley made upon him, it would illumine the subsequent destinies of them all.

"And it does. Mr. Wroot said 'he didn't fit in at all with the folks.' Mr. Rhys didn't even try to fit in. He wanted to get away at once. New York might be not so dusty; but this raw Americanism, this open-faced hospitality that gave him not a moment of privacy, this astounding system of serving food in a lot of little oval dishes arranged around a mother

dish loaded to the guards with provender, convinced him
that he was a sort of knight errant rescuing a beautiful dam-
sel from a whole mountain range full of ogres. He made it
clear that he wanted to take his bride out of that as soon as
possible. And the fact that Martha wanted to go too, more
than anything else in the world, did not prevent her from
seeing how revolted he was in his mind at the sort of background his wife had. He was too young and too inexperienced
to know that it was the best background of all because it
left her without any prejudices against his own background,
and gave her to him full of vitality and rich good-will to be
molded to his heart's desire. It was his tragedy that he did
not see it, and I dare say it haunts him now, and puts an
edge on his hatred of Americans. Neither of them knew how
profoundly that attitude of his towards her people and the
rather daunting scenery of those parts affected their lives.
They went away, to New York and across the Atlantic, to
London, where Martha Rayne Rhys, as she insisted on
calling herself, saw Society at close range and tried hard to
fit into it.

"Of that I don't know. I only go by what came of her
efforts. There was something wrong with the union from
the beginning. I don't mean because she was an American.
American girls were popular in England. Gibson girls were
all the rage. Young fellows stood in crowds every night at
the stage door of the theater in the Strand to see Edna
May come out after *The Belle of New York*. That wasn't the
trouble. I think young Rhys really went to America with
the romantic idea of going West, buying a ranch, and becoming a landowner far from Rhys and Robinson's drapery
emporiums. It was the regulation thing to do if one had a
row with the pater. Instead of finding Indians on Broadway,
he had gone to a house on Lexington Avenue with steam
heat, a colored cook, and a smart waitress, and had fallen
immediately in love with the most beautiful and vital creature he had ever seen. There is no doubt of her beauty.

She had black hair and gray eyes and a voluptuous body. And she might have been a success in London if she hadn't been inspired to rampageous exploits. The life in Berkeley Square suffocated her. Her views and actions inspired a gentle amused irony from old Mrs. Rhys, who had not expected her son to bring back an American wife.

"When the baby—Athalie—came, it seemed as if the wild oats were sown and there would be a serene acceptance of the Berkeley Square life. But when the child was less than a year old the war in South Africa broke out, and young Mr. Rhys enlisted in the Imperial Yeomanry as soon as possible. It wasn't an impulse. He would have gone off to Jamaica, or to Canada, or some other distant place, if the Boers hadn't declared war on England. He joined, and sailed. You may not remember those days. He was one of Mr. Kipling's 'Absent-minded Beggars.' He left a lot of little things behind him, which we, who were not heroes, were commanded by the Poet of Empire to look after while they did our country's work.

"To Martha Rayne Rhys the whole thing was inexplicable. She was an average American girl of those days, and it was inexplicable. She had never heard of the Transvaal and was utterly unable to understand what it was all about. She didn't know where Africa was, let alone the Orange Free State. The tramp of armed men, the hauling of guns through the streets, the brass bands and the seeing off of soldiers at Waterloo for Southampton, was very exciting. But when he was gone she had a subtle conviction that he was glad to go. She had a sense, too, of a door closing, a curtain rustling down upon a finished scene.

"Mr. Wroot had no information for me as to what took place in London while Captain Rhys was at the front. The Boer War was a long business. It took years, and Rhys remained out there. Whether he had any intention in so doing I doubt whether he himself could say in so many words. A soldier's duty is in the field. He was serving Queen and

Country. And so on. He had a perfect alibi for staying out there until the last Boer commando was rounded up and captured. It would have been perfectly all right if he had decided to settle there and had sent for his wife and child. He may have done that very thing, but Mr. Wroot, telling me the story, had no information. All we can say is that his wife did what she would have done if he had sent for her. She ran away. She left a note on her dressing table when she went out to dine at the Savoy one night with friends. The following Saturday she sailed on the Lucania from Liverpool, and after an interval that wasn't entirely occupied by the voyage in a twenty-one-knot mail boat, she appeared in Shap on a visit to her folks.

"Her father by that time was living in Pittsburgh, where he was a vice president of the road, or assistant to a vice president. I am quite helpless among the officers of an American corporation. I am reminded of *The Mikado* at every turn. Vice presidents are like Central American generals. I am dazzled and abashed by the formidable desks at which they sit and the splendor of the odalisques who take their dictation. You can imagine for yourselves that Mr. Rayne was by that time an important executive. But he is of no importance to us because he didn't even know his daughter had run home. She vanished again and turned up in Reno, where she began an action for divorce on the grounds of extreme mental cruelty and desertion.

"Who paid for all this we can't set down in black and white. Mr. Wroot says she had an allowance from her father, but the fact no doubt is that the man she ran away with, who was on the Lucania, who had been living for some months at the Savoy, and who met her later when she reached San Francisco, a divorced woman, was the real inspiration of her break-away. It is curious that she should have run off with a man who was what her husband had wanted to be before he met her. She became the chatelaine on a vast estate in California, an estate with a ranch of cattle and orchards as large as an English county, where were grown those enormous apples which look so magnificent and are so desolate to the taste. They seem to have been conceived in a dream by Bouvard and Pecouchet, those twin growers of fabulous vegetables in Flaubert's novel.

"So there was the girl you knew on the Camotan, an infant, with her runaway mother married to a stranger and her father on a crowded transport approaching old England, unaware of the situation. She might almost be said to have no father either, for the bronzed major with the bleached hair parted in the middle, who picked her up and held her in his arms for a moment when he arrived, had never seen her before. All he had seen was a sleeping infant.

"What he thought we can only conjecture from his life. He was in his thirties then, and his suddenly discovered freedom from a bond he had found intolerable ever since the novelty of Martha's brilliant personality had faded had the effect of expanding his ideas. He returned from South Africa an imperialist, and the impetus gained by his new position as a seasoned soldier with no ties save his infant daughter drove his thoughts outward to the lands across the sea. His mother approved. There was the hereditary estate in Jamaica, the remnant of plantations that came into her family when one of the Mortimers married the daughter of a great city merchant in the eighteenth century. He could go out and take care of Caerleon Pen, as it used to be called."

"Hadn't he any paternal feeling at all?" Mrs. Kavanagh inquired.

"Paternal feeling in military gentlemen in the thirties is never very strong," said Mr. Spenlove dryly. "I would say that paternal feeling is a much overrated emotion anyway. Especially when it is supposed to be inspired by a baby. In ninety-nine cases out of every hundred it isn't paternal feeling at all, but something else, like family pride, or the pride of possession, or even plain egoism. A man is fond of

children or he is not. It has nothing to do with paternity.
I have known men adopt kids and treat them far better than
others treat their own. I mean take more interest in them.
Most fathers care nothing either way so far as paternity is
concerned. Was there ever a greater failure on earth than
the attempt to deify Father's Day? And rightly so. Fathers
have no spiritual existence. The nineteenth century was
better informed. They called fathers 'the authors of our
being' and let it go at that.

"So, with both parents safely out of the way, Athalie's
grandmother had a free hand with the girl's education and
upbringing. I shall always regret I never met the widow of
the wealthy founder of Rhys and Robinson Limited. She
must have been a character. She had a sort of salon, to which
artists, authors, musicians, and even actors came. The girl
was sent to a school for the daughters of gentlewomen near
Brighton, and it was run by a clerical person with advanced
ideas of education. He believed in love as an inspiration and
vital principle. There were neither punishment nor imposi-
tions at that school. The teachers were to rule by love.
Mrs. Rhys thought it a good scheme. Or was she only being
gently ironical?

"When Athalie left that school, or even before she left it,
her mind was a mass of confused sensuous images and fantastic ideals. To say that she expected a fairy prince would
be inaccurate. What she expected was a fairy emperor who,
like Roman emperors, was also a god. She was even more
lovely than her mother, with a tousled mop of tawny hair,
a skin of transparent purity, and a body like one of those
eighteenth-century bacchantes. She had a blending of furious
Celtic strains, with a dash of Anglo-Irish blood from her
American grandmother, and at fourteen it was already
carrying her far beyond the regions where most schoolgirls
dwell. It brought her, at her mother's house in Kensington,
into the range of 'the great love' of which she spoke to me.

"She was still living with her grandmother, but the house

in Berkeley Square was leased, and they had what I imagine was an even more romantic domicile, for a girl of that nature, in Onslow Square. I once had lodgings in Sidney Street in Chelsea, and I know Onslow Square well. I used to pass along the east side of it to reach the South Kensington Underground station to go to work. Onslow Square was the perfect setting. I wouldn't mind going through the experience of 'a great love' myself in Onslow Square. It was, in my youth, my conception of an ideal locality. Even now, if I were to inherit a fortune from some distant cousin in New Zealand, I would look favorably on Onslow Square. Berkeley, Eaton, Grosvenor and Belgrave Squares are ultra ultra, of course. Onslow Square, that select, unobtrusive, architecturally refined rectangle of yellow-painted stucco, with Regency porticoes and exemplary mews, appeals to my middle-class capitalist soul! What perfect neighbors one would have! A retired admiral of the line, a colonel of guards, an elderly Lady of the Bedchamber who has a private income of her own and so does not need a Civil List pension or a suite of rooms at Hampton Court. No doubt a first secretary of a foreign embassy, or even a chancellor, might be expected near by, leasing annually. I am now revealing to you my most cherished dreams, never to be realized, for I haven't any cousins in New Zealand! But the mention of Onslow Square always arouses in me a few harmless but very clear ambitions. It represents for me the finest sort of habitation a civilized man can use. I wouldn't give tuppence for your idiotic Fifth Avenue 'mansions' and the summer hotels people call homes on Long Island. You might as well expect me to want Chatsworth or Balmoral. Oh no! Onslow Square for me.

"It borders on Chelsea too. Out of the square you are instantly into that select thoroughfare that runs from Knightsbridge through Brompton to the Cromwell Road. You cross it at once, and you walk down Sidney Street, which is the last word in discretion. The lady who had the

first-floor front in my boarding house—I was first-floor back,
impressed me as being the most refined upper-class female
I had ever met. I was in the early twenties, you see, and full
of charming illusions. And you have no idea how really
virtuous I was in those days! Her maid was a severe creature,
like a governess, who came in by the day. For months I did
not understand the status of the gentlemen callers who came
home with the lady in a hansom. If I hadn't seen her entering
the Alhambra one evening I might never have guessed her
profession. She had a face like a baroque saint, her black
hair drawn back in a bun. Her eyes were downcast as she
passed me on the stairs with a faint whiff of chypre. The
exemplary rectitude of that line of houses, rented in flats or
furnished rooms, was beyond all description. It faced a
church of entirely correct perpendicular Gothic. The demi-
mondaines who rented the first-floor fronts could gaze down
upon their gentlemen friends being married!

"At the end of this romantic thoroughfare was the King's
Road. You crossed over and passed down Oakley Street to
Cheyne Walk and the river Thames. I mention this because
I had occasion to go there. I went down into that august
region to call on 'the great love.'"

"You!" said Mrs. Kavanagh. "You really found the man?
The one who . . ."

"Yes. I called on the man who inspired the furious passion
in her. I used to wonder why she became religious, and I
imagine it was an instinct that made her do it. Her immense
capacity for passion demanded some sort of spiritual govern-
ance, and she found it in the genteel and human Catholicism
of the Church of England."

"You call it that!" said Mrs. Kavanagh, amused.

"Well, they claim the Apostolic Succession, you know.
I learned quite a lot about it while talking to young Nevile's
father down at Ufford. It suits us! You remember what some
papal legate said when writing to Rome in the time of Elizabeth. He said Englishmen were naturally against Rome. He

probably knew what he was talking about, for he was plotting against Bess at the time. He produced it as an argument in favor of a foreign army landing to impose his religion on the nation. Well, I can feel in my bones an antipathy that enables me to understand that papist. He felt himself in contact with a tough, coarse-grained national character, insensitive to his Italian subtlety of spirit. You must bear that in mind, for in this case I am narrating there is nothing of Latin emotion at all. It is Celtic, and English, and, if you like, American. So she found solace in going to church when she was left alone."

"But how did you venture?" said Mrs. Kavanagh.

"I had a great curiosity about him. Young Nevile had been quite certain that Athalie did not love her husband any more. I was quite positive that she hadn't ever loved him, that he was something I had to account for in some other way. When she spoke with a certain pride of this Fakenham, and with a touch of desperate nostalgia in her voice and face, I was conscious of one of those affairs of the heart that are independent of social inequalities and even outlive the loss of all illusions about the man himself. Sometimes I envy a man who has been singled out by fate for such a love. He can do the vilest things, and she thinks he is admirable. He can abandon her, take her money, kick her in the face, sleep with another woman, and command her to bring them breakfast in bed, and she will worship him on her two white knees! And then, on reflection, I feel glad I am not one of those men. The responsibilities are too heavy. To be worthy of such a woman's love one would have to be a god anyway, so a mortal is bound to fail. When the woman is a lusty, oversexed Celtic romanticist of fourteen, the burden, unless one were an extremely intelligent amorist, would prove insupportable. It does, in many cases, and the result is suicide, or homicide, or infanticide. Only an artist in the fullest sense of the word can handle the situation.

"But I must explain here why I spoke of Captain Wensley,

with whom I went over. He's in the London office now, assistant to the director of new tonnage, and I can say what I like about him. He wouldn't care, though. I told you he was an excellent raconteur, if one behaved and did not interrupt. He hates interruptions. Several times on the voyage, in the smoke room, while he was telling us a story, someone burst into our group, or one member of it would get up, or the harmony was destroyed in some way for a moment. Wensley would never resume. He just dried up, and we had to finish the yarn ourselves. He didn't protest. Just dried up.

"But on one occasion he told us one of his experiences, and no one interrupted. He sat there, cigar in hand, everybody attentive, and told us the incident. We had been discussing what the French call l'idée fixe; obsessions, bees in one's bonnet and King Charles's heads. All that sort of thing. One of the company had spoken of his house man at home who was obsessed with the notion that he would find the place on fire. Always prowling around searching for incipient blazes. I told the story of old Ridyard, the almost legendary chief engineer in the African Royal Mail, where I once toiled, and how he would appear before the coal passers in the bunkers, a miner's safety lamp in his hand, his white beard in a green baize sack and dark glass goggles on his eyes, searching for spontaneous combustion and so forth. He would frighten those simple West African blacks into stark staring immobility, their eyes rolling and teeth gleaming. Even the white men, oilers working in the engine room, had a turn when they encountered that extraordinary old chap in the dark of an alleyway. He was popularly supposed to have communication with the spirits in the mountains when he went on shore in the Niger region hunting for ju-jus and idols and the fantastic regalia he used to take home and present to the museum. He had been reported as coming back from the jungle to Old Calabar followed by two leopards!

"Well, there we were, swapping yarns, and Wensley said, 'I had a man some years ago who had the same obsession. He was afraid of fire.' And he went on to tell how, some years ago, on the Celerosa it was, he had a bosun's mate who became so celebrated for leaping out of his bunk in the petty officers' quarters and shouting 'Fire!' that they complained to the bridge. Wensley had him up on the carpet. The man was a gray old badger with a taste for drink. But Wensley told us he was a good painter. He had the knack of mixing paints, keeping brushes in trim, and covering a panel on the promenade deck without a blemish. I knew what Wensley meant. The man was a tradesman, and we have progressed so far in our modern destruction of the handicrafts that a man who knows his trade is treated with the same consideration that the Medicis gave Michael Angelo. He is cherished. Wensley had him up and wanted to know 'What's your story?' The others who slept in the room, boatswain, carpenter, plumber, and assistant master-at-arms, all said the chap was crazy. Wensley didn't mind if he was, so long as he retained his painting ability, but he had to sift the evidence. Sometimes, said Wensley, who had never heard of psychoanalysis, when a man can tell his story it helps to calm him down.

"So the old fellow, name of Roscoe with the Christian name of Somers, told the captain his story. He said he had been the center of an extraordinary affair. A year previously he had been on the booze a good while and couldn't get a ship. He didn't belong to the local New York unions, so he couldn't get a job as a painter. He was living in what he called a flop house, but it was known that people would call up there if they needed hired men. One night he was thinking of turning in when the night manager sent for him. Said there was a man on the telephone inquiring if they had anybody who could paint a house. Somers Roscoe said he could paint anything. So the man said he would call in his car and take the painter along, as the job was in the country. He would pay five dollars a day and board. As the house was empty Roscoe could sleep there too.

"It sounded like a fairy tale, but half an hour later the man turned up in a big open car that had been a costly affair once, and Roscoe threw his sea bag in the back and climbed in beside his new employer. He was a tall, dark, rather good-looking chap, Roscoe said, but only in a certain special way. He was a devil! Roscoe shouted at Captain Wensley, who told him to pipe down or he'd go into the brig to do his shouting. But he was so impressed with his discovery of satanic qualities in a human being that he had difficulty in keeping it to himself.

"They started out from New York late at night, and whether Roscoe already suspected the other of being Mephistopheles or whether he built it up in his mind later we shall never know. He told the captain he thought that guy had a funny look from the first. Yet the guy was kind enough, with plenty of cigars, and Roscoe had an unfortunate weakness for cigars that he couldn't afford. Then they stopped at a place in Harlem, and the guy went away and brought out a paper parcel that contained a jar of wine. Must have been a gallon of red wine. And when they were out in the open country beyond Pelham he stopped the car and they had a good swig. At Rye they had another, and at Port Chester another. Good stuff, too, said Roscoe, making him feel pretty sleepy but very pleased with himself. Once, somewhere about Sound Beach, I fancy, they turned along a shore road, and Roscoe had a fine swig while the guy was pumping up a tire. Roscoe was feeling too good at the time to wonder why the guy hadn't stopped at a service station for air.

"So they went on and came at last to Norbury. Roscoe remembered how they turned off the Post Road and took the shore route again. Said he could smell the sea. It was very dark and nearly one o'clock in the morning when they turned off the shore road and followed a dirt track that ended in a dark silent house. He sat watching the guy unlocking the garage, which was under the house, owing to the rise of the hill behind, and the headlights showed a big cellar stacked with cut logs, and wooden crates, and a bench standing in a great heap of shavings, as if carpenters had been there at work. Pots of paint and cans of oil on shelves. The guy came out and drove the car in. He got a big red portable electric lamp and led the way up the cellar steps into the house. They took the jar of wine with them. It was half empty by that time.

"There was no current on, and the furnace was out of order. The guy said he had men coming in the morning to work on it. He brought up armfuls of shavings and logs and started a big fire in the living room, and they had a good swig at once. There were some sandwiches in the kitchen, and they had those. The guy sat munching and taking a drink of wine and telling how he was moving in with his family pretty soon and wanted the place painted up good. All of it, all over, inside and out. Ladders and planks all ready. And two hundredweight of white zinc paint. Five gallons of turps and any amount of oil. Ha-ha! old Roscoe laughed as he told his captain the amount of oil. The guy had gasoline down there too. The job would take several weeks, he said, and he would pay a bonus too.

"Old Roscoe must have been pretty drowsy by this time. He said he wanted to turn in and as the place wasn't very completely furnished as to bedrooms, the guy made him up a bed on a sofa. He said he himself would sleep on a cot on the porch. Roscoe had had a lot of wine, and he lay right down by the roaring fire and slept. Roaring fire! he repeated to Wensley, and his face became absolutely demoniacal. He described the guy going to and fro, getting things ready. He said the guy knocked a picture from a table, and when he picked it up Roscoe saw it was a big photograph of a beautiful dame with a little girl at her knee. The guy said, 'That's my wife, damn her!' Roscoe protested earnestly at this. He was feeling benevolent and wanted to look at the pretty dame. He told the guy he ought to be ashamed to speak like that, but the guy went on arranging blankets and cushions. And

Roscoe dropped away into the warm oblivion of drugged wine.

"You can imagine Captain Wensley, solid as a seated granite effigy of an Egyptian deity, listening to this yarn of an old gaffer who had been making the lives of his bunk mates a burden to them. The carpenter, who had been a long time with Wensley, told him the old fellow went over the tale again and again, bringing it up on any or no provocation, besides rousing them up with his nightmares yelling 'Fire!' and 'Jump, damn you, jump!' For once in his life he had had a clear glimpse into an evil mind, and he kept on talking about it. 'Tried to murder me, he did! Aye, and would ha' done too, if I hadn't had me wits about me.'

"He had fallen asleep facing the roaring fire he spoke of and was dreaming he was 'bein' roasted in a oven' as he put it. He fell off the sofa with his face in the blankets, which probably saved his life. He got tangled up with something which turned out to be the picture of the beautiful dame. It must have been laid beside him while he slept. The room was full of smoke, and there was a great roaring below. The heat, he said, was too much, too much! He rushed to the window and got it open, shouting 'Help! Hello, help!' but no help came then. The garage and cellar below were a roaring furnace. He said the flooring cracked and burst into flames as he stood gulping air. His head was so thick he 'thought he had died and gone to hell!' He had no time to philosophize. The heat behind him, as the floor gave way, was beyond endurance. He jumped, shouting curses on the murderer. It was a good deal further than he figured, and he came down on one foot and broke a leg. He scored his hands and face on gravel and groaned, but he crawled somehow beyond the range of that heat. He was alive and—he was 'going to get that bastard.'"

"I remember now!" said Mr. Kavanagh. "All clear now. I remember the case well. He was a newspaperman, wasn't he? He got ten years. He'd insured his life and . . ."

"That's why I'm telling you this yarn of Wensley's," said Mr. Spenlove. "Wensley has never had any idea that the yarn of his bosun's mate's obsession had anything to do with the passenger he called Wilmarth's bit of skirt. It owes its quality and deep authenticity to Wensley's pontifical faith in the uniqueness of anything happening to *his* bosun's mate. He carried conviction in the same fashion that Homer did, I suppose, when he told his tales. He had been there himself. And old Somers Roscoe, with a gift of the painting craft, was equally convinced that nobody had ever tried to kill anybody before. Not in that particularly fiendish way, of course. The tale was double-distilled conviction as it came to us in the smoke room of that Cunarder.

"They caught Wilkerson going on board an obscure steamer in New Orleans bound for British Guiana, of all places. I suppose he meant to transship to a steamer bound east to Europe. He was the sort who would head as quickly as possible for Paris. She was to meet him there—after the insurance money had been paid. He believed, he believed that he could dominate her as he had always done, her and any other woman who came under his spell. They caught him and brought him back; and old Roscoe, on crutches and in bandages, white with rage and almost useless because of his self-importance, was the star witness.

"The sensation in court when it came out that he had placed his wife's picture, Athalie's and her child Ginevra— Fakenham's child, beside the doomed Roscoe, so that when the charred body was found, near it would be found the metal frame of what Athalie would identify as the dead husband's wife's portrait. What a perfect touch! What genius in detail!

"In a general way, however, it was a curiously clumsy crime. It was the conception of a bold, reckless, unscrupulous, imaginative, but inexperienced mind, and that describes Wilkerson from the day he practically picked up a fifteen-year-old English girl in Paris, a girl who was being rushed by an uproarious crew of enlisted men. He picked her up and carried her under his arm to a taxi, walking backwards and holding them off with his service revolver. The taxi was under a lamppost, and the sound of the taxi horn squawking brought the military police at the double. That was how he met her, taking her to the hotel where her father, Mortimer Justin St. Cyr Rhys, was then staying.

"I said the crime was clumsy. It was full of holes, yet I have no doubt he had often thought of himself as able to conceive the perfect crime. Supposing he had brought it off, even an elderly unemployed painter would be missed and the circumstances of his vanishing quickly assembled. He forgot that of all institutions, the hardest to cheat and the most implacable in pursuit are life insurance companies. Above all he gambled madly on the assumption that Athalie, of all the women living in the world, would do his bidding and dutifully follow him into the shocking desolation of nameless exile. Yet he had so gambled. The intoxication of a hundred thousand dollars was too much for him. To him it meant rehabilitation, freedom and—for once—success. For Wilkerson is a failure if he still lives. He has never put anything over. He is one of those who, when they succeed, tell reporters that money is nothing. They mean it, and he would mean it too. What he has always wanted is to achieve something beyond the ruck of his companions. And always, though he would destroy a life and flaunt society, it has eluded him. His grandiose schemes burst with a faint pop, or no pop at all, and left him in a débris of foreclosures, receiverships, repossessed motorcars and office furniture.

"And yet, when I remember him as I saw him on the one occasion we met, I am puzzled. He has style and a presence. He was, in some period of his life, a gentleman. He has that subtle faculty, even after years in a penitentiary, of ease among strangers and of assuming the pose of a superior man. I have met pro-consuls and governors of distant possessions who had no more of it than he as he sat on a chair arm, inhaling cigarette smoke and demanding money from his wife so

that he, a prisoner on parole, could go South for the winter
—because his chest was bad!

"But I am running ahead of the story. I told you I had a
great curiosity about his predecessor, the painter Athalie
had mentioned to me with such tender pride. And when I
was in London I saw the announcement in the paper of a
show of pictures by Harold Fakenham, at the Fantome
Galleries in New Bond Street. The name burst out of the
paper at me as I sat at breakfast. Harold Fakenham. I made
up my mind to go and see his pictures. Perhaps they would
tell me something about himself.

"In those few lines in the *Morning Post*, which caught my
eye as I breakfasted on my first morning in London, I found
my curiosity rising again. Here he was advertising himself.
I didn't even have to hunt him up. I looked again. It was
the man I wanted; not Gerald, the celebrated painter of
Daddy's Best Girl, the picture of a blue-eyed tot with her
arms around her handsome father's neck. No, it was Harold,
and he was billed as an experimental portraitist. There were
also 'abstractions' on view at the Fantome Galleries in New
Bond Street. Admission one shilling.

"I went that afternoon. I paid a shilling. I walked down a
lighted corridor lined with orange velvet and occupied by a
dozen bronze heads on pedestals, as though Harold Fakenham had carried out a raid on the studios and had decapi-
tated his rivals. At the far end was the gallery, and here again
I had a faint impression of entering the stronghold of a successful barbarian. Two stunning blond girls like Valkyries
stood by a table selling catalogues and photographs, and also
a pamphlet by Harold Fakenham. Admission a shilling,
catalogue a shilling, photographs sixpence each, and the
pamphlet two shillings. Those two perfectly matched Nordic
creatures were probably worth the money. I mean I looked
at them more than at Harold Fakenham's astonishing modernistic 'portraits' and 'abstractions.' One is always being
swindled nowadays by the very people who attack business

men and capitalists for dishonesty. Artists, sculptors, musicians, and poets are not only unprincipled but impudent. I remember one portrait labeled 'Lloyd George.' There was no face—only a brilliant spectrum coiled upon itself like a clock-spring with the outer end flung at a tangent in a smother of comets' tails and polychromatic sparks. It was, according to the catalogue, 'a rendition of the soul of a statesman.' Another was 'the ghost of a steam engine' which intrigued me because it was so entirely just and accurate. It was only a steam engine diagram such as I take every voyage myself. The clever fellow had had a clever idea. I heard a woman say, 'Steam engine! It looks like an old shoe drawn by a small boy.' Which is just what it looked like to me without my knowledge of where the artist had stolen it.

"I thought, well well! I was inclined to think I had made a mistake. Athalie would never be in love with a fraudulent lunatic, surely. I walked towards the Nordic goddesses. They might know if the artist was likely to attend. It was only the second day of the show, and artists, even more than criminals, haunt the scenes of their crimes.

"I saw a small middle-aged woman coming in without paying. The Nordic goddesses were tolerant of her in a distant fashion, and the sharp look she gave them, putting them in their places, made me look at her with some attention. She was a little person with a lot of very expensive and tasteless clothes that seemed to have been wrapped about her body by the lucky fortuitousness of a gale of wind. She had black flat-heeled shoes a little run-over, black stockings that hung loose on thin shanks, and on her bosom beads. Her hat was a flop—though you mustn't imagine I enjoy making puns or even making fun of a woman. It flopped over one eye, a black nemesis of a hat. It was the one thing that harmonized with her sallow, sharp little face and belligerent brown eyes.

"She walked, her petticoat showing about a quarter of an inch on one side, slightly round shouldered, examining the pictures. When she came to the one that had a red stamp stuck on the frame, the Portrait of a Bigot, she put a soiled white glove finger on the red spot and looked round at the two Nordic ladies in waiting. There was a queer expression of triumph on that sallow wizened face and large puckered mouth.

"I was interested, believe me. She was somebody. She had some place in this crazy cosmos on New Bond Street. As she came my way I was inspired to utter an 'Excuse me. Er— could you . . .'

"She gave me a sharp but not unfriendly look. I suppose she sniffed a buyer. She waited, a receptive scare-crow. I mumbled something about being a friend of a friend of the artist.

"'Sure you don't mean Gerald? This is Harold,' she piped in a thin voice. Her neck was sallow and corded. I said no, it was Harold. A friend of his, an old friend, in New York. Would she . . . ?

"'I'm Mrs. Harold Fakenham,' she said in a whistling soprano. 'What name, please?'

"I had a card, by good fortune, and she examined it with the aid of pince-nez she took from a mangy pocketbook that glittered with cut-steel ornaments. It was extraordinary how everything she wore was good and expensive, yet her ensemble recalled something fished from an ash can. She had a disintegrating effect upon everything she put on.

"'Oh!' she said, and looked at me again. 'I didn't get the name of your friend.'

"'You wouldn't know it, perhaps,' I said. 'She was a Miss Rhys.'

"The change in her attitude was instantaneous. She smiled, but it was one of the least beautiful expressions I have ever seen on a human face.

"'Indeed!' she said and looked all around the gallery before going on. 'Oh yes. I think I've heard of *her!* What was it you wished to know? Have you a—a message, for instance?'

"'No,' I said. 'No message. I happen to be in London,

and seeing the name in the paper this morning, I thought I
would call on him. She is a friend of mine in New York, you
see.'

"She went on looking at me, and through me, and the
force of her character became a shade more evident in her
face. People passed close by us as we stood talking, in a low
tone of course, as befitted a temple of the arts. Two severe-
looking dames entered, and Mrs. Fakenham turned to them
for a moment. Then she said, 'Harold won't be here today.
The strain of getting this show ready has made him seedy,
so I made him go down to Godalming. We live at Godalming.'

"I said I was sorry not to have the pleasure.

"'Oh, you can come down with me this afternoon,' she
said, 'if you'd care about it. It's only an hour or so in the
motor. He hates Americans, but then you're not an American, are you? You only live there. And I know Harold would
be simply charmed to have a message from . . .'

"'No message,' I said. 'She spoke of him, in admiration
of his talent. Genius was the word she used.'

"Mrs. Fakenham approved of the word. She nodded, and
one of the abstractions, which was an elongated oval with
triangles for eyes and a parabola for a mouth, seemed to wink
at me as it caught my eye over her floppy hat. I explained
she was going to marry a friend of my own, and so . . .

"'Again!' said Mrs. Fakenham, studying the toe of a not
very small glacé kid shoe. Then she said, 'It will be delightful. Shall we say half-past three? I have a little shopping
first. Yes, outside the gallery. So glad . . .'

"I had less than an hour to wait. I walked down into
Piccadilly and through the Arcade. I was so interested in
Mrs. Fakenham I could hardly wait. She was somebody. She
was a woman who had not only got her man but kept him.
And when I looked at her again as she sat in the large black
six-liter Bentley limousine, waiting for me, I was ready to
hear a heroic tale. A woman of less character would have
evaded my allusions to Athalie. She would have bounced

those perfectly matched Nordic girls and hired an austere, capable virgin with an Oxford degree, who would have failed to draw a single Brazilian millionaire into the Fantome Galleries, who would have been regarded as a dry husk by the young esthetes from Bogotá and Montevideo who thought Modigliani a great painter. Mrs. Fakenham possessed that driving efficiency which only flowers when a woman has a man to take care of. Once she has him in her possession, and he has given up all thoughts of escaping from her, she puts forth incredible energies for his advancement. She believes in him and in the credulity or gullibility of the public. She subordinates herself and everybody else to the problem of his worldly success. And she inspires men like me with a belief in witchcraft!

"There was a chauffeur, of course. There was a monogram on the door panel. The interior of that car was upholstered in a way that seems impossible to introduce into America, whether on trains or in motorcars. I sank into cushions of amazing comfort. The car moved as though floating soundlessly on moonbeams above the earth. Down into Piccadilly. I don't know how it is, but in such a situation I always feel slightly out of the picture. I can't live up to it spiritually. I never feel that way over here, no matter how regal the setting. If I could discover the source of such an emotion as I felt sitting beside that dowdy little Englishwoman in her sumptuous limousine, threading the traffic of Piccadilly, I might be on the track of an important distinction between the two countries. Or perhaps I would only classify myself a shade more definitely!

"It was odd that with all her dowdiness and her utter incapacity to present any reasonable resemblance to one's abstract conception of an artist's wife, Mrs. Fakenham was yet very much in possession of all her faculties. Such as they were. She was sharp. She was intelligent in the sense that women who live on men are intelligent, though I'm not suggesting Mrs. Fakenham did anything of the kind. In fact, it was her money that was running everything. She was financing a genius. But she had that kind of intelligence which comes to its finest flowering in the successful madam of a high-class house. It is a concrete, materialistic intelligence, suave and implacable. By the time we had passed through Kingston and were on the main road to Guildford I had learned that Mrs. Fakenham knew all about Athalie Rhys as she was at the time of which I was speaking. Athalie was probably less trouble than some of the others. At that time she said, 'Harold used to have too many distractions. It was very bad for his work. He hadn't found out his own special line then. You couldn't tell his portraits from anyone else's in those days. They were like Christmas Supplements!'

"I wanted to say they were distinctive enough now, but I was too deeply engrossed in this little woman's story. She spoke of her husband as something she had made. What he had been in other days was of no importance now. He was, in fact, her chef d'œuvre.

"'It was so bad for his work,' she went on. 'He's susceptible. Women got hold of him. And he would have adventures at Brighton. So silly, when he has his work! He is really great.'

"I said, of course I understood that the girl had been very young at the time. Mrs. Fakenham gave a trill of laughter. 'Oh, quite,' she said. 'A minx, I assure you. The war had just begun. Girls were running simply wild. She got hold of him.'

"This was something I couldn't harmonize with the picture I had in mind of Athalie at fourteen and an artist who was probably a dozen years older. Girls of fourteen don't get hold of men, do they? I was so obviously puzzled that Mrs. Fakenham let out another trill.

"We were going with remarkable speed and comfort. The car wove its way through the traffic with effortless ease. We floated onward. In the country I had the sensation of passing other cars as though we were incorporeal. I craned my neck to see the dial. It stood at seventy-five, and Mrs. Fakenham sat placidly smiling at Epsom Downs flowing past us like the waves of the sea in a fabulous fluid universe.

"She let out another trill. It was evidence of a triumph of some sort, and I waited. Then she said, 'What is she like now? I suppose she is enormous. I can imagine . . .'

"'Enormous. No, not at all. In fact, Mrs. Fakenham, she was on the stage—beauty chorus, you know—not long ago. Not enormous!'

"She was still smiling at the countryside—we were rushing towards Guildford now—and the large glacé kid shoe moved up and down quickly, kicking the hassock she used for a foot rest. The car seemed to cleave a way through a clot of cyclists with jingling bells, swiftly separated a jungle of houses into two equal parts, and sped up a hill in silence. I lit a cigar as she nodded permission.

"'You'll never get us to believe that,' she said in a queer voice. 'She was very robust, very mature for her age. Harold always said she would get heavy. She had the sort of prettiness men always make fools of themselves about. He painted her portrait, you know. He was drawn in. . . . Her grandmother, old Lady Rhys, never restrained her at all. The girl had no chaperon. She came to the studio—he was in Chelsea then—without a chaperon. It might have ruined his professional career, running round with a chit like that.'

"'Was he, by the way, married then?' I asked. 'To you?'

"'A long-standing engagement. Of course, I know men. I understood how it was. Men are only big children. They run after a new toy. I've never reproached him. He is great! He will be recognized as one of the greatest of the moderns. But we must have America.'

"'America? You mean American recognition?'

"'Yes. I am corresponding now with an American professor. He wants to write Harold's critical biography for a new series of art manuals. He has asked our permission. Of course, I shall give him all the details. I thought, as you were interested, I could give you an introduction to Professor Kidder. Is he well thought of in the States?' she inquired keenly.

"I said he was. I had never heard of him, but I was quite safe in saying he was well thought of.

"'I'm always so glad to get in touch with Americans interested in Harold's art.'

"I said I feared she was under a misapprehension about me. I wasn't a collector.

"'But you know them, of course?' she said. 'You live in New York.' She took out my card again. It bore the address of our downtown office. 'Whitehall!' she repeated in a respectful murmur, thinking of Whitehall in London just behind us. 'Harold hates Americans. So I do all the work. I see the dealers and make all the arrangements. I give teas at Claridges. To the Press. I mean the critics. The pressmen, the gossip writers, I know most of them personally. Lord Dumbelly, who does "Pistols for Two" in the *Morning Chronicle*, is an old friend. But it's an awfully difficult job. There's always his brother Gerald in the public eye.'

"We flew on serenely. I was able to understand, by the time we reached Guildford, that I was in the grasp of a woman completely absorbed in a dream of achievement, and I personally, as well as the girl in the background who was responsible for my presence there, was of no particular importance at all. I suppose you can call her an artist too, for she was molding Harold Fakenham into a celebrity, a great man, in the modern manner, by publicity; by dogged industry digging a tunnel under Parnassus and boring a subterranean passage to the top. What she meant by the top was a one-man show in New York, interviews, reproductions in the newspapers, purchase of his pictures by a millionaire or so and also by an art gallery. She had no other ambition. She corresponded with art critics in Berlin, Paris, Rome, and New York. At any rate, she fed them with the stuff she and her secretaries, the two Valkyries, ground out and mailed. Now that I look back and see her in perspective, she is heroic. She has a mission. Athalie was a mere joyous interlude, a flash of madcap gayety in Harold Fakenham's career. And yet . . . I wonder!

"'I saved him,' Mrs. Fakenham said just before we reached the house. 'I saved him from all the distractions and follies that were taking him away from his work. It's a great responsibility being the wife of a man of genius.'

"It's all very well to laugh, Mrs. Kavanagh, but Mrs. Fakenham had the strength of faith. She was a fanatic on this subject of her husband's art, and for her there were no other subjects in the world. And if you grant that his lunatic interpretations are the twentieth century's contribution to art, then she is the wife of a man of genius. I would say you must be a genius to draw a picture that means nothing no matter which way one holds it. I pulled myself together to play the part of a visitor from the States to an artist genius.

"I was surprised when I saw him. What did I expect? I don't know now. I can't recall how I had imagined a painter of abstract portraits and experimental wash drawings would look. What I did see, as soon as we entered a large comfortable country mansion in a marvelous garden hidden by ten-foot box hedges and red-brick walls, was a small blond man with a neat golden mustache and quick blue eyes who came forward and kissed Mrs. Fakenham with a 'Hullo, dear' and then held out his hand with great cordiality. 'Awfully good of you to come. My wife telephoned about you. You'll have a wash? And look here: I've some jolly good Hollands. How about a gin and bitters?'

"He took me into a nice big bathroom leading off his dressing room and presently reappeared with two gin-and-bitters on a tray. I was using his silver-backed military brushes before the mirror. I saw his face in the glass, and he was examining my own with a certain strange, quick interest.

"'How'd you like my show?' he said, looking towards me ceremoniously as we raised glasses. I said I was interested, of course, but did not pretend to understand what he was trying to do. I said I belonged to the pre-war generation and so was unable to perceive the allusions in modern art. But I got a glimpse, I told him, in his Soul of a Steam Engine. I inquired if he was serious in such things.

"He smiled to himself and took a quick walk, hands in pockets, head down, along the rich flowered carpet. He nodded. 'Yes,' he said. 'You say you are an engineer. You've got me there. But if you were a chemist and spotted some idea I had taken from—oh, the nucleus theory—ions or electrons perhaps—that wouldn't negative the value of my painting for the public.'

"I wouldn't argue this. I was aware that he had something on his mind and was only playing for time to speak to me about Athalie. He had given me several keen glances. We drank our gin-and-bitters. The comfortable silence of an English country house, the exquisite coziness of a genuine home, was all about us. The house was rather cluttered up with a great many things that don't appeal much to me, but they are sacred in my country. The accumulations of half a century stood on shelves and tables and on the walls. The house was a nest which Mrs. Fakenham had inherited, and like many nests it was fashioned of an enormous number of odds and ends—china figures, brass pots, stuffed birds, heads of beasts, what-nots loaded with mementoes of Cromer, of Bournemouth, of Geneva, of the Highlands, of Aberystwith and Torquay. There were photographs and walking sticks, a ship in a bottle and a frame full of butterflies on pins. There was a faint smell of lavender, and a satin quilt of strawberry color contrasted with the nearly black wood of the bedstead. Outside the window a creeper framed the view of a garden so densely cultivated it seemed to have been forced up into ridges of bloom. There was a sundial on a short column, and a conservatory with curved glass against the north wall.

"I said, 'You are pretty snug here.'

"He raised his shoulders slightly and seemed not very elated at the suggestion. He glanced at me in the long glass in front of which I was standing at the moment. He had the same strange expression in his eyes, while his mouth twitched at the corners.

"'You know Athalie?' he said abruptly. 'My wife told me over the telephone. I'm interested.'

"'How?' I inquired. 'She spoke of you with a sort of pride. It made me want to meet you.'

"'I don't understand,' he said. 'Why should it?'

"'She spoke as if she had expected you to take care of her, but the war came, and so . . .'

"'That's right enough,' he said. 'The war did a lot of things. It did that to her. Do you know what the war did to me?'

"I didn't, of course, and waited. He swung to and fro, his head bent towards the carpet, his cigarette held on a level with his shoulder. He looked up suddenly as a deep booming came from the dinner gong in the hall downstairs.

"'Look here,' he said. 'Can't talk now. Dinner. You in town for long?' I said I would be in London for a week. 'Then come and see me at my studio. Glebe Place, Chelsea. Just off the Row. I'll show you Athalie's picture I painted in the summer of 1914.'

"'I'll do that,' I said. 'Are those girls at the show your models?' I couldn't give up the idea that he was a great ravisher. He stared. 'The two young goddesses,' I explained. 'Models for what?' he said. He shook his head. 'No, I never have women in the studio at all, except socially. No! Good God!'

"He gave a rather nasty laugh.

"We went down to dinner. Mrs. Fakenham was in black with some costly antique jewels on her thin bosom and arms, and the conversation became impersonal until Fakenham opened a bottle of old sherry. Mrs. Fakenham kept her eye on the maid for a while, but presently she looked at me with intention.

"I was thinking of the sound of his voice as he said, 'Good God!' What did he mean? I decided in my simplicity that here was a tragic affair! I thought I saw it all at a glance now. He had married in a reaction from his folly with Athalie and now cherished her in his heart. But he could not give up the profound economic security of a rich elderly wife who controlled his destinies. Even Nordic goddesses no longer had any power to lure him away from the imagined ecstasies of a life with the girl he had loved. Only in some such way could I account for the tone in which he had exclaimed 'Good God!'

"Mrs. Fakenham said, 'You must tell us all about Athalie, because when she writes she never gives us the slightest information about herself.'

"I said I understood from my friend Captain Nevile that she wrote beautiful letters. They chorused together, 'She does! That's perfectly true,' and Mrs. Fakenham went on, 'That's all they are. They might be written from the Feejee Islands or the middle of China, for all the news she gives us of herself. She had a crush on Harold before the war. You know the way schoolgirls become infatuated with men much older than themselves. She still writes to him occasionally, and her letters arouse our curiosity very much. She seems quite undiscouraged by getting no replies.'

"'You mean you don't answer her letters?' I said to him directly. He made a gesture. 'Just a line. Or a picture postcard if we go to Paris or Nice.' And he went on with his dinner. Mrs. Fakenham was watching me. I fancy she detected some sort of consternation in my face. She smiled. 'She's quite unable to understand that Harold is married. We only heard indirectly that she was married herself. Now you tell us she is in love with another. But when she has written she never mentions such things. She writes to Harold as if she and he were the only people alive in the world.'

"'But what of it?' I said. 'I don't suppose you want me to

understand she is indiscreet.' There was a silence. I added, 'I'll never believe she is anything but good.'

"'She wants to keep up an old affair,' said Mrs. Fakenham, smiling formally. 'It's amusing. Because Harold is married. And he's certainly got over all that kind of immature sentiment.'

"And she smiled towards her husband as she uttered this statement as though she were only echoing his words. He nodded, and she turned her smile on me.

"'But you haven't told us about her,' she said.

"'Well,' I said, 'I don't know much, but she was a passenger on a ship to Jamaica.' I looked at both of them back and forth as I explained how I came to be on that ship. 'I am here, you see, sitting at your table, under a misapprehension on your part. I'm not a collector of art. All I collect are curious specimens of humanity.'

"'And you thought that anyone Athalie Rhys might have known in the past would . . . ? Don't apologize!' Mrs. Fakenham's black eyes were humorous, but they certainly had a slight gleam of amused resentment.

"I said, not at all. I said Miss Rhys had made such a deep impression on me that I had been only too eager to learn more of her background, as it were.

"'Which is what you wouldn't get from her,' said Mrs. Fakenham. I protested. I went on to tell her just how I had come into the life of those two. They listened, the Fakenhams, while I talked, and dinner progressed to sweets and cheese, after the immemorial custom of the English. Cherry tart and cheddar, I remember. And a glass of port with the cheese. Mrs. Fakenham rose and ordered coffee in the drawing room. As I held the door for her, she and her husband exchanged a glance. He stood there, small, dapper, and neat, touching his small golden mustache with his napkin, watching her pass out. I closed the door, and we sat down to another glass of port which he drank right down and at once refilled his glass. He had no cigars, so I lit one of my own, and he drew out his cigarettes. It was one of the unusual comforts of that meal that they did not smoke during dinner. He drew up his chair on my side of the table and drank again. He became aware of the fact that I didn't want any port and at once rose and went to the sideboard. Using his keys, he opened a door and drew out a bottle of brandy. For half a century that benign liquid had awaited my arrival.

"'Hard to explain just why,' he said, in my ear, 'but I can't talk about her in this house. I might be able to in the studio. This house is—I haven't much to say here . . .' He poured out some more port, holding it up to the light. I tried to rationalize what he said, but it made no sense. I waited. He was obviously one of his wife's possessions, but that didn't explain the freedom with which they both spoke of Athalie. She might have been a pet animal they had once known. There was something missing here, and as the little man at my side gazed somberly through the ruby wine I tried to think what it might be. But he spoke of it himself at once, while putting down the good red wine.

"'Don't mind me,' I said, 'I can understand perfectly you might not want to discuss her here. Why anywhere? You say you don't answer her letters. She didn't tell me that. Perhaps you are wise, since nothing can ever come of it. And she has a man now.'

"'Well,' he said, 'then why did you come and see my show? Didn't she ask you to? She must have told you a lot about me for you to . . . eh?'

"'No,' I said. 'She said very little. She's rather a mystery to me and to her friend who wants to marry her. I saw your name in the *Morning Post* at breakfast. She gave me the impression that you were part of the mystery, because although she has more than enough reason to divorce her husband she won't, not even to marry a man she is in love with.'

"'She was in love with me once,' he said in a dull, miserable tone. I said I knew that. He glanced at me, and then his gaze hung between us in a vague way, as though he had forgotten where he was. Slowly he came back to the present and drank down the wine.

"'Yes?' he said. 'She never mentions the child.'

"'Nor to me,' I told him. 'It was a girl, I understand. Fifteen years old now.'

"'God!' he said under his breath, and put his hand out for the bottle. I took a glass of brandy, to keep him company, for I wasn't in the mood for conviviality. Mr. Fakenham was going to pieces inside. 'I painted Athalie's portrait at that age.'

"'You didn't know?' I said.

"'Yes and again no. She doesn't state definite facts. She writes—well—poetically. Pledge, she said. Pledge of our passion. And it doesn't matter! Did you know I got mucked up in the war? Bloody well mucked up!'

"'Your wife said something about it,' I said.

"'What did she say?' he asked, bending an ear, his eye on the table. The maid, who had stolen a sly look in my direction as she removed the cloth and replaced a fine epergne on the polished mahogany, had gone off to the kitchen. A neat minx, I had thought in passing, though the look wasn't quite comprehensible at the time. 'What did she say?' he asked, as if it were extremely important for him to know. 'H'm, just a general remark,' I told him. 'Gassed and wounded.'

"'Did she tell you how I was—wounded?' he inquired. It was my turn to look at him with some attention. At this moment the maid came back into the room and put something away in the sideboard. She gave me the same impudent look after flinging a glance at my host. Her master, that is to say. I had a flurry of cockeyed suspicions just then. No, I thought, no; that's no explanation. He has some antipathy...

"'No,' I said to him, 'I thought being gassed was enough. She said you had a long spell of convalescence.'

"'Convalescence! I was off my head. I remember absolutely nothing from the time I was gassed until after the armistice. Nearly a year. And when I was able to go home, I found I might as well have died anyhow.'

"I watched him drink some more port. I had no answer to such a statement because I hadn't guessed what he meant. He looked at me and gave a very dreadful little laugh.

"It was rather distressing, and I was glad when Mrs. Fakenham opened the door and suggested we go into the drawing room for coffee. He had had nearly half a bottle of port after the sherry. He nodded and said, 'Righto, dear.' He took my arm as we rose.

"'Tell you all about it at the studio,' he mumbled. 'Can't invade the what you call it—the sanctity of the home with all the desolation of old wars, what? Love's torch, stinking and stale . . . Kipling hit the nail on the head there. Stinking and stale . . .'

"He took another nip before joining me at the door. He seemed full of a noble desperation now, walking with his head erect, one hand feeling in his pocket for cigarettes. I saw him glance at the big brass salver on which a score of visiting cards lay scattered. An unexpected Irish terrier rose from a mat the same color as his own honest red coat, and after a sidelong glower at me, followed his master into the drawing room. Mrs. Fakenham handed me a cup of coffee.

"'There's a train at nine-thirty from Guildford,' she said. 'I'll drive you in. Harold goes to bed early. He doesn't drive. Since his breakdown he has to be careful, you know.' She looked at him. 'Darling, hadn't you better . . . ? You'll be so tired in the morning.'

"He went to bed shortly after this. 'See you in town,' he said. He seemed to have become completely deflated, as it were. All light had gone out of his eyes, all color from his voice. I explained to Mrs. Fakenham, after he had departed, the terrier close behind. I said he wanted to show me a portrait he had painted of Athalie Rhys.

"'It would do for a Christmas Supplement,' she said in her cultured, carefully articulated voice. For some reason she gave me a tragic glance. She said, 'I suppose you think it strange that I am not jealous.' I said, 'I haven't thought of that. I was thinking your husband shouldn't brood over what is past. He seems restless. Perhaps what he went through in the war . . . Well, he has something on his mind.'

"She gave me a swift glance of alarm, or perhaps it was suspicion. 'He didn't tell you, did he?'

"I had to say, 'Tell me what? He told me he was gassed and wounded. As you did, you remember. He didn't say how he was wounded. I don't want to know, if it is something you don't speak of. Only, when I told him Athalie's first child was fifteen, he was very much upset. Much more upset than a man usually is when he hears of a girl he has known having a child. Is she his child? That was the impression Athalie gave me. And he thinks so. Well, if it is true, he must have become accustomed to the idea after all these years.'

"She finished her coffee and glanced at her wrist watch, and then she rose.

"'You'll have to excuse my hurrying you,' she said. 'Your train. I think, after all, I'll get Colebrook to take you in. I was going to drive the two-seater, but I'm rather tired.'

"'You've been most kind,' I said. 'I feel an interloper. And I've upset your husband, talking about the girl.'

"'He'll be all right tomorrow. When you see him in town, he'll probably want to talk a lot about her. It's quite all right. He broods. He is really a great artist, but he broods. His former life, when he had no ambition and was attracted by every pretty face, seems to haunt him—well, like a ghost.' She frowned, her fingertips on the table. 'Yes, it haunts him, and he doesn't want to go on. But he must go on now. He has burned his bridges behind him. But sometimes he broods—on that girl. It would do him good to have a good talk and get it out of his system.'

"'I would have thought it would make matters worse,' I said.

"'Not him,' she assured me. 'I am not in the least afraid

of what you are thinking. That is all past and done with. I am thinking of his own future. Nothing like that can affect him any more.'

"'Mrs. Fakenham,' I said, 'you are both very hard to understand.' She smiled without looking at me.

"'I dare say,' she said. 'I'm sorry. It's really quite simple, but we don't discuss it. Tell me before you go. This girl, Athalie Rhys, is she the sort of person one can know socially?'

"'Mrs. Fakenham!' I said. I was astonished. Not hurt, you know. Only astonished.

"'I hardly know how to express what I mean, quite,' she explained. 'Americans are so different from us. I know that. And you, in your life, often have to meet people who are not . . .'

"'Don't apologize,' I said. 'I get the idea. I was only surprised you should think Miss Rhys was not . . . not . . . The man who is in love with her is English. He says she is a saint.'

"'A saint!' Mrs. Fakenham echoed the word with a faintly rising inflection. 'And you? Do you think she's a saint?'

"'Yes,' I said, 'so far as my experience of such beings goes.'

"'Oh! Would you mind touching the bell? I think I hear Colebrook. Thanks.'

"'She still has only gentle thoughts of the past,' I pointed out.

"Mrs. Fakenham didn't reply to that. She went with me to the door, holding a lace shawl about her thin shoulders, her eyes black in a sallow face.

"'So good of you to come,' she said. 'Do call and see Harold at the studio. It will do him no end of good to talk. Good-night.'

"I got into the car beside the chauffeur. The last I saw of her was her prim black figure silhouetted against the lamplight in the hall, rigid and unsmiling, motionless save for the closing door. So she passed, she and her secret, and I never saw her again."

IV

FOR A MOMENT Mrs. Kavanagh did not speak. The chiming
of an old clock by the door began as Mr. Spenlove paused.
It was eleven. Mr. Kavanagh compared the time with his
own thick silver wrist watch. The kitchen had long since
become dark and vacant, and Mr. Spenlove, going silently
out there to get fresh ice while the chimes still vibrated above
the rafters, had the air of a benevolent shade retiring into
the past he had evoked by his voice. Mr. Kavanagh took
another cigar from the box and bit off the end as he gazed
with mild eyes into the glowing heart of the fire. He had
heard a great deal about Mr. Spenlove from his wife since
that trip to the West Indies. He had heard about the Fishing
Club from Terry and was hoping to get down there some
time. Terry could fix it, maybe. And he recalled, also, his
wife's excitement when she came across that item in the newspaper about that girl. She had been on the ship. For some
reason Norah could get worked up about a thing like that.
It was, she said, human interest, and therefore "copy" for
her books. Norah was always on the jump for "copy." She
was like a terrier with an old sock when she got hold of an
item like that. Mr. Kavanagh wondered mildly why they
were all making a fuss over the girl. The husband, if he was
out on parole, might be interesting. He had built up a nice
little machine down here at Norbury. Mr. Kavanagh was
interested in nice little machines. That fellow Wilkerson had
uncovered a lot of graft. He had got all the well-to-do innocent intellectuals from New York to finance his reform
movement. He had even made it extremely uncomfortable
for the local politicians who were protecting the beer runners.
Mr. Kavanagh was moved by the revelation that Wilkerson,
behind his adventures in Norbury, behind his peculiar career
in New York previous to that, had had a romance. Mr.
Kavanagh struck a match and glanced at his wife. She had

told him she wanted to find out everything she could about that girl. That was why they had come over. This fellow Spenlove had the damnedest way of talking. . . . He had to bore a hole through every episode and fit it on the string in its right order, by golly. . . .

He lit his cigar, and Mr. Spenlove, as he came in with ice and a tray of sandwiches, smiled upon his guests.

"I still don't believe it," cried Mrs. Kavanagh. "You and your saints! What did she do that you men must fall down and worship her? All of you, it seems! Even Terry. He wouldn't say anything except that he was scared of her. And as for her not making any claim, isn't that the line those girls always have? Isn't that what sets decent women against them? To tear their eyes out!"

"So?" said Mr. Spenlove as he bent over his fire with a faggot in his great hairy hand. "All women say that, and you are all wrong. I can explain it to you if you will have patience. A line! A line! If speech was given us to conceal our thoughts, American has been devised to obscure your emotions. Now say I'm crazy! Do you ever hear yourselves? Do you ever stand away, for a moment, from your towers of babel and contemplate them?

"No, she hadn't any line in that sense. She was what the girls you speak of pretend to be but never are. They do not believe in God. They miss the very quality they strain after so passionately. I can speak with confidence because I have been in such intimate contact with that girl's mind. I have seen her in such circumstances as you have no conception whatever! Circumstances that would make your girls with their insufferable 'lines,' as you call them, take to open prostitution instead of the relative variety. I tell you she had a sense of honor and an immense capacity for love. Nothing could rob her of her faith in the power of goodness—not even the power of evil her husband exerted over her. It was only when she imagined the man she loved no longer believed in her, because she couldn't bring herself to tell him the truth, that she gave up. And then—did she give up as if she had a line?

"Mind, I don't say that she was revealing any miraculous virtue of wisdom when she made no claim on Fakenham. . . ."

"She hadn't any claim," said Mrs. Kavanagh viciously, and both men made a faint gesture of protest. She waved them away. "No claim!" she insisted and her chin sank on her hands as she leaned forward to stare into the fire.

"Well, let us agree about that," said Mr. Spenlove. "Didn't I say she made none? And never did!" His voice rang out for a moment. "No word of reproach for those whom she loved. It was only the silly, fatuous sensualists, who thought she had a line, and was only keeping them guessing by a pretense of virtue, whom she assailed with a sort of girlish anger. If you will not misunderstand me, I would say she was cross with them. Or merely impatient. Irritated at their stupidity because they imagined she had any time for what they called love. Love for her was a deep devotion unto death, but instinctively and from bitter experience she found that men did not understand it that way. Even the best of them! She not only made no claim, but she had no hatred. With her first love she might have shown fight and so forth. Should she? What's the use of a man if a girl has to snatch at him? She had a deeper sagacity than your modern girl, who always gets her man. What she imagined, I think, was something as much beyond the usual relations of married people as heavenly harmonies are beyond the scratchy crackling of a radio."

Mrs. Kavanagh raised her left hand and let it drop into her lap, shaking her head with a slow, wise smile. Mr. Spenlove smiled too.

"Of course! She was incurably romantic. But that isn't a line, and it isn't a crime. She was essentially good, and in the valuable sense, virtuous, with a lusty adoration of vitality. That's the only way I can define a romantic woman in the modern world. She is the predestined victim of her own instincts. Wait just a little. I am coming to that. I was going to speak of the portrait he painted.

"I told you I knew Chelsea. I kept my appointment and walked from Sloane Square Station, down Tite Street to the Embankment. The afternoon sunlight struck along the river, which was at high tide. A tug with a string of barges was coming down from Hammersmith, black blobs on a golden stream. I always permit myself a tender sentiment in that neighborhood. When I was young and working in the city, I would make furtive excursions into Chelsea. To me those artists who lived there were enchanted dwellers in paradise. They were bohemians. When I saw a girl run out of a tumble-down rookery without a hat and hurry into the little shops of Church Street, that for me was romance. I would sit on the seats on the Embankment and dream of an adventure with a beautiful model who would love me devotedly on a pound a week. I saw Cheyne Walk and the tumbledown rookeries through the eyes of Murger's Latin Quarter. The artists and models, when they saw me, a young mechanic, sitting gazing romantically at the river, probably saw me through the eyes of Ibsen and Shaw. So we never understood each other. I escaped romance in spite of a natural bent for it. My romantic swans were really socialistic geese.

"When I took my way up Cheyne Row to Glebe Place, I saw those early days in a mist of sentiment. I thought I understood how his affair with Athalie must appear to Harold Fakenham. What I was not so sure of was Athalie's reason for writing him letters which he only answered per-functorily, or by a postcard from Paris, or not at all. What I was vague about was his whole philosophy. He seemed to hold an anomalous position in the world. All very well to wink and nod and say he'd feathered his nest by marrying a woman with lots of money. Chelsea artists had done that often enough. Chelsea socialists did it. They seemed to ex-pect it. But Fakenham had a touch of bitterness about him.

A touch of misogyny. I thought of the word as I rang the bell of his studio. Misogyny, a hatred of women.

"The immaculate white enamel with its shining brass fittings swung inward, and a young man in a white jacket ushered me in. 'Mr. Fakenham's very sorry, sir,' he said, 'but he had to go out of town. He was called away unexpectedly. He left word to show you the portrait he mentioned, sir. And to make yourself at home, sir.'

"I walked into a large high chamber with a gallery at one end and a small kitchen opening out behind. There was a picture on an easel, covered with a sheet. It stood a little way under the gallery, and there were screens on either side of it. The young man offered me some tea. He had a good face. He had the indefinable air of the enlisted man, so that I was not surprised when he admitted he had been in the army.

"While he was getting the tea I looked at the drawings on the wall. I was impressed with my own feeling of relief that Fakenham hadn't remained to show me the picture. It was her picture I wanted to see. These things he drew now were like those in his show—monstrous and not entirely comprehensible commentaries on humanity. I noticed a couple of pairs of compasses walking arm in arm, and a shapeless human figure adoring an enormous engine in a power plant like an inferno. There was a clever semblance implied between that incredibly lofty engine and the huge seated figures of stone in the Valley of the Kings in Egypt. He had ideas, I tell you, but there was only derision of the human race in his heart.

"I said, when the man brought the tea, 'What was Mr. Fakenham in the war?'

"'He was in several things, sir,' he said. 'He wasn't accepted at first on account of his chest, and he did camouflaging for the War Office. Then he got into the Air Force, having very keen sight, and he was an observer until he was shot down. He was gassed that time. They'd just laid a barrage of gas down, and they had no masks, and the two of them was wounded as well, so they couldn't take any precautions, sir. He was invalided home, of course. Mrs. Fakenham has a villa on the Riviera, and they were goin' down there as soon as she could get a permit to travel, when he was struck in an air raid.'

"'You mean he was wounded again?' I said.

"'Very seriously, sir. Very seriously. He's never been the same since.'

"I said I was very sorry to hear this. It put another construction on Harold Fakenham. Here was a genius caught in the wheels of war, with a difference.

"'You mean the gassing, I suppose. I've heard men are never the same after gas if they get it bad.'

"'That's right, sir. He has to lead a quiet life, and for a number of years he never smoked or drank nor had any exercise, because of the gas in his lungs. It 'angs round, you know, sir. But there was the wound in the air raid. It incapacitated him, sir, if you know what I mean?'

"He stood there, and when he had finished speaking he left his mouth open, as if he had a hope that the words he had uttered, once I had understood them, would fly back into his throat and be forever hidden.

"'Good God!' I said and I just looked at him without making any further comment. It happened that I knew very well what he meant. I had seen the thing happen in an air raid. I had been getting into a boat in front of the Navy House in Port Said when a bomb from a lone Turkish raider struck the stone quay not far away from where a sentry was on duty. I saw him double up and collapse. I heard about him later, in the hospital. I remember he had strutted along to the end of the jetty and had right-about-turned, facing the explosion as it came. Slivers and flakes of riven metal that slice muscles in one's shoulder, sever fingers, and hamstring animals like razor blades. That had been Harold Fakenham's fortune at a time when he was saturated with poison gas.

"'It was a shocking thing for them, sir,' the young man remarked, moving away.

"'What's your name?' I said. 'Are you an old comrade in arms?'

"'No, sir. Carter's the name. My mother used to take care of Mr. Fakenham's studio on the Walk. I was in Mesopotomia. Basra, and then Kut. Before that, Palestine.'

"'You didn't have any luck either, then?' I said. I knew what had happened to the poor devils in Kut. They had had to walk, as prisoners, from Bagdad to the Golden Horn. 'It was nothing to write home about,' he remarked without bitterness. 'I was luckier than Mr. Fakenham, anyway. Wouldn't you say so?'

"There was no sense in discussing it. I had not expected that my shadowy forebodings would suddenly sharpen into a tale so charged with grief. I had a shamefaced reluctance to make any further allusion to Fakenham. When you can't do anything to diminish a tragedy, it is humane to get away from it. Do you think I am callous, to skip briskly out of range of human sorrow? I call it being humane as well as intelligent.

"I did then. I set down the teacup and pointed to the easel. 'What's that?' I asked him. Carter, whose mother had 'done' for Mr. Fakenham in the old days, lifted the covering from the canvas.

"'It's what you came to see, sir,' he said."

Mr. Spenlove paused and pulled his beard as he gazed benignly at the fire.

"It was the bravest thing!" he said. "She had been standing in a garden, with the sunlight filtering down through the leaves, the blue Welsh hills far away behind her. There was a rose in her hair. She stood there, laughter in her gray-green eyes half closed, the yellow cotton dress slipping from her shoulder, a coral bracelet on her upper arm, and that scarlet circle made her arm seem whiter than any flesh could be. The breeze blew her dress against her body and limbs, and she held it down with one hand on her thigh, while the reddish gold hair tumbled about her face.

"Yes, it was brave, and as the picture stood a little beneath the gallery with those screens on either side, it seemed to hold a radiance of its own. It glowed. I turned to get further from it for a new view and caught sight of another of his modern monstrosities—a wooden-jointed Lady Godiva riding naked on a rocking horse.

"She was all there in that picture—all I had imagined her as I sat in her apartment in New York and listened to her faint bell-like voice telling me of her 'first great love.'

"I thought, forgetting the faithful Carter, 'How could he leave that girl the way he did? The war!' Well, he had been all right in the war, and what had happened to him was horrible. But what *had* happened to him? What, I mean, when he had the love of that lovely young thing fluttering like a bird in his hand and he had run off to marry another woman? What had scared him?

"Carter stood looking at me and then back at the picture. I suppose he had formulated his own explanation of an elderly stranger being shown the portrait of that girl. I was so preoccupied with my own thoughts I forgot him. I was in a sort of rage that a man could be so unaware of what he possessed. For that was the only solution. Fakenham hadn't comprehended what she was because of her youth. He had supposed she was only what appeared on the surface, a silly chit with a crush. Now he did know, and he gazed out upon the fair domain of a lost paradise from the anchorite's cell in which he was forever immured. He did not answer those tender letters, breathing a gentle hope that he would come to her again. Wait! Wait! I will tell you how I know. I am trying now to recapture my own mood as I looked at her portrait and reconstructed the idyll in the Welsh Hills.

"Carter stood looking at me, and at last I did what he was expecting and possibly hoping for. I asked him, 'Do you know who that is?'

"'Oh yes, sir,' he said. 'I remember when she used to come down to the studio from Onslow Square. I was a young fellow then, and my old lady often spoke of her. She'd come on horseback after she'd been in the Row, walkin' her pony all the way along Royal 'Ospital Road, the groom just behind. I used to work in the King George at the corner then, sir, and the studio was almost next door. She was just like that, sir. It's a very speakin' likeness, I'd say. The groom 'ud come into the King George and have a wet with me while he was waiting.'

"'She was being painted then?' I said.

"'Mr. Fakenham did a proper picture of her, sir, in riding 'abit, with a crop and a little top hat with a cord, for her grandmother, old Lady Rhys, in Onslow Square. This one was done at their place in Wales, I understand, when Mr. Fakenham was down there, just before the war.'

"'And is that all you know about her?' I said. 'I know her, you see, Carter, and what you tell me is very interesting to me. I suppose Mr. Fakenham won't think you are abusing any confidences, will he?'

"'Not at all, sir,' Carter said. 'Mr. Fakenham gave me practically carte blanche, as the Frogs say. He told me you were an old friend of the lady's, sir, and I was to give you any information in my power.'

"'Only he didn't feel up to being here himself.'

"'That's about the size of it, sir. He never shows this picture to a soul. When he said to me: Get out that one there, Carter, and put it up there, I was quite surprised. He looks at it himself sometimes, but when he's alone, always. And he's always a bit under the weather at such times, sir, if you know what I mean.'

"'I see,' I said. 'Can I have another cup, Carter? You are an excellent host.'

"'Don't mention it, sir. Might I ask if the young lady is all right, sir?'

"'She's married and has two children, Carter. She has a daughter about the age of that picture.'

"'Is that so, sir? In the States, of course. Well, I did think of goin' there myself when my old lady passed on, but it isn't so easy as it used to be. I suppose she's changed a lot, sir. We're all gettin' on, I mean.'

"'No change at all in essentials,' I said, very much moved. 'She's like that, except perhaps she's not a child any more. She has had a lot of trouble, one way and another, but it hasn't changed her.'

"'Well, there you remind me of what I used to say, sir, when my old lady spoke of how she'd act so daring, not going home till late. Say what you like, sir, it's a pity there was a prior attachment. It might have changed everything if only . . .'

"He lifted the tray in his brown capable hands and glanced at me respectfully.

"'It's all very well to say you've been given carte blanche,' I said, 'but you seem to me to discuss your employer as if he was dead and gone! In another world, like Miss Rhys.'

"He walked slowly toward his kitchen, holding the tray against his middle with one hand as he opened the door with the other.

"'Now you mention it, sir, isn't that just about what it amounts to, when all's said and done?' He pushed the door further open with his foot. 'And what's more, speakin' for meself, sir, I'd just as soon *be* dead and gone!'

"As he backed through, he looked from the picture to me and then, dropping his eyes discreetly, let the door, dark-green baize with brass nails, swing shut between us."

Mr. Spenlove took the whaling iron and prodded the logs into a heap. They burst into a straight white flame that licked the soot-coated kettle on the chimney crane. He ignored the two silent people behind him. Mrs. Kavanagh sat on the hearth rug leaning on one hand, the other in her lap.

Mr. Kavanagh smoked solemnly at a pipe. Mr. Spenlove took a fresh cigar and bit the end meditatively.

"So I had what I'd gone for, and more! When I cast myself for the rôle of private inquiry agent I had no idea of turning up a corpse. A skeleton in a cupboard would be frivolous by comparison. At first I didn't believe it. In my experience, women get just what they deserve—if one only knows what has gone before. Or I can modify that by adding that in most cases they get a jolly sight more than they deserve. So I could not believe that the girl in that painting, the girl I knew in New York, had been taken for a ride, as you say, more than once, by fate. What made my blood run cold, as I journeyed north to take charge of my new ship, was that she did not know why Fakenham stood her off. She did not know. Wait while I tell you! And sometimes when I am at sea, remembering her gentleness before that hard-boiled ticket-of-leave husband of hers, with his peculiar air of a deteriorated diplomat, I am glad after all she never did know, and hadn't that sorrow to bear.

"Oh yes, she would have understood—a little. But it would have been too much, added to what she had to contend with. The only armor she had in these fights was her own goodness, which is why I say she was a saint in spite of those externals that so offended you, those disguises that she borrowed at times from the chorus girls and the wantons. And the money of her own that she had held on to, and which had diminished as the years passed, until the bank, in whose stock most of her money was invested, toppled into ruin. And even then, with a certain steadfastness and innocent gayety she carried on until the last stroke of all brought her to her knees and she turned to God. . . ."

"There can never be any justification for suicide," said Mrs. Kavanagh obstinately.

"I certainly want to agree with you," said Mr. Spenlove. "We can leave the justification in more competent hands than ours."

"The last stroke—what was that?" Mrs. Kavanagh asked. Mr. Spenlove held up his hand for a moment.

"A trifle. Something you, if you had a rebellious child, would take in your stride as a capable matron. The two of you would have a dozen ways of dealing with it. But they were not open to her, as it happened. I'll tell you.

"I journeyed north. But before I left London I had another experience. I had written a note to young Nevile's sister down in Suffolk, mentioning the time I would be in London, and the name of the hotel. Ursula Nevile. I didn't suppose for a moment I'd get a reply after all these years, but I did, from a flat in Bloomsbury. She was married and signed herself Ursula Cahen. Could I not come to dinner? I could and did. She lived just off Russell Square, in a flat at the top of an old house, a flat made out of a high-pitched attic. One room had had a north light let into the roof, and in it her husband did his work, which was largely posters and advertising designs of a high-class nature.

"I suppose there was a faint doubt in my eyes when she came in. The neat maid had led me into one of those immaculate English rooms with tall bookcases and unobtrusive pictures. It didn't look as if it had come straight from a store or a museum, as so many American rooms do. It had the air of being used—at intervals—by refined beings of perfect behavior, as the Cahens were and their two children also, a boy and a girl. When Mrs. Cahen came in she said, 'You didn't expect to see an old woman!'

"She wasn't an old woman, but compared with Athalie Rhys, who was practically her contemporary, she was very mature. She wasn't aged, but she had no glamour. She was perfectly at home in the post-war world.

"Ursula had become what she would be, inevitably, when the right man came along—a happy matron. She was married in a way young Nevile could never be. She had the man of her heart, who had arrived at exactly the right moment, and who had exactly the right temperament to bring out all that was in her. When her husband came in, just before dinner, and I was introduced, it was easy to see she adored him and thought herself the most fortunate woman in England. He is a quiet competent fellow and makes a tidy income. He may think himself the luckiest man on earth, but he would never reveal it to a living soul. With her it shone out like a luminous cloud—I—I am the chosen of my king, my lord! And her two children were like models constructed by an intelligent English deity for use during lectures in advanced eugenics. I had reason to remember that family group when I came back and saw Athalie's children, because of the contrast.

"Mrs. Cahen said: 'And I have news for you of Sidney. Do you know he is going to be married again? To an English girl. I'm so glad! That awful American creature . . . !'

"'Ada was all right,' I protested, 'except that she wasn't married to the right man.'

"'I shouldn't think any man was the right man for a girl who acted the way she did. Of course,' she went on, 'I've only Sidney's side of the story; but she couldn't have had the slightest sense of loyalty to him. I know Sidney. He's very loyal to those who are loyal to him. Do you know the new one? This Miss Rhys? He says she's the real thing.'

"I recognized the phrase. I said I knew her, and what did Mrs. Cahen suppose he meant by the real thing?

"'I couldn't possibly define it,' she said, glancing around the room, 'but I know just what he means. He says he's been looking for it all his life, and now he's found it he is going to get it. Dear Sidney! He hasn't had such a happy life so far, has he? He says he had some rotten luck, but he won't say what it was. He resigned from the Company. But he seems to be doing awfully well now, in Jamaica.'

"'Doesn't he say he's very anxious to get back into the Company?' I said. 'He is. Being manager of a club patronized by wealthy patrons is not so good a billet as captain of a liner,' I went on.

"'No, but he's on British soil down there,' she argued. As if that mattered a fig! I suppose she saw me smiling and said gravely, 'Some of us still believe in the Empire, Mr. Spenlove. The time may come . . .'

"Mr. Cahen agreed with her. We ought to stay within the Empire. They sounded like a couple of later Roman colonists, living frugally in Sicily while the barbarians in Rome were taking over the administration of the empire. Neither of them has the faintest notion of what is going on in the world. We spoke of the Dole, and Mr. Cahen was roused to add, 'Panem et circenses.' He alluded gruffly to 'five shillings in the pound. There's an income tax for you!' Ursula nodded. But they are doing well enough. He makes a lot of money. They showed me magazines with his designs. One of them had an interview with Gerald Fakenham, now Sir Gerald. He was photographed in his paddock with his little son perched on a hunter and a regal collie under his left hand. I glanced at the reading matter. 'Those who aspire . . . After all, the public is the best judge . . . the good, the true . . .' And so on. A lady interviewer with wide starry eyes, and not much behind them.

"I said, 'I've met his brother Harold.' Mr. Cahen gave a short laugh and put his hand to his brow. '*That* chap! Off his nut.'

"'Yet there was a time when he could paint,' I said. 'Before the war.' He nodded.

"'Did you ever hear of a picture he did called Shell Shock? He took a small gallery and exhibited just this one picture, set up at the end of what looked like a dugout. It was a geometrical design, but when you'd looked at it long enough you saw the lines were barbed wire over a window —and inside a large room a lot of men hung head downward, from rafters, like bats. And they were all giggling. The picture revolved slowly so that the top became the bottom. It was a mild sensation. But now he has gone Dada, or whatever it is, the fellow's cracked. You say you've met him?'

"'Introduction from a friend in New York,' I explained. He nodded.

"I had a nice evening. I was leaving next day, and I asked for any messages for young Nevile.

"'Oh, I write regularly,' Ursula said. She had no intention of surrendering her brother to anyone. 'I do wish he could come back to England to live when he marries this girl. By the way, is it true she is a divorcée?'

"'Not so far as I know,' I said, a shade mendaciously. I didn't want to get into an argument with a monogamist like Ursula at that moment. If young Nevile hadn't seen fit to tell her the whole story she could live on in innocence.

"'I doubt if he could,' I said. 'If he gets his job back, which I doubt, he will be in New York again.'

"'What was the matter?' Ursula asked with a frown. 'Nothing professional, I hope?'

"'No. Rather social. A passenger lodged a complaint, and to save trouble for themselves the office requested Captain Nevile's resignation.'

"'An outrage!' she said indignantly.

"'It might have been worse,' I pointed out. 'He accepted a position in the ticket office and made a jolly good thing of it too, until this club business came along.'

"'I was afraid he was asked to resign for something like the yacht—you remember?'

"'Perfectly. No, it wasn't like that at all. It was plutocratic rather than aristocratic, this time.'

"'I wonder what you mean,' she said, eyeing me, but without wondering in the depths of her mind. It didn't really matter what I meant because she had so sure a grip on life. The Prayer Book and the Empire, panem et circenses, and those two 'ducks,' as she called them. She meant her children, Jock and Winnie, twelve and thirteen, with perfect manners and with a copy of Kipling's 'If' over the boy's bed. Winnie was a Girl Guide and knew more about fishermen's knots and the habits of the otter than one would believe possible.

Jock was equally wholesome. I felt a pariah among thorough-
breds, one of the lesser breeds without the law. I was glad
I hadn't spoken of Athalie. Ursula is an extraordinarily
intelligent and understanding woman, but her mind would
be so clouded by the facts of the other woman's life that I
doubted. As I feared, she adverted to the matter herself.

"'What I didn't gather from Sidney's letters,' she said,
'was why this Miss Rhys is living in a place like New York.'

"From the way she said it you would have concluded that
New York was a collection of a dozen hovels in Tierra del
Fuego or Turkestan. I said New York was a natural enough
place for lots of people. Even artists of various kinds. And
she, the girl, had been on the stage.

"'An actress! Sidney didn't mention that.'

"'Only in the chorus,' I said.

"'Oh!' Ursula Cahen gave me a strange, far-away look.
She was thinking, 'Sidney is in the clutches of another
creature!' I could see it like a foreboding coming up in her
mind.

"'No!' I said. 'He didn't give you that impression, did he?
—that there was anything to be ashamed of.'

"'Is that why he has been writing Percy to send him
money?' she asked blankly. 'Percy tells me he has had several
letters asking . . .'

"'For his own money, I believe,' I said. 'I remember that.
He could do with the money, naturally. For himself, I mean.
She wouldn't take it. She has an income.'

"'It's very confusing,' she confessed. 'I do hope you'll
advise him for the best.' She frowned. I could see she was
wondering about Percy, the brother who had borrowed
young Nevile's savings and 'invested' them for him. Ursula
is so straight herself she is always finding things confusing.

"'I wouldn't worry about Sidney,' I said.

"'Is he in love with her—really in love?'

"'And she is with him. They met on my ship. Her father
has a plantation in Jamaica. They are connected with the

Caerleon family. Look.' I showed her the coat of arms young Nevile had given me. 'Why don't you look them up?'

"'In the peerage?' she said, looking at it.

"'Or the College of Arms,' I said.

"'My husband knows a man at the College of Arms,' she said looking at him, and he nodded.

"'I do those things for publishers,' he informed me. 'The man I know is assistant Chester Herald. Lots of people use crests who have no right to them. He can identify any crest if it's genuine. If it isn't on record at the College, it's a fake.'

"'But why . . .' Mrs. Cahen stopped herself and seemed to be meditating. 'Did Sidney give you this? To find out?' I nodded. 'It's a perfectly sensible thing to do,' she said firmly.

"'That's what I thought,' I said, 'and yet personally I haven't the slightest doubt that she is truthful.'

"'You really believe that? I should hate to have Sidney make another mistake. I must write him again.'

"We left it that way. I took the train to the north, and my holiday was over. The ship was being fitted out on the Clyde, and I found Wensley, imperturbable and dominating, waiting for me. He had no curiosity as to what I had been doing with myself in London. If he gave the matter any thought at all, he would have arrived at a totally erroneous conclusion. And because he had no use for young Nevile it would have been hopeless to make any allusions to my adventures. We were too busy with our own affairs on the ship. I got lodgings in Radnor Street, and until the ship had run her trials I had no time to reflect upon the fate of anybody else but myself, for I had seventeen thousand horsepower and an engine room crammed with gadgets, very new and very efficient, and not always familiar to me. I felt an old fogy at times, for the young fellows were on easy terms with the new machinery. They had never known anything else. For that very reason they could not have the same feeling for the ship that I had. Wensley expressed the gentlemanly attitude of the new generation in his own way when he said to me, 'As soon as they get a license their hands drop off at the wrists.' For all his majestic demeanor and air of being a god, Wensley had worked in sail and as mate in steam. He knew what work was. I fancy it was primarily because he knew young Nevile was a steamer-bred sailor that he disliked his success and had been complacent about his downfall."

"What difference could that make?" asked Mrs. Kavanagh with impatience.

"Everything, to Wensley, because he belonged to another generation, almost another religion," said Mr. Spenlove, smiling. "We had so many of the new school on board the Salvadorena that Wensley took refuge in silence. He left the sea in time to save himself a lot of grief. When we arrived in New York he was appointed superintendent, and we had the captain of the Pamplona, next in line for promotion, take over our command.

"This was an incredible piece of bad luck for young Nevile. He had put in his application some time before, and it had been favorably received and tentatively approved by the personnel board. But now it was blocked. Wensley was definitely against having a commander back whose resignation had been demanded and accepted. Wensley's position was that young Nevile had officially left the sea by taking jobs ashore. It would have been no use reminding Wensley of famous admirals who had been on shore and then returned to their ships. The application was filed and would have stayed filed if Wensley hadn't been sent back to London as assistant adviser on new construction. That's all you need know of Wensley. He has a billet perfectly suited to his talents, and he has nothing to do with us any more. So young Nevile's chance came after all.

"But while it was hanging fire I had two experiences.

We were still in New York and I was determined that if I had the chance I would go and see Athalie. Before the chance came a letter was forwarded from here. Young Nevile had written me from Jamaica very urgently. Would I see what had happened to Athalie? She had not answered his last two letters. The letter was a fortnight old. He had misjudged our arrival date. This was a good excuse for action. I called her number, and after a while I was told she had been disconnected.

"There was nothing to do but go up and find out for myself. For some reason the disconnection of her telephone aroused my old distrust. I recalled your feeling about her and the memory of the time I saw our Mr. Wilmarth's limousine outside, with Mr. Wilmarth himself emerging from her door. It all came back, even the scene on the train, when she was obviously frightened to death at meeting me. So I went up, far from easy in my mind, and found another name on her letter box. She was not there any more.

"Gone! I rang the janitor's bell and after a long wait a ferocious-looking native of mittel-Europa emerged, sending out a powerful stench of garlic. Like many of his kind he had only a sketchy knowledge of English and no control over his pronunciation. He was hopeless, and communicated his hopelessness to me. At last I gathered that what he was trying to say was I ought to see the manager. He lived on the first floor two doors away. The squat heavily mustached janitor waddled down out of sight again. The manager was without enthusiasm one way or another. He said he had no authority to give addresses. Letters could be forwarded. As he told me this his wife came into the office. When she heard I was inquiring about Miss Rhys she gave me a look of close scrutiny and then spoke to her husband. It had evidently been a matter of argument between them. The man stood by his desk, not asking me to sit down, his eyes on the papers under his hand.

"'There's two months' rent due,' his wife explained to me

in a frank quarrelsome voice. Yet she was not ill-natured.
She was convinced somehow that her husband was taking a
wrong line. 'Miss Rhys couldn't keep on with the apartment,
and we had a prospect at a better rent. Miss Rhys promised
to pay up pretty soon. Maybe you're one of her gentleman
friends?'

"Her husband growled something to her that I couldn't
hear.

"'Oh, her gentleman friends are nobody's business,' she
repeated a shade shrewishly, yet with what I call humanity.
She turned to me.

"'I'm a friend, certainly,' I admitted. 'Whether a gentleman or not I can't be sure.' The manager glanced at me
at this. 'I have a rush message from her sweetheart in
the West Indies. He has had no answer to his last letters
and . . .'

"'There you are! What did I tell you?' she said to her
husband. She turned to me again. 'My husband's very
particular,' she informed me, 'and it makes him suspicious.
He's afraid the neighborhood's getting a lot of these girls
with too many gentleman friends.' She went to the mantelpiece and took up some letters.

"'She could have come for her mail,' her husband grum-
bled. She waved an impatient hand towards him.

"'Miss Rhys had a bit of trouble lately,' she said to me.
She glanced at her husband as if in challenge. 'It's that boy
of hers. Don't ask me what it was. Not her fault. It's not
so easy to make out when you're in her position. And she's
been a good tenant for three years. Never any trouble.
Gentlemen friends of hers have always been gentlemen.
And if she was what he thinks'—pointing to her husband—
'she'd have paid the rent.'

"'That will be taken care of,' I said. She handed me the
letters, saying again to her husband, 'There you are! What
did I tell you? This gentleman'll fix things.'

"It didn't seem a sound policy to dislodge myself from

the status she had given me. She was evidently a citizen of the world. She was able to make extremely fine distinctions when estimating tenants, finer than her husband could appreciate. She gave me an envelope with an address on Eleventh Street.

"It wasn't very far—a few blocks south and west, near Seventh Avenue. A brownstone walk-up—one of those gracious mansions of the 'eighties which have so miserable a destiny, but which at least have noble ceilings and tall windows. They have so sour a smell and furtive unwholesome humans in their basements. There was a vertical row of small bell pushes with smudgy cards almost beyond hope. The top one of all had a slip of mauve paper with the single word written in microscopic letters of blue ink. Rhys. I pressed it and waited. A woman opened the heavy half door and let herself out. She gave me a dazed, puzzled look, as though the sight of a middle-aged man at the top of the brownstone steps was an insoluble problem. She started down into the fine spring evening, and suddenly, with that temporary recovery of the wits which marks the New Yorker she turned and informed me that the bells were all out of order. 'They don't ring,' she added as a further lapse into coherence. 'Go in,' she suggested. 'Door's not locked.'

"Five floors again. Wide stairs, with smooth empty niches at the angles, as though the statuary had fled secretly, in shame of the stale odor of lost hopes. Little medallions on the doors with names. One door ajar, with a severe-looking young woman on a sofa sitting well away from a young man who was wearing blue suède shoes and improbable socks. At the top a skylight revealing four doors, a strip of linoleum instead of carpet, and on one door the little poem of welcome in its frame. There was also a tiny brass knocker shaped like a ship on that door. I knocked. And waited.

"I heard a gramophone inside and a mysterious crepitating sound. Then abruptly both stopped as I knocked again. A silence, and 'Who is it?' came through the door in a voice

I didn't recognize, a young peremptory voice, not to be trifled with.

"'Spenlove's the name,' I informed the door. Another silence, and then it opened gently, and Athalie Rhys looked out at me.

"She put her hand to her face in a conventional stage gesture, unsmiling—yet she opened the door to admit me.

"I walked into a large room in which the carpet had been rolled up under a day bed. A portable gramophone stood open on a side table. The chairs had been pushed against the walls. She brought one or two of them towards the window and invited me to take one. I handed her the letters.

"She was changed. There was a sort of desperate gravity in her face now, a sweet yet austere recognition of grief. It made her even more desirable, for it gave her a sensuous spirituality. When she took the letters she did not speak but bowed her head and laid them aside for a moment.

"'I heard music,' I said. 'Don't stop on my account.' She smiled faintly.

"'We didn't know who it was,' she said. 'I'm glad they gave you the address. I shouldn't have liked to miss you.'

"'Read the letters,' I said severely. 'I mean Sidney's.'

"'I sent him a cable,' she said in a low tone. 'It's quite all right now. He's so impatient!' She spoke as if of an infant.

"'We—you said—who's we?' For a moment I thought young Nevile had come to live with her. Athalie rose with her finger on her lip.

"'Impatient!' I said. 'Aren't you impatient?'

"'Oh yes,' she said faintly, 'but I have things to do.'

"She walked over to a door that led to a bedroom, I suppose, and opened it only enough to slip in. I lit a cigar. There was a perfume hanging in the air that reminded me, like a gong sounding, of Elli Phalère. She mustn't use that scent, I thought. I hadn't detected it on her before. She must get rid of it before young Nevile got wind of it. What a strange effect it would have!

"She was away a little while. The delay roused my silly suspicions again. Why had she omitted to write and then spent perhaps a couple of dollars on a cable? She was always doing such things. And not paying the rent!

"The door opened, and she came in, leading the original of the painting I had seen in Fakenham's studio. The exact replica then, in a yellow dress that had been so hurriedly flung on that one white shoulder was bare. She was wearing toe dancer's slippers on her bare feet.

"'This is Ginevra,' said Athalie. 'Ginevra was practising when you knocked.'

"The girl came forward like a young lithe animal with a mop of russet hair and ice-green eyes and shook hands. 'I've heard a lot about you,' she said. 'Mother talks a lot about you. I'm very pleased to meet you.'

"She was about fifteen, I would say, but she had a great deal of character even at a casual glance. She had a trick of immediately sinking into immobility and meditation when she was not speaking, as if she had already acquired the habit of reserving her vitality for the terrific demands of her art. She walked with a sort of mincing precision, yet with feline grace. There was strength in the arms and the supple loins and shapely knees. She sat with her feet poised for flight.

"'She's been at school,' said her mother, 'but I couldn't afford to keep her there any more. And anyhow she hated it.'

"'Hated school?' I said, assuming an expression of anguish. The child shot a long level glance at me from under lowered lids. She knew me already very well.

"'She wants to dance,' said Athalie. 'Nothing but dancing. She's taking lessons in New York.'

"'To be a dancer?' I said.

"'I'm afraid so,' Athalie confessed. 'It's her passion.'

"'You'll have dinner with me,' I said. 'Both of you.'

"'I don't know. I may be engaged,' Athalie said uncertainly. Ginevra got up and suddenly, to my astonishment, rose on her toes and pirouetted across the room like a butterfly flitting across a bank of blooms. Her mere motion evoked perfumes and flowery meads, romance in formal gardens and the darts of love in white bosoms. She seemed to hover on the doorknob, and as she passed into the bedroom she threw me a daring, almost professional glance of allurement.

"'No,' I said. 'I'll take no denial.'

"'My husband,' Athalie said in a faint whisper, 'may come in.'

"Ginevra had closed the door on herself. *She* was perfectly sure of her power over men, I thought. I made no reply to that astonishing statement of Athalie's. I sat smoking my cigar, wondering what sort of chaos I had got myself into.

"'Tell me,' I said finally. 'I'm completely in the dark. Are you reconciled? What are you going to do about Sidney? Where has your husband come from?'

"'He will not be here long,' she said in a low tone. 'He is trying to find a position.'

"'You'll have to be perfectly frank if you expect me to remain your friend,' I said. 'I've got to get all this straight now, or quit.'

"She looked extremely distressed and agitated.

"'I'm sorry,' she said. 'I suppose you heard something from those people over on Park Avenue.'

"'The woman is your friend, I'm sure,' I said. 'She wouldn't break any confidences, but she was almost shouting at her husband that she was right and he was wrong about you! What's this about your boy? What did she mean?'

"'Morty didn't mean to do anything!' she said quickly. In any other woman you would have been able to say she flared up in defense of her child. Athalie only said it quickly. I waited. 'They shouldn't have put temptation in his way,' she went on, looking at her own very small feet. 'He's a very spirited boy. He's like his father, very high strung and impulsive. Anyway, it's all over now.'

"'Where is he now?' I inquired.

"'I don't know,' she confessed. 'He went away . . . to get a job. He's been getting rather hard to handle, and when this trouble came he said he didn't care, he had to have some money. He's fourteen and awfully big for his age. I don't think he'll ever work for anybody else. He's too bossy. Like his father.'

"'I thought he was at school,' I said.

"'Well, he was, but I've had some financial worries lately, and so . . . it doesn't matter. He ran away before. He's got so much personality.'

"'But surely you must want to know where he is.'

"'In a way I do. I mean he has so much personality he prefers to be on his own. I sent him some money. He's at some country club. He's awfully good at golf already.'

"She smiled at me and added, 'Then his father came, and I didn't have enough money to keep on that other place.'

"'He isn't living here—your husband?' I said. She nodded towards another door.

"'In there. Ginevra and I are in this room.' She said in a low tone, 'That's all.'

"'I'm sorry,' I said. 'I promised those people the rent would be taken care of. I had to, because I believe in you, you know.'

"'You believe in me! Oh, I knew it,' she cried and then began to weep softly. 'If only *he* did!'

"'Sidney?' She nodded. 'Doesn't he?'

"'He doesn't understand! He thinks everybody's life is simple like his own. Morty got into trouble—and his name, his father's name, was in the papers. Those horrible newspapermen!' She clenched a small fist and trembled a little. 'And then my husband came back. Sidney thinks all I have to do is pack up and marry him. He doesn't think of me. He—he can't.'

"'Do I understand it was . . .' I began.

"'Don't you remember the day you saw me on the train?'

she said. She hurried into the bathroom to bathe her eyes. I waited, feeling somewhat inhuman at causing so much misery. She came back again, calmer. 'I was so frightened. I was afraid you were watching me so you could tell Sidney. Because I was going to see my husband. Visit him. You know, don't you? Do I have to say it?'

"'No,' I said. 'Please forgive me. But now he is here, is he going to stay?'

"'It wasn't really his fault!' she insisted, like a mother bird guarding her young with her own breast. 'They hounded him! He didn't know what he was doing that night. He never meant to . . . Oh!'

"She clasped her hands and bent her head over them in prayer for a moment.

"'You see,' she said, 'how can I tell Sidney all this? He would never have anything to do with us again.'

"'He knows you have children,' I said. She waved that aside gently.

"'He doesn't *realize* them,' she said. 'And if he heard about Morty, what would he think? And he doesn't understand that the children don't *know.*'

"'About their father?' I whispered.

"'About my husband. I have to bear this cross. Perhaps, who knows? it will work out. But Sidney writes to me: Explain! Explain! He wants to know everything about everything! He says I know all about him!'

"She rose and walked agitatedly about the room. Her voice never rose above a sort of chirrup. It was very clear and musical and I marveled at her self-command, her spiritual stamina.

"'He won't come in while I'm here, will he?' I inquired with a certain interest. I meant her husband.

"'He has a key,' she said. 'After all, shall we go to dinner? Ginevra will love it.'

"They hurried to get ready. It was growing dark as we went down to the street. We took a taxi uptown. I had the inspiration to give them something unusual. We went to a big restaurant on Broadway where there was a floor show, and we had a good table. I watched Ginevra with fascination. She was elated, but there was a cool, calculating look in her eyes as she watched the performers. She was estimating professionally just how good they were. And Athalie, when I looked at her, smiled with ravishing sweetness. Sometimes her eyes were wet, but in some mysterious way she would recover and indulge in a sort of exquisite ecstasy. There was nothing professional in her attitude, though she had been on the stage. Ginevra seemed to have taken over the major rôle. But they both loved it, as Athalie told me.

"'Some giggle water,' I suggested, but she shook her head. Yes, perhaps Ginevra would like some.

"'Only a little,' said Ginevra. 'It's not good to drink if you're a dancer.'

"'Well, this is a special occasion,' I said. 'One of these days we'll be drinking champagne out of your slipper.'

"They were entranced. I had a good time. Only the shadows bothered me at times. I had a feeling I was in the company of two fairy beings who had been released for a while from a dark cavern. Athalie, in the taxi going back, said, 'You are a good fairy! We've had such a good time.'

"'Not the last,' I said. 'When Ginevra's a famous dancer!'

"Ginevra's ice-green eyes slanted towards me. I saw them glittering in the lights of Sixth Avenue.

"'It takes years,' she said gravely and with complete composure.

"As we came along towards the house where they lived Athalie craned out to look. She said in a low tone, 'Couldn't you say good-bye now?'

"'No,' I said. 'I'm all right. I'd like to meet him.'

"It was too late, anyway. The taxi slowed to the curb and stopped. We got out, and as I followed them up, I saw a tall man rise from the top step, where he had been sitting and waiting for us. It was a clear bright evening, and he was plainly visible in the light of a street lamp. This, I thought, is the core of the whole thing!

"The strange thing to me was the instant feeling I had that he was a gentleman born. And he is. No mistake! He received us as though the brownstone steps were a throne and he of royal blood. I heard Athalie say faintly, 'My husband!' Ginevra had thrust forward and was opening the door with her mother's key. I saw a tall clean-shaven man with handsome ravaged features and iron-gray hair, dressed in dark clothes and a ready-made spring overcoat. He wore gloves, which he removed before shaking hands. His bow was courtly and inborn. He made a gesture for me to go in first. We proceeded up the stairs in single file, and I heard him coughing a little behind me. I said the night air was chill. 'When you're not used to it,' he answered. I wondered why he hadn't gone indoors in that case. 'Oh,' he said, 'I don't like being indoors. The Greeks had a name for that!'

"I thought to myself, Good God!

"When I saw him with the lights on, the peculiar effects of what he had gone through were more obvious. He had become, as it were, etherealized in outward appearance. All dross seemed to have been fined away from his face. And this, of course, was illusory, for there had been no inward resolution, only the scarifying effect of incarceration. He gave a disturbing impression of being an anchorite without a soul, of nobility without honor.

"It was Athalie's demeanor that made me feel one of the lost. She never glanced at him. Ginevra vanished into the bedroom after her mother and did not appear again. I saw Wilkerson's glance shoot after her with a demoniac gleam in his eyes. He said he was sorry he had nothing to offer me to drink. 'We haven't any money!' he said in a refined voice. He sat on the arm of the ottoman swinging his leg, coughing violently as he lit a cigarette. 'Clothes don't fit, no money, and God hates me! You're a friend of my wife's, I suppose.'

"I told him, concisely, how we had met on the Camotan,

when she went down to visit her father. He shrugged his shoulders at the mention of Major Rhys.

"'I ought to go South,' he said and coughed again. 'My chest is bad. But . . .' He shrugged again and gazed at the floor.

"Athalie came back into the room, holding a handkerchief to her lips. She smiled at me.

"'I was saying I ought to go South,' he said to her. 'In fact, I'll have to go. I'd like to try my luck in Havana.' He looked at me and held my gaze with a long enigmatic stare. There were so many things in that look of his that I was spellbound. It was a flash of his old personal magnetism, that had lured so many men into his phony schemes, and it was also compact of impudence, roguery, and matchless courage to face emotional odds. He dared me, in that look, to associate him with the felon who had served years for a shocking crime and who was now at large to begin life afresh. No, he was my equal, possibly my superior.

"And I grant it, if I admit his point of view. I grant you, and anybody else, that in his circumstances I would have destroyed myself. I would have hidden from the very face of mankind. I would have run away into the desert and cohabited with shrieking ghosts. I hadn't the stuff in me to be a devil. I could never have done what he did, when he pulled Athalie towards him and flung an arm around her and made the humorous suggestion that she had some money hidden away in some bank, money that would save his life. He coughed, his eyes still with that gleam in them. He glanced toward the room where Ginevra lay in bed.

"I rose. I said I had to get back to my ship. He said, 'I'll go along with you,' and rose. His arm left Athalie's form as though he had been embracing inanimate wood or stone. He dragged on his cheap overcoat and opened the door. I hardly remember what I said to her in parting. She smiled a farewell and turned away.

"I didn't want him, of all people on earth, to walk with

me along the lighted streets. I have my limitations, and
they begin this side of a man like him. But he was oblivious.
What he wanted was, precisely, what I had. He wanted the
company of a man utterly beyond his own world as he had
made it. He wanted my principles, my lifelong fussy preoccupation with solid work and incorruptible integrity. He
was aware of these things, make no mistake. Prison makes
men clairvoyant in such matters. And he intended to make
use of me, to my distress.

"'You know,' he said in a low husky growl, as we walked
towards Seventh Avenue, 'they say anybody can stage a
comeback. I've been out of the game so long I'm beginning
to wonder if they're right. What I'm thinking of is an absolutely clean slate. Did you know I'm a good printer? I was
a printer in . . . never mind . . . a very large establishment.'
He smiled into the night. 'And a good printer. Do you know
they use Garamond French, old style, for their menus and
weekly bulletins in that institution for the active-minded?
A fact. Well, that's that. I want a job, not in New York,
as a printer. Like old Franklin; Poor Richard, the old crook!
You can stand me a drink, can't you? In here.'

"He surprised me. I thought I knew New York, but he
surprised me. Somewhere on Tenth Street he thrust a door
inwards, and we walked along a passage into a crowded bar-
room with a lunch counter, humorous signs over the bar
about 'In God we trust; all others cash; no checks accepted.'
There was an alcove containing tables with red-and-blue
checked cloths and doll-like women being made love to
by elegant satyrs in tight-waisted suits. The bar was long
and cluttered with women whose lipsticks stained the glasses
from which they drank and whose finger nails shone like
carnelian claws. Wilkerson, his hand on my elbow, guided
me to an opening at the bar and ordered two straight ryes.
I decided to humor him. He was a special case. He might
suffer from claustrophobia, but it didn't apply to this illegal
secret tavern where all you had to do was walk in. I might

do Athalie some good, get some information, by being hospitable.

"'A printer,' I said. I didn't catch on at first. He eyed me shrewdly.

"'I need a change,' he said, and his shoulder shook for a moment as he coughed. 'You've no idea how bloody much I need a change. I've been a—what you call it—a shut-in!' He coughed again bending over and releasing a long spittle into a cuspidor. 'Ah! A shut-in. A sea voyage, the doctor said. That bastard always had a joke for us patients. He'd threaten to send us a bill for violet-ray treatment. Yes he said a sea voyage. Now what do you say?'

"'I haven't the slightest idea what you want me to say,' I said. 'I'm not in the printing business.'

"He tapped me on the shoulder, 'Buddy, I didn't suppose you were. But you're on a ship, aren't you? And they use printers on ships. I haven't crossed the Big Drink several times without finding that out. Why, it's an ideal set-up,' he reflected, turning his empty glass around. 'An ideal combination! Do I make myself plain?'

"It wasn't any use pointing out that my powers in that direction were limited. He did not know enough about what he wanted to understand how little I could do. But he kept on talking about it. Finally I told him that he could tackle the Victualing Department if he wanted to apply. It was none of my affair.

"He had several more, and spoke largely of the tragedy of coming home to a family that was not very glad to see him.

"'You must give them time to get accustomed to you,' I said.

"'I'd like to wring both their necks,' he told me confidentially, as we walked along. I would have felt a certain pleasure in wringing his. I kept an eye out for a taxi.

"'Good-night,' I said as it came alongside. 'Keep cheerful. Your luck may turn.'

"'I'll use your name,' he said.

"I didn't quite understand at first. Then I decided I'd warn Romaine. You remember the chief steward on the Camotan? He is now head of his department. I'd warn him. He might hardly be proof against a good printer.

"But the Salvadorena took all my time, and I forgot. That is how Wilkerson, unknown to me, got a position on the old Pamplona as a printer. He had found my card among Athalie's belongings. I had written my sailing date in pencil on the back of it for her convenience. He had soon got rid of the pencil marks and replaced it with a 'Introducing Mr. James Wilkerson' in a convincing scrawl. I learned that later after the affair on the Pamplona. He must have been a good printer too. He held his job.

"If I had only thought of it I might have helped him. It let Athalie and her child out of the hell in which they lived with a paroled prisoner in the house who would have been glad to wring their necks. What he meant was that if he could have obliterated them and gotten hold of Athalie's poor little income, he would have done so. There is nothing so paralyzing as an atrophied personality. Wilkerson had ideas of grandeur as to his own capacity before he committed that major crime that put him away. Mr. Wroot of Shap, Virginia, told me of several grandiloquent schemes Wilkerson promoted before he came to Norbury and started his Norbury *Times-Leader* career. He had got some of Athalie's money by some trick, and leaving her in her apartment with the two children, had come down here to make a conquest. I suppose he had read of Americans doing such things in movies and he never was able to keep fact and fiction separate in his mind, which I suppose is a good enough definition of the American spirit. Another characteristic was his utter inability to believe that he was ever guilty of anything. He was convinced, I fancy, in his own priceless phrase, that he was 'as clean as a hound's tooth.'

"Yes, he got some of her money. She was defenseless in

many ways. If you were a cad and could bring yourself to do it, she had no defense. Ginevra has more character by far. Athalie could plan to conceal her resources, but when he found her with the money in the apartment, he merely took it, and she could only submit. He had that blackjack of her past to swing down on her heart, and I believe he used it. What? I mean Ginevra. He had a sort of cold, villainous sexual continence, and he regarded Fakenham's daughter as a shocking affront to his sense of greatness.

"I sailed in the Salvadorena bound for a cruise de luxe and forgot him. It was young Nevile's job to shoulder the responsibility of Athalie's future. And where was he? She had sent him a cable, collect no doubt, and perhaps this had quieted him. I was due at Kingston in a week, and I sent him a radio the day before we docked. He was waiting for us and came up to my cabin.

"He was very bronzed and good-looking in fresh white linen and a pith helmet. He even had a flamingo-colored tie and a small red flower in his buttonhole that matched it perfectly. But he was very much upset by the love affair that seemed to be going to pieces in his hands. There was hurt pride in his face as well as consternation when he sat down in my sumptuous brown leather armchair in my suite on the boat deck. His brow cleared for a moment as he looked around.

"'They are doing you very well now, Fred,' he said. Then he sighed. I could see the nostalgia sweeping over him as he realized how passionately he wanted to be back in command of a ship.

"'That's only one thing more,' he muttered, meaning Wensley's having the power to postpone any decision in his favor indefinitely.

"'Yes,' I said, 'you're out of luck there. He doesn't like you and never did. You aren't his style.'

"'He's a stuffed image,' said young Nevile, and without

any personal animosity either, though I wouldn't have blamed him. He really believes that Wensley is a stuffed image and has got by simply because nothing ever happened to test him. It may be so. A mate of Wensley's agrees in that decision. We shall never know. But because of what happened on the Pamplona, nobody can say young Nevile wasn't tested.

"When I told him I had seen Athalie, he started up. 'How is she? Why doesn't she write now? I haven't had a letter for two weeks!'

"'Be patient,' I said. 'She's had some sort of trouble.'

"'There it is!' he cried. 'That's all I get all the time. Some sort of trouble. *What* sort of trouble? Can't I be told? She wanted to know, while you were in England, if I could spare—well, some money. I naturally asked what it was for. I'm not a kid to send money all over the place without knowing what it is for. I haven't held back anything about myself—though as a matter of fact she never asks—and I can't stand all this mystery.'

"'Well, I know she has had some sort of financial reverses and has had to move.' I gave him the address. He put it down in an expensive memorandum book with his monogram on one corner. 'One of my guests gave it to me,' he said. He had a gold-plated fountain pen too, another guest's tribute. I went on: 'She's had to take the children away from their schools, and the boy has been troublesome. He seems a bit of a handful, from what she said. The girl is very pretty, Sidney. I don't know . . .'

"'Is she?' He was thinking. I added that Athalie had had to leave some rent unpaid over on Park Avenue.

"'Why on earth didn't she say so?' he stormed. 'What would it be, do you think, Fred? Suppose I send her, well, three hundred?'

"'Don't send it. Give it to me. I told the people when I called it would be taken care of. Better not send it.'

"'But why not?' he insisted.

"'There you go again,' I chided him. 'You seem to be a success down here, Sidney, but in dealing with a woman you're more of a kid than I'd think possible with all your experience.' He flushed under his tan.

"'What you call experience is no good with Athalie,' he said, and showed he wasn't such a fool. Then he gave a short laugh.

"'A success! You think I'm a success! A beachcomber with a flunkey's job! I'd rather be mate of the old Manola any day. Fred, do you think I'm a fool to quit?'

"'At present, son?' I said. 'I suppose you'd shy at starting in another line.'

"'I'm thirty-seven now,' he said. 'Nearly thirty-eight. I'd be seventy before I got a command in a new outfit. No. I'll not give up hope. Wensley may burst with his own importance . . . !'

"He laughed boyishly. I admired his pluck because waiting for Wensley to burst was a job that would last him well beyond the seventy years he had mentioned for the other scheme.

"We stayed overnight in Kingston. I went ashore with young Nevile, and he drove me over to the Club. He had his own quarters now, secluded from the members' quarters, a bungalow with a private dock below a terrace on which stood modern chromium-plated chairs and lounges with waterproof cushions and a portable electric wine cooler that was also a table. He had a colored man who waited on us. After dinner we sat and looked out across the lagoon. I said he might make this job do if he got married.

"'Even if she would, I wouldn't,' he said doggedly. 'You only see the externals, Fred. She wouldn't fit in here.'

"'Well, she can't just at present. She's in a jam.'

"'What about me? If I help her out of that hole you spoke of, what does it get me? I have a chance to think things over down here. I'm no nearer having her than I was. Less! She will have to make a decision between us. I'm coming up in a month or two, to see her, and the vice president. I want to make sure Wensley is going to hold me up. I know a side of the business the Wensleys never get conscious of—if they're ever conscious of anything but what wonderful deck ornaments they are!'

"'I liked Wensley,' I warned him. 'He never interfered with me.'

"'All right! All right! But I'm going to test his powers to do me dirt. And when I see Athalie I'm going to put it up to her. Even if she wants to have it all over with. I'm going to get on a ship again. I can't afford to let her make a mess of my life now. I've got to be the boss.'

"'Well, if you were in her place, with two children in their teens, would you want them to learn all about their father? It's a rotten story, I can tell you.'

"'I know this, I won't hang on and off all my life,' he answered. 'I want her more than anything in the world. I can hardly bear to think what it will be like, to have her. . . . But this is real life, not a storybook. She mustn't think I am less important than her kids.'

"'But I am afraid you are,' I said. 'Less important than Ginevra.'

"'Why her especially?'

"'She is just like herself. Ginevra is a very lovely girl.'

"'Is she?' He glanced at me: the old look.

"'She wants to be a toe dancer.'

"'Really! Of course . . . yes . . . h'm.' He became lost in thought. So did I for a moment. I realized I was in the presence of a man whose familiarity with life was authentic enough, and yet he was continually opening vistas down which were enormous mysteries. He had just glanced down one of them. He had just perceived that if he became the stepfather of a beautiful girl who was a dancer he might not prove very expert in his own part. Fifteen was an age, in a girl like Ginevra, with her peculiar existence at an expensive school, with a vagabond father who had suddenly appeared after a long absence (which her mother explained as 'desertion')—fifteen was an age equal, in relation to a man, to twenty. I could feel it while in her presence. She looked out at life appraisingly and with the courage, not of a saint like her mother, but of a skillful swordsman who knows just how to use his weapons in attack or defense.

"Young Nevile said 'H-m' again and caught his chin in his hand.

"'You'll have your hands full,' I said seriously. 'The boy I've not seen, but it's a man's size job you will take on.'

"'I don't care about that,' he said, 'I'd not interfere with Athalie's affairs. I'll be able to cross that bridge when I come to it. I'm jolly sick of being down here. Don't misunderstand me, Fred. I'm not sighing for love in a cottage. I want to be on a ship. That's my idea. Come into port, go home and have a week's domesticity. Then back to work.'

"'Oho!' I said.

"'Why oho?' he inquired. 'Is it so very unusual? I'd never lived ashore before they kicked me out, and I'm safer at sea. Look at Farriday, who came over with me in the Santander. He's got the old Pamplona now. He left his wife and two children in England and, between voyages, he lives in a cheap hotel in Brooklyn or on the ship.'

"'What's the matter with Farriday?' I inquired.

"'Nothing, except that he has a girl in Havana and another girl in Cristobal. Jack ashore! I can't live that way. I saw Farriday his last time in, at the hotel. He'd had several planter's punches in the bar. He drove away in a gharry and he wasn't going down to the ship.'

"'What makes you bring him in?'

"'Oh, as an example of what to avoid. As a man who doesn't know how to handle himself. He'll be out, next thing you know.'

"I had to get back. Young Nevile was sending a colored chauffeur with me.

"'Let me know by radio if you have any news,' he said.

I already had the money he was sending to Athalie. 'I'd like to come North with you on the way back, but I can't be sure. I'm not going to chuck this job until I'm sure of another.'

"I took a look around at the bougainvillaea climbing the trellis that hid his kitchen quarters and the semicircle of club bungalows, the calm mirror of the lagoon in which a young moon was reflected, the speedboat in its shed hard by, the sound of music in the clubhouse, and the Chinese lanterns in the trees, and I wondered why he could not be happy without reaching out into a girl's life, a girl who had so much to agonize over besides her love for him. As I drove back to the ship I wished I had the power to immunize him from this curse of love!

"That was all it was at that time. They had gotten themselves into a perfect closed circle of misunderstanding and misery. They were both idealists and the forces of Mammon were thrusting them apart.

"Think of the consequences to them that streamed from the act of a man neither of them had ever heard of, a man in London who had a heart attack and decided to retire! He did retire, and the chairman of the board, who had once made a round-the-world cruise with Wensley, cabled that Wensley should succeed to the position just vacated. He became assistant director of new construction. And Captain Sylvester, whom we all liked and who had taken young Nevile's part when he had to resign, was appointed superintendent.

"I heard the news when we were docked on the Pacific side. I sent a cable to young Nevile from Panama City. I knew it might mean his application would go through. The old story was being forgotten. Spottiswood was in his grave. Virginia had already begun to divorce her prince. The Company had a score of new ships on the routes, and many of us had never heard of Captain Nevile. The question was, would Sylvester be able to give him back his seniority?

"And what would young Nevile do when he reached New

York? Suppose Wilkerson was around when he turned up. We did not call at Kingston on the way home, and I couldn't give way to my desire to radio Athalie. Wilkerson again.

"There was another problem. If young Nevile got started on a ship once more, he would have to avoid any complications. And Wilkerson was a complication. The man was an incalculable quantity so long as he was in that house. Obviously she gave him money, or he wouldn't remain, and if she did that anyone else who poked his nose into their affairs would be without any standing at all, no matter what his intentions might be. I did not see young Nevile putting Wilkerson outside. He hadn't the experience, or the temperament, to ease a desperate man like Wilkerson out of the picture. He was much more likely to fade rapidly out of the picture himself. In fact, I know absolutely he would, if he had ever met Wilkerson as I met him."

Mrs. Kavanagh was about to speak when she saw her husband nodding his head in recognition.

"I'm remembering the Pamplona now," he said. "There was a lot of funny business about that story. It was killed. I heard the boys talking it over."

"Yes," said Mr. Spenlove grimly, "the boys would rather have a lot of passengers killed than a good story. It was killed because it happened to be not true."

"They were saying the captain was for setting the ship on fire and then jumping overboard."

"I know the true story," said Mr. Spenlove. "I had it from the chief engineer of her, who is an old friend. But it's off the record, remember, Mr. Kavanagh. It was the news story that was killed for once, not the passengers. Barratry, they were calling it. But you can't bring in a charge of barratry against a man who has vanished. And hardly a single passenger was aware anything had happened until next morning. Only one had anything to tell the reporters, and he had the story wrong way round. I have it the right way round.

"When we docked in New York Mr. Romaine, who used to be on the Camotan with me, came into my cabin and had a drink. He is head of the victualing department, which is a branch of Maintenance and Supplies, and he enjoys pretending he is back on a ship again. Don't we all? No, not all, but all that count.

"I gave him a drink, and we had a talk. We always got on well under Wensley. He said a fellow had come in with a card from me to get a job, and as he was a good printer, which he demonstrated to Romaine's entire satisfaction, he was assigned to the Pamplona.

"'I never gave anybody a card,' I said. 'I wouldn't do such a thing. You ought to know how I regard such interference.'

"He said he had been surprised, but the card seemed genuine. However, he had kept it. Chap's name was Wilkinson.

"'Oh,' I said. 'Wilkinson. Not Wilkerson?'

"'Some such name,' Romaine said. He is aware of many things, including the way men change their names with chameleon-like rapidity. 'Some such name. Where did he get the card?'

"'I have a suspicion,' I said. 'I know him slightly. He asked me to get him a job, and I refused. I told him to apply to your office. Nothing more.'

"'Well, he is suspected of smuggling dope,' Romaine said, 'nothing against him. But they have reason to suppose . . . I'll leave this card here.'

"'Reason to suppose?' I repeated. Romaine gave me one of his quiet glances. He has a great regard for me, as I told you, because I suggested selling his stock at the peak. The broker was urging him to hang on until Christmas when it would go over a hundred. 'He's a Jew,' I had said, 'and Christmas has nothing to do with Consolidated Utilities. Get out with me.' He did, and is forever grateful, for he bought at 22 and sold at 89. He has a couple of nice houses on the south shore and a bungalow at Fire Island. When I tell him the industrial revolution will take it all away from him and send him to work as mess man in a Soviet forecastle, he doesn't believe me.

"But this phrase of his, 'reason to suppose,' disturbed me. I knew he meant that Wilkinson, or Wilkerson, was acting as a screen, or perhaps as agent for someone else on the ship. This was a source of endless harassment for our people. Latin-American ports are the intermediate depots and clearing houses for the drugs which so many Americans find indispensable if they are to face existence in God's country. You hear of 'rings' being broken and 'master minds' being arrested by Federal agents. But it is only a drop in a bucket. The ease with which the stuff can be carried in small compass, the vague ethical attitude of so many of us towards the traffic, and the incredible money to be made by an astute agent, make the whole thing hopeless, for the governments of small republics have no objection to making a profit out of it.

"I knew all this, and Romaine knew it, and his words conveyed to me that Wilkerson (or Wilkinson) was thought to be a blind. Then perhaps I wasn't so responsible after all. After one has the peculiar experience of seeing one's own personal mess man taken off the ship in handcuffs, as I have, you become philosophical about human behavior. I made it plain that I was in no way responsible for the Pamplona's printer.

"'He's married and I believe separated from a girl I know,' I explained. 'He used to be in the newspaper game but has come down in the world.'

"'He'll find himself in the penitentiary if they catch him,' said Romaine. The words depressed me, and I let the matter drop.

"We had to go over to the yard for some minor defects, and the Pamplona was in drydock close by us. An old ship that had seen her best days. I was looking at her hull being scraped and painted and saw my friend the chief, perched on a shaky ladder, poking his nose among the barnacles on her stern tube, when young Nevile, in an ulster and a green fedora, swung along the dock sill and reached out to shake hands. He looked strange with that lean brown face among all the yeast-colored complexions in Erie Basin.

"'You got the Pamplona?' I said.

"'No,' he said, 'mate! I'll explain it all when I see you. I've got to get on board. Anyhow,' he blew out a great breath, 'here I am. Mate! God, it's the happiest day I've spent for years! Back to the army again, Sergeant!'

"I believed him. He took the gangway across to the Pamplona's well deck in three strides. His very back looked happy to me as he disappeared into the ship. Back to the army again, he said. I guess it was, for him. I wondered what he would say if he knew that Athalie's long-secluded husband was now on the ship's staff as a printer. But what would it matter to him? He had his job. Still, I thought, he will not find it easy to be mate after being a crack commander. Standing rigging makes damn poor running gear, as I know, for I've been up and down myself.

"I was reading the newspaper when he came on board. There was a headline about a bank. Banks at that time hadn't made a habit of getting onto the front page by smashing. And I had never consciously heard of this bank, the American Union Trust. Anyhow, it had closed its doors. There was a picture of a lot of people clustered around the closed doors reading a notice which was obligingly shown in an enlargement. Someone had started a run. Banks are like women's stockings in several ways, and they certainly seem unable to deal with runs. I had a momentary qualm. What of my own bank? That was a more serious matter than this affair on Lower Broadway. Some of the people in the picture, if they really were depositors, were a scratch lot. They looked as if they had deposited the results of pocket-picking or

panhandling. Perhaps I malign them. The newspaper photograph does few of us justice. I threw it aside when Sidney
came in. He gave me a tremendous grip.

"'Once aboard the lugger,' I said, 'how are you going
to live on a mate's beggarly stipend? Two hundred a month
will seem like chicken feed to a myrmidon of the idle rich.
Did you feather your nest at the Club? What? No pickings?
And you expect to be an American citizen and one of the
boys? You're a renegade!'

"He waved all this away. He knew I was glad to see him
when I accused him of grafting.

"'Listen,' he said seriously. 'Sylvester has sent me to the
Pamplona to find out who's smuggling drugs ashore in New
York. He says, if I can find the leak he won't stop me getting
a good ship. They're all steamed up in the office. The Federal
men have found evidence, in a raid on a Syrian hotel in
Greenwich Street, that it's coming in on the Pamplona.
They've shadowed several of the crew and found nothing.
Now they've invited active coöperation. What do you
think?'

"'Why don't they invite the captain's active coöperation?'
I said, half to myself. But I knew the answer to that. Farriday was not persona grata with Sylvester. Farriday had
sort of a position, due to the fact that he was in command
all through the war and would have been senior commander
if he hadn't gone haywire after the armistice. They sent him
back to us as mate on the Santander, and gave him the
Pamplona. But he didn't belong with the new men. What
he ought to have done was to bring his family over to live in
the country where he earned his wages. He always had some
excuse about the authorities refusing a permit, and another
excuse about his wife not wanting to leave Bootle. He even
had a third excuse, that it would mess up the children's
schooling. The fact was, Farriday had no desire to see them
again. He was due for vacation then, but everybody knew
he wouldn't get past Atlantic City or some hotel in the

White Mountains, where he could meet one of his girl friends and drink more than was good for him. He was the sort of skipper who never looks twice at the most beautiful lady passenger, but who is in some place in the Calle Zuleta a couple of hours after he has docked his ship in Havana, with his arm around a girl who knows more about castanets than bridge parties.

"That was young Nevile's temporary commander. He had a pair of hard blue eyes in a face that might have belonged to a Wall Street man who never went out in the open air. You wondered what any girl would see in a man of fifty who had neither hair, good looks, nor conversation. His was a furtive sort of life, for he had no contacts with any of us. He was supposed to have done pretty well, getting high pay all through the war in transports and living very thriftily. How his family lived, nobody could say; but the story goes that his wife wrote the office to know what her husband's salary really was, as she could not make ends meet on ten pounds a month. He was getting four hundred dollars a month at that time, which was over a hundred pounds with the pound at three fifty. So the office—so the story goes—suggested he could send his wife a little more. It is in character, even if it isn't quite true. Captain Farriday, of the Pamplona. Chief officer: Mr. Sidney Nevile. The chief engineer was my friend Jim Cassell. He told me all about it afterwards.

"But young Nevile sat looking at me when I asked that question about his captain, and then he shook his head.

"'A captain doesn't have the opportunities to see things the chief mate does,' he said.

"'That's right. Farriday's too busy investigating the joints ashore, I suppose. You'd think he'd get tired of negresses and Cuban yellows and Costa Rican mestizos whose grandfathers were Chinese laundrymen.'

"'They tell me he has cut it all out,' he said, smiling. 'They hardly ever see him. And stays on board.'

"'Does he, by Jove?' I said. 'Can they hear him saying his prayers? Does he stay on board alone?'

"I was surprised Nevile didn't say anything about Athalie. I asked him, and his face fell.

"'It's rather unlucky, my coming back just now,' he said. 'I have to meet her somewhere in town. She says it's impossible for me to visit her at present. On account of her husband. Fred, am I being just a damned fool? What's the mystery? Is she giving the money I give her to—to him? I get so I feel ready to chuck the whole thing. I would if I didn't love her so much. I wish I didn't love her, because it's a curse. It is going to mess up my life. She has moved again. Did you know that? And when I meet her, she asks me to be patient because at present she is in a difficult position.'

"'She is,' I said. 'I happen to know that her son as well as her husband is giving her unhappiness. Don't you see? She has to keep her husband's past from the children?'

"'She doesn't have to keep things from me, does she?'

"'Maybe she's wise at that!' I said. 'She doesn't feel sure you don't idealize her too much.'

"'You have to have confidence in each other, don't you?' he demanded. 'Some,' I admitted, 'but you can't get it by holding the other person up, Sidney.'

"He shook his head. 'Who else has to take a girl's word for so much?' he inquired dismally.

"'It is probably all the more worth waiting for,' I suggested. 'You'll be back in five weeks.'

"'She'll have another reason for putting me off in five weeks.' He took his lower lip in his teeth and pondered. 'Well, I'll take your advice, Fred. I feel too good about getting back to sea to make myself disagreeable. I'm going to meet her tonight at a place uptown. I'm going to rent a room, you know, sort of crow's nest, so I can have a place of my own.'

"'Would she go to a man's rooms?' I said.

"'She'll have to, or I'll quit!' he exclaimed, and stood up to go.

"'Your sister Ursula wouldn't understand that,' I said. 'I saw her in London. You never told me she was married. She's very conventional.'

"'I forgot,' he said, smiling. 'It's such a long while ago. Ages ago. And Ursula doesn't understand life over here. She doesn't know a thing about it.'

"This was a new Nevile. It registered a development in his character as a lover. I could see he was in love with Athalie as much as ever, but his conception of love had been hardening into something more suited to 1930 than to the age of chivalry. When he was gone I picked up the paper again. Neither he nor I realized that right on the front page was the answer to some of his perplexities. I glanced at the news about the American Union Trust and turned the page. That evening as I passed up into Broadway I saw a small crowd around the closed bank reading the notice on the doors. Another twinge of anxiety about my own bank, and I forgot the matter. I wanted to come down here to Norbury, but had no time. I wanted to see Athalie and Ginevra again, but when I walked down Eleventh Street the apartment was vacant. I wondered about the rent there. It struck me that unless I went over to Park Avenue and saw the manager's wife myself she wouldn't be paid. And I had thought it would be a much better plan to let the girl do it herself. It was funny, the perplexity young Nevile was in because he couldn't get the two antagonisms of this world, Women and Money, correlated. He was still simple enough to believe that merely because a woman was a saint she had the same view of money as a man. He was still youthful enough to imagine that because Athalie loved him she had no feeling for anyone else and that she must pour out everything in her life before him. He assumed that because she was a person of quality, persons of quality are invariably persons of stainless honor and incorruptible integrity. It didn't occur to him that a person of quality might have something to conceal. Nor that so far he himself hadn't shown much consideration or achieved any remarkable self-sacrifices. In fact, he had done nothing except pester her to gratify his curiosity. He was thinking of her exclusively from his own point of view. He had graciously enthroned her in his imagination as the queen of heaven, 'what I've always been looking for,' as he called it in his own jargon, and in return for this high honor she was to dash naked into the street, abandoning her children and every other tie, to hold onto his stirrup while he rode proudly along, a hero. He didn't really mean this, but it came out unconsciously in the superb masculine egotism of his mind.

"He was off to sea in the Pamplona before we had our turbines all right, and I stayed by the ship most of the time. I was secretly wishing, I remember, that I could call up that girl on Park Avenue and take her to dinner, as I had done before. I couldn't make a satisfactory explanation of why things had changed so much for her. I had expected that when young Nevile arrived, a storybook ending of the better sort would ensue. And here we were! I went uptown alone.

"It so happened that one evening I had an invitation from a passenger on Park Avenue, a broker who lived in one of those apartment hotels above Forty-fifth Street. I wasn't very keen about it, I may tell you. I had been there before. He had been a rather boisterous passenger, and the stewards had overheard him, in their suite, shouting at his wife because she was 'dumb.' A little of her dumbness would have been admirable in him. She was a quiet, frightened kid who didn't catch onto the rapid life he loved. Of course, they didn't know I knew of his shouting, but I had small relish for the evening. He was a bully, and all he had ever done was to guess luckily that Air Reduction was going up, or some such imbecile evolution of the market.

"I had plenty of time and got out of the subway at Forty-second Street. I walked east, and as I passed one of those large five-and-ten-cent stores it was closing for the day, and a torrent of girls poured out of a doorway. They flowed over the sidewalk, like a river, on high heels, with cheap little jackets and hats, in coats not so cheap and rather puzzling on eighteen-dollar-a-week bodies, if you don't understand how those girls do their financing. I was, for a minute or so, almost carried away in a tide of girls. Then a lot of them were sucked down into the subway like water down a scupper, and some began to climb on the Third Avenue trolleys.

"I was making for a speakeasy near that avenue a few blocks uptown. And suddenly, as I crossed to the north side of Forty-second, I recognized, under an old but extremely expensive felt hat pulled over to one side of her head, Athalie Rhys. She went past me rapidly, headed across Third Avenue, and I followed her on the other side. She was moving so fast I had to speed up. I was determined not to let her slip.

"I was very shocked. I had heard shrill laughter among those girls about something. One of them had made a remark that set them cackling, bitter, trilling derision. What was that? I must have been almost touching Athalie in the first spate of girls that swirled among us passers-by. Now she was alone. Block after block she hurried, never looking to right or left, oblivious of glances or the children that roller skated past her. And then, all of a sudden, she slowed down.

"I was not only shocked but bewildered. There was a line of about a dozen poor folk waiting in front of a sort of restaurant. On the window I saw the words *One Cent—Vital Food Only—One Cent. Eat Cracked Wheat for Vitality.* In smaller type you were told that 'the addition of a little cream makes it delicious.'

"Apparently it was the idea of some bold capitalist to keep the proletariat alive a little longer. It was extraordinary to behold such a thing in the streets of the richest city in the world, the city that held nearly all the gold in the world and numbered so many owners of multi-millions. Only two blocks west lived an old woman with a hundred millions who never went out of her house or bought a new dress, and who kept a priceless patch of ground boarded up on Fifth Avenue to give her poodle a place to play. While I watched, other shabby people joined the line and waited. And then an elderly creature with a bristly chin came out of the restaurant and walked down the line handing each member of the line a coin. Whereupon they filed in and went to a counter to be fed on the vitality-crammed cracked wheat.

"This was awful. I found myself wildly wondering whether Athalie was having cream to make it delicious. Nothing mattered to me now but to get hold of her. I waited. There was a dingy restaurant on my side of the street, and I went in and bought a cup of coffee and sat down near the front, where I could watch.

"In a few minutes she came out and looked up and down the Avenue. She came across the street and looked up and down again. Then she began to walk south. I was up and after her. She walked quickly but kept looking back, as if for the trolley. I seized my chance and overhauled her. I took her arm firmly and brought her round to face me.

"At first she was frightened. When she saw who it was her face cleared and she smiled, and then turned away to hide her sudden crying.

"'What's all this?' I said very sternly. 'Where are you going now? I emphasized the 'now' to show her I knew where she had been. She said, 'Home. Please let me go!'

"I kept firm hold of her arm and hailed a taxi crossing in front of us. He swung to the curb with a howl of dry brakes and opened the door. 'Get in,' I said. I didn't give a damn for my dinner engagement. I felt positively murderous towards people who spent a hundred dollars a day living in an apartment hotel because they knew when Air Reduction was going up. I thumbed my nose at the whole bestial crew.

"She got in, and I followed. When I looked at her for instructions she said 'East Eighth' in a faint voice. I said, 'East Eighth. We'll get out at the corner.' The driver, whose name I saw was Karl Marx, and who gave us a shrewd yet tolerant glare, started with a jerk and set off with desperate speed downtown.

"I began to laugh. It was the best thing I could have thought of, but the cause of it was the contrast between that one-cent restaurant of cracked wheat—as if the whole damned town wasn't completely cracked—and the windows of the floor above it. They were large store windows, and behind them stood rigid men in tin armor, with dingy red crests on their helmets, a pierrette's costume of red hearts on a yellow ground with blue sleeves, and a portrait of an eighteenth-century gentleman in a lace collar. Some theatrical costumer's, I suppose. It made me laugh, and she laughed too, laying her hand gently in mine.

"'I'm afraid you're not to be trusted to look after yourself,' I said. 'Do you work in that five-and-ten?'

"'Oh no! I . . .' She stopped and nodded. 'I suppose,' she said, 'when you see me doing that you think I'm on the way out.'

"'I hadn't any thoughts at all,' I said. 'Why have you hidden from us?'

"'I had to. I couldn't face things any more.'

"'You have to face them now,' I said. 'I'm not going to let you go until I see you are all right. How is Ginevra?'

"'Oh, she's fine!' Her face, very pale and without any cosmetics, lighted up as she spoke.

"'Where is she? What is she doing?'

"'She's at a dancing school.'

"'And the boy?' Her face fell slightly.

"'He's going to school soon.'

"The cab plunged and leapt. We were nearly thrown against the glass when he stopped for a red light. At Fourteenth she said, 'Please let us get out here—at Ninth.'

We were already at Tenth, but I let him roar on, and we got out at Eighth.

"She turned eastward again, taking my arm timidly. You know, under that old but good coat and that three-dollar frock she was as lovely as ever. Another block. Here were strange ravaged commercial houses and garages for trucks and teams. We turned into an area that smelt strongly of manure. Vast wagons were stored there, and beyond in the murk you could see the rumps of great horses. We opened a battered door and climbed a dirty, uncovered staircase. At the top she took out a key, and at that moment her door opened and Ginevra stood before us in a short blue sleeveless frock, her yellow-gold hair tied in a ribbon, and old pink mules on her bare feet. She jumped when she saw me, but the pleasure that showed at once in her piquant little face was my reward.

"'Oh Mother!' she said, and stood back.

"They led me into a large bare room that must have been originally a hay loft. It had been papered over wide planks, and the ceiling was of rough beams. There was a gas radiator in one corner, a screen tried to conceal a sink, and their clothes hung behind a calico curtain on the wall. A day bed of large size stood along the wall. I saw the prie-dieu and the picture by Lawrence, but the little poem of welcome that had hung outside her door was gone.

"'Now,' I said, 'you two are coming out to dinner with me.'

"Ginevra said, 'I'm sorry. I can't. I've got a date.' Athalie smiled at me.

"'She's working on an act. She eats later.'

"'Then,' I said, 'you.'

"She said, 'Ginevra works so hard. She wants to earn money, to . . . to . . .'

"'What's become of your money?' I said.

"'The bank,' she said. 'The American Union Trust. I had stock in it. It was left that way. Years ago. The dividends got less and less, and now—well, even the depositors don't get their money. It had a good name. Well, it left us a bit short for a while. So I got a job.'

"'You didn't try to get back to the stage?' She shook her head. 'It's bad in a store, but it's better than the chorus. And I'm no good for anything else. To undress gracefully.' She smiled gently again. 'Now, Ginevra's got talent. She will succeed, I'm sure. So I let her go to the school. It's rather expensive, but we manage.'

"'And the boy?'

"She wouldn't speak much of him, evading my cross-examination. While we were talking he came in.

"He was so like his father I was speechless for a moment. He had run up like a weed, and his haggard, aristocratic face was spotted with pimples that had induced an expression of permanent annoyance. His wrists protruded from the short sleeves of his jacket, and he had plastered his hair down with water. There was nothing wrong with him save that he was growing too fast and was desperately unhappy about himself, for he gnawed a finger when he became rapt in his own thoughts. Yet the inherited easy grace of an accomplished charlatan emerged unconsciously when he came forward to be introduced.

"'This is Morty,' his mother murmured, and I looked upon the latest scion of the house of Caerleon, the ruthless Welsh border earls, and the equally ruthless Welsh draper of the London outskirts. Perhaps, also, of other ruthless forbears on his father's side, who had peddled wooden nutmegs and patent medicines, with abrupt, disconcerting excursions into distinguished service and fanatical integrity. Master Mortimer Rhys had all these strains tearing at his gangling personality as he sprawled and twisted in his chair, but he was probably only conscious of a passionate resentment at his poverty. The contrast between him and his sister was so great that it seemed improbable that they could belong to the same animal species. At fifteen she was complete in her precocious sophistication. Her conscious powers of rhythm and poise, her absorption in a difficult art, gave her a mature dignity. The extraordinary clarity of her skin and the wisdom in her ice-green eyes set her apart. Morty will one day be a hand-some devil, but he looked like something the cat had dragged in, that evening. They are both dynamic possibilities, which makes it all the more interesting for Captain Nevile in his new rôle. The blood of old Rhys, of that vivacious Martha Rayne, of Shap, the hill town in the Appalachian ranges, is blended with the restless ambition and resourcefulness of their father.

"'What do you want to do?' I inquired. I expected to hear he wanted to sell something, but he scowled at the floor and announced that he wanted to go into politics. I was as-tounded. He looked up at me defiantly. 'Like Jimmie Walker,' he said. He had clippings of Jimmie in an old atlas. Something about that elegant symbol of New York had captured the imagination of Mortimer Rhys. And he had been hanging around doing odd jobs for the local Democratic headquarters, distributing circulars and running errands. 'But I want to study law. You have to study law to get into the game. So I'm going to school pretty soon.' He glanced at his mother for a moment. His gray eyes were not easily fathomed.

"It was characteristic of her that she should think it a fine thing to follow the footsteps of a showy politician. She took all that as she found it. She was, as I said before, very much a female person, and there was no penetration in her attitude towards the world of men. She lived in her own world, and if men shattered it she could only meekly sub-mit.

"All the same, I was relieved when she was ready and we could leave. I saw her give the children money for their dinners. It was curious how those two moved around each other like animals, without animosity yet without conscious recognition. I found it hard to believe they ever spoke to each other. I suppose they did. I even admit they behaved in as civilized fashion as I ever could manage in a loft over a stable that held a strong ammoniacal odor and shook as the great teams rumbled out underneath.

"I didn't see why I should let on I knew where her husband was, so I inquired hypocritically, 'Does he come home at all?' She shook her head. 'He only threatens to,' she said, with a queer irony that came into her voice at times. 'Why does he seem to enjoy tormenting you?' 'It's Ginevra who torments him,' she said. 'He has always resented Ginevra. When the children were little, he wanted me to have her brought up by someone else. And when he had his trouble—when they hounded him into doing something desperate,' she explained loyally, 'he said I didn't back him up enough. I couldn't have done what he wanted me to. It wouldn't have been quite right.'

"It was like hearing an angel explain why she couldn't conscientiously steal church offerings.

"'But he won't come back now, will he?' I said.

"'I hope he doesn't do anything unwise,' she breathed and then sighed.

"'You must get a divorce,' I insisted. 'Never mind the children. Or rather, explain to the children.' I forgot, even when she sent that blush over her face, how it would appear to her when the children thought of her afterwards.

"'Yes,' she said. 'Perhaps it would be best.'

"'And tell Sidney where you live.'

"'Oh no! Wait until I get on my feet again. Please! You've been so kind. If he loses faith in me, I guess I must bear it. But he doesn't understand how I feel. He never has.'

"I knew that. Men in love never do. I concentrated on giving her a good time. She was so naturally abstemious that I suspect she had mesmerized herself into enjoying cracked wheat. I asked her, 'Suppose you owned that five-and-ten and could spend millions, what sort of dinner would you order?'

"She smiled and put her finger to her lips.

"'Oh!' she said. 'Just what you're giving me here.' She had the wing of a chicken, a piece of brown bread, and a glass of milk. Later she dissipated to the extent of a parfait. I felt as if I were of a Rabelaisian grossness gorging on a chop with baked potatoes and a pint of claret, with apple dumpling and Roquefort cheese to follow. And yet I believe her attitude was genuine. My coffee and cognac seemed indecent, like a glass of beer on a church altar.

"She had to go to a show as well, for I had the suspicion she was spending all she had left on her children. And it was more than a suspicion that she had given her husband money. He would never have gone away unless she had, and without admitting it even to herself, she knew that.

"She went home loaded with a box of chocolates, some roses, and an armful of magazines. She also had in her pocket-book the money young Nevile had given me to pay her rent. 'You do it,' I said, 'and remember, I shall tell him where you live. I'm taking the address. And you're not to run away again.'

"'Where could I go?' she smiled.

"'I don't know,' I said, 'but you're so ingenious you'd find some hiding place, and we'd have to find you, no matter what happens.'

"'I'll be here,' she said. Only when I came back did I understand how she meant those words. She was there, in a way, as we now know."

Mr. Spenlove took a long swig of his drink and waved his guests to help themselves.

"That voyage," he said, "was dedicated to some celebration, the four hundredth anniversary of some historical event or other, in South America. We were away much longer than usual. In Rio we heard mysterious hints of something that had happened to the Pamplona. It was summer time up here, you see, and summer means fog. But the yarn, as we received it through a young American in the Rio agent's office, hinted at a fog that was a blessing, for it had concealed a very unwholesome episode in our company's career. It concealed the final fade-out of Captain Farriday.

"We were unable to make head or tale of it. Captain Farriday had vanished from his ship in a fog off Barnegat. That much was easy enough to understand. But what of the fight down on the lower port section with a madman who was trying to set fire to the ship? This, mind you, while the ship was proceeding dead slow in a thick fog and the passengers upstairs knew nothing about it. We gave it up. But I was in a stew to know how young Nevile had come out of it. It was a baptism with a vengeance for a returning prodigal. It made one feel faint to think of it.

"It was all the more astonishing to receive newspapers that never even mentioned the affair. When we steamed into Cristobal, Canal Zone, bound north, and saw the Pamplona coming in, bound for west coast ports, we decided that our friend in Rio had spun us a good yarn. But neither Captain Farriday nor his chief officer was on board, I heard. New men.

"I decided to go on board and see Jim Cassell. No romancer he, but he could be depended on to know every last thing that happened on his own ship. 'She's a bitch,' he told me once, 'but you can get used to her, as I tell my wife.'

"He was sitting in his cabin down in the working alleyway, the same as the Camotan, a red-faced, parrot-beaked man about my own age, filling a white tunic as tight as a bale of cotton in its bands. In fact, Cassell is very much like a bale of cotton, compressed and immovable. He is made in muscular chunks stiffly hinged in various places, and his stiff black toothbrush mustache is quite capable of running the Pamplona's engine room by itself. He was silently glad to see me. He had been out of the company for a year or two, or he would have had a newer ship. But he is one of the old school. He takes whatever comes, and God help any junior who doesn't know his work. Cassell knows it, and he can work

forty hours on end without much beyond a very foul old pipe
and a pouch of shag. He's the only man I have left on my
calling list who smokes that noisome compound.

"'Yes,' he said, 'we had hell popping for an hour or so.
In fog too.'

"'Where was the old man?' I demanded.

"Cassell made a complicated gesture symbolizing a man
going down for the third time.

"'Game was up,' he said, 'and he knew it. Didn't you
know he'd been bringing in the hop? Suitcases full of it. Who
would search the commander's baggage when he's going
ashore in New York? With the Federal Prohibition boys
sitting in his room drinking double Scotches while their men
search the ship for liquor? He used to go ashore with them on
each side of him, their vest pockets wedged tight with perfectos out of the box the Company paid for, and his little
overnight bag had a small fortune stowed away under his
pajamas. Yes sir.'

"'Where'd he get it?' I inquired.

"'Curaçao mostly. Sometimes Havana; but there was too
many chiseling in on him there. Half his woman-chasing was
a blind for the other thing. He had a chink girl in his cabin
one night. One of the lady passengers told me; and my god-
father, how shocked she was! But it was business. She'd
brought some dope in a laundry basket. She cheeked the
quartermaster who stopped her coming on board and made
him take her to the captain. The captain said he'd deal with
the matter. The lady passenger butted in while the chink was
top side getting paid. Old Farriday always thought women
passengers the lowest form of life, anyhow.

"'Well,' said Cassell, 'we all had some sort of a hunch, but
you'd go balmy if you worried about the other fellow's graft.
Anybody who's fool enough to use dope can have all he
wants, and kill himself if he wants, for all I care. Serve 'em
right, the damn fools! Farriday never interfered with us. He
wasn't so bad, now I come to think of it. Beyond "Are you

ready?" or "How long will you be?" he never opened his trap to me.

"'The trick was,' went on Cassell, 'that he never went ashore in these places. Most of the time he had nobody from ashore who would be selling it to him. He was clever too. He would lay off the trade for a trip or two. He must have had a lot stowed away in his digs in Brooklyn now and then. So the anti-narcotic boys ran themselves ragged trying to locate the agent on the Pamplona. They arrested the bartender once; but God knows he has enough ways of gettin' rich without going in for that. They copped a guy ashore who confessed he got it from the bartender of our ship. When he was confronted with our Shanty Irishman he said he'd never set eyes on him before. A case of mistaken identity. He said the feller he traded with had a beard. Can you imagine a bartender with a beard?

"'Then we lost our printer. He was paid off one trip and went ashore late Saturday night with his dunnage, and he never came back. If you ask me, he knew a lot more about Farriday's private affairs than he ever let on. He was the one who did the loading for Farriday, and I fancy he double-crossed the old man that last trip. He probably thought he could get away with it, and he did. We had a new printer, and the night the old man went over—the night we had a fire in the glory hole while we were stopped in the fog—the printer vanished at sea. He and the old man, you see. He had something on the old man. Young Nevile took charge.'

"I stared at him. What was this? 'Tell me the whole thing, man. I know Nevile very well.'

"'It was his show,' said Cassell, and his statement was all the more convincing because he made it so bald and so devoid of emotion. 'We were off Atlantic City when they rang Dead Slow and then sent down to have her go a bit faster to keep steerage way on her. That was in the middle watch, and the old man was on the bridge soon after midnight. The second mate was with him and an extra sailor. The whistle went

"*Whoo-oo!*" every half minute. "*Whurroo-oo! Whoo-oo!*" All round us they were. You could hear 'em and even see 'em, when they scraped our sides, almost. Yes, the other ships.

"'Well, the second mate suddenly heaves up out of the fog and rings Stand By on both engines. He says to the sailor "Fetch the captain!" Opening the chart-room door the sailor sees nobody there. He looks into the old man's cabin. Nobody. Then he opens the door into the wheelhouse where there's nobody but the helmsman. He runs out and tells the second, who had the ship stopped: "Can't find him, Sir." "Jesus Christ! then call the chief officer." The idea that he was alone on the bridge in command of the ship nearly gave the second a heart attack. He's never had charge of a fishing smack yet.

"'The gob runs into Nevile's room and yells to him to show a leg. "Captain's disappeared, sir. You're wanted on the bridge." Nevile was out there in his pajamas in three shakes. "Now what?" "I can't find the captain, mister."

"'Nevile tells the sailor to go fetch his clothes, and he dresses himself on the bridge while the whistle goes *Whoo-oo!* over his head, and two seamen, able seamen they call them, started to search for the old man. "God Almighty, he was here a minute ago! I heard him go into the chart room." The other sailor says, "Heard him? I seen him!" And he had, too.

"'The ship was moving dead slow again. It was the Stand By that made me come up. I'd tried to get an answer out of the second mate on the telephone, and he sounded crazy to me. I said, "Where's the old man?" and he said, "We're lookin' for him." I slapped the thing back on the hook and I was just starting for the ladder when the automatic fire alarm showed red and began to buzz like mad. We started the fire pump slow, and up I went. On the promenade deck a sailor grabs me in the fog. "Seen the cap'en, sir? We can't find the cap'en." "How in hell would I know where he is?" I says, and he runs off wringin' his hands. It was a hell of a job for the poor son of a bitch, lookin' for the old man in a fog.

"'I found Nevile putting on his overcoat on the bridge. Four stripes on the epaulettes. Hadn't had it on since—you know. I asked him about the old man.

"'"We seem to have mislaid him," he says, very quiet. "And there's a fire on D Deck. Chief, will you take charge down there? This is a very serious matter. I can't leave the bridge. You understand? I can't leave . . ."'

"Cassell went down at once and found the chief steward and the kitchen hands with extinguishers fighting a fire in the glory hole. No, he said, it was a matter of about ten minutes and they had it under control. It had started in the room where a pantryman bunked with the printer, next the second steward's store and office. The pantryman had been nearly suffocated in his bunk and was being given first aid by the doctor, but the fire was stopped before it took hold of the inflammables. The night pantryman had seen the printer go along the alleyway and out, just before the fire started. Once he saw there was no chance of it breaking out again, Cassell went back to the bridge. He is not an imaginative man, but he was appalled by the position of the chief officer. It was this that carried him up, against his will almost, to see young Nevile again. The fog was as thick as ever, and the ear-splitting roar of the whistle up there, invisible yet shaking the very heart in his breast, impressed him with a dread he had no words to express. He just shook his head at me and made a slight downward motion of his hand. 'No good!' he said.

"What made him afraid was the absence of the captain. When Cassell got on the bridge, young Nevile was standing by the engine-room telegraph, staring into the fog and listening with an expression of cold, immobile severity on his face. When the whistle roared, he frowned. He saw someone standing beside him in the darkness. He inclined his ear. 'Well?' he said. Cassell said, 'It was nothing. Out now.' 'Make a report,' said young Nevile without moving. 'The captain is not here. The ship is being searched, quietly. No excitement.'

"He had the ship moving slow. 'Are you all right down below, Chief?' Cassell said everything was O. K. 'I think he's gone,' young Nevile said. 'The captain, I say—I think he's gone.'

"Cassell asked him what made him think so.

"'Isn't it obvious?' young Nevile inquired. 'He had a radio last night. I've taken charge of it. Besides, where would he be if he was on the ship?'

"'Well, he may have fallen overboard in the fog,' Cassell suggested, though he did not believe any such thing. He knew Farriday hadn't fallen into the sea accidentally.

"Cassell stayed there, with an occasional visit to the engine room, until daylight. The fog lifted at times and then shut down again. The news spread through the ship that the printer couldn't be found. A sailor who had been on from twelve to four told young Nevile he had seen the printer on the top deck near the captain's cabin. Young Nevile was not so surprised at this as Cassell would have expected. 'Yes,' he said, 'but if you can't find the captain anywhere on the ship the printer will have to wait.'

"Cassell said he couldn't sleep even after the fog changed to haze and the engines were at half speed. He sat in his cabin thinking of the man on the bridge. 'And they tell me,' he said as he gave me the story, 'they tell me the blamed fool chucked a shore job in Jamaica to get back on a ship!' Cassell went up in the afternoon as the Pamplona was making time to reach Ambrose Light so she could dock first thing in the morning, and he saw young Neville on the chart-room settee, his face gray with stubble, his hair a shade grayer than ever before, and lying as though he had been flung there by an indignant destiny, lying like a dead man, so complete was his exhaustion.

"'That's why you didn't get the real story,' he said. 'The office had sent Farriday a radio saying his attendance was imperative at the Federal Building as soon as he docked. No excuse was accepted for noncompliance. And Farriday's goose was obviously cooked. What did he have to say to the printer who had been his associate in the peculiar business he had drifted into? What happened in the fog to make a commander forget everything he had ever known in his professional life? And what were the thoughts of the other man when he saw that once again his enterprise and daring had failed, and had carried him at last over the edge, out of our world and perhaps into eternity?'

"'And where's Nevile now?' I asked Cassell.

"'He had to lay up for a day or two,' he told me. 'Sylvester's giving him a ship.'

"'Well,' I said, 'he's not a beachcomber any more. They won't talk about steamer-bred men in the office any more. He's been tested this time.'

"'He was certainly tested,' said Cassell grimly. 'It turned him gray.'

V

"A WEEK LATER we were in New York again. There was a letter from young Nevile. He wrote from an address on West Forty-eighth Street where he said he had an apartment. Would I come up? He was waiting for a command. He wanted to celebrate. Athalie and Ginevra would come too. Ginevra, he added, was 'marvelous.'

"It sounded like the old exultant note. I was amused. He would always have his enthusiasms, no matter how sorely he might be tested. So he will always have the materials of happiness within reach. To love women and be loved by them, yet to have one's heart in one's work—is not that all the happiness possible in the world?

"Well, perhaps there is also the happiness of seeing the sons of the morning make fools of themselves. There is the pleasure of brooding over folly and noting how little it changes through the centuries and how indomitable is hope. Always at the next bend in the road he expects to catch sight of the topless towers of the city of eternal love. Each magic casement frames the face of the ultimate perfection of which he dreams. And to each one he sings the same old song.

"For me also, perhaps, there was another pleasure, of seeing Athalie again. I had the suspicion that alone of all the men she had known, I realized her true quality, the fineness of her character beneath the superficial mannerisms and girlish whims. I was not always able to convince myself that she knew this, or even that she was able to gage her own quality herself in spite of her conviction that she was 'a lady of quality.' The real quality lay even below that. It lay in her Christian meekness and fortitude, in her selfless constancy to an ideal motherhood without ever speaking of it. It lay in her uncomplaining submission to the hard rules of a world where money dominated, and where everything that made up her spiritual life was regarded as dross. She was like a princess who seemed a hag in tatters to the drunken revelers but who was a glorious creature in robes of light to a discerning eye.

"I wondered how much, apart from what he called 'love' young Nevile could see. Apart from a faintly snobbish fondness for someone who was 'different,' what did he see? I phoned him, and said I would be there. In fact, I left the ship in time to reach Athalie's place on East Eighth before she would be leaving. It was Ginevra who opened the door to me. She had a comb in her hand and was drawing it through and through the thick golden masses of her hair.

"'Mother hasn't come in yet,' she said, letting me in. 'I hope you'll excuse us. We aren't very tidy here.'

"I said, never mind about that, and she sat down near me with her comb and went on endlessly drawing it through the short locks. She began to brush it with a brush whose heavy silver back bore a crest. I spoke of it, and she showed it to me.

"'It's Mother's,' she said. Her hair seemed to grow more and more lucent, as though she were charging it with some electric radiance. She had nothing of the conventional 'chit' about her. She seemed as old as her mother and smiled rather than tittered. She had an air of capacity and poise. In her wrapper, which hardly covered her bare knees, she resembled a siren combing her hair by the shore, to lure mariners to their doom. She was infinitely poetical, yet without any consciousness of poetry save through the rhythm of her body. All her remarks were commonplace and practical. When I made a joking allusion to her making a sensation among the boys, she gave me a sidelong glance out of her narrow eyes.

"'I don't like boys,' she said calmly. 'I like men. Boys make me sick.'

"'Aren't you too young to talk like that?' I said. She was a new species to me. She did not answer save by a faint smile and another glance from the ice-green eyes.

"We got on very well, but I had the impression of being shut up with a charge of high explosive with whose character I was not familiar. There was an air of repressed vitality and perfect awareness of the world that daunted me in one so young. When Athalie came in, the difference between the two women was dramatic. She put her hand to her lips and started back exactly as ten thousand movie virgins have done since the cameras began to grind. Nor was this affected. It was from her generation that the cameras stole the technique. And then, when her little play and pretense of alarm (if it was pretense) was over, she was so very glad to see me.

"The ingenuities of those two in living in one room transcended human belief. The calm way they adapted themselves, like some glorious species of insect, to the interstices of our decrepit economic system, which they were not responsible for, was amazing. But I could see the lines on the mother's face, very small, fine lines etched on either side of the mouth. And sometimes she became absent from us for an instant, as though her spirit were taking little trial flights into the infinite in preparation for the last great renunciation. She only smiled when she caught my look and said, 'We'll have a good time. A hot time in the old town to-night!'

"I said, 'I wanted to have a talk with you. Can I talk freely before Ginevra?'

"'Oh yes. Ginevra and I have no secrets now.'

"'Does she know? Do you know? About your husband?'

"She inclined her head very gently. That was one of her characteristics. She could receive information like that and reveal nothing of it to the world unless an occasion arose, and even then she never ranted or stood in the spotlight.

"'Then you have nothing to fear any longer,' I said. 'You can live happily ever after.' She smiled and seemed to reflect upon what I said, but she only made a vague motion of her head, as though she knew more about happiness ever after than I did, and how it was to be attained.

"Yes, she had given up the job in the five-and-ten and was in a photographer's office. Hence the nice new dress and the new hat, which did not suit her like the battered old English felt she had been wearing.

"When they were ready, after a great deal of disappearing behind screens and going in and out of a small alcove, we started. They were like grisettes, whose every centime has to count, yet they had mysteriously achieved perfection. Ginevra carried a small brown satchel that aroused my interest, but her mother said, 'She always takes her dancing things with her. She likes to dance.'

"And indeed, of that evening, with the dinner in a small cabaret downstairs on Forty-sixth Street, where young Nevile danced a little with Athalie and a great deal with Ginevra, I remember mostly Ginevra's dance to the music coming in over the radio in the apartment when we returned there. It was the subtle change in the atmosphere that I remember, as though Ginevra had worked an incantation and transformed herself suddenly into something we were all afraid of, yet were enchanted by her magic.

"It was almost as though she had changed young Nevile into something I had never seen before. Because he was changed. He became, while I was away on that voyage, what he is now, the confident, extremely good-looking middle-aged commander with his hair touched with gray and his face sharp under the bronzed tan of the tropics. And his achievement, in getting back his command, reacted in a quiet tolerance, almost condescension, in his manner. I realized later that he had been under a certain restraint all his life. It wasn't that he wanted to prove to others that he was genuine. Until he had that sudden, soul-freezing crisis on the Pamplona, he hadn't been able to prove to himself he was what he wanted to be. And at this moment of triumph he met Ginevra.

"It put him into a turmoil. He did not know himself what he was trying to do. Without being aware of it he thought of Athalie as Ginevra's mother. He wanted Athalie because of Ginevra. That evening he was very gay. And when Ginevra suddenly came out of his bedroom in a gauzy dancing frock of black chiffon without sleeves or back, and with a short ballet skirt that stood out stiff like a ruff, he was struck momentarily silent. She walked to the radio and turned the knobs, listening, and then suddenly she rose on her toes and became a thing of light and beauty.

"She fixed those ice-green eyes of hers on Captain Nevile and went through the intricate evolutions of her dance, as though for him she was doing it and from him came the inspiration. And he was entranced. He sat absorbed, while Athalie sat back with her face in shadow and followed the seam of leather on the chair arm with her fingernail. When at length the music finished Ginevra spun rapidly towards him on her toes and came to rest, laughing, on the arm of his chair.

"Here, if folly was what I needed to divert my soul, was

all I could desire. Yet they could not perceive it. Each of them had the power of self-deception. Only Athalie, perhaps, with the clarity of vision instinctive goodness gives to those who cherish it, had a glimpse of reality behind the appearance. For see how it came disguised—that reality. It came disguised as paternity. Ginevra, he said, must go to a school where she would be thoroughly educated for her career. She must be given every advantage he could afford. And Athalie agreed. 'Oh, that will be splendid!' for the deepest instinct of her nature, even if she were unaware of it, was to give everything to Ginevra.

"And it appeared to young Nevile as an objective, a means by which he could reach out and influence the life of another. To have that girl dependent upon his generosity and his success as a man of the world was delicious to him. It was disguised as a sort of paternity. He saw himself the patron and protector of a girl whose own success would reflect back upon himself and reinforce his personality. It became the central thought in his private life. It progressed side by side with his sincere plans for Athalie.

"But—and here I have to tell you what I learned later from Mr. Floyd Wroot, who came East when he was telegraphed for—Athalie raised difficulties young Nevile could not understand. She said she would take nothing from him for herself. When he wanted to know why, she said she did not believe her husband was dead and she could not be moved by any arguments. She had, she said, a conviction. And in addition there was Morty, who had run away for good. She had, after a struggle with herself, notified the police, but they had heard nothing of him.

"She and young Nevile had a quarrel before he left on the new ship as captain. He was a little out of himself during those days, I fancy, finding the achievement, of what had been his waking dream for so long, hard to believe. He became peremptory that Athalie and Ginevra should move into his apartment. With a gentle refusal she turned down the proposal because she was not yet able to consider herself free.

"I asked Mr. Wroot, as an attorney who knew Athalie's mother and the intricate background of the whole case, how much of her refusal was genuine. He was a little startled by that aspect of it, not because he disagreed with me, but because it had lain deep in his mind without having ever risen to the surface where he could see it. He is a conventional man and thinks in conventional phrases. He sat in this room and explained what I was unable to understand when I heard what had happened.

"He was a little startled, but he saw what I meant and how I meant it, which was clever, because a fool might have imagined I was hinting Athalie was a posing hypocrite who had been tricked by her own daughter into losing her man.

"'Why,' he said, 'there's no doubt that the trouble she had was a mite too much for her reasoning faculties, and she was a little strange. She struck me as strange when she came to see me.'

"'Why?' I said. 'When was this?'

"'Oh, a good while ago,' he said. 'She wanted advice, but of course she didn't take it. She wanted to get a Mexican divorce without letting *him* know about it. She wanted to marry again. This Captain Nevile hadn't come into the picture then.'

"'Oh, another!' I said, rather taken aback.

"'Some fellow who had a lot of money,' Mr. Wroot explained, 'but it never came to anything because the man shied. He couldn't place her in his cosmos,' and Mr. Wroot laughed. 'I could never make up my mind whether she was a child trying to be a woman or a woman playing at being a child,' he said. 'She had the little girl with her, and of the two the daughter was the woman, it seemed to me. But she never acted anything more than just unusual. So I figure, when she lost her money, and the boy got into that trouble, so that she had to replace some cash he'd lifted, and with *him* getting out on parole, she wasn't quite responsible for her actions. I think she was distressed in her mind.'

"'I urged her strongly to get a divorce,' I said.

"'So did I,' Mr. Wroot agreed. 'But women only take advice that is no use. She had an obsession that if she divorced *him* he would find some way of fastening bastardy on the girl. And that if the children found out where their father had been all this time, and what he had done, it would ruin their lives, and they would blame her.'

"'I gathered all that,' I said.

"'Well, she was capable of any sacrifice. But she ought to have taken Captain Nevile into her confidence, because it wouldn't have made any difference to him if she was divorced. I never knew a man yet who cared what his predecessor had done. In fact, it's all the better, in my experience, for a woman to have her worst bargain first, if she wants to keep the second.'

"'That's sound worldly wisdom,' I said, 'but Athalie was not worldly. It was the secret of her life, I think, that she had not a single thought for herself or any other pride but that of birth. I doubt if any woman she came in contact with ever understood a thing about her.'

"'Or men, either,' Mr. Wroot said. 'She never said anything you could make an affidavit of, yet she never falsified. It was a way she had. In that way what she said to Captain Nevile was genuine enough, but she could—well, she could deceive herself as to her motives. Lot of people do that.'

"'Ah!' I said. 'And she was an exile in a strange land, for all her American parents. I think myself she was really an alien to her children. Morty, now . . . Morty seems to me a very simple problem. It wasn't his absent father that would bother him. It was his mother's resignation when they lost their money that made him a problem. He has a sound modern instinct that if you haven't money you ought to get some. He probably has an instinctive and subconscious conviction that this is the ultimate ethics of his age.'

"'It's the New York ethics, anyway,' said Mr. Wroot. 'Maybe he'll make good. His father was smart in his way.'

"'Do you believe she really thinks he is still alive?' I said. 'That he hid on the Pamplona and got ashore?'

"'It's possible she had some reason to think so. All I know is, a law firm in Forty-second Street—all Jews—made an inquiry for a client, they said, as to the heirs to the property. Maybe they had a contingent interest. Those people take up a case fifty-fifty. But the will she had me draw is unbreakable. Everything to the two children in trust, with the captain as guardian.'

"And that is," Mr. Spenlove continued, "the captain himself told me, exactly as he would have had it left. When he came home from his first voyage as commander I was away. I didn't see him until a couple of months later down in Havana. When I climbed up to call on him he was having a nap in the afternoon. He looked as peaceful and dominating as a crusader's effigy in the old church at Ufford. He jumped up when I was announced, all drowsiness gone.

"'I didn't expect you in till the evening,' he said, 'or I'd have been looking for you. Fred,' he said, 'what'll you have? You know I don't drink much, but let us make a night of it ashore. I mean, have a good time.'

"'For one frenzied moment,' I said, 'I thought you were suggesting a night of wine, women, and song.'

"'Wine and song if you like,' he said, 'in a good place. No women.'

"'Same old Sidney,' I said. 'I suppose the passengers are as troublesome as ever.'

"He laughed and told the boy to bring some ice and glasses. 'Oh no,' he said. 'That's all water over the dam. I've got an object in life now, Fred.' He looked at me. 'Ginevra.'

"'Good God!' I said. 'What about her? Are we beginning again in the schoolroom?'

"'She's a long way out of the schoolroom, old man,' he said coolly. 'We are really friends. . . .'

"'You talk as if everything had worked out for the best,' I remarked. 'I don't think you would ever have married Athalie. You'd have taken her long ago.'

"'You say that!' he said. 'You don't know, Fred. I suffered horribly down in Jamaica. But what could I do? The more I tried to find out where she stood and who she was the more mystery she made of it. When she was there with me—staying with her father—I was really happy. I'd have chucked everything to go with her. She was a fairy child! But as soon as it came to getting anything definite out of her about herself she went dumb. You'd have thought money grew on trees and we could live in a tree. She told me once, when we were married we could go back to Wales and live on her estates. Well, I suppose we could if I had a fortune and bought them! Now do you see how I felt when you told me she'd moved because she couldn't pay the rent? I was absolutely on the level all through, Fred, but God knows I never expected she would destroy herself after I'd sent Ginevra away to school and offered to give her my place to live in until she could get a divorce.'

"'You know, I think you never understood her.'

"He waited until the boy had gone out again, closing the door, when he said quietly:

"'And whose fault was that? I didn't make any of the complications, did I? It wasn't my fault she was in such a fix. Be reasonable, Fred! I have to take care of myself now. I've had a hell of a time with women. You don't know the half of it. And all because I played their game. Never any more! No sir! I told Athalie I wasn't a junior third officer who had never known any girls to speak of. I was sick of being made a fool of because I gave my so-called gentlemanly instincts full play. I wasn't going to put my head into any noose without knowing what I was in for. If you want to know!'

"'And so,' I said, 'you have no regrets?'

"'Don't say anything so foolish,' he protested. 'I'll never forgive myself for not being much harder and insisting, yes, insisting, on a full explanation. But what can you do if she hands back your ring and letters the minute you want to know who she really is and where she has been all this time in America? Think I didn't know something about Wilmarth? Hah! But no! All I got was an offer of ring and letters, as if Queen Victoria was still alive. I didn't care a damn about the ring or the letters, come to that. What I wanted was confidence.'

"'And now it's Ginevra,' I mumbled.

"'Yes,' he said. 'Now it's Ginevra. We are really wonderful friends. She writes to me from that school at Dobbs Ferry. She'll be a marvelous dancer. Well, there it is. Fred, you're cold-blooded.'

"'I was thinking you are getting pretty sophisticated yourself,' I said, 'but all I can suggest is—take care of yourself. You won't find Ginevra as easy to handle as Athalie. If you fall in love with her, I mean. I doubt if you get an offer of the ring back, and she won't keep your letters. Not for a week!'

"He looked at me as he raised his glass steadily, a successful gentleman adventurer, no longer a stray beachcomber or a man without a name. And then he laughed.

"'You're right, Fred. She won't get any letters. It will be something worth while, though, something I've done myself. I'll know who she is. I'll know who the man is too. Myself. Don't forget I'm her guardian.'

"'Let's go ashore, as you said,' I suggested. 'I'll watch your career, from a safe distance, with considerable interest. Watch out!'

"'One hand for myself and one for the ship,' he agreed, and downed his drink. 'Let's go. Fred, do you remember that time in Malta? Elli Phalère? Wasn't I the damnedest young fool?'

EPILOGUE

A<small>ND THAT</small>," <small>SAID</small> M<small>R</small>. <small>SPENLOVE</small>, "is all. But did you ever know an elderly man with a passion for other men's lives who could rest while there were attics unexplored? Last trip, before I took my vacation, I was at Kingston, and we docked early. Do you remember? And my mind had been running on that tall elderly man in the well-worn khaki who had been down to meet Athalie. Major Mortimer Justin St. Cyr Rhys (retired) of Caerleon Park. What would he think if an inquisitive stranger poked his way up into the hills and paid him a call? It was rather awful, when I came to think of it, that he could remain so long outside of everything that had happened to his daughter. If so, he had solved the secret of serenity and earthly peace. Never to let anyone break in upon one's life—never to step out of one's own magic circle and permit loving arms to drag one down into the miasma and quaking bogs of human misery. You can say what you like, but many of us would do it if we could. But since we can't, we make a virtue of our humane instincts, which are often no more than curiosity and a hope to be in at the death. Yes! We fool ourselves.

"It was better than stewing on the ship all day or even lounging in the hotel. I struck a bargain with a colored gentleman who swore he knew where Caerleon Park was, and we started off in his antique car. I may tell you it would have been a long way even if we had known the shortest route. My chauffeur got into the hills above Williamsfield and made a number of errors in direction. We would dismount at a wayside store, and he would fetch me a rum punch while he beat the neighborhood for information. It was very hot, and I considered the prospect of being out on the hillside all the afternoon and getting hopelessly lost on the way home. But he found a young nigger who said he knew Majah Rhys' place, and he swung aboard as a pilot. We traveled a good many miles even after that, my old bones bumping cruelly in ruts and against a rocky surface. We left the road and drove into the bush, always climbing, until we reached an entrance that filled me with awe. I think of it even now as one of my extraordinary experiences. It was like entering the gates of the past.

"They were of iron, and shockingly corroded, with some of the bars no more than a dark red and black filigree, hung askew between broken columns of stone topped with strange mutilated griffins holding, one a moldering shield, the other nothing, for the shield was gone. They were rusted into a half-open position, like the gaping, toothless mouth of a very old person of dissolute habits, so that my man had to use care in edging his car past them. The wall on either side ran low and broken into a jungle of vegetation, so that the full irony and futility of the princely gates, with the ornate C in their central panels, was apparent in the mule track that went through a gap in the wall and rejoined the green rutted track through the overhanging trees. Here and there I could see mounds of greenery that were ruined cabins fallen in and filled with rotting vegetation or fragments of masonry. We passed a tennis court so overgrown that only the two posts with a tattered net strung on the top wire gave me a hint. A broken deck chair without a seat had fallen over and was being devoured by ants.

"We went on, not as you progress along a path, but as one seeks a passage through an unknown wilderness, by trial and error, backing out of blind alleys and trying again a little further up, until we started a flock of goats stampeding ahead of us. We followed with toots of the horn, gaining a wider track bumping over tree roots and a hidden curb that was the buried ruin of an old aqueduct, and finally came suddenly into a grass-grown courtyard before a ruined house.

"I hushed the raucous snarling of the nigger's horn and waited. This was an adventure. Who could live in that elegant survival of an older era, whose high front door was approached by a stairway so perilous I could not believe my eyes? In the stables, open to the winds, stood an elderly English car without wheels, propped up on rum puncheons and with chickens roosting on the tattered, folded top. There was a sugar house across the yard with the stack of the boiler inclined and holed with rust. A nigger woman suddenly was there, startlingly white as to apron and stockings, and so black in face she was difficult to account for. She seemed blacker than anything I had ever seen in Africa. She stood wiping one black wrist on the white apron and exchanged unintelligible words with my man. She held up an arm indicating I was to ascend, and vanished among the crates and vine-hung trellis behind the house. I got out.

"The house had had no paint for what seemed to me a very long time, and the boards were so weather worn and thin that it assumed the crazy impermanence of a sun-dried carton on a garbage heap. It leaned. I could almost declare that when one spoke it trembled. The first step I trod on moved ominously. Yet I reached a sagging landing under a portico and looked for a knocker or a bell on the high mahogany doors bleached white and scarred by generations of pawing dogs.

"I knocked and fumbled for a card. This, I thought, was a far cry from Berkeley Square, the great house with the polished brass name plate of Caerleon, so that the old earl's tenants could find his lordship when they came to town. It was a far cry from Park Avenue; but not so far, perhaps, from the room over the stable on East Eighth. There, in fact, I think lay the key to both Athalie and her father—a sort of patrician obliviousness of one's physical environment that is an enigma to a middle-class bourgeois person like myself. It inspires me with a sort of fanatical anger, and the memory of it remains in my mind a long time. I cannot rationalize it. And when that damaged door opened quickly and Major Rhys in a frogged dressing gown looked out at me I was confronting that enigma with a vengeance.

"'Who's this?' he said, in a voice strangely reminiscent of Athalie's—not angry or even ill-natured, but aristocratically peremptory, as though his ancestors had had minions bending low and vassals paying tribute. He was not dressed, but wore pajamas and old red-leather slippers. It was afternoon and hot. He blinked at my card. 'Oh!' he said and made way for me to enter. 'Not very settled here,' he added in what I suppose was an apology. He need not have apologized. It was something beyond all apologies. He pointed to a chair and looked at my card again.

"He seemed to have just aroused from a sleep from which he never wanted to awake. There was a distinct air about him of having been disturbed in committing suicide, and he wanted to learn my business, get me out of the place, and return to the job as soon as possible.

"'Oh,' he said again, when I explained I had known his daughter.

"'She was a special friend of mine,' I said. 'I saw her only a few weeks before . . .'

"'Did you really?'

"We were still standing in that astonishing room. He looked again at my card. I told him his daughter had introduced me when he met her on the dock. 'The Camotan,' I reminded him. He nodded. 'Oh yes, I think I'm beginning to understand. We don't get many visitors up here, you know.

'Fraid I'm a bit rusty about you. Yes, the Camotan. What can I do for you?'

"I thought to myself, 'I wonder what he can do for a single soul now.' He was the grandfather of Ginevra, who could sail the stormy seas of life without his help. And of Morty, whose ideal was Jimmie Walker and who would seem like a wild animal to this withered aristocrat on his sun-scorched plantation.

"'I came to see you,' I said, 'because I was so interested in Athalie and hoped you'd tell me something about her. Her youth and early marriage.'

"He made an abrupt movement. 'Do sit down,' he said. 'I'm not very polite. Sit down. That chair is all right. I live alone, you know. I'll get a drink. Would you have a drink? I'll call the maid.'

"He went out, shuffling over the uneven hardwood floor and left me to look around. It was, I say, astonishing. The wall paper was a dingy design of red-and-white stripes with purple urns full of blue grapes. There were old engravings hanging there, of the sort you see in second-hand furniture stores on Royal Street in New Orleans—French sentiment. Le Bouquet est Bien Reçu was one, and two plump girls by a stream, Les Pêcheuses, was another. There was a portrait of George V cut from an illustrated paper, and a fly-blown, light-brown photograph of H.M.S. Hydrangea, which must have been taken a quarter of a century ago. And there was another photograph so perished he had scrawled underneath it 'Garden at Caerleon Park, Wales, Eng.' In case he himself forgot what it had been, I suppose. And there was a framed certificate declaring that Maj. M. J. S. C. Rhys (retired) was a member of Island Institute.

"And on a small table against the wall, close by my chair, was one of the most disturbing collections I have ever seen. There was a morocco case of miniature dress medals such as officers wear, the ribbons very much tarnished and stained. There were two miniatures in a double frame, who he told me later were his parents. There was a box of cigars, a cartridge case full of flowers from the garden, and a small toy locomotive on circular rails that ran around among the other articles. Backed against the wall were three books with the bindings gnawed by insects: an Edgar Wallace thriller, Omar Khayyám, and a novel called *Torn Sails*.

"I was entranced. The chair creaked. For that matter, the floor under it was none too firm. How? I thought . . . hurricanes! How?

"There was a hurried conversation going on outside. Then he came back. 'We'll go on the gallery,' he said. He had a bottle of rum in his hand and was waving a corkscrew. 'Sorry we have no ice. As an American, you'd like ice?' He pronounced the word with vigor and precision as though he had discovered and identified the germ that was destroying American life. I said he needn't bother as I was still English enough to do without it. Privately I wished there were ice.

"He said, 'Why didn't you say so before?'

"We walked out onto his 'gallery.' It was none too firm, but he sat negligently on the old rail and held out his arm to show me the beauty of the world that fell away over his treetops waving at my feet. Far away the blue sea lay like a floor of cobalt. There was a breeze, and the veranda was in shade. He seemed to think it didn't matter what sort of place you had if you could enjoy a view like that. Perhaps he is right. He has a view. It is all British, including the three miles of ocean on the rim. That is satisfactory to Major Rhys (retired). He is, I found, an imperialist. It is his diversion to contemplate an unalloyed vista of land and sea unsullied by tourists or white men of any kind. The stout black woman in the snowy apron and stockings brought us glasses of odd sizes, limes, sugar, and a bottle of cold water. Major Rhys began a ritual of preparing his own punch. The house responded in every beam as the woman clumped downstairs again.

"'Yes,' I said. 'You have a wonderful view.' It turned out

to be wonderful rum, too. He said he had had it ten years in the cask down in the cellar before he began to use it.

"He became confidential. His long legs perched on a three-legged stool, he extended himself in a cane chair that set up marvelous complainings. At the end of the gallery was a string hammock in which he had been reclining when I knocked. An old pipe hung on a shelf near at hand. A copy of *Punch* lay on a bamboo table within reach. But now he became confidential and said that trade was not very good. Coffee and sugar. Ugh! You couldn't have two more miserable crops. Every damned fool in the world seemed to be growing too much coffee and sugar.

"'But you do well enough to stay on,' I said.

"'Oh, I couldn't leave now,' he told me. 'I'm used to the place after all these years, and the place is used to me. I like it. But you were speaking of my daughter. We never saw very much of each other. My mother took care of her. Her mother—my wife—was dead. Dead to me, anyhow. And I couldn't live in England. I went abroad. I was on service. When the war started she came to Paris and married that rotter. I wasn't even consulted. I was very busy, of course. Married him and went to the States to live. I know he ill-treated her, but I gave up interfering in other people's lives thirty years ago.'

"He reached for his pipe and began to fill it from a ragged old semicircular pouch with a monogram, such a pouch as went out of style a quarter of a century ago, when he renounced the affairs of mankind. As he talked to me he would break off to converse with an invisible Negro foreman under the gallery who would go off into the plantation again. Major Rhys seemed more comfortable since he knew I was English.

"'I don't even ask about people any more,' he went on, without being personal, for he was almost enjoying a soliloquy. He was expressing the foundations of his philosophy. 'Leave other people alone,' summed it up.

"'That rotter she married,' he went on, 'was always trying to borrow money for some scheme or other. I wouldn't trust him with sixpence.'

"'He is supposed to be dead,' I said.

"'I doubt it,' he replied sarcastically. 'You can't kill that sort. They should never have let him out. I wanted Athalie to come down here to live. But she wouldn't leave her children. She wouldn't leave him, come to that. Very well, I said, you've made your bed, lie on it.'

"'I admired her enormously,' I said.

"'Oh.' He gazed at the landscape before striking a match. 'That's very good of you. You probably knew her a lot better than I ever did. She seemed to like living in New York.'

"'It gets people,' I said.

"'It didn't get me. I hated it when I was there. You know, I married an American girl. H-mph!'

"The sound he made seemed to indicate he had never been able to understand his own folly.

"'So I suppose Athalie got it from her mother. I've given up roaming. I've been all over the world. This is our place. A hundred and sixty years. The maid's grandmother was a slave on this estate. Did you see the huts?'

"He gazed out, placidly imperial, oblivious of the twentieth century. He defeated me because he was no fool, after all. His gods were not mine. It was like being entertained by a Thibetan lama or the monks of some order in the savage Caucasus. He had attained contentment. He did not go to the trouble of registering emotions he did not feel. He was a moldering rampart of empire. You could no more deny the dignity of his personality than you could sneer at the beauty of his useless iron gates because they were crumbling away. It just happened that what you and I call happiness, the modern world with its fast steamers, airplanes, and mechanical agitations, doesn't appeal to him at all. Even less does he want to know anything about our souls, and the restless evacuations of American minds he regards as he would the horrors of African devil worship and the dark mysteries of a Russian madhouse.

"He made me stay to an early dinner. I half expected him to put on evening dress, but he found, somewhere, after much conferring with the maid, whose name was Josephine, a suit of white drill. He let me wash my hands in an anchorite's cell, where he slept. There were khaki blankets on a bed which had a kerosene lamp with a blackened glass chimney on a shelf so he could read. In there he had two large old leather trunks of solid cowhide with brass corners and his crest on the lids. I mention them because he opened one and took out a miniature case with a portrait on ivory of his daughter. She had been about twelve. 'My mother sent it to me,' he said. 'She didn't change much, did she?'

"Yes, and he showed me, with a perplexing lack of reserve and yet with dignity, his sword. It was tarnished, of course, being in the tropics. He showed me his name engraved on it —Mortimer Justin St. Cyr Rhys. 1914.

"'For King and Country,' he said, slipping it back into the scabbard, and put it away. He seemed to forget I was there as he meditated upon the past. But when I expressed surprise that Athalie had appointed Captain Nevile guardian to the children rather than her own father, he said:

"'That was because I refused. I refused to be drawn into any such engagements. I wrote to Wroot and said as much. She was her mother's daughter, and Wroot was the man. As for Captain Nevile, she gave me to understand she was going to marry him. I didn't see much of him. That club of his, tourists coming down to fish and all that sort of thing, we don't want. Keep out, is my motto. Kingston's bad enough. Let them go to Bermuda if they want to kick up a fuss.'

"'He's on a ship again now,' I said. Major Rhys glanced at me and then hurriedly back to the blue distance as though he grudged the time away from it. 'Is he? Good position and all that? He might have . . . H-m, I don't know. I saw very little of him. I didn't interfere. He wanted to speak to me, permission to pay attentions and so on, but I refused to be drawn into it.'

"He gave me a dinner of goat cutlets, new bread, and tomato salad, with rum in water. Fruits and coffee. 'Grown here,' he warned me. 'Roasted and ground today. None of your filthy tinned stuff.' He even grew his tobacco, and rolled a cigar from the leaf before my eyes. We gazed upon the dying day from his gallery, and it was dramatic to see the night pass over the scene like a curtain being drawn.

"'I never tire of it,' he said. 'Pity you can't stay and see the sun rise too. I suppose you must go back. Your man is having dinner with Josephine.'

"That was a day for me! He attended me to the car with a lantern and stood in tall, silent dignity while my man got ready to depart. Major Rhys said:

"'Glad you came. Don't see many people from outside. Appreciate your interest. What I mean is, don't think I'm made of stone. Not quite. But from long experience I've given up prescribing for other people. Take your own medicine and keep a still tongue in your head. That's my motto. And there's too much rascality in the world up there for me to take a hand in it. I'd be done, for sure! I don't understand what's going on nowadays. We were getting the world into some sort of order. Now everything's gone to pieces. I'm too much of an old crock to go and do anything about it. I've seen the world—most of it—and there's nothing anywhere that I envy. I'll go down to the gate with you.'

"He got in beside me, his lean hands resting on an ebony cane with a vast curved handle of semi-transparent horn. We drove down through a tunnel of light in the green gloom. He seemed lost in thought. At the gates, when we were safely past them, he got out.

"'God bless you,' he said. 'Come again and stop longer. Always glad . . . Good-bye!'

"Of course he did not mean it. He does not want to see

any of us again. We left him there, leaning on his stick in a
faint unearthly moonlight, gazing at us, backed by the rotting iron gates of his ancestral lands, with the gray griffins
on their moldering pylons lifting their heads in stony contempt of the departing barbarians."

The fire was all red ash now as Mr. Spenlove stood up
and stared down upon it. It crumbled and threw up a little
flame and died again. It was very late, and his guests made
ready to go home.

"And that," said Mrs. Kavanagh, "was that. But I don't
agree with you. You're much too tolerant. You'd make
excuses for the devil himself!"

"And you," said Mr. Spenlove, smiling, "would have the
last word with him."